iN THE
HEART OF
TEXAS

iN THE HEART OF TEXAS

GiNGER MCKNIGHT-CHAVERS

swp

SHE WRITES PRESS

Published 2016
Printed in the United States of America
Print ISBN: 978-1-63152-159-1
E-ISBN: 978-1-63152-160-7
Library of Congress Control Number: 2016943333

For information, address:
She Writes Press
1563 Solano Ave #546
Berkeley, CA 94707

Cover design © Julie Metz, Ltd./metzdesign.com
Interior design by Tabitha Lahr

She Writes Press is a division of SparkPoint Studio, LLC.

To My Family
And
My True Believers

CHAPTER 1 ♡

It's crazy to light a cathedral's lot of candles in a small makeup trailer. But that's not stopping Olga from igniting a thicket of scented pillars amidst the tubes and bottles and other cosmetic clutter she has strewn across her narrow table.

"Olga, you may wanna trim the wicks before you *liiight* those things."

My drawl is slipping again. Sometimes this early in the morning I have a hard time controlling my natural tendency to stretch every single syllable of speech into two or three. Even though I've worked like the dickens to suppress it since I left Texas some twenty-odd years ago. Usually my lapses into Texan prompt a tease from Olga, but today she's ignoring me. She's absorbed in attacking the mishmash of tall cylindrical candles she has assembled with a cherry-hued, plastic lighter that matches her shock of red lipstick.

"What are you, a witch?" I ask, not entirely kidding.

Olga's tall, lean figure is draped in black, sorcerer-like garments that resemble singed stalks of willow. Sheer, dangling shreds of dark fabric from her tunic-draped arms float perilously close to her assortment of rising flames. If this film were a Grimm's fairy tale flick, her getup would be perfect. Maybe her mastery of makeup artistry extends to the dark arts. But I know better. Olga has Soviet roots, but she is actually the embodiment of Zen. She's keen on environment and can't work without creating the right atmosphere for inspiration. I like this about her. And I certainly benefit from a bit of aromatherapy at this godforsaken hour of the morning.

I stifle a yawn, but I can't complain. I love my job. It smells good.

"Ylang Ylang," she says as if reading my mind. "And lavender. A *leetle* sage. Good for you and me. We carry too much fire."

I don't know what that means, but I accept it. "Fire" has been used to describe me my whole life: "spitfire," "firebrand," "hothead." And Olga and I have worked together often enough that I trust her. On one film she had to cover my entire, naked body in sparkly gold grease paint every day for a month, when I played an alien assassin having an affair with my human target, Colin Farrell. So Olga may know me better than I know myself.

Suddenly Olga leans toward me. Her fierce, Kohl-rimmed eyes narrow, and her tight-lipped expression is a mystery. Her blue eyes are cold and penetrating, dramatized by the sweep of her eyeliner, which resembles an image in an Egyptian artifact.

"Your *skeeen*," she says, her lips inches from my own. "Too dry. No wrinkles, but you need moisture, Jo. Over forty we need more."

"Olga! I am NOT over forty!" I shout. "Why do you think I'm over forty?"

"Actresses lie," Olga shrugs.

It's not a good sign when the woman who applies my makeup every day thinks I'm over forty. Even if it's true. And she said it so casually, like, "oh, you know how it is when we're over forty." Whatever happened to "Black don't crack?" I don't look old, do I?

It's all starting to make sense. I bet that's why Michael Mann gave that astrophysicist part to Meagan Good instead of me. She's a sweet girl, but it's ridiculous that a child barely out of diapers is better suited to play the head of NASA. Shouldn't the head of NASA be old? Oh, shit.

"Coffee?"

"What?" I snap.

"You want coffee?" Olga asks, raising a silver Starbucks thermos in my direction. She seems completely unaware of the damage she has done to my ego by correctly guessing my age. I shake my head, unable to speak. Olga shrugs again and takes a sip from a small, silver-toned cup. She hums softly to herself while sorting through the contents of the rolling bag she uses to carry her kit to and from the set every day.

Olga has unleashed my demons, and I doubt the hint of sage burning in her candles is sufficient to keep them at bay. This is a disaster. Even when I had trouble getting parts because I wasn't a "Julia" or a "Sandra," at least I had my looks. My Yale drama degree is irrelevant in L.A., but my resemblance to what my agent, Jen, calls "a poor man's Halle Berry" (with no sense of irony) has always helped me keep a roof over my head. Maybe I should move back to New York.

I lean forward in my canvas seat toward the shrill lights of the makeup mirror. I don't see any lines. OK, a few hairline streaks in the forehead, but otherwise good. I still look good. I think. I don't look twenty, but I don't look forty, do I? I wonder if that's why Jen keeps pressing me to read for that judge role. It's a good script, but that's usually the beginning of the end, when you start taking those judge roles. But Jen's a good agent and an even better friend, so she would tell me if I *needed* to read for judge roles, wouldn't she? And I got this *Obsessions* part, didn't I? It's a lead! With a love scene! I press my index fingers against the edges of my eyelids and give them a little tug.

"Don't get eyes done," Olga says as she jabs the igniter of her Bic lighter with her thumb and lights the last few torches. "These women, they ruin themselves with too much work too soon."

The tiny flames glimmer; a golden glow that fizzles in the glare of the brassy bulbs of the makeup mirror. Olga pulls a CD out of her bag and slips it into the carriage of her Sony boombox. Deepak Chopra's baritone wafts through the small space like a trail of incense. *"With your toxic emotions, toxic environment, toxic habits, toxic substances, the key is to experience inner silence . . . "*

What I'm experiencing is anything but inner silence, and the white-hot glare of the fluorescent globes is bothering me. It's too severe; more suited to an interrogation than a beautification. So I close my eyes.

My senses are on edge, and my scalp itches. I inch my fingers underneath my wig and scratch the skin beneath my short, squiggly strands of real hair. I dared to shave my head for that Colin Farrell movie, and it's taking forever to grow back. I lopped off my locks, despite Jen's warnings that short hair is the death knell of the career of any Black actress other than Halle Berry, even the poor man's version. You not only need youth, but you need "good" hair and an even better bod to get work these days, no matter how prestigious a drama school you attended. But I beat out a boatload of younger actresses for that part, so I was feeling brazen. Maybe it wasn't the best idea, since I could have worn a bald cap. But I've spent my entire life obsessing over my hair, and I needed a break. Though now I'm anxious I might not get another one.

Eyes still shut, I feel something soft and cool stroking my face and neck as Olga gently sweeps them in a circular motion with a toner-soaked sponge. I suddenly feel an equally soft bit of pressure on my forehead as Ravi kisses me hello.

"Just had to see you before the madness starts," he whispers. "Director's prerogative."

My eyes flutter open to the sight of his coppery reflection gleaming in the lighted mirror. Dull dots of black and silver stubble speckle his chin. Ravi experiments with various stages of shadow, beard, and bare face, as he can never quite decide who he wants to be. Today he's got a Don Johnson shadow that most likely resulted from his late night in the editing room, not some attempt at a fashion statement. His long, black hair is pulled back in a haphazard ponytail that he has tucked underneath a faded baseball cap featuring the logo of a surf shop near his house. We admire each other in the mirror without looking at each other directly.

"We missed you last night," I say to his image. "I wanted you to meet my best friends, Jen and Rudy. You haven't passed inspection yet, and Rudy goes back to New York in a couple of days."

Ravi's eyes turn dark and uncertain. Olga is here, the soiled sponge still pinched between her fingers and poised to cleanse me. I knew this would happen at some point. One of us was bound to slip up, even though we said we would keep "us" under wraps until the film was a wrap. Which is usually a taller order for me than Ravi. Unlike all the prim and proper women in my family, I've never been good at hiding things or holding in my emotions. But film romances can be distracting to everyone on the set, even though they crop up so often that they're almost expected. And Ravi's divorce isn't final yet, which is an even bigger problem than the distraction. Though I don't know of any L.A. relationship that isn't messy, so I should stop stressing. But when your parents have been married for forty-five years and complete each other's sentences, it's hard not to have high expectations.

The trailer door creaks and shudders. It's stuck, as usual. Yanked hard, it abruptly swings open, and our producer, Regan Coleman, steps up into the trailer. Dark slashes of her red bob are plastered against her head from a recent shower, like dripping strips of tinted papier-mâché. Her unlined, makeup-free face squints in Ravi's direction.

"How was dinner with Danielle last night, Ravi? You work things out yet?" Her narrow mouth can barely contain the smirk that is threatening to escape.

"I was editing . . . "

"Relax!" Regan says, the smirk now released. "As long as it doesn't affect my movie or my inheritance, I could care less about what you and my mother do or don't do. I'm sure Danielle has a good prenup. I mean, she has always been good at taking care of *herself*."

What is she talking about? I gaze at Ravi. He looks as anxious as I feel.

"I just came to talk about the rushes from yesterday," Regan continues. "I like the melodrama and think we should amp that up. The dark, indie film vibe looks good but is kind of a snooze, don't you think? I think we should go more soap than filmie, you know? I know some folks at Lifetime. With a few script tweaks, I think we can interest them in turning this movie into a nighttime soap. I mean syndication, residuals, hello? Danielle's romance novels are a better fit for TV than the festival circuit anyway." Her hazel eyes shift from Ravi to me. "And you're good. I know you do a lot of indie films, but TV is a good place for older actresses."

From the corner of my eye I notice Ravi's narrowing stare. Olga raises an eyebrow, sponge still squeezed between her fingers. But Regan's expression seems affable, not critical.

"TV's good for all of us except for that hussy, Meryl Streep," I deadpan. "Who did that woman blow to get all of those great films? And you'd think she could share some work with the rest of us seniors. Tsk. Selfish!"

Regan smiles without smirking this time. Her eyes soften and she grins like a toddler with a fresh balloon. It's disarming, because she usually seems hard edged and hard to reach.

"I *love* you, Jo!" she giggles. "You're crazy!"

"I'm from Texas," I say with a wink. "Crazy is in my DNA."

"Ha!" she laughs. "OK, so I'll let you get back to it. Ravi, we'll talk later. This is going to be awesome!"

Regan bounds out of the door. Ravi slumps and leans against the wall of the trailer.

"What a *fuuucking* nightmare," he mumbles in the direction of a spot above my head in the mirror. Living in L.A. for so long has screwed up Ravi's speech. His Anglo-Indian, London-bred accent is moshed with stretches of slow Southern California intonation and invectives, so talking to him is a bit schizophrenic.

"This thing is becoming a *maaajor* drag, Jo," he drones. "Regan and those other producers are *reeal* morons. This thing is supposed to be satire. It's supposed to be clever. A send-up of all the reality TV bullshit and drama. You understand that. *Everybody* understands that except the stupid investors. I just . . . I can't take it anymore. I mean, why do they think some network will buy *fake* fake-reality TV with union actors when you can make *real* fake-reality TV for *waaay* less with some bloody chavs that would pay *yooou* to be on television?"

I notice red streaks in Ravi's eyes and faint lines in the corners of his lids. His slender face is drawn, his expression tired. His shoulders slump as he slides into the empty chair next to mine. Olga drops the sponge and rummages through her makeup case, as if she is searching for the most important thing in the world instead of listening to our conversation. She removes some round pots of color and begins to spread and mix little bits on a board resembling an artist's palette. Ravi ignores her. He places an elbow on his armrest and drops his forehead into his palm.

"And they say reality stars don't work for a living," I joke.

Ravi doesn't move or speak. He hates to be reminded of the fact that he was on *Real World*.

"Ravi, I was just kidding, you know." I tuck stray strands of his hair into his baseball cap.

He finally raises his head, this time staring directly into my eyes instead of my negative image in the makeup mirror. "It's not that. It's just . . ." He glances in Olga's direction. "I'm *reeeally* stretched to the limit, Jo. I've put everythin' into this project. I'm forty, and I can't be known as just another reality TV loser for the rest of my life. Forty is pretty old not to have made it in this town, you know. And I've got to . . ." Ravi leans toward my chair and lowers his voice to a whisper. "I *muuust* get Danielle off my back and out of my life. I can't take her anymore."

"Why is she still torturing you?" I lower my voice and lean my face closer to his. "She can't file for divorce and then blame you for moving on with your life."

"I'm working for her, Jo. Regan gets the producer credit, but we *allll* know Danielle is bankrolling this thing. I'm still her *freeeakin'* lap-dog. But I don't have a choice do I, love? I know this thing will do well for all of us, but until then I can't afford for her to pull her money out of it. Maybe I *aamm* just another reality TV loser."

"Look, Ravi, if she's funding this, then it's in her interest for it not to fail, right? And I wouldn't get so upset about Regan's TV idea. There's some great satire on TV. And TV may be more cutting-edge than film these days. You started in reality TV, so you're the perfect person to poke fun at it."

Ravi's head drops back into his hand.

"Ravi, I'm sorry." Why do I always say the wrong thing? How many times has Mommy told me that truth is best served in small bites, not gobbles? "Hey, Ravi, I didn't mean . . . "

Ravi raises his hand, cutting me off. "It's OK, Jo. I'm just tired. Since I can't buy Danielle out yet, I still have to listen to her. And I also have to listen her crazy daughter that doesn't even get along with her and keep the peace with everybody. Regan's annoying, but Danielle's a *huuge* pain in the arse. My lawyer's trying to get this divorce done, but she's using this movie to get to me."

"I'll bet she's more interested in your *arse*, sugar plum, than the movie."

"Well, perhaps," he says. "But *sheee's* the one who broke it off."

"That doesn't matter, Ravi. People want what they no longer have, even if they threw it away in the first place. My Uncle Buddy back in Midland says, 'a dry well teaches 'ya the worth 'a water,'" I drawl. On purpose this time.

Usually my Uncle Buddy's Texanisms make Ravi laugh, or at least smile. Today he remains grim. "I need to get rid of her, but I *caaan't*, at least not right now. I've tried to find other investors to buy out her share, but she *woon't* do it, even if there's a profit in it. And the film's based on her book anyway, so I'm stuck with her."

Ravi searches my face as intensely as my earlier search for wrinkles. "W-well . . . ," I sputter under the heat of his gaze, "you know I've never read any of her stuff. I mean, other than this script. I guess I prefer chick-lit to romance."

"But of course you do," he says. His voice gains a bit of levity, despite his weary expression. "You're quite the modern girl, aren't you Ms. Randolph?"

"Don't tell my mother." I force a smile and wink at Ravi. "You haven't met her yet, but she's pretty old school."

"I guess I better go now." Ravi stands and pats the top of my wig like a puppy. "*Maaaybe* we'll see each other tonight," he murmurs, this time back to the mirror as he turns and leaves the trailer.

Olga silently approaches me with a foundation-doused sponge, and I close my eyes again and try to focus on Deepak.

"To help you quiet your emotional turbulence when your needs are not met . . . accept your feelings without judgment . . ."

Ravi has been wigging out. And I barely see him anymore, even though we work together every day. We used to find a way to see each other all the time, no matter how busy we were, no matter how stressed.

He used to just appear out of nowhere when I was shopping, lunching, buying coffee. Now he's a phantom, obsessed with his editing and rewrites until all hours of the night for a project that's just not that deep. It's not Scorsese. And it's definitely not Shakespeare. It's a fun, over-the-top riff on soap opera-type dramas and reality TV characters that he has glossed with a music video finish. It's like spinning cotton candy—we're making a fun bit of fluff on this set. *Obsessions* is not art. It's not life.

That being said, we both have a lot riding on this. Unlike Ravi, I've been pretty lucky in this business and haven't had to wait tables since my early twenties. Though he's right – forty is too old not to have made it in this town. The big opportunities, the big roles, are fewer and farther between for me. Even the good small parts are growing scarce. My sister is only two years older than me, but she's a successful dermatologist back in Midland, with a huge house, a family, and enough money to take care of herself comfortably in her old age – with or without that grumpy spouse of hers. I'm not destitute by a long shot, but my life is by no means "set." Certainly not by L.A. standards. Not even by my bourgeois Midland, Texas, Black-doctor's-daughter standards. If *Obsessions* is picked up by Lifetime Network and turned into a cable series that eventually goes into syndication, it would become a nice retirement plan for me and for Ravi. Especially since he's divorcing a Beverly Hills-dwelling, best-selling author who could crush his career in the sieve of her lawyers' stealth bombs if she wanted to.

"I be right back," Olga startles me. My eyes fly open as her willowy presence floats out of the trailer.

I feel jittery, like I'm juiced up on caffeine, even though I haven't had a single cup since we started shooting, to save my veneers. I pick up one of the gossip rags Olga always brings to the set and randomly flip the pages. 2007 isn't turning out to be a good year for women in show business or for reality TV "personalities," as they prefer to be called. Britney Spears is bald and busting up her man's car. Nicole Richie and Paris Hilton have done time. Lindsay Lohan keeps hopping from rehab to jail and back to rehab. This magazine is bad karma, and I don't want to jinx my luck. I'm forty-one with a sullen but otherwise wonder-ful boyfriend and a romantic lead in an indie film, or possible made-for-TV movie that could become the biggest nighttime soap since *Knots Landing*, if we play our cards right. I follow Deepak's suggestions and take some deep, drawn-out yoga breaths to calm the rat-a-tat of my out of control heartbeat.

Olga returns and resumes my makeover. Though I may be long in the tooth, it doesn't take her too long to transform me from forty-something to fabulous. I smile at Olga and hoist my weighty *Obsessions* script off my lap as I slide off the chair and make my way out of the makeup trailer.

It's really hot today. Much hotter than usual for L.A., particu-larly at this time of morning. It's almost Texas-hot. My head is boiling underneath the wig of long, synthetic strands that's hiding my increas-ingly frazzled curls. The morning sun is as merciless as a late morning in Midland, and I feel myself "glowing." "Horses sweat, men perspire, and women *glow*," my high school French teacher, Mrs. Bonner, used to emote when the unforgiving Texas heat left us all drenched and soggy. To keep my lovely, white wrap dress from being dotted with "glow" stains, I take shade in the shadow of a tall, translucent scrim at the edge of the set. I scan pages of my script while I wait to rehearse and shoot my scene.

I lean against a tall lamp and enjoy a bit of peace. My nerves calm as I transform my persona from Jo Ella Randolph, single actress, to Latricia von Sturm und Drang, the scheming fifth wife of the elderly Baron Felix von Sturm und Drang. It's relatively quiet in my corner of the set, the silence disturbed only by the whisper of my own voice as I recite my lines to myself, and the rattle of my stockpile of gold bracelets that jingle every time I turn a page or mop my brow with the back of my hand.

Suddenly a loud shriek pierces the silence. I look up from my pages but all appears ordinary. There's just the familiar buzz of the crew: the camera operator adjusting his end marks, the sound men testing mic placements, the lighting crew raising light meters and moving large set lights into position. Ravi is across the set from me, gesturing with his hands as he chats with the Director of Photography. Production assistants, mostly young women in ponytails and T-shirts, bustle about the set, toting scripts, handing out water bottles, placing props.

Another shriek. The single shriek turns into a continuous loop of ear-splitting screams that grow louder and closer with each passing second. I jerk my head from side to side, but I can't see the source of the clamor. I'm not the only one – crewmembers pause what they're doing and scan the surroundings in response to the racket.

"Jo, watch out . . . "

A leathery stick figure careens around the side of the makeup trailer and charges in my direction. Her tan face is contorted and changes rapidly from a deep, chestnut color to a bright shade of crimson. The screeching beet woman lunges at me with both arms extended, shoving me back into a scrim and knocking me, the scrim, a couple of lights, a director's chair, a speaker and an unfortunate boom operator one-by-one onto the ground.

I fall backward, and pages fly everywhere. I hit the ground hard, scuffing my elbow against the asphalt. I hoist myself upright with my hands, wincing from the burning sensation of the long scrape on my arm. Suddenly my torso is slammed hard against the ground again from the weight of the wild woman. Covering my body like a thin blanket, she stares at me with a confused expression. Too stunned to move, I stare back into her unnaturally unlined face. She's familiar, I know her, but I can't distinguish her face, as so many women are so identically ageless these days.

I twist and squirm and finally jimmy my arms from underneath her body. I press my hands against her shoulders and push hard, but the woman grabs my back and won't let go. We roll around on the ground, exposed skin pinched and scraped by the rough asphalt underneath us. I yank at her honey-gold hair extensions and block her flailing hands with my elbows to avoid being clawed by her nail tips. One of her bony hands slips through my shield, and she swipes my cheek with the point of her large canary diamond ring. My face tingles, and I wince and clutch my cheek. Free from my grasp, the woman grabs my wig and rips it clean off my head.

The wild woman pins my arms against my body with her legs, using all the strength of her sinewy muscles to immobilize me. Her personal trainer would be proud, for as much as I twitch and twist, I can't break free of this stringy-limbed stranger. This is like that Joan Collins–Linda Evans catfight on *Dynasty*, minus the shoulder pads and big hair. Well, I guess mine has turned pretty puffy from the heat, but the scrawny woman's hair is flat-ironed to crepe-like thinness.

"What the . . . ?!!!" I yell in a muted shout muffled by the bony palm pressed against my mouth.

"Hey, stop!" I hear Dave the cameraman's voice somewhere nearby. I hear random shouts and footsteps racing in our direction but can't see past the mat of corn-silk hair blocking my vision.

"*Ravi!*" the woman yells very close to my ear. "I am *not* paying for your nappy Black bitch!"

I jerk my arms free from her grasp. "Who are you calling a nappy Black bitch, you shriveled-up whore?!" I start pounding her legs and sides with my fists as hard as I can. She clutches her waist and doubles over, and I'm finally able to push her off of me. I roll on top of her and slap and pound her prone body. I don't see where my floundering arms land. I just sling them in a random, blind conniption of emotional defense.

Suddenly one of my flailing punches connects hard against a slender slant of bone. I draw back from the sting, shaking and flexing my throbbing fingers as the woman starts screeching again. She rolls from side to side on the ground, crying and moaning and clutching her broken nose job. The blood trickles through the spaces between her fingers, and I'm almost moved to help her. But the "nappy, Black bitch" shriek rings in my ears, and I struggle to constrain my urge to jump up and kick her in her nonexistent stomach.

I slowly lift myself off of the ground, brushing gravel and dirt and bloodstains from my arms and clothing. Everything is fuzzy and out of focus. Finally my eyes zoom in on the large, elevated camera where Ravi is seated, his eyes wide and wandering like a caged animal.

"*Ravi!* Who is this crazy, Klan bitch, anyway?"

Ravi's head drops, the brim of his cap and stray wisps of his long black hair shielding his eyes from my blazing, direct stare. I glance at the woman, who is still on the ground, crying and curling into a fetal position as she cradles her shattered septum. "*Ravi!*" I shout again. "Call security, dammit!"

Ravi doesn't look up. "I can't, Jo. That's Danielle."

What the hell has she done to her face? Why is Ravi just sitting there? "Ravi, I don't care who she is," I shout. "*Get rid of her!!*"

Ravi's voice lowers to a whisper. "I can't, Jo. I can't."

"Why not?" I yell. "Look, Ravi, I'll borrow money from my family. I'll ask my agent for help. This is *crazy!*" I shift my focus back to Danielle. "You *ever* touch me again, I'll call the cops!"

"Stay away from my husband, you *whore!*" Danielle's voice is muffled behind the hands still cuffing her face. But her words are clear.

"*Look*," I shout at her writhing figure. "If you're having second thoughts about your divorce, work that out in therapy! Keep your hands off me, or I'll have you arrested!"

"I *own* all of this," Danielle sneers through her sniffles. Her reddened eyes narrow, and she releases her mangled nose. She rolls herself upright and reaches her bloodstained hands, zombie-like, in my direction. "I will *kill* you! Get off my set! And leave my husband alone, you desperate bitch!" She doesn't have the energy to stand, so she sits there, arms and hands stretched in my direction, her bloody fingers wiggling frantically, as if the tiny motions will generate enough kinetic energy to do me serious harm.

"What is wrong with you?" I shift my focus back to Ravi. "What's going on, Ravi?!"

"I'm . . . we're . . . I mean . . ." Ravi finally raises his head, but he doesn't leave his chair. His hands clutch the armrests, his eyes uncertain. I finally understand.

My head throbs like a hangover. I'm standing upright, but I'm dizzy, and I can't feel my feet. A rush of passion, steam, anger, despair overwhelms me, but I can't move or speak. The set is eerily quiet, everyone appearing as stunned and speechless as I feel. Regan's eyes are wide, a glimpse of her smirk returned. Though standing less than ten yards from her mother, she doesn't reach out or move in her direction.

Two burly, black-clad guys with headsets trot toward me and seize my arms in their oversized hands. They hold me so tight I can barely move. I twist and turn to free myself from their straightjacket grips, but it's no use. Another guard moves in on Danielle and extends a hefty hand to steady her and help her to her feet. A production assistant jogs over toting a towel, which she presses against Danielle's nose.

This situation is unreal. I can't think, and I can't move. All I can do is yelp like a West Texas prairie dog. I bark out a string of really stupid plastic surgery slurs and obscenities; any stupid thing I can think of just blurts out of my mouth in a diarrheic stream.

"That chipmunk-cheeked bitch jumps *me,* and you're letting her *go?!* Chip & Dale had better *watch it!* I will *kick her Michael Jackson ass!*"

I struggle to wiggle my way out of the guards' clutches. I finally slither one hand out of my vise just enough to grab the heel of one of my slingbacks and hurl it in Ravi's direction. The guards pull me away, and I shriek Ravi's name over and over again.

"Ravi! *Ravi!!*"

The guards' thick fingers circle my forearms, and they lead me, limping, across the set, through the stage lot, and out of the studio gates onto the parking lot.

"Which one is yours?" The guard is holding me so close that I feel his deep voice roll within his chest as he speaks.

I point in the direction of my ragtop BMW. The guards slightly slacken the tension on my arms. A chance. I yank free from their grips and bolt, half-barefoot, back to the action, back to the set. One of the guards grabs me roughly, jerking my arm and shoving me against the hard metal of my driver's side door.

"Get in the car, miss!"

"Wait, I . . ."

"Get in the car!"

"*My keys! My keys, you moron! My purse . . .*"

One guard pins me against my car with his wide, strong arm while the other makes a labored jog back to the set.

"Calm down, miss, just calm down!"

"But . . ." I plead, the tears pricking my eyelids.

"Look here, miss." The megaphone of the security guard's voice quiets to a low rumble, and his oversized face draws close to mine. I catch a waft of spearmint Tic Tac on his breath as he nears. His walnut skin is rich and smooth, his nose long and pointed. He reminds me of my cousin, Memphis, back in Midland. If Memphis gained about 150 pounds, that is. The guard's voice is a gentle contrast to his hulking physical presence, with the silken, staticy quality of an old Johnny Hartman record. "You don't want these white folks calling LAPD, do you, dear? Why don't you just go home and cool yourself off?"

I nod mutely as the other guard lumbers back and hands me my bag. I slide into the tight little space of my front seat and start the ignition, the huge men watching my every move. I drive away, the hot breeze from my open window drying my tears before they have a chance to fall. All I feel is heat, the hot air, the pliant leather seats melting into the backs of my legs, the simmer of my stomach that threatens to boil over and tinge my throat with acid. I drive straight ahead, straight through the passionate climate, with no thought to where I'm going.

CHAPTER 2 ♡

I leave Culver City and crawl down Venice Boulevard toward the Pacific. The ocean will calm me down. The ocean is always the Tiffany's to my Holly Golightly, the Rx for my "mean reds." My day has gone from a tranquil, Tiffany shade of blue to mean red in a matter of minutes, so I need a dose of the sea to restore my sanity.

"*Come on baby, come on baby, do the Conga . . .*" Maybe Jen is right, and I should change my ringtone. My cell phone sings over and over again, crooning for my attention. I tap a button to light up the smartphone screen. I have seven "missed calls" from Ravi. There are just as many texts from his screen name, "Brahmaman."

I have to call my sister. At the sound of her voice, I begin to cry.

"Jo Ella?"

"Ann Marie," I rasp. "I . . . I just needed . . . I just broke up with . . . I needed to hear a friendly voice."

"And you called me?" she asks, though I know she's kidding. "What happened?"

"I don't even know where to begin," I say, and it's true. "The guy I was seeing . . . my director . . . he was supposed to be divorcing his wife. But it looks like he was lying, or it's not happening or . . . I don't know what. But she just threw me off the set."

"How can she have you thrown off the set of your movie?"

"She . . . she's financing the movie."

There is a long pause before Ann Marie speaks. "I know this is the wrong time to say, 'I told you so,' but how many times has Uncle Buddy told us not to shit where we eat?"

I don't respond. I know she's right. And I know that my sister knows that I know she's right.

"Anyway," she goes on, "I'm sure you feel like you just got the crap kicked out of you, but it will pass. And hey, here's another cliché for you—'there are a million other fish in the sea!'"

"I'm forty-one years old, Ann Marie."

"And your forty-one-year-old prom date, Willie T, is still single. And remember Curt? He just got a divorce. Move back home, darlin', and the world is your oyster. Oh damn, another cliché. The longer I live here, the more I talk like Mommy."

I almost smile. "And you wonder why I left Midland."

"Now I know how emotional you can be, Jo Ella, so don't do anything crazy. Don't go slashing the man's tires or keying his car or anything, OK?"

"Ann Marie! When have I ever done anything like that? I'm emotional, but I'm not a psychopath!"

"Hmmm," she says. "I think the jury's still out on that one."

"Ha, ha, very funny, Ann Marie. Why did I call you again?"

"I'm just teasing you," she says. "Look on the bright side. At least you've *had* more than one boyfriend in your adult life. I'm stuck with the same guy I've dated since we had braces on our teeth. I don't know whether to be grateful or to put my head in the oven."

"Thanks, Ann Marie," I say after a long pause. "I love you."

"Love you too. Now remember, no tire-slashing!"

"As if," I say and end the call. Suddenly, an Aston Martin screeches its brakes behind me. The sleek roadster veers sharply into the opposite lane to speed past me, almost sideswiping me in the process.

The beach isn't so carefree anymore. Laid-back surf towns where sunny, middle-class kids like Gidget & Annette Funicello lived in the movies of my youth have been overrun with the abhorrently affluent, whose needs always come first. Ravi's neighbors in Manhattan Beach paid two million dollars for a teardown, and my favorite beachfront burrito joint lost its lease to a Jamba Juice.

I should have punched Ravi's nose instead of Danielle's. Why was I yelling at her, when I should have been yelling at him! And he had me dragged off the set! He could have stopped them, but he didn't. I should have done something. I should have called Jen. I should have called my lawyer; threatened to sue. I didn't start the fight, and the whole thing is his fault anyway, so why am I the only one they hauled away?

The heat is creeping up the base of my spine toward my head again, and I can't do anything to douse the fire. I see the entrance to the 405 South and swerve over two lanes to get to it. The next thing I know, the Beemer is blazing down the Santa Monica Freeway toward the South Bay. I hit Inglewood Avenue, speeding past storage lots and Shell stations and Subway sandwich shops until I make it to Manhattan Beach Boulevard. I hook a right toward the ocean and race to the last street before the sand.

I skid into an empty parking space before a slender, shingled three-level house that sits so close to its neighbor that one can barely walk between them. Out of the car, I head to the tiny patch of flowers near the front door and fumble through the shallow soil with my fingers to fetch the spare key from beneath a smooth, polished stone. I peek through the glass-paneled door and see only darkness, so I press on, unhinging the lock and dashing into the stone-floored foyer. The air is bitter and chill, but it provides me with no relief. I fan my hands before my face to fan my fever as I hobble on one heel to the kitchen.

Opening and slamming lacquered white drawers at random, I seize a pair of kitchen shears and hop up the stairs to the master bedroom. Flinging open bureau drawers, I pull out a passel of expensive silk socks and cut off all the toes. Snipping and snapping the scissors, I turn all of Ravi's expensive briefs into thong underwear. I move on to the pricey watch collection laid out neatly on the dresser. I grab his favorite time-piece and shove it into the pocket of my dress, where it scratches against the face of my smartphone. I also pocket the iPhone I recently bought for him, and a small pack of sugar-free gum. I pull together a mis-matched collection of Ravi's personal effects—shirts, sweaters, shades, iPods, silver cigar tubes—and shove them out the bedroom window.

Back down in the kitchen, I find a virtual armory of ammo in my spurned-woman war on terrible boyfriends. I dribble soy sauce on the creamy upholstery of the fine furnishings and splatter pricey, corked balsamic vinegar on the milky carpets and porous stone floors. I uncork a few bottles of obscenely expensive Bordeaux, sipping one while simultaneously pouring the others all over the plush throw pillows downstairs and the crisp Pratesi duvets and shams in the bedrooms above. I turn his place into a Pollock painting, though I don't disturb the art. I could never wreck his Basquiat sketches or his Schnabel plate paintings, though I secretly believe them all to be overrated.

Clutching the two remaining bottles of Bordeaux, I tramp out the sliding glass door and plop down on the soft, imported Ipe wood of the deck. I search for comfort from my ocean view, but there is none to be found. I take out my phone and begin to text "Brahmaman," but my fingers are shaking, and I have nothing to say to Ravi anyway. I make a lame attempt to type a message to my agent, Jen, instead.

JoMaMa:	How mny matchs 2 torch a wistwatch!
JenPhen:	What? Where R U?
JoMaMa:	Nair's house. Gess I cld drown t. Panerai's wrpf?
JenPhen:	What's wrong w/U? Sounds like U shld get the hell out of there!
JoMaMa:	Jin this IS hell. Also cant fin me shoe.
JenPhen:	R U drunk? Put the bottle down & get your barefoot butt home!

Neither my friends, the wine, nor the ocean view calm my nerves or quell my fire. I spot an open book of matches on the patio table and reach for them. I cradle the book in my palm and examine the sketch of a gryphon on its underside. I heard once that they used to call matches "Lucifers." A fitting, though useless, piece of trivia I picked up among all the other useless stuff I've collected in my travels and years of play-acting. Everything in my life appears worthless and obscure from my point of view right now. The water fades in and out of focus in the distance as misty clouds of fog roll in from the horizon. My ocean view is not calming the Furies I seem to resemble. I can't see myself clearly in the sliding glass door, but I certainly feel like a Fury of myth, eyes dripping blood and head wrapped in serpents, spitting out poison all over the place.

I kind of feel my fingers, so I light a match. It dies a swift death, the tiny orange flame a mere speck against the backdrop of the churning, cold sea. If I can concentrate my explosive, scattered energies like the phosphorus on these match tops, then maybe I can figure a constructive way out of this mess. Or I can forget constructive and just torch the ugly stick sculpture on Ravi's coffee table and call it a day. That fucking thing has always bothered me. When I think about the godawful sum of money Ravi spent on that pile of twigs, the whole thing just pisses me off. My six-year old nephew could have made that stupid thing from the sticks he scoops up in Mommy's backyard with his Fisher-Price rake. For all of his whining about how Danielle held him back and inhibited his creativity, he didn't seem to think twice about spending her money on some nonsense. Not to mention how much money she probably spent on this place for him. Money he could have invested in his projects and his future. But for the Santa Ana winds, I would burn those stupid twigs right here and now.

"Damn it!" I say out loud and strike another match. I try my best to remember what happened in that Farrah Fawcett movie where she burned the bed. I don't recall the fire affecting the rest of the house, just the bed and the son of a bitch lying in it. How did she pull that off? Leave it to another Texan to find a way, when the will for revenge rears its tousled, feather-banged head. Brainstorm—I don't have to burn the twigs to get back at him. I can just toss his fancy watch into the ocean. Better yet, I can toss it into the toilet! In plain view where he'll know it was destroyed and not just misplaced!

I guzzle wine straight from the bottle, despite the smiling reminders from the little pixie sitting on my shoulder named "Mommy" to "use a glass, Jo Ella." Hard as I try to ignore her, she keeps coming back to pester me, flicking tidbits of advice and commentary around my head like tiny flecks of fairy dust. Legs neatly crossed at the ankle and hands clasped in her lap just so, she grins at me in the same way that she did whenever I tried to sneak a swig from the milk carton back home. The smile that sheaths daggers. The smile that says, "Jo Ella passed up law school and a respectable life for drama school and a life of sin, so the least she could do is show that she has some home training." Well, I hate to disappoint Mommy, but I think I broke all of the glasses.

"Ow!" The forgotten flame I am holding singes my fingers. I drop the wine bottle onto the soft, shadowy wood of the oceanfront deck, though I'm too low to the ground to break it. I wipe my hand on the front of my dress, smearing blood-red drops of Bordeaux from the tips of my freshly manicured nail on the poly-silk fabric. I can't distinguish the wine from the blood stains, though some of the older spots are beginning to brown. Mommy would love me in this dress, but it's ruined, so it doesn't matter if I treat it like a dishrag.

I try to get up, really need to get up, but I can't feel my feet. My feeble attempt to evolve into a species capable of standing upright fails miserably, and I land back on my butt with a thump. Well, if I can't sink the watch, then maybe I'll just burn the T-shirts I threw out onto the deck and let that be the end of it. That will work just as well, since these are no ordinary t-shirts. They are creamy, white $80 James Perse tees that Ravi wears every day under his slouchy Italian blazers and distressed leather jackets. He buys them in bulk from Jim at Maxfield as if they were Fruit of the Looms. Purchasing piles of James from Jim every month isn't so funny, though I always used to giggle every time he laid that lame line on the salesman. The thin-haired dude always smiled back at Ravi from behind the sleek sales counter that separated their stations as he carefully wrapped the stacks of new T-shirts in rich, black paper. Now the joke is on me, because Jim was always just playing along with the game, whereas I was like a kid with an Easter basket, eating up every morsel of wit and pre-packaged Hollywood charm he tossed from his lips like so many jelly bean treats.

How did Jo Randolph, 1985 Valedictorian of Midland Lee High School, graduate of some of the East Coast's finest institutions of higher learning, and girl who was raised to know better, get herself into this predicament? I always thought of myself as no-nonsense and smart. Savvy enough to weed out the louses. But, despite his flashy wardrobe and reality television past, Ravi was never lecherous. He worked hard. He was generous with praise and treated all the actors and crew with kindness and respect. He knew every member of the crew by name and always asked about their spouses and kids, whom he also knew by name. He was thoughtful. Without my asking, he arranged a VIP tour of Universal Studios for my sister and her kids when they visited me in the spring, though he had never met them. He was funny and well-read, and I would often find books that I "*muuust* read" and clipped articles about art exhibits and concerts he wanted us to see in my dressing room. He had a great sense of humor. And we were great together.

I shove my foot against the base of a brass gong propped on a little stand on the deck. The gong crashes with a noisy clatter, shaking and vibrating in sync with the waves shattering the surf just beyond the deck. Ravi once told me it was a gift from some Tibetan monk he met on his journey to enlightenment or the Atlantis or wherever the hell he was headed for all that time last fall after he brought me in to do a table read for the film and help him with the shooting script. It was so weird that he left in the middle of pre-production, and his adventures sounded far-fetched. But I never said anything, because he was so nice and was trying so hard to impress me. I'm not sure why he wanted to impress me. Why he tried so hard. With all the wealthy divorcées to pad his pockets and pretty young starlets out there for the picking, why did he have to choose my heart to break?

I reach for a clump of costly shirts and fling them into the gong. I light more matches and toss them in as well, but they merely poke parched pinholes into the fabric.

I somehow find enough equilibrium to rise to my feet, not just to stand but to actually move with some sense of direction and without too much difficulty. I find some newspaper and toss a stack of it atop the T-shirt pyre. I roll a newspaper into a cylinder and light another Lucifer, touching the roll with a tiny flame that expands erratically as it eats its way through the paper. Blackened shards of paper lift into the air and disintegrate into charcoal dust that I watch the wind carry out to sea. I toss my torch on top of the newspaper stack, and it starts a surge that's finally strong enough to ignite one of the tees, though the shirt simmers more than it flares. The newspapers burn, however, creating frolicking flames that shift and shimmy this way and that with the rising force of the wayward winds.

Senses stoked by the fire, I make my way across the deck and through the sliding doors back into the house. I shuffle my way over to the coffee table, grabbing a couple of the larger branches of the elaborate twig sculpture. I clumsily drag it outside to the deck and pitch it into the fire pit.

I don't realize the power of the parched wood until it makes contact with the flames. It flares up into a frightening firewall that towers taller than all the height I'm able to muster in my single stiletto. A warm rush of air strikes my face like a slap. Sizeable sparks flicker onto the deck and the long, tall slats of the seaside structure. Small flames pop up here and there on the planks of the house, growing in force and fury as they make their way up the sides of the house to the roof. In an instant the back facade is circled in a virtual clown wig of fire that cackles and crackles and pops sparks my way as it rapidly expands before my eyes. The yellow-orange flames eagerly meander their way across the roof to the rest of the house, like a festive Chinese dragon snaking its way through a merry New Year's crowd.

"Oh shit! Oh shit! Oh shit!" I race to the edge of the deck and scurry down the steps to the beach. "Oh, God, what do I do?!" I pace back and forth, gnawing my nails into nubs. The air is tinged with the acrid scent of soot. I have to get out of here. I pull Ravi's iPhone out of my pocket and tap '911' on the touch screen.

"Uh, I'm calling to report a fire in Manhattan Beach . . ." I bark the address to the operator in a low, scratchy growl. I toss the phone into the ocean and then race around the side of the house to get back to my car. I don't wait for the fire trucks to arrive. I thrust my key into the ignition and peal away in the opposite direction.

I don't know if anyone saw me drive up. The neighbors are all weekenders, but what if someone saw my car? Who can miss a fire-cracker red, convertible BMW? Daddy told me to buy a Taurus, but how could I hold my head up in L.A. driving a piece of shit like that? OK, my piece of shit BMW needs a new transmission, but at least it's a BMW. Oh shit! Oh shit! Oh shit!

Tearing down the Boulevard, I search for the pixie on my shoulder, as she'll certainly know what to do. But Mommy is gone.

CHAPTER 3 ♡

The late afternoon sun is low but blinding as I race up the winding drive to my Hollywood Hills bungalow. The jagged orange streaks of its rush hour glare splice through the tree branches and strike the windowpanes of my little hacienda with narrow beams of light. My Spanish-style cottage is like a grown-up dollhouse, with fluid arched doorways and cute, miniature painted tiles of blue and white and ochre flowers that I bought candles to match.

I want to dive under the covers of my unmade bed and shut out Ravi, the fight, the fire. How could I have been so stupid? What if the neighbors were home? What if their houses caught fire? I didn't hear anything about it on the radio in the car, but what if this turns into one of those major wildfires from the evening news? *What if I killed people?!!!*

And what about Ravi?

I can't process it all. It's just too much. I shove my shoulder against the door of my Beemer and slowly unfold myself out of the car. I sniff my clothes as I limp across the pebbled driveway in one five-inch heeled slingback and one bare foot. A trace of smoke lingers in my dress that could be mistaken for a hint of cigarette.

The tiny stones begin to crunch noisily, like a garbage truck chewing refuse. A wide Crown Victoria enters the driveway, rumbling ominously as it settles to a stop opposite my car. Two policemen emerge. Mirrored glasses hide their eyes while revealing how guilty I appear in their reflection as I limp lamely on one shoe in a mysteriously stained party dress.

I slap my hand over my mouth and inhale to see if I still reek of booze. I freeze as the officers approach me, unable to move and barely able to breathe beyond the stream of shallow breaths I blow into my palm. I try to play it cool, but my image in their lenses looks like one of those crazy Hollywood mug shots where even the most glamorous people are disheveled and unkempt. I don't dare look down at the blood, wine, and soot—the evidence of my indiscretions—splattered all over my skirt. Instead I wrap my bare foot around the heel of my shod one as if nothing's wrong with this picture. I clutch my handbag against my stomach to stop it from churning.

One of the officers crushes purple bougainvillea petals under the thick-soled heels of his boots as he trods on the flowerbed I planted along the edge of the carport with Mommy when she visited me last summer. "Are you Jo Randolph?" he barks as he shakes the soil and damaged flower petals from the spit shine of his large, black boots.

"Yes, that's me." I say in as innocent a voice as I can muster. "Can I help you with something, officers?"

"Miss Randolph, we'd like for you to come with us down to the station. We have some questions about an incident that happened this afternoon."

The flower squasher looks me up and down, but he doesn't say anything about my ragged attire or the reason he's standing in front of me. Where the hell is my shoe? Did I leave it at Ravi's? Did I throw it at him on set? Why can't I remember? Will one of these mirror-eyed guys whip it out in an "aha" moment before hauling my ass off to the slammer?

Be cool, Jo. I try to remember what happened that time I was arrested when I played that high-class escort on an episode of *Boston Legal.* The TV cops read me my rights, and I didn't talk to anybody but William Shatner, who played my lawyer and most loyal customer. I try to remember what Captain Kirk told me to do, but I'm drawing a blank, and I'm running out of time, as the mustached policeman reaches for the handcuffs hanging from his belt. All I know is I better not run or make any sudden moves. I've watched enough reels of *Cops* and the Rodney King video to know better than to run from these guys.

"What incident are you talking about?" I ask. I try to appear confident and at ease, but unfortunately my voice doesn't cooperate with the program. My casual question comes out more croak than cool.

"Look, Miss Randolph, why don't you just get in the car? You can ask whatever questions you want down at the precinct."

"Why can't you ask me whatever you need to ask me right here?" I ask as I try to keep my tote from sliding off my shoulder. I fail, and the bag drops to the ground with a dull thump, so I bend at the waist to pick it up.

"*Stand up and keep your hands where I can see them, Miss Randolph!*"

I feel like a nor'easter has whipped my face, a brusque chill that brings tears to my eyes, though I'm not actually crying. Tiny trickles run from the corners of my eyes down the sides of my cheeks. The rest of me remains motionless, as one officer's hand moves from his cuffs to his gun holster. I start to speak, but the words are locked in my throat, afraid of setting off the guys with the guns and becoming another random, big city statistic. The mustached man approaches me while the other continues to pose with his hand on his hip holster, never taking his sunglasses off me for a second. I don't look at the mustached man as he steps behind me, but I feel the sour heat of his breath against my neck.

"Miss Randolph, you have the right to remain silent. Anything you say can and will be used against you . . . "

I lose all feeling in my limbs as the officer lodges my hands behind my back and secures them in handcuffs. Though he's still talking, the sound is muted, as if someone turned down the volume of my reality with a remote. I say nothing as the cop grabs my bag and ushers me across the carport to the police cruiser, where he guides me into the back seat, head first.

As we pull away, I feel myself shrinking into the landscape, growing smaller and smaller to the point of disappearing like so many lost and unrealized dreams in this stupid town. L.A.'s glitz and gloss appear dreary and covered with grit as we leave the Hills and head south toward the rugged flatlands of Lynwood. We pass bored teens strolling down the cracked, grimy sidewalks of Hollywood's nether regions, dribbling basketballs on downtrodden courts, slinging shallow backpacks filled with very little knowledge. Passing through neighborhoods you never see on the sitcoms, L.A. appears as bleak and hopeless as the Texas town I ran away from some twenty-odd years ago. My eyes glaze at the never-ending stream of harshly-lit fast food drive-thrus, tire shops, garden apartment complexes, and modest frame homes – Midland-like scenes that I thought I was escaping when I chose this life and this place. I rub my eyes, hoping to remove the film and let in more of the warm, California sunlight. But all I can see is the L.A. fog that burns off later and later with each passing day. All I can think of are the L.A. dreams I burned to ashes with the strike of a match.

We arrive at the Century Regional Detention Center, and I immediately recognize it as the women's prison where Paris Hilton and Nicole Richie and all the other famous for being famous people did their time. I hope they put me in the special holding area they reserve for celebs and drunk cops' wives. Maybe it won't be as bad as it seems. Maybe they'll have mercy on me. Maybe I'll have a second act where I can do better and be better the next time. A redemption story, like *Shawshank Redemption*. I'll bet Jen will want to hook me up with that artist that does those silkscreens of the stars' mug shots, adding a Warhol glam to their misdeeds.

Who am I kidding? What I've done can't be scrubbed up or airbrushed or made pretty. I don't deserve mercy.

I'm led through dim corridors to a buzzing, open area with a long counter and a scattering of desks. I'm handed over to a balding, brown-suited hulk in rubber-soled shoes, who takes me to a long, metal table. He smothers my small fingers in his indelicate grasp, pressing each one on a blotter and marking my prints on a stiff white card. Then he shoves me in front of a bulky, old camera with a large numbered sign shielding my chest. It's rare that I meet a camera that doesn't entice me to grin and mug like the Texas prom queens I grew up with, but all I can affect is a droopy-eyed stare, chin lowered and shoulders slumped into submission.

"I told you, I ain't stole no money! That fool owed me twenty dollars." Standing nearby is an overweight and rather vociferous woman, similarly handcuffed and wearing a similarly dubious costume. Though her attire makes me question her color perception, not whatever antics landed her in this place. A graffiti-like swirl of purple, red, fuchsia, gold, and lime green curly-cues splatter her velveteen hoodie, which she has paired with skintight black jeans flecked with gold specks and sequins. She's wearing sunglasses, though her faux-Versace, Medusa-adorned spectacles are clear and only slightly tinted rose pink; her expressive, heavily shadowed eyes plainly visible through the lenses. As the seething woman glares at the officers through her possibly designer shades, that Notorious B.I.G. song, of all things, pops into my brain; Biggie's round cheeks puffing out "I'm clockin' ya, Versace shades watchin' ya" over and over in a continuous loop in my head.

Versace-Shades-Watchin'-Ya bangs her handcuffed fists against a desk without fear and yells, "I got a job! I pay taxes! Got my own house. So why y'all bring me down here over some damn twenty dollars? Y'all never come to South-Central when we call y'all to pick up them people who up to no good! It don't make no damn sense that he kin go round beggin' and stealin' to drink 'n smoke reefer all day while I go to work, but y'all drag my ass down here instead 'a his!"

Versace is the most reasonable person I've encountered today by a long shot, but three cops rapidly move in on her. They grab her meaty arms and shove her, with some difficulty, out of the booking room.

The brown-suited man stifles a yawn and rubs his red-streaked eyes with the back of his thick hand. "Look, miss, you might want to do yourself a favor and just admit to this thing," he says. "I checked you out, and you don't have a record, so I'm sure the DA'll go soft on you. By the way, weren't you in *Swamp Sisters*?"

I nod and flash my veneers at the detective. A faint blush spreads across his cheeks that matches his sunburned dome and the lines in his eyes. "I just rented it this weekend," he smiles, sharing a shy glimpse of coffee-stained teeth.

Maybe this is a good sign. Celebrity can get you everywhere in L.A., no matter how miniscule or D-List your stardom might be. Emboldened by the attention, I say, "Look, man, how can I admit to something when I don't even know what it is?" I add a wink and a gleaming, red carpet-worthy smile to my suggestion, but the flicker of friendliness that appeared in the detective's demeanor is gone.

"You assaulted a very famous woman today, girlie," he snaps. "You wanna act like that didn't happen?"

"Huh?" I'm confused.

"Danielle Coleman?" he sneers. "The woman you attacked on the Sony Pictures lot today?"

"That bitch!" I blurt, unable to control myself. "That goddamn bitch jumped me, not the other way around! I don't believe . . . "

I don't get a chance to explain what it is I don't believe, as the detective and his brown-suited buds drag me off in a similar fashion to Versace's ignoble exit. They pull me into a small, windowless room and leave me with two husky, uniformed females, who remove my cuffs and order me to take off all of my clothes, underwear included. I stand, feet shivering against the cold, hard tile, as they pat me down and feel me up, opening my mouth and peering inside with the aid of a flashlight. This is probably what it felt like on the auction block back in the bad old days, minus the flashlight. One of the burly babes straps on a surgical glove and examines my rectum. Finding no contraband there or in any other orifice, the ladies dump the contents of my tote on a bare-topped table. They bag my belongings in clear plastic bags while I stand buck naked in the middle of the room. My bare butt quivers, and, though I rub my arms rapidly, my hands wouldn't generate enough friction to warm my forearms. As I shiver, one guard leaves the room and returns a few minutes later with a pair of white slippers and bright orange scrubs.

"We're keeping the dress for evidence. Put this on."

My breath stops and my heart pounds hard, jabbing rapid one-two punches within the cavity of my chest. I'm really going to prison. All I know of prison is the fake, plywood backdrops we use on TV. Does prison smell? Will I smell? Without adequate Black hair products or a wide-toothed comb, will my hair grow into long dreadlocks like some sort of Bob Marley on estrogen? Will I get beat up for looking at someone the wrong way, even though I don't know right from wrong?

I'm led out to a counter with a bulky, black telephone. My fingers shake as I dial Jen's cell and pray to hear her voice and not her voicemail.

"Hello?"

"Jen, it's . . . it's me, Jo." My tears return and run rapidly down my face.

"*Jo!* Where the hell are you?! Rudy and I have been looking all over for you. We must have called and texted you a million times! And Ravi has been driving me out of my fucking mind, calling me every five seconds. He's freakin' hysterical, and . . . "

"I'm at Lynwood," I cry. "Jen, They're putting me in jail for . . . Can you help me get a lawyer or something? I'm sorry, but, I don't know what to do-oo-oo."

The lady cop reaches for the phone, but I clutch the receiver tighter within my fists. "Jen, they're gonna lock me up!"

"Jo, just calm down, honey. Rudy has lawyers that handle criminal stuff for his clients, so don't worry. We're coming down there. Now don't say anything to those people, Jo, and try not to let anybody touch you. I'll bring you some hand sanitizer, so don't touch anything 'til I get there, OK? I saw this thing on *Dateline* about staph infections, and . . . "

I guess it's too late to tell Jen about the cavity search. I sob as the officer takes the phone from me and shuffles me down a long, gray corridor in my orange prison pajamas to the cell.

The cell is no celebrity chamber. There are eight other women in the small space, though I'm the only one in prison garb. Versace is here, relieved of her shades-watchin'-ya, but otherwise intact. Versace is sitting on a long, narrow bench, arms crossed over her broad chest as she mumbles obscenities to no one and everyone.

Versace appears to be the most normal of the bunch. One woman I can't make out at all, as she is stretched out face down on the floor, only the stringy strands of her dull brown hair and the equally drab hue of her T-shirt and sweatpants visible from my vantage point. From their style of dress, four of my cellmates appear to be hookers, though none of them resemble *Pretty Woman*. Without airbrushing or adequate dental care, these ladies resemble characters from an HBO documentary as opposed to an HBO movie. And where their clothes and tall-heeled boots are secured with the assistance of safety pins, it looks nowhere near as cute as when Julia Roberts did it on film. In fact, cute is not a word that enters my mind when I look at them.

As for my other mates, one resembles a housewife, with sensible Aerosole shoes, tan slacks, and a yellow blouse. But the dark circles under her eyes and the steely, beady-eyed stare beneath her straw-like, silver-streaked mane suggest serial killer, not Susie Homemaker. The one other woman is stick-thin and pacing back and forth in soiled, baggy jeans and a loose-fitting grey T-shirt that was probably white in another life. Her ash-blond hair is matted and unkempt, and, like Versace, she is mumbling to herself as she paces the width of the cell, though the language is so unintelligible that she might as well be speaking in tongues. It all sounds like so much "mish mash mush bejeez" except the word "*Fuck*," which rings out loud and clear.

Versace seems safe, so I sit next to her while I scan the room and decide who it is I need to become. The desperate housewife is staring at me sinisterly from the bench opposite ours, her lips pressed so tightly together that they have formed a thin line, like the mouth of a Muppet. Perhaps I can just shrink into myself and become as invisible as my life feels. But that can't happen in such a small, confined space, where the hookers keep stealing glances at me, and the deranged starer won't take her eyes off of me.

"What the fuck are you lookin' at?" Versace screams at the subdivision serial killer. Versace is one tough cookie, so I decide to stick close to her. Poor Versace is badly in need of electrolysis, with sideburns worthy of an Elvis impersonator. But that extra bit of testosterone is exactly what I need in a prison pal, so I decide to watch her back, though she doesn't appear to need my help.

"Yeah, your crazy ass better find something else to look at if you don't want me to come over there and kick your ass." Twisting my neck and gesturing cockily in the deranged housewife's direction with my hands, I project far more ghetto-tude than I've ever been exposed to in actual life. But no one laughs out loud or tries to stab me with a pencil, so maybe the ladies accept my performance.

"*Fuck!*" yells the pacer.

"Crazy bitches," I hiss under my breath to Versace, who smirks and nods her head in apparent agreement.

The housewife doesn't say a word or move a muscle for a long time. She continues to stare in my direction, though her gaze grows distant. She finally turns her eyes away from me toward the hookers, who are standing in a circle in the back corner of the cell. Though serial killer has stopped looking at me like she wants to chop me up and eat me in sushi, the hookers have now replaced her steadfast stare in my direction. I try to make myself invisible, despite being the new girl who needs to be no shrinking violet and who happens to be covered head-to-toe in the neon orange color used to stop traffic in emergencies.

"What you do, skinny girl?" A curvy Latina in a super-short gold lamé skirt and false eyelashes speaks to me in a scratchy voice that makes me want to hand her a lozenge. I can't read the edge in her voice, so I'm not sure if she's trying to provoke a conflict or a conversation.

"Ain't I seen you before? Over on Sunset?" A blonde with very dark roots and a definitive Deep South accent chimes in to what seems to be a conversation, though it's still too early to tell. "Hey, y'all, I thank I saw'er over on that corner by the bank."

"Naw, Britanee, that ain't her. That's Chyna you thinking of," a Black woman in white patent leather go-go boots and a platinum blond wig offers. "She look kinda like her, but Chyna got bigger tits. And Chyna got braids. Hey, skinny, your man ain't bought you no tits yet?"

"You think I need a man to buy me tits?" I sass back, though as soon as I say it, I wish I could take it back.

"Well all right, Mommy," trills a pink-haired prostitute in a tube dress that matches her tresses and a rhinestone tiara to top it all off. She winks at me, and I notice her pink sparkle eye shadow and a rhinestone sticker shaped like a star on her eyelid. "Why don't you come over here with us. We don't need no man neither. At least not until the judge sets our bail." She blows me a pink-lipped kiss and winks at me again.

"She's cute, y'all," drawls the half-blonde. "She get herself some boobs, then we won't get no work no more."

"Naw, honey," the go-go girl objects. "Blondes like us always work. So what, skinny, you do girl dates? She look like the type they always ask for, don't she?"

The pink lady nods her head, and the others join in as well.

"I don't need a girl either. I don't need anybody, got it?" I'm not really cut out to play tough girl, but now that I've started down that path, I can't exactly turn back. I figure my best bet is to stay on this road until it turns treacherous, and then take a detour down crazy street.

"Damn, skinny, why you all hostile and shit?" gold lamé girl sneers. "This bitch must have PMS or some shit."

"I've got some shit all right!" Mimicking Versace's seated stance, I cross my arms over my tit-less chest and lean my back against the cold concrete wall.

The pink lady's sparkly brows rise expectantly, and the others' faces perk up as well. Even the pacer stops to stare at me.

"Hey, Mommy, you got some shit to share with the rest of us?" My mates' hardened expressions now appear hopeful, and all eyes are trained on mine, with the exception of the facedown girl, who never comes out of her coma, and Versace, who resumes her hushed obscenities to herself.

The whole thing reminds me of my prison scene in that *Boston Legal* episode. My hooker character ended up having a psychotic meltdown that enabled William Shatner to plead an insanity defense. My lines pop into my head as clearly as the day we shot the scene, though I probably need to improvise and amp up the profanity to make it work for me here.

What do I have to lose? I jump to my feet, shaking and agitated, my arms still embracing my chest as I begin my detour. "No, I don't have any shit to share with you. I've got shit . . . I've got this *shit .
. . this shit in my head!* I've got shit in my head, that's . . . I'm not

talking to you! I'm not talking to any of you! You're just gonna talk to them, aren't you? You're gonna tell 'em my shit . . . you . . . you . . ." *"Fuck!"* The pacer interrupts my meltdown and resumes her back and forth stride across the cell. The hookers huddle together and inch as far away from me as possible, turning toward each other to talk about my crazy ass in hushed tones. I sit down and rock back and forth, hugging myself. The housewife's stare slips back into a stupor, and Versace slides her rear down the bench a bit to avoid sitting so close to me.

I silently rock back and forth for God knows how long. I have succeeded in getting my prison pals to leave me alone, but now I'm left alone with my thoughts. I can't get the sight of the flames out of my head. Those damn Lucifers. The magnitude of what I've done is so huge that I can't even connect back to what I was feeling about Ravi and Danielle before I lit up those Lucifers. A sharp pain stabs my stomach as I imagine charred wilderness and orphaned animals like the ones on the TV news during California's annual forest fires. I imagine the cartoon image of Smokey the Bear pointing at me—only *you*, Jo Ella Randolph, can prevent forest fires! Or boyfriend beach house fires. I wish I could just wake up and start the day over again, like Bill Murray in *Groundhog's Day*. I wish I could make it all go away as easily as I made it happen.

I have to find something else to occupy my brain before I take a real detour down crazy street. I start to quietly recite my lines from *Obsessions*. It passes the time, and I don't have to think. I don't know what I'll do when I run out of scripts and plays to recite, but I'll cross that bridge when I come to it. I've been working a long time, so I have a lot of material to work with. I make it through the entire film script and then launch into Shakespeare. I start with my favorite, *Twelfth Night*. I was the understudy for the lead role of Viola in Shakespeare in the Park the summer Jen and I moved to New York after grad school. It was one of my luckiest breaks in this business. I smile as I remember it, which works because it makes me appear even nuttier to my prison comrades.

The smile fades fast as my feelings keep intruding on my monologues. What would Dr. and Mrs. Randolph think if they could see their baby girl in jail? The girl for whom they sacrificed their hard-earned, West Texas salaries to send to fancy New England schools. The girl they enabled to graduate with no lingering student loans, just like the Miss Porter's girls and all the other rich preppy princesses. The girl they lavished with dance lessons, music lessons, summers abroad, anything they could afford, just to give her opportunities and chances in life that their segregated upbringings didn't allow. All so I could become an adulterous arsonist and second-rate actress who does time with a bunch of hard-faced hookers. Perhaps my big sister was right when she used to say they shouldn't have had a second child.

I finally finish my recitation of *Twelfth Night*, and one of the prison guards brings us bologna and bread. I ignore my ration, preferring to disappear. I embark on *Othello* instead of my sandwich. Though I played Desdemona in a Harlem production of the play, my situation inspires me to channel Othello himself, the Black one who "loved not wisely, but well."

Suddenly, a figure appears at the door of our cell.

"Jo Randolph?"

I nod mutely at the guard.

"Come with me," she snaps. I hurry out, never looking back as she leads me back down the long corridors to a small, windowless room, where two suited gentlemen are seated around a metal conference table. One is navy-blue suited with a plain white shirt and museum gift shop tie, while the other sports a slim black suit and black open-collared shirt more suitable for club hopping than the county lockup.

"Jo, I'm Allen Simmons," the party-suited man says, smiling confidently as he stands and extends his hand to me. "Your friend, Rudy Wellington sent me. I think we've worked this whole thing out, haven't we?"

"Yes, yes, I suppose so," smiles the navy-suited gentleman, though he doesn't appear quite as self-assured as Rudy's pal. "I'm Assistant District Attorney Wilkins. You're free to go, Miss Randolph. Ms. Coleman has decided not to press charges against you for assault. So, if you're amenable and don't want to press charges against Ms. Coleman either, the DA will drop the whole thing."

That's it? I can just walk out? *What about the fucking fire?!* I raise my handcuffed hands to suggest the questions I can't bring my lips to ask. Allen shakes his head ever so slightly as if to signal me to keep my big mouth shut and count my blessings until I'm out of the building. The uniformed lady unlatches me and hands me my plastic-bagged belongings. I quickly change into my soiled street clothes and sign some papers I don't take time to read.

The guard releases me through a heavy locked door into a large room the color of putty. I immediately spot my best friends, Rudy and Jen, seated close together in stiff, metal chairs. In their stylish "Industry" uniforms, they're a complete contrast to the vision of Hollywood I left behind in my cell. I feel dirty and cheap in comparison. Jen's high-heeled curves are packed into pencil-straight jeans and a delicate silk tunic, cinched by an exotic, Moroccan silver link belt that I saw her buy on the street in Marrakesh. Intertwined loads of chunky silver chains and leather cords circle her neck, and her freckled, russet face is framed by a short, black bob. Rudy is sitting stiff and upright in an elegant, black linen blazer and bright white slacks. He scowls as he brushes real or imagined traces of grit from his pristine trouser legs.

On sight of me, Rudy and Jen rise from their seats. I rush over and drape my arms around Rudy's slender shoulders and plant a generous kiss on the ridge of his cheekbone. His teak-colored skin is smooth and cool despite the dank humidity of the waiting room. Jen wraps her arms around my back, enveloping me in her scent of gardenia and rose petal.

They quickly shuttle me out of the building to Jen's gleaming Mercedes sedan. We settle into our luxurious leather seats for the drive back to my place. Jen takes the freeway, circumventing the blighted, local path that led me to prison for the fast route back to the Hills. But it's not so fast. Though the still-dark sky is barely flecked with pinpricks of early morning light, LA's rush hour crawl has already begun.

"You need to go home," Jen says, her eyes fixed on the snarl of traffic, her manicured fingers tightly gripping her leather-wrapped steering wheel. "Tonight."

"I need to go home now," I say as I try to smooth the creases in my disheveled mess of a skirt. "I don't know what you had in mind, Jen, but I really need a shower and . . . "

Rudy cuts me off, reaching forward from the back seat and tapping my shoulder with a folded white sheet of paper.

AA Flight 5787/United Flight 3927, Los Angeles (LAX) – Houston – Midland, TX (MAF), 8:15 PM – 8:54 AM.

"Your crazy ass is going home."

CHAPTER 4 ♡

I guess I'm on the lam. An odd expression, "on the lam." Almost quaint. It's rarely used anymore, though everyone's familiar with it. Like an over-forty film actress. I looked up "on the lam" in Mommy's *Dictionary of American Idioms* last night. Seems it was a common expression back in the nineteenth century, used by thieves to indicate a "hasty departure." But I'm no thief. I'm just a fool.

Lord help me!

Mommy's trying to ignore Aunt Lula. My great-aunt Lula is chanting, "Lord Help Me" over and over again from the second pew, like a broken gospel record. It's a quiet but well-known secret among bourgeois Black folks that too much shouting and carrying on in church is just not appropriate. Especially for Methodists, like us. *Lord help us.* I haven't told Mommy about my Buddhist chant phase or my ceremonial circles in Santa Fe. Some things are better left unsaid. And Mommy's having a hard enough time staying composed in this god-awful heat in her saffron silk suit, matching wide-brimmed hat, and ribbon-tipped, suede pumps she bought on sale at Neiman Marcus' Last Call.

It's one of those hotter-than-Hades, West Texas summer days, in which the broiling morning sizzles into white-hot noon and simmers down to a smoldering slumber long after darkness falls. The heat is tangible and close, and it penetrates the entirety of St. Luke's United Methodist Church this morning, torturing the congregants into submission even more than the minister's sermonizing. Between the feverish temperature, Aunt Lula's moaning, and Daddy's outrageous snoring, Mommy's doing good to avoid a seizure, much less fail to break a sweat.

Lord help me.

Daddy lets out a long snort. His head drops and threatens to bang against the hard, walnut edge of the pew in front of us. Mommy's doing as well as a one-legged man in a butt-kicking contest when it comes to keeping Daddy awake in church. His slender, seventy-something face is the color of dark coffee, and his deep, childish dimples fade and reappear repeatedly as he breathes heavily through his mouth. His lips move sporadically, and he appears to be mumbling, though that's just how he dreams. His silver-streaked hair, slick with Murray's pomade, doesn't move an inch, though there's one mischievous curl that he can never tame, despite Mommy's best efforts to flatten it into submission.

Poor Mommy. She was so proud that she not only dragged my depressed ass out of pajamas and away from the television, but that she also got Daddy to church as well. OK, football and basketball seasons are in recess, of course, and she did threaten to throw the ham she baked for Sunday dinner out the window, but that's beside the point. Here Daddy sits, in full view of the Good Reverend Doctor, with his head weaving and bobbing and his mouth wide open, rumbling like an August twister. But if I know Mommy as well as I think I do, she'll play it off with a big ol' Texas, beauty queen beam.

Oh Lord! Help me!

I run my fingers through what's left of my hair. It's stiff and spiky from the decades-old mousse I found in the bathroom I used to share with my sister. Mommy is even less enthusiastic about my new 'do than Jen. She gives me the once-over, from my blond-streaked buzz-cut to my unstockinged gams. Her eyes settle on my obsidian toenails peeking out from the wide straps of my thick-soled sandals. She looks up and flashes me a toothy grin from her campus queen days, with a wink no less. Visions of "*Serial Mom*" flash through my head. For his own protection, I try to nudge Daddy, but he just snorts and lolls his head from left to right in response.

Mommy's smiling but sinister gaze invites explanations and excuses, but I have none, whether it relates to my lack of employment, my lack of will to do anything but watch television, or my choice of church attire. Bourgeois or no, one does not sport platform shoes, bare legs, or black toenails in an African-American church. I feel the urge to babble about the rage for dark nail polish in all the fashion magazines, and the pedigree of my chunky sandals, culled from Miuccia Prada's recent runway collection. They're very chic in my adopted hometown and very hard to come by. But Mommy rarely understands my sartorial selections any better than she gets my career choices or choices in men, so I don't bother. Besides, I'm not supposed to chat in church.

Mommy's gaze finally returns to the pulpit. I drop my eyes to my lap and pick at my gothic manicure. Why am I back in the Bible Belt? Rudy and Jen think it's a good idea for me to lay low and stay out of the limelight until the scandal loses its sizzle. It's hard to work on the "what nexts" in the midst of so much noise. But couldn't I hide out in Brazil or some remote South Seas Island? Rudy's response, of course, is that West Texas is more remote and removed from the real world than Vanuatu. I honestly can't argue with him.

Luckily no one was injured in the fire. The damage to Ravi's house was extensive, but the fire didn't spread to other houses. The tabloids are ripe with speculations and theories and innuendos, but no police or lawyers or formal inquisitions have come to get me. At least not yet. Most of the media attention has been on Ravi and Danielle's marital troubles—and my role in them. For some reason the fire hasn't been the focus. Rudy and Jen tell me this is a good sign and even more reason for me to keep my mouth shut and wait for the media mania to blow over. But it's maddening to do nothing. Not that I know what to do.

My cell phone is near the top of my open handbag. I slowly inch my fingers into my purse and cover the phone with the palm of my hand. I quickly remove it and hide it underneath my church program. I type an awkward, one-thumb text message to Rudy.

JoMaMa:	2 wks an im still n midlnd
HiFiNY:	You're just now figuring that out? Brain damage worse than I thought.
JoMaMa:	m goin crazy rudy.

HiFiNY:	Going crazy? Baby doll, you've been long gone ever since we met @ Dartmouth.
JoMaMa:	what does law shark say. did allen hear anything
HiFiNY:	Good Lord, girl, he's your lawyer. Call him! Law Shark says stay put. He's working on it.
JoMaMa:	wrkin on what
HiFiNY:	Be patient, sweetie. Me & Jen & Law Shark have your back & are looking out for you. Law Shark never steers me wrong.
JoMaMa:	isnt law shark entertain lwyr not matlock
HiFiNY:	You know most of my label artists are hip-hop. You don't think my lawyer knows a thing or two about rap sheets? Sit tight my love.

I feel Mommy's eyes boring into the top of my bent head before I even look up and catch a glimpse of her smiling wickedly again in my direction. I drop the phone and the program into my bag and avert my eyes. I don't want to stare at Mommy directly, lest I turn into a pillar of salt. Or is it a pillar of stone? I always get my myths and my Bible stories confused.

My widow-black dress of form-flattering jersey, which seemed so smart and hip and cool on the rack at Fred Segal back in L.A., is plastered to my back and backside. It's probably not fair to expect Mommy to appreciate my appearance when my garment looks like a wrung-out mop, and my hair looks like a whiskbroom. My *Blade Runner* spikes are OK when I'm playing the ubiquitous Black sidekick in one of those "ironic" independent films. But they're comical in the West Texas savanna, where Black women miraculously keep their upsweeps and pressed and parted 'dos in place in spite of the oppressive heat and profusion of sweat. Though I seem to be the only woman sweating in this camp. I fan myself with a yellowed photo of Dr. Martin Luther King, Jr. stapled onto a Popsicle stick and wonder what I'm going to do with myself.

"Lord! Help me!"

I'm in hell. This resembles a house of worship, but it is actually hell. I should be home. My *chosen* home, not Midland, Texas. How can I resolve the mess I made in L.A. from the middle of the West Texas desert? How can I get my life back on track when I'm so disconnected from it? My parents don't have Wi-Fi, so my only Internet access is the slow-ass, cable connection in the kitchen. Between my chores and '70s sitcom marathons, every day I scour the Web for news of Ravi, Danielle, me. There are anonymous accounts of Danielle screaming at Ravi and shutting down the set. Rumors of cost overruns since the crew and cast are on hold until shooting starts again. Speculations as to what will happen to the movie; is their marriage kaput; and where is Jo Randolph?

Reverend Bumpers bellows, *"Sin will find you out!"* at the congregation, and seemingly at me in particular. He doesn't read *Variety*, does he? I'm sure it's just a matter of time before they come for me. Maybe Rudy's Law Shark can make some sort of temporary insanity argument in my case. Though I don't know how well that excuse works these days, at least not in this State. If it didn't work for the psycho Texas cheerleader mom or the Houston woman who trammeled her husband with her Mercedes sedan, I sincerely doubt it will work for me.

I try to peel my damp dress from the front of my thighs and avoid the withering glare of Mommy's obstinate gaze, which now resembles Jack Nicholson's Joker from the Batman movie or that crazy character from *The Shining*. I focus on Mrs. Good Reverend Doctor's impressive beehive, which reminds me of the elaborate coif of my all-time favorite heroine, Lt. Uhura of the Starship Enterprise. If asked, I always profess my number one role model to be Barbara Jordan. The governor named me a Lone Star Scholar for an essay I wrote on the late Texan legislator during my senior year in high school. But secretly, in the dark recesses of my heat-warped imagination, it has always been Lt. Uhura's miniskirted *Star Trek* adventures I've really aspired to. How can I face a second go-around in the barren wasteland that Midland can be for a Black girl that dreams of being a Starship officer?

The congregation nods knowingly at Pastor Bumpers, as if they're all sharing a secret, and I'm the odd man out. I glance around at the rows of pastel day suits and floral chemises and feather-decked hats and crocheted tams. *Lord help me.* I don't care what everyone says. It was an awful idea for me to leave the promised lands for these badlands, no matter how difficult my life had become. And to make matters worse, Mommy has started making noises about me working at the "Big House." This name is well-deserved by my high school alma mater, considering the huge Confederate flag that flew in front of the school and past throngs of rebel-yelling fans at football games in my youth. When a southern Negro hears a yell, particularly of the rebel variety, it's usually a good indication that you are someplace you don't belong, whether it's 1897 or 2007.

I guess I never fit in as well as my sister, Ann Marie. Ann Marie was a high-kicking Dixie Doll and the only Black homecoming princess the Big House has ever seen. I glance over the back of my pew to look at her. Her flawless, bronze skin gleams in the sweltering air of the sanctuary. From her smooth hair to her silk knit, St. John's suit, Ann Marie remains fresh and composed, in spite of the heat. Her long-lashed lids are solemnly closed as if in prayer, though I know better. Ann Marie never wakes up to join us as we all kneel before the crucifix on our velveteen-covered benches and pray aloud from our United Methodist Books of Worship.

As we leave our knees for our rears, a fly starts buzzing around my head. I try to use Dr. King to swat him, generating an even chillier, more sinister grin from my mother. Following the fly's gyrations, I glance over my shoulder and catch a glimpse of one of my fellow House Negroes. Willie T., the undertaker's son and my old prom date, is sitting a few rows back and staring at me with a grin on his face equal in size to Mommy's, without the Mr. Hyde undertones. Willie T. looks good. He looks great, actually. And there is no visible gold in his mouth, at least as far as I can tell from this distance. So I grin back, though I quickly regret it, as I haven't yet confirmed whether his shoes are tasteful black or brown or some awful, Dirty South-style metallic, Lego-colored or gator-aded numbers. I recall a sloppy semblance of a kiss we snuck while sitting on the diving board of our pool during Ann Marie's senior year-end blowout. But the memory is more "American Pie" than poignant, adding to my discomfort.

I'm saved by my badass nephew, Trey. He has been sitting or, more accurately, *agitating* in the pew behind me and is an even bigger pest than the fly circling around my head like a dented halo. Trey bonks me hard on the head with a Methodist hymnal. Mommy, Ann Marie, and most of the people around us turn their attention to the little tyrant, as bad children are almost as unforgivable as bad manners in this part of the world.

Uncle Buddy reaches over and hands me a candy. "Don't give none to the baby," he whispers to me with a big wink. My great-uncle Buddy is ninety-five years old and the most handsome, charming man alive. He is very tall and very thin with a shock of frizzy curls and a snow-white goatee. His erect, regal carriage and sly smile bring flutters to the heart of every woman he meets, regardless of age. He uses a walker to get around, but I'm convinced that he really uses it to compensate for his inebriation, not his lumbago. Uncle Buddy loves his scotch whiskey, cherishes pound cake, though he never gains a pound, and carries a pistol everywhere he goes, even to church. The beauty queen adores him as much as I do, and Mommy even refrains from giving him a hard time about the concealed flask and concealed weapon he insists on toting into the sanctuary every Sunday.

I pop the candy into my mouth, and I jump in my seat with a start. My eyes fly wide open, and my throat burns from an odd toxic-sweet sensation. This candy tastes exactly like a tequila shot. In fact, *it is* a tequila shot!

"I made those myself," Uncle Buddy stage whispers with a big, broad grin.

I can't stop coughing. Mommy's evil eye darts back and forth between me and her grandson in a frantic attempt to determine which of us is the bigger nuisance and embarrassment. Trey starts reeling on the floor underneath the pew, the hard soles of his penny loafers whacking and wrecking the L'eggs of the gentle old ladies seated behind him.

Mommy and Ann Marie direct their devoted attention and decisive horror to subduing Trey, while Willie T. continues to stare and smile in my direction. He ignores the spectacle of my sister grabbing my nephew by his heels and dragging him down the center aisle of the sanctuary like a squirming sack of potatoes, disrupting Pastor Bumpers's searing sermon on sin.

I am amazed that so many of my contemporaries, people with choices like my sister and Willie T., never left Texas. Especially when so many of our ancestors had to hightail it out of here if they wanted to live a decent life and make a decent living. And the West Texas economy isn't exactly soaring these days, despite the presence of West Texas oilmen in the White House. But suggesting that someone leave Texas seems to provoke a stronger reaction and a greater sense of bewilderment than a bearded lady or a buck-naked cowboy prancing down Main Street. But like the Midlander-in-Chief, I guess I now have a pretty compelling reason to use Hell on Earth as a retreat from the limelight during the most miserable time of the year. Who's going to follow me here?

So I'm back in Texas. Smack dab in the middle of the snorer and the beauty queen. Back in my old room with the "Midland Lee Rebels" and Dallas Cowboys pennants over the bed and my wooden rackets leaning against the bookshelf with my tennis trophies and worn copies of *Jane Eyre* and *Mrs. Dalloway*. Eating iceberg lettuce instead of mesclun and rib eye instead of tuna rolls. Drinking DQ Blizzards instead of wheatgrass juice (OK, I never really bought into the wheatgrass thing, though I faked it). Not to mention Bud instead of Sauvignon Blanc. A lot of Bud, actually, sitting by the pool with my cousin, Memphis. Swatting flies while we wonder how inevitably hot the next day will be.

Lowering my head with the rest of the congregation, I thank God for the existence of satellite TV, the Internet, and air conditioning, despite its apparent absence in the sanctuary of St. Luke's on this particular Sunday.

Lord help me.

CHAPTER 5 ♡

What time is it? The last thing I remember was the holographic glow of the TV screen hovering like a poltergeist against the darkness of my parents' family room. There was an infomercial for a motivational book and DVD by that actress that played Thelma on *Good Times*. A still-stunning, Julliard-trained actress shilling mumbo-jumbo at 3 A.M. on BET. If I avoid prison, is that what I have to look forward to?

I never gave the future much thought after I left Midland. I always assumed that once I got out of Texas and became an actress, it would all work out, my life. I would see the world, perform, act, act out, and get paid for doing it. I would avoid the nine to five, the ordinary day-to-day, and the judgments of others about what roles I should play and what life I should lead. In the process, a glorious, prosperous life would magically unfold, like the plot of a Kate Hudson movie. I never developed a Plan B. I prepared no Ice Age scenario for when the meteor hit and my dreams and life as I knew it went the way of the dinosaurs.

I'm surprised Mommy hasn't come in to wake me up and command me to take a shower. The fluorescence of the late-night screen is gone and has dissipated into a swath of Texan sun that is flooding the family room. Its goldenrod hue suggests A.M., but I don't have a clue how long I've been lying here. Long enough for the scratchy fibers of the twill upholstery to etch an elaborate pattern into my cheek. Long enough for crusty flecks to collect in the corners of my eyelids. But I still taste an acerbic trace of generic red table wine on the surface of my tongue, so either it's very early in the morning, or I drank too damn much. Again.

I peel my face from the sofa and slowly sit up. I shake my head and stare at the smudged marks my fingers left on last night's wineglass. I try to recreate in my head exactly what happened to my life, the series of steps that got me to this place, but my recollection of my past is as cloudy as my fingerprints and my future. I remember the image of the day I met Ravi when I crashed a party at his house. I remember the setting, the orange-red sun dipping into the ocean beyond the deck of his house, the white-shirted waiters passing shimmery cocktails from silver trays, the muted glow of the day's last sun softening the sharp edges of his features like a jelly lens. But the words, the conversation, the details of what we talked about are fuzzy. Except for the movie. I had a cocktail in my hand, one of Jen's discarded designer creations was flattering my figure, and Ravi told me I would be perfect for his film. He remembered me from *Young and the Restless* and loved the way I played the crazy nurse stalking the town surgeon.

I don't know what to believe. I'm a professional actress, but I couldn't have faked my way through a performance as intricate as Ravi's for an entire year. And Ravi and Danielle didn't live together. Nothing makes any sense. I have to think about something else. I grab the remote and start scanning channels.

Ravi's face is suddenly before me, his angular bronze features filling the entirety of Daddy's 49" flat screen. Sporting a scraggly beard, his head and the brim of his baseball cap are lowered, and the palm of his hand is raised in an unsuccessful attempt to shield himself from the relentless scrutiny of the TMZ cameraman that is chasing him down Robertson Boulevard.

"Is it true that your wife has sued you for divorce and shut down your movie? Is it true you were having an affair with your lead actress?"

"No comment."

I drop the remote and grab my cell phone off of the coffee table. I pad, barefoot, outside to the brick-lined back patio and flop my foul body onto a white, wrought-iron chaise lounge. My cousin, Memphis, emerges from the pool shed and plops onto the lounger next to mine. He's supposed to be cleaning the leaves from the pool, but he hasn't made much progress. Clutching a coffee can in one hand, and a beer bottle in the other, he spits streams of tobacco phlegm into the tin can between sips of beer. It looks like a cliché, but this is my new reality.

"Hey, Jo Ella. What's cookin', good-lookin'?" Memphis smiles and spits again, narrowly missing the tattered yoga pants I've been wearing for the last two days.

I can't help but smile back at him. "Not much. Just checkin' in with my agent." I wiggle my cell phone in front of him. Memphis raises his beer bottle in a mock toast, as I select Jen's name from my favorite contacts.

"Jo, I was just about to call you," Jen says without a hello. "Did you go out in public?"

"I went to church the other day," I respond. "Why?"

"Well, it looks like some church lady sent pictures of you to the tabloids. I haven't seen them yet, but they'll be in supermarkets by the end of the week. Girl, I told you to keep your butt out of sight until we figure this whole thing out!"

"Jen, I'm not exactly in the witness protection program. And try telling Ella Randolph that I can't go to church with her because I'm hiding out from the police and my boyfriend's wife!" Shit! I forgot about Memphis.

Luckily, Memphis is distracted. Our next-door neighbor, Billie, has appeared on the other side of the fence and is flashing her enormous dimples in Memphis' direction.

"Jo, are you there?" Jen's piercing voice snaps me back into attention.

"I'm here," I groan. "You know, Jen, I can't stay in hiding forever. My family, and I'm sure all of Midland, knows I'm home. You expect *my* mother, of all people, to keep information like that under wraps?"

"Maybe not, but at least we could have bought more time. Luckily we got you out of town before the story gathered enough steam for anyone to pay attention to you. But now your cover's blown. We'll just have to deal with it."

"Blown cover? Jen, you've been watching too much *Law and Order*."

"Well, fact is resembling fiction right now, my friend. You haven't called Ravi, have you?"

It takes me a few seconds to answer. "No. Ravi leaves me messages all the time, but I haven't called him."

"Good girl. Look, Jo, we'll just put the best spin on it that we can. Maybe we'll leak some pieces to the press ourselves. Something about Ravi leading a double life, using Danielle for money. People are already speculating that he set the house on fire to collect the insurance money so he could divorce her. The press has been on his case, man, much more than you. For a change they're not making the women the bad guys."

My stomach lurches. The focus on Ravi isn't making me feel any better, even if it helps me. He's no saint, but he didn't deserve what I did to him. I cover my eyes with my other hand so Memphis won't see the tears I feel.

"Jo?" Jen prods.

"Um," I stutter, "d-do you think people will start hanging outside my parents' house? Are they stalking my place back in L.A.?"

"Well," Jen pauses a moment. "Not really. I mean, a couple of folks have asked the gardener questions, but they're not exactly camped out at your house. I mean, this story is interesting, but it's not as interesting as Charlie Sheen peeing on some photographer last weekend. Or David Hasselhoff eating that hamburger off the floor. Did you see that shit?"

Lord, help me. Drunk-ass white men engaged in drunk-ass behavior are more significant than the disintegration of a marriage, a love affair, a career, a film project that employs hundreds of people.

"Hey," Jen continues. "Maybe you should do that drama thing with the kids that your mother keeps bugging you about. That could be a good move. You know, a 'giving back to the 'hood' kind of thing. I like it!"

"But, what about the movie?" I ask.

Jen pauses again. "Jo, I think you're going to have to accept that the movie is done. You're going to have to move on from this movie. And from Ravi. You're gonna have to focus on the rest of your life and what's left of your career. Not to mention avoiding prison."

I can't speak.

"Look, Jo, take care of yourself. I gotta run, but we'll talk later today, OK?" Jen hangs up without saying goodbye.

Eyes still covered, I drop my phone into my lap. My nerves are frayed, but I'm too weary to cry. I peek through my fingers at Memphis, but he's not paying attention to me. He's still focused on Billie next door. He lowers his big, Bootsy Collins sunglasses and winks at her. Billie has a sweet, little girl's face, which starkly contrasts with her brassy, peroxided finger waves and the Day-Glo colors she prefers to wear. Today, it's a neon pink T-shirt with matching Capri pants, which encase her like a plump sausage, and metallic gold sneakers to match her stiff, blonde waves.

"What y'all doin'?" she calls in our direction.

"Nothin'," I groan, though she's not really talking to me. Y'all is both a singular and plural pronoun around here.

"Waitin' for you!" Memphis drawls as he moseys over to the fence, shoving his longneck into the deep back pocket of his jeans. A lush smile spreads across his smooth, unlined face. For a man of forty who spends most of his time in the sun, his skin is inexplicably youthful. Perhaps it is his young-at-heart spirit simmering to the surface. Or perhaps it's just true what they say about melanin.

Billie giggles, her light laughter piercing deep pits into her cheeks as Memphis leans lazily against the chest-high fence that separates them.

"Where you goin' all cute 'n' stuff?" Memphis asks.

"Nowhere," Billie gushes in response, eyes and dimples twinkling as if she just bumped into Billy Dee Williams back in the day.

"I'm just hangin' out here with Jo Ella," Memphis volunteers. "Keepin' her company so she won't get too lonesome."

"When'd she get back, anyway?"

"Couple weeks ago." Memphis' gaze is direct and laser-like, admiring the large, round bottom and fleshy hip on which Billie has placed her claw-like, rhinestone-tipped nails. His smile, however, is soft and whimsical, like that of a child flipping through the toy section of a thick Sears Wish Book.

"You know, Memphis, I get kinda' lonesome too sometimes," Billie suggests seductively, licking the traces of bright red lipstick that have begun to melt into the corners of her mouth from the searing southwestern sun.

Memphis is quite successful with women. His popularity among the ladies of Midland remains a complete and utter mystery to me, youth glow notwithstanding. I sigh and squint at the wide, open sky. I've never been to Montana, but I don't see how it can possibly surpass our baby blue expanse. They don't call West Texas "The Land of the High Sky" for nothin'.

"She some kinda movie star?" Billie sucks her teeth. "I've never seen her in nothin'."

"Now, Billie, you have too." Memphis removes a long blade of grass from his mouth that he has been using as a toothpick and continues to lean against the back fence. "You saw her in that soap opera with the Black folks on it. She was the sister who was kinda off who tried to poison the other sister and steal her man."

"That was Jo Ella? She looked crazy in that. She too skinny for all that hair she used 'ta have."

"Now, you know they made her look more crazy for that part. Jo Ella's gonna be in some new movie, too. *Hey! Jo Ella!*"

I bury my head into a copy of *US Weekly* I find lying on a nearby patio table. I pretend not to hear Memphis yelling my name at the top of his lungs.

"*Jo Ella!*"

"Memphis, when you gonna take me to the movies . . ."

Billie saves me from having to discuss my shaky screen career and sordid love life. I flip the glossy magazine pages and pour over the luxurious-looking lives and stylist-created miens of "stars" and the people who pay publicists to pronounce them as such. Some I've worked with. Some I found inconceivable to associate with until a couple of weeks ago. And now I would give my eyeteeth for a spot on a reality show. Getting photographed buying coffee, opening nightclubs, and cruising boutiques while dressed like a video vixen past her prime is shameful, but it's not prison.

Maybe Jen and Rudy are right, and it will all work out. The fact that I punched out a best-selling romance novelist and slept with her husband and trashed his beach house to high heavens doesn't have to mean I'll never see the light of day or work in my adopted hometown again. If Russell Crowe and Courtney Love and the rest of Hollywood's nutcases can bounce back from their temper tantrums and public meltdowns and indiscretions, why can't I? Ernest Hemingway turned getting wasted and slugging people in bars and cafés into a romantic, perfectly acceptable thing for an artistic type to do. And besides, nobody has known or cared about the personal lives of writers since Hemingway's day, so it's possible that Danielle's woman-done-wrong story will fade into the sunset as soon as Paris Hilton or Lindsay Lohan or some other starlet falls down drunk in a nightclub or flashes her crotch getting out of a limo, which seems to happen on a daily basis.

I lift myself out of my lounger and head back inside the ranch house. I slide open the glass door to the kitchen and find all 5'6", 135 pounds of Mommy whipping up a trough of ambrosia. She is adding what appears to be a ten-gallon, Sam's Food Warehouse-sized tub of Cool Whip to the combination of fresh and canned fruits, coconut flakes, chopped pecans, and maraschino cherries that make up her specialty dish. "Oh, Jo Ella! I know you've been trying to eat healthy, so I made you some fruit salad," she chimes in a sing-song-y voice.

Even if I'm ever able to show my face in L.A. again, who knows if I'll get any work after a stint in this place, unless I'm willing to settle for the funny fat girl parts that everyone over a size four in Hollywood is relegated to these days. I love my parents dearly, but if I don't get out of here soon, I may explode from the exponential increase in my calorie intake that has occurred since I arrived back in town. My parents actually eat very little and regularly scoff at the folks that fill their little hors d'oevres plates to the point of overflow at sorority banquets and church socials. But they have been cooking for me as if I just returned home from the battlefields with a regiment in tow. Sugar Busters and heart-smart health be damned, with nightly slabs of pork chops, pork ribs, pulled pork, honey-cured ham, broiled steaks, chicken-fried steaks and BBQ of all shapes and varieties, with heaping sides of molasses and bacon-laden beans, creamy mashed potatoes and mayonnaise-rich coleslaw and potato salad. And don't get me started on the junk food. I'm not sure that a single, solitary steamed vegetable exists in West Texas, much less a portion size smaller than Super Duper.

Mommy looks so happy, however, that I give her a big kiss and thank her for my thousand fat gram health snack.

"Baby," my father says from behind his newspaper. "You know you can't spend your life lying on the sofa."

"Now, Walter," Mommy smiles and sets her spoon on the counter as she leans in Daddy's direction, affecting a "whisper" that's not only loud enough for me to hear clearly but is probably audible to Memphis and Billie out in the backyard. "She's feeling low because she was *fired* by that movie company. You know how hotheaded she can be. Remember when she got kicked out of the French Club?"

When will I have to stop reminding these people that Mrs. Bonner did not kick me out of the French Club? I *resigned* from the French Club after she accused me of lying about French teenagers drinking wine with dinner when I spent the summer at the Sorbonne. "Madame" Bonner, a devout Southern Baptist who had never stepped foot outside of Texas in her entire life, was convinced that I made up this immoral tale to justify why we had filled up our Dixie cups with Gerald McDougal's mama's box wine at our annual crepe-fest.

"Mommy, I didn't get fired. My part got cut short. Script changes, you know. And I, uh, I just . . . I kind of need a little break from L.A. before I start another project."

"You could make your next project helping out the drama program." Daddy sets down his paper. "You know you're probably an actress today because of that program. Think of all the kids around here who don't have the same opportunities you had. And your mother keeps telling you how much they need English teachers for the summer. So desperate that they'll waive the certifications if they think you're qualified. A bunch of kids won't graduate next year if they can't take English this summer, but they don't have enough teachers."

"Daddy, I don't have the energy to teach a bunch of juvenile delinquent teenagers to read at a third grade level."

"It's summer school, Jo Ella, not reform school." Mommy picks up her spoon and returns to stirring her salad. "You know, I remember when teaching was a pretty good job."

"Jo Ella, in our day, teaching was one of the only ways smart Black folks like your mother could use their brains for a living. And teachers make a difference in people's lives. How many actors can say that?"

"Though, Walter, I sure did like that Gregory Peck in *To Kill a Mockingbird*. I always hoped you would go to law school, Jo Ella. I wanted to be a lawyer, but not too many law schools admitted colored girls back then. And I couldn't afford to go to Howard." Mommy doesn't look up from her stirring, even as Memphis passes her to grab another Lone Star from the fridge. He sticks an unwashed, soil-coated finger into her fruit bowl and then distracts Mommy with a light kiss on the cheek and his childlike smile.

"The pool's gonna be cleaner than when you built it, Aunt Ella. Jo Ella, wasn't you a swim teacher in one of them movies you did? The one about the guy with chain saws for arms at that summer camp?" Before I can answer, he scoops another marshmallow with his index finger and disappears out the sliding glass door.

Daddy stares at me. "How long you gonna keep this acting thing up, baby?"

"Um, as long as I can, I guess."

"You know, Jo Ella, you're not getting any younger," Mommy says in the saccharine, pageant voice she affects when giving directions disguised as suggestions. "Maybe while you have this little break, you can think about things like your career, family . . . Maybe you can catch up with a few of your old friends while you're here. Some of them aren't married either."

"Look, Mommy, if I wanted to be Ann Marie . . . "

"Nobody's telling you that you need to be like Ann Marie, Jo Ella. We just worry about your future." Mommy is staring straight at me, and she isn't smiling. Her mouth is pinched, and I notice tiny lines at the corners. Mommy is still beautiful—everyone always said she looked like Lena Horne in her prime. She still does, but for perhaps the first time I notice that she is now the *Lady & Her Music* version, not the

Stormy Weather ingénue. Her cheekbones are high and pronounced, her skin relatively smooth, but the laugh lines at her eyes have deepened and do not disappear when her smile fades. There is a weariness, and possibly even fear, tugging at her perfectly made-up eyelids that I never notice when she flashes her movie-star smile.

I have nothing to say, and I'm relieved when Mommy drops her eyes back into her salad bowl. Even if they're in the dark about all the details of my current predicament, I can't blame my parents for their doubts. I remember when I flew them to L.A. for the premiere of my big-budget movie break in *Jurassic: The Revenge!*, just for them to see my head torn off by a pterodactyl in the first five minutes of the film. At least I didn't subject them to my full-frontal nude scene in that indie film about Amazonian eco-terrorists that never picked up a distributor at Telluride. That may have been too much for them, though at least I wasn't eaten alive by piranhas like my co-star. And now I've given them something much scarier than computer-animated dinosaurs and flesh-eating fish to worry about.

"OK," I say. My parents' eyes meet mine. "I'll talk to whomever about doing some stuff at Lee this summer. Working with the drama program or whatever."

Mommy smiles broadly, though this time her smile is sincere, not sinister. "Oh baby, that's wonderful," Daddy says as he claps his hands in applause. "I'll call the Superintendent right now!"

Daddy bounds out of my parents' harvest gold-hued hangout. Mommy begins to hum as she opens a tin of mandarin orange pieces to add to her salad bowl. I need a drink. I grab a Lone Star from the fridge and walk toward the sliding glass door to join Memphis back at the pool.

"Oh, Jo Ella," Mommy calls out. "I forgot to tell you. I'm having a little get-together on Saturday to welcome you home!"

"Wha?"

"Just a few friends and family, Jo Ella. There are so many people that have been asking about you and wanting to see you that I just *had* to do something. I'm calling it a 'cocktail barbecue.' What do you think?"

"Huh?" For some reason, the English language keeps escaping me.

I can't find words to adequately express how I feel. I'm sure my mother told people that I was home, that I wanted to see them, and that she was having her "cocktail barbecue" because she just *had* to do something to help me out, but that's just details. Truth is relative around these parts. My truth is that I don't want to be confronted by all the people I grew up with who'll flood me with questions that will cause me to have to come up with plausible-sounding lies and half-truths. I just want to hide out here in the hacienda with Mommy and Daddy and eat enormous amounts of ambrosia salad and watch old episodes of *Three's Company* and *What's Happening!* until things calm down and I can finally return to L.A.

"You can go to Sam's with me and Daddy this evening to shop," Mommy continues. "Don't look so worried, Jo Ella. You don't have to cook anything. You're the guest of honor!"

Mommy blows me a kiss and returns her attention to the Cool Whip barrel. I can't think of a single thing to say. But I'm in Texas now. Mommy's domain. So nothing I say will make a difference.

CHAPTER 6 ♡

In a span of three days, I've made five insanely chaotic trips to Sam's Food Warehouse with Mommy and Daddy, two of which occurred on the same day. (How on earth could we have forgotten the Nacho Cheese Doritos that we easily could have picked up at the 7-Eleven around the corner but instead chose to drive for twenty minutes and stand in line for an hour to secure for some fifty cents less?) I now find myself hunched behind the steering wheel of the noisy orange, vintage BMW model 2002 that I gave to Memphis years ago when I bought the red convertible that is sitting in my L.A. carport. I am attempting to navigate the no-longer familiar streets of Midland in search of the place where I spent nearly every weekday of my adolescent life.

The first school orientation for summer faculty is this morning, and I hope not to be late. I dusted off my Bobbi Brown compact and even applied my own makeup for a change. Though I still have to wipe the Dorito dust from the front of my blouse. My dietary habits are in a free fall and are completely spiraling out of control.

I'm scared. And not just about my expanding waistline. The consequences of screwing this up are more significant than forgetting my lines in some forgettable horror film. I have no clue what I'm doing. This wouldn't be a problem back in Hollywood. But in the real world, I'm not so sure.

After several wrong turns, I finally roll up on the massive low-rise structure, which reminds me of the state pen in Huntsville. I slide back into the demure Nine West mules that Ann Marie picked out for me—the style, that is, not the bright orange color to match my car and my nacho sprinkles. I smooth the wrinkles from what started out as a crisp white shirt and khaki pants, Gap-issue, that I borrowed from Ann Marie. Ann Marie and Mommy effectively persuaded, OK bullied, me into adopting a more conservative, soccer mom style to counterbalance my erratic *Eraserhead* hairdo, since they couldn't convince me to get a perm. They know I hate to comb my hair, but they don't want me to scare the white people unnecessarily.

The metal doors are heavier than I recall, the hallways darker. The harsh fluorescents give the place a dim, asylum feel. I breeze into the auditorium, my little heels clip-clopping against the hard gray linoleum, where I'm greeted by a sea of pale grimaces. OK, maybe I should have gone for the perm.

"Don't worry, it's not you," says a nice baritone behind me. I turn to face Dennis Quaid's schoolboy grin melded with a slightly scruffy, Beach Boys-era Brian Wilson, circa 1964 or so, with a green short-sleeved knit shirt, the same Gap khakis I have on, and flip-flops to match. Handsome, though something about his face is off-kilter. The bridge of his nose is slightly crooked, as if he has just been through a brawl.

"No one deals with the summer heathens very well," he says as I stare at his nose. "I'm Davis. Music and Chemistry."

"Jo. English and Drama."

"Davis! Where's that sumbitch cousin of yours," growls a gravelly-voiced, ruddy-complexioned hulk in dark red polyester shorts and a white "Rebel" polo.

"You mean sumbitch Dean or sumbitch Duke?"

"Dukey-boy. S'he gone get back on the wagon long enough to be my off-ensive coach? Practice is already started! Whar the hell is that boy gone off to anyway?"

"Don't rightly know, Coach. You probably talk to him more than I do."

"You tell that sumbitch to learn to hold his liquor like the rest of us and stop being a sissy and get his ass to practice, ya hear?

"Coach Buck, this is . . . "

"Tell 'em I'm lookin' for 'em!" Coach points a beefy forefinger in Davis's direction as he lumbers off in the direction of matching polyester shorts.

"Sorry about that. Let's grab a seat together before we have to talk to anyone else."

A friend perchance? I clip-clop behind surfer dude to locate some empty seats among the rapidly filling rows of putty-colored, folding chairs.

"So, Davis, but for your accent, I would guess you're not from around here."

"Because of your accent, I would guess the same about you, except for the fact that I used to sit behind you in art history class."

I stare blankly.

"I was one of those anonymous, skinny band guys everybody ignored back then."

"The guy with the bad acne who used to say hi to me all the time? Oops."

"That's the one," he grins. "I *love* reunions."

Suddenly, a short-sleeved Van Heusen shirt with Ken Doll hair rises to greet the room.

"I hope everybody's having a fine summer. As you all know, I'm Principal Hardy, and I want to personally welcome y'all to Lee High for the start of what's sure to be an exciting summer, Lord willing. Before we begin, let's bow our heads."

The hairs at the back of my neck practically stand on end, less from the heat this time than my new boss' decision to pay no heed to the First Amendment. To my knowledge the Constitution hasn't been altered or amended recently, no matter what the First Midlander says to the contrary. Did I miss something? I mean, no one else seems to be surprised or bothered by our nonsecular practices on public property. And even I can't help being distracted by something of far lesser consequence, but of equal fascination, and that is the unnaturally molded, immobile quality of Principal Hardy's hairdo. Not a strand moves out of place as he lowers his head to praise Jesus.

"Hairspray?" I whisper.

"Dippity Doo. I see his wife buying tubs of it at Walmart. I think he and Trent Lott must share the same barber."

"Or the same gene pool."

"So, you've obviously met him."

I smile again, bowing my head with the crowd to suppress a giggle. Talking to Davis reminds me of being with Jen and Rudy. I miss having a good friend to joke around with. Now all I've got is a PDA to keep me company and keep me sane. That and my new email buddy, Mrs. Hightower, though our online exchange is driving me *in*sane.

I'm supposed to take direction and advice from Mrs. Hightower, but I haven't learned much about teaching from her yet. My bag is stuffed with reading comprehension exercises and State exam questions she sent me to review before summer school starts. But didn't we analyze books and write papers about them when I was in high school? Good books with dictionary words in them? I know I spent a lot of my college freshman year in a Heineken-soaked haze. But I do remember having picked up enough literary skills from this outback, country high school to ace all of my English courses at Dartmouth, notwithstanding a pervasive hangover and the pub-induced massacre of a good amount of brain cells.

I guess the only upside of my online exchange is that I've only had to sit down with the woman in person once. She was far too cheerful and friendly for my present state of being as she walked me through endless lists of multiple choice questions whose strongest relation to English comprehension was that they were all written in English. I suddenly spot Mrs. Hightower across the room and slink down into my hard, metal seat. I shift to the right a bit in the hope that Davis' tall torso might shield me from her view. It's too late, as she has already spotted me and is waving in my direction. As a reflex, I lean closer to Davis for support, my shoulder brushing his forearm.

"Sorry," I whisper. "I'm trying to duck Mrs. Hightower. I think she wants to give me a tour or something."

"Well, you're toast. She definitely sees you." Davis leans in a little closer, his lips very close to my ear, which causes more eyes than Mrs. Hightower's to look our way. "Wanna grab a drink after? You'll probably need it."

"Bless you."

"Don't mention it. Meet me at Chimichanga's when you finish up."

I nod, surprised that Davis has suggested a place near my neighborhood. When I was growing up, most white folks I knew were afraid to come to my neck of the woods, even though at the time it was tamer and cleaner than the set of *Leave it to Beaver*. I was used to being the one and only in their world, but it was usually a one-way street.

I haven't been to Chimichanga's in a long time, perhaps not since my neighborhood pals and I used to meet there on breaks from college. They had two-for-one tequila happy hours with free trays of nachos and stuffed chiles and overflowing ramekins of queso. My Chimichanga days were happy days. I celebrated there when I found out that I made it into the graduate drama program at Yale. I was home from Dartmouth, and after a few too many tequila shots, I jumped on the bar and performed excerpts from the satirical monologue I created as part of my entrance application. I had seen Whoopi Goldberg on Broadway during college and was inspired to create my own one-woman montage of quirky Texas gals living through the Reagan-Bush era. In a twist on Gil Scott-Heron's "Winter in America" from the Nixon years, I called it "Summer in the Southwest."

At the entrance of Chimichanga's, the tequila drinks of the day are scribbled in white chalk on a board by the front door. I'm intrigued by the "Adios, Motherfucker!" The prices of the drinks have doubled since I used to come here, but the décor of this hole-in-the-wall is exactly the same. The same brick-red walls and dark wood-beamed ceiling, and a few too many rustic square tables and stools stuffed into such a small space. Lynryd Skynyrd or some such southern rock band is blaring across the room, where I see gnarly, tattooed guys with silvery moustaches and camouflage caps and small groups of Latin men, their tawny faces reddened by the many bottles of beer scattered across their tables. A dark, heavyset man sporting an '80s-era jheri curl sits by himself, sipping something brown. Thin gold rope chains circle his neck, and he extends his pavé diamond-ringed pinky in the air as he drinks. I don't see Davis, so I take a seat at the bar. The simple wooden bar stools with the red pleather cushions are a bit worse for wear, and I try to pick the least tattered one.

A bandana-ed bartender of indeterminate ethnicity wipes the area in front of my seat with a rag. He is wearing a black Jack Daniel's T-shirt that stretches tight across his muscular chest and black terrycloth bands around his wrists. "What you havin,' darlin'?" he says to me as I stare at his hands.

"Adios Motherfucker! Please."

"Comin' up," he smiles as he slaps a plain paper napkin in front of me. A Celtic cross is tattooed on the top of his hand, and a small water bird is etched on his index finger.

Many of the men in the room glance my way, and I suddenly realize that I'm the only woman in the bar. My skin tingles, and I feel itchy, fidgeting a bit in my seat. I'm not certain whether it's best to keep my eyes focused down on my drink or to stare straight ahead at the long rows of bottles shelved behind the bar. I take a quick glance at the front door to figure out the best path to it. I see Davis chatting with a tank-topped man wearing a large, gold dollar sign necklace. They engage in one of those half-handshake, half-hugs that guys like to do before Davis walks over and touches my arm.

"Sorry, Jo. I had to make a phone call, but I couldn't hear in here. I've got a table over there."

As we move to a booth near the window, I yell over the music, "You know that guy?"

"Yeah, I know him." Davis' lips form a straight line, though his eyes dance. "You seem surprised."

"I . . . I mean . . . oh, hell, I guess that was pretty judgmental of me, wasn't it?"

"On many levels, yes, but I'll forgive you this time. I know it's hard to leave L.A. with your brain still attached." Davis releases his lips from their lineup and allows me to sit before he slides into the bench across from mine. "Mr. Johnson has a son who's in the band at Lee. I'm teaching him the trumpet."

"You come here often?"

Davis' face reddens. "I haven't been here since college. The crowd was a little different back then. I should've picked someplace nicer, but I just moved back from Austin about a year ago, and I don't get out so much."

"No worries," I smile. "This is actually convenient to my house, I mean, my parents' house. I just won't be coming here by myself."

"As well you shouldn't." Davis signals for the waiter to bring him one of what I'm having.

"You know, Davis, you seem too big city for this place. You're not like any of the teachers I remember from high school."

"Maybe I am like them, but we just saw all the teachers as too old to be interesting back then."

"No, I would have noticed if a Hardy Boy was teaching me the periodic table. My chemistry teacher wore powder-blue slacks and thick, black glasses. And he had this really greasy hair that I don't think he washed once the entire school year."

Davis takes a long swig from the glass that the waiter places in front of him. "Well, after graduation, I said I was leaving and never coming back. I went to UT Austin and got involved in the music scene down there and played in a couple of bands. We never sold many records, but we did a lot of studio work with some famous folks. And we had nice little followings in places like Dallas and Nashville and ski towns out west."

"Wow! So you were a real musician? Not one of those unemployed, forty year olds in a Lou Reed T-shirt that still lives in his parents' basement?"

"Ouch!" Davis clutches his stomach in mock anguish. "Yeah, I was a real musician, am a real musician, even though I do live at home and own a Lou Reed T-shirt."

"That's what I get for stereotyping." Not paying attention to what I'm doing, I spill drops of my drink on the front of my blouse, which is now flecked with watery-blue spots to go along with the Dorito dust. I must look a mess.

"It's a fair stereotype," Davis says as he focuses on my face and luckily not my untidy attire. "Though, to be honest, I make a better living from writing songs than singing them."

"You write songs too?"

"Oh yeah." Davis's eyes drop into his drink. "I probably like writing more than performing, even. But I've been kind of stuck lately . . . " his voice trails off, and he seems far away. He scrapes a few chunks of salt off the rim of his glass with his index finger and presses them between his lips.

"What, you weren't tortured enough by bad band jokes as a teenager? Seriously, Davis, how could you leave what sounds like a pretty nice life in Austin to come back to a place like this?"

"Well, my teen years were torture, all right." Davis swirls his glass as he speaks. "But my mother got really sick, so I came back and took care of her 'til she died. It's not like anything was going on for me in Austin anymore—I had just left my band, and I couldn't really write anything. I guess I kinda needed a break from it all."

Though I wait for more details, in true man-fashion, none are provided. Seconds turn to minutes as Davis continues to sip his cocktail in silence, not seeming to notice that he opened Pandora's box without releasing any of its contents. I now see what Ann Marie means when she complains that talking to her husband, Little Claude, is like talking to the doorknob.

"When did your mother pass away?"

"Last August."

"So what are you still doing here?" I blurt.

Davis's eyes are not large, but they do not lack for expression. They either dance or brood, betraying what actually lurks behind the cool blue irises and the dry, poker-faced wit. His eyes appear darker and more distant as he pauses and thinks before he speaks. "I loved Austin," he sighs. "To be honest, I really miss it. But I had to get away from that place for a while." His eyes return to the room and brighten a bit as he notices me again. "What about you? What's the big Hollywood actress doing in Midland teaching summer school?"

"Not so big."

"Hey, I saw you in the *Jurassic* movie."

"Then you must not have blinked in the five seconds it took for them to kill me off."

"Ya know," Davis drawls, "I knew you were destined for big things when you played the Wicked Witch of the West in the school musical."

I laugh at the memory. "My mother was mad that they gave the Dorothy part to that blonde cheerleader that couldn't act her way out of a paper bag. When she couldn't remember her lines, she would just shake her boobs around like this." I pucker my lips and shimmy in my seat, but I stop as suddenly as I started. This may not be the sort of thing one should do in front of one's work colleague in the real world.

"I remember that too," Davis laughs. His eyes are dancing again. "I thought it was on purpose, though. Like one of those campy, *Rocky Horror* kinds of things where Dorothy is a hooker instead of a schoolgirl. But, hey, you're a big-time actress now. That poor girl gained about 100 pounds and works in the lawn and garden department over at Walmart. She sold me a sprinkler last week."

"Serves her right! Though, I have to admit that I like playing a Wicked Witch better than a Dorothy. Unless it's a campy, hooker Dorothy. You know, I've had a lot of small, weird parts in big things and big, weird parts in small things. But I still have to rely on breath mint commercials and teaching Bel Air anorexics how to do downward dog to disco music to keep the lights on a lot of the time."

"Don't down yourself," Davis smiles. "Look what commercials did for the '*wassup*' guys and those Geico cavemen."

"You mean, people actually remember who those guys are?"

"No," Davis grins slyly and extends his glass to the waiter, who has reappeared with a cocktail shaker to refill our drinks. "I was just trying to make you feel better."

I can't help but grin back. "So, I guess you've confirmed for me that it wasn't such a sacrifice to give my SAG card and my passport a rest for the summer." My grin fades. "I guess I finally need to figure out what to do with the rest of my life other than just slog through auditions and run around collecting interesting cocktail recipes from bars around the world."

"Experiencing bars around the world seems like a worthwhile activity to me." Davis raises his glass in my direction.

"It usually gets me into trouble, but I guess it does have its merits. Cheers." I raise my glass back to him.

"If it's any consolation, it's actually kind of good for the soul to get off Sunset Boulevard or Sixth Street and just sit still for a while. I turned forty last year. It sounds like a cliché, but it's been a big transition for me. Especially since I've been living on the road for so long. I don't feel old, but it's like I can't run away from the fact that I'm a grownup anymore. I've got responsibilities I didn't have ten years ago, hell, five years ago, and I've had to force myself to settle down and sort out some things. There's not too much to distract my attention here in Midland, so I have plenty of time to think about how I want to spend my adulthood, if you can call it that."

I contemplate the quiet of Davis's face, his calm, slightly sad eyes focused squarely on my own. "Davis, did you come up with that speech yourself? Can I borrow it sometime for my own selfish purposes? Everything I say or do to explain my behavior either comes across as incoherent or downright loony."

"No problem," Davis grins. "But you may have to pay me royalties if it works out for you."

"If I could find a way to make sense of my life, Davis, it would be worth a fortune to me."

"Now I'm no lawyer, but I'm not sure it's such a good tactic to put all your cards on the table like that. I hope for your sake that you don't start out all your negotiations that way."

"Unfortunately for me, I do. I can never hold anything back."

Davis laughs and winks at me. "Me neither. You see, I'm not as perfect as I look."

"Then we're probably going to get along very well, my friend," I laugh along with him, and we clink our glasses together. "Hey, Davis, this is a weird question, but would you be interested in going to a 'cocktail barbecue' my family's having this weekend? I know we barely know each other, but I'm desperate for company to help me get through it. You seem to fit the bill, even though you do frequent Walmart."

"Don't knock Walmart, smarty pants. The essence of America, not to mention twelve thousand varieties of deodorant and peat moss, can be found at Walmart." The faint lines at the corners of Davis's mouth deepen, and his slim, sandy brows rise quizzically. "Now this gathering, does it involve other faculty?"

"No."

"Margaritas?"

"Absolutely."

"Done. I'm there."

Maybe Midland's not going to be so bad.

CHAPTER 7 ♡

I am now wearing a white, off-the-shoulder peasant blouse embroidered with images of Technicolor desert flowers, cactuses, and, inexplicably, tropical birds. Why does Ann Marie get to wear the cute, sorority-issue Mexican dress with discreet little embroidered flowers running down the front while I get to look like a waitress from El Chico? And Mommy expects me to greet people I haven't seen since the Mesozoic era in this getup? Never mind that everyone else will be clad in similarly ridiculous attire. I really need to get out of this place before I explode into something uglier than my shirt.

I peek through the open kitchen door, afraid to go in. Mommy and Ann Marie are preparing trays of food, arranging flowers in colorful glass vases, and adding festive Tex-Mex touches to the tables. Uncle Buddy is fast asleep sitting straight up at the breakfast table, a skill he perfected in church. Aunt Lula is sitting three inches from the kitchen TV set, riveted to a marathon of *Wheel of Fortune* re-runs on the Game Show Network. Memphis is busy unfolding chairs and card tables outside, a Texas flag folded with military-like precision tucked underneath one arm.

Daddy and Uncle Harvey, the family Republican, seem oblivious to all the activity around them and are deep in debate over the conspiracies behind America's drug epidemic. Uncle Harvey, a conservative who, inexplicably, cannot stand Caucasians, agrees with Daddy that the influx of drugs into impoverished communities is a purposeful exercise of ethnic cleansing on the part of the federal government. They merely disagree over whether it was "that redneck" Lyndon Johnson or "that hateful bastard" Richard Nixon who started it. As this discussion will continue for the rest of their lifetimes, I decide to exit the scene before anyone notices me standing in the doorway.

"Oh, Jo Ella, there you are." Mommy blurts from behind the pre-made guacamole trough she is shoveling into a ceramic serving dish shaped like a chili pepper. "Take this outside for me, will you?"

I enter the kitchen and take the dish from her. I grab a celery stick from the relish tray – finally, a vegetable not smothered in orange cheese food or deep fried!

"Willie T. will be here," Mommy sings in my direction. "You know, Jo Ella, he never married."

There goes that wink again. I duck out to the patio with Daddy. I set the guacamole on a long, folding table and then help Daddy fill Mexican flag-adorned plastic cups with frozen green goop. It looks like the slimy synthetic stuff that oozes out of Trey's terrifying toys, but it's actually the byproduct of Daddy's most recent infomercial purchase—a large, rather unstable-looking, stainless steel margarita machine. Thank God Daddy is afraid of Mommy's computer, as his proclivity toward late-night instant purchasing would become really dangerous if he could maneuver the Internet. The frozen refreshment looks suspect, but Daddy unloads two gallon jugs of tequila into his magic mixer, so no worries there. We don't really care what it looks like around here so long as it's lethal.

Trey, meanwhile, zigzags across the parched grass kicking anthills with gusto. He punts one near my foot, and swarms of the little buggers scurry under one of the serape-draped picnic tables. His brow is lined with streaks of determination as he terrorizes the little creatures and then shifts his focus to a somewhat larger little creature, his younger brother Mitchell. When he thinks no one is paying attention, Trey kicks Mitchell hard in the shin. Though I am sure this is a sign of future felonious tendencies, I can't blame my nephew for his hardly repressed anger. His grandmother has forced the poor boy and his two younger brothers into straw sombreros with wide red bands around the brims and tight black gaucho pants with epaulets and matching vests. She let them keep on their Nikes, however, finally giving in to Ann Marie's calm but determined suggestions that the boys might dirty their Sunday School shoes. Little Mitchell and Martin suffer in silence, but Trey vents his rage on the animal kingdom and his fellow little men.

"*Uncle Wee Wee!*" Memphis hollers across the backyard. "Where the good beer at? The Coronas. We need to crunk up this b___. . . Hey, girl! You look good, but we need to get you into some mini mini skirts or Daisy Dukes or sump'm. *Trey! Cut that out now, boy!*" Memphis yells in response to Mitchell's howls. He kisses the wailing tot on the top of his head and hands him a maraschino cherry, followed by an orange slice. "Girl, you ain't gone catch you no man wearin' no muumuu. Oh, Jo Ella, this here's my podner, Boo."

"Nice to meet you, Boo." I mimic Mommy's Donna Reed demeanor and smile, extending my hand politely.

"Yeeeah!" Boo nods and ignores my right hand, using his to raise a longneck to his lips and take a long swig.

Memphis slaps him upside the head, pretty hard actually, though Boo doesn't seem to notice.

"Mind ya manners, boy. My cousin here is a educated woman. A college lady. Have some respect up in my auntie's house before I have to whoop your country ass."

Boo apologizes sweetly and bows gallantly in my direction. The rush of blood and alcohol to his lager-sodden head causes him to tip over like a sleeping bovine.

I inch away as Memphis grabs Boo's careening beer bottle in the nick of time, sets it on the umbrella table and only then extends a hand to his stumbling buddy. When they're not looking, I turn and run smack into Davis's chest.

"Whoa, there. Where's the inferno?"

"Oh, thank God!" I gush. I rush my new colleague too aggressively, like a linebacker too anxious to wait for the snap, ignoring our relative unfamiliarity and the narrowing, Eastwood-like stares of my family at the sight of me throwing myself at this white man. Davis returns my wide-armed bear hug with an equally wide grin and smooch on the cheek. My family's cautious glares become wide-eyed gawks. As liberal as my family professes to be, Uncle Harvey notwithstanding, they are always a bit shocked and awed at the sight of public interracial-ness. Or perhaps the overly enthusiastic clinch hold I have exerted on this poor man has caused my family to wonder how I landed what appears to be a boyfriend without them knowing anything about it.

I stammer to eke out some semblance of an apology to Davis. He waves it off.

"Family makes me crazy too. Now, which way to Margaritaville?"

We turn directly into Mommy's steely, slanted grin. No longer a head-on beauty queen beam, but more of a twisted glimmer.

"Mommy, this is Davis, who teaches with me at Lee. Davis, this is my mother."

Nothing. No comment, no change in expression, nothing. The Joker, not the beauty queen, is still in the building.

"Mommy, remember I told you I invited one of the other teachers to come over today?"

A glimmer of uncertainty changes her visage ever so slightly, but she's still channeling Jack Nicholson, not Jackie O.

Davis extends his hand. "Why Mrs. Randolph, Jo told me all about you, but she made no mention of the fact that her mother was, well, *stunning!* I appreciate it so much that you let a pitiful old soul like me impose on you good folks. You know, I lost Mama last year. I really miss being in such a warm, family environment."

The iceberg is melting faster then you can say "global warming." Relief, or maybe good manners, or maybe just vanity, overcomes her. A rosy expression reemerges on Mommy's face.

"Imposition? Why no, darlin'. You just come over here with me and have some of my famous bean dip. Don't ask me the recipe, now, because ladies just have to keep *some* secrets, don't we, Jo Ella?" Mommy winks at me. My mouth opens but no words come out. What does she know?

Davis and Mommy circle arms and beam at each other like new-found loves. They stroll away, leaving me stranded in the dust and the demolished anthills with my own set of secrets much darker than Mommy's black bean dip. I almost don't mind, as anything that takes my family's focus off of me for a moment is a godsend.

Mommy and Davis haven't been gone for two seconds when I'm accosted by Uncle Harvey.

"Now, Jo Ella, I hope you know what you're doing."

"Huh?"

"You see, Jo Ella, you have to understand that it's the *white man* that's the real weapon of mass destruction in this world." Uncle Harvey hisses in a hushed, conspiratorial tone, as if the NSA has bugged Mommy's palm tree.

"But, Uncle Harvey, you voted for Bush."

"True. I voted for Bush. I voted for Bush because I know he ain't gonna try to give me nothin'. Them Bush people, that Cheney, they're some ruthless sons of bitches. I can respect that. It's honest. I don't trust anything the white man says he's tryin' to do for me. They just want to *enslave* the Black man! Nope, I don't trust 'em as far as I can shake a stick at 'em. You gotta be careful with them people, Jo Ella. You know, they took your grandmother, Gun's land. Her very own relations took the land right out from under her, and there wasn't a dang thing she could do about it back then . . . "

Noticing the look on my face, Uncle Harvey shuts down his rant. He flashes me his warm, wide grin and throws his arm around my shoulders, hugging me tight. "Now don't frown, baby. You know I love you and am just lookin' out for you."

"I love you too, Uncle Harvey."

Unlike Daddy, I never argue with Uncle Harvey. He's actually a sweetheart when he isn't shakin' off The Man.

Uncle Harvey strolls off to search for a Coors, as he doesn't trust the Corona people. I grab another cocktail and decide to lift my chin out of my cup and act like all the other Randolphs instead of a curmudgeon or a fraidycat. I bravely march over to Big Claude, the Cadillac Baron of Midland, and his vivacious, not to mention significantly taller, wife Alma. Standing behind them, sulking as usual, is Ann Marie's significant other. My brother-in-law chauffeured his parents to the picnic in their vintage 1959 Eldorado convertible that Big Claude lovingly restored or, more precisely, paid Memphis to lovingly restore for him. I almost forgot that Little Claude is a pretty handsome guy. He scowls so much these days that it's hard to see the attractiveness lurking behind the grimace. When I look at Ann Marie and those three beautiful banditos of theirs, I don't quite get what's bothering him so badly. Though one could say the same thing about me, so I'm not going to press it. Maybe Little Claude has finally realized how hard it is to live in Midland. Or maybe he's just finding it hard to live in Big Claude's formidable shadow.

Though he leaves a large impression, Big Claude is actually a very little man, bearing a striking resemblance to Little Richard. All five foot two of him is exquisitely dolled-up in a lightweight Guayabera shirt and pleated linen trousers. Circling one wrist are three heavy gold link bracelets; on the other, a large-faced watch with so many dials and details that it can probably be used to navigate planes. Big Claude has wildly luxuriant eyebrows that render his expression alternatively mischievous or pleasantly surprised. In contrast to his shockingly shaggy eyebrows, his pencil-thin moustache is so slender and symmetrical that it appears painted on with an eyeliner brush. But his most distinctive feature is his hair. A flourishing, highly stylized coif that swirls and twists and curls into a swerving peak that never moves in the wind. Neither Al Sharpton, Prince, nor even Little Richard himself have a thing on Big Claude in the 'do department.

The only person in Midland more resplendent than Big Claude is Alma. To enhance her already impressive altitude, Alma is wearing an enormous, conical hat festooned with brightly-colored, Mexican-inspired paper sunflowers. The height of her hat makes her seem ten feet tall, particularly in contrast to her diminutive spouse. Alma McKlintock is wearing a sweeping, sequined prairie skirt and a flowing, feather-decked blouse, set off by a multi-colored, braided leather belt with a wide brass buckle. The outfit is enhanced by Alma's Technicolor blue cowboy boots and the abundant, overlapping, turquoise squash blossom necklaces she has draped around her substantial throat.

"Hello, Mr. McKlintock. Mrs. McKlintock. What a beautiful hat you're wearing."

"Oh, Jo Ella. Sweetheart, how are you doing? We are so glad to see our little movie star back in Midland." Alma grabs me and flings me against her broad bosom, holding me so tight that I am overpowered by the scent of her "White Diamonds" perfume.

"Memphis tells me you might be needing a new car," Big Claude grins and pats me heartily on the back.

Alma straightens and looks me up and down, like a Miss Texas judge sizing up an eager, grinning contestant. "Now, why haven't you gotten married, sugar? You should be, thirty-five, forty . . . *forty! Jo Ella!* What are you waiting for? You don't even have a beau yet, do you?"

"Now, Alma, mind your business. She'll tell us all about that Caucasian boy when she's good and ready. By the way, Jo Ella, what does he drive? He looks mighty prosperous . . . "

"You know, I don't understand you young girls. Forty-five is too old not be married yet. Not even once."

"But I'm not . . ."

"Now, Alma, you watched that *Sex and the City* on HBO! These young ladies don't have to get married 'til they're good and ready. Heh heh hee. Yes, Lord, those girls seem to have a good time, don't they? Jo Ella, you used to live up there in New York, so I bet you know all about that—don't worry, child, I won't tell your mama. You know, girls even buy their own cars these days . . ."

"*Jo Ella!!!*"

Oh God, not that squeal. My childhood playmate and former neighbor, Lou, has greeted me with the same high-pitched shriek ever since elementary school. Lou approaches me, arms outstretched. Lurking behind her is my childhood nemesis, Paula Harris, whom I used to tease unmercifully during carpool about her "baby fat." Unlike Lou, she's not smiling or apparently happy to see me, though I can't really blame her. Our eyes meet, and she immediately looks away with an expression closely resembling the face of a pug.

"Girl, you have been in town for weeks now, and you haven't even called me!" Lou shouts, grabbing me and embracing me in a tight hug. "Girl, what have you been up to?"

Trying to be recognized as a forty-year-old woman of the world who doesn't look her age, but who can make her own decisions and live her life as she pleases and be successful at something, instead of just a girl from Midland who is hiding out in her parents' house because she lost her job and almost got herself indicted and doesn't have a boyfriend, much less a husband, and can't afford, and doesn't even want one of Big Claude's fancy new Cadillacs, but I digress again. I try my best to plaster together a weak reproduction of Mommy's famous grin. I look more like one of those tight-faced Beverly Hills matrons, but this mug will have to do for now.

"Girl, you know, me and Paula just went on that Tom Joyner cruise. We saw some folks with crinkly hair just like yours down in Jamaica, didn't we Paula? Have you been to Jamaica? Ooh, girl, you gotta go. It's beautiful! Me and Paula don't have husbands to tie us down anymore, so we just go. Just like you. We just up and go. We're going to Cancun for Columbus Day. Girl, you should come with us! It's one of those 'chocolate singles' weekends. The men will *be there*, honey. Now, I'm sure Pastor Maples won't like it so much, but we bring our bibles, now. We don't just go buck wild down there. But I had to tell Pastor Maples that we can't keep showing up at the Baptist Singles' Ministry with the same old tired folks over and over again. How are we supposed to build us a sacred family unit if we . . ."

I am not at all keeping up with Lou's endless chatter. Not even Big Claude and Alma can keep up—they conveniently saunter away without Lou even noticing they were there in the first place. I, however, have no means of escape. I notice Davis kneeling on the ground, engrossed in conversation with my youngest nephew, Martin, who is proudly showing off the colorfully painted little guitar Ann Marie bought him in Acapulco. Davis places the tot's tiny fingers on the wobbly plastic strings, and they pretend to pluck a little tune, both of them completely oblivious to the fact that this little souvenir isn't designed to play much music.

Nowhere else to turn, I follow Lou's lips, which move rapidly while

I nod and continue my Botox grin. Lou means well enough, but even as a child I could only take so much of her bottomless pit of conversation. Though I have to admire her enthusiasm for, well, everything. From new shoelaces to a new beau to a virgin sunrise, Lou expresses childlike wonder and zeal for all elements of life, great or small. You can't help liking her, though it is extremely hard to listen to her run-on chitchat. But maybe I'm just jaded. L.A. will do that to you.

Memphis cranks up the volume of the already torturously loud music a couple of notches. It drowns out Lou's chatter but sends Mommy into a fit of apoplexy and practically gives Aunt Lula a coronary, as the chorus of "I kick yo ass bitch, you motha' fuckin' bitch . . ." blares out to Mommy's distinguished cadre of chocolate singles and couples, plus Davis. Mommy streaks across the lawn, wielding a cactus-adorned serving knife in the direction of Memphis and his boom box.

"Mommy, please. . ." Ann Marie pleads as she takes up the rear.

Mommy waves her knife uncomfortably close to Memphis' skull while she gives him a piece of her manicured mind. Mommy is of that generation that not only remembers Black music with no cussing, but also the desire of the community to be better, more proper, more respectable than the white folks that tried to put them down or hold them back. The crudity of Memphis's musical selections has completely offended Mommy's straight-laced sensibilities, not to mention those of the Good Reverend Doctor, the ungodly language being the only thing at the party that diverts his attention from his heaping plate of chili-powdered buffalo wings.

Ann Marie struggles to wrestle the Tex-Mex cutlery from Mommy's hand before she can smack Memphis upside the head with it, or worse. As I watch my sister give my mother the sumo security guard treatment to keep her from killing Memphis, Davis sidles up to me. "You don't have to say anything, Davis. Just run for your life while you still can." I shake my head at the sight of Ann Marie trying to place Mommy in a hammerlock. Perhaps this explains where my violent tendencies come from.

"As long as she doesn't come after me with that knife, I think I'm OK," Davis drawls.

"You know, the sad thing is, that was probably a love song. But the real problem with this picture is that I agree with my mother. Is that part of the aging process, or have I just had too much to drink?"

"You think this song is bad, just wait 'til school starts." Davis takes another drag from his flag cup. "They should make people get a license to procreate."

"If only we could trust the judgment of the people handing out the licenses."

"True," Davis laughs. "You know, this reminds me of being around my family, if you remove the warmth and kindness."

"You say that about a woman who just threatened her nephew with a big, prickly plastic utensil? Besides, I would have taken you to be from the mannered set."

"Oh they have manners, but they have no genuine pleasantness on the inside. Except for Mama, of course, but she's gone. So I just avoid my family altogether or drink heavily enough to become as obnoxious as they are. Here I can drink for fun . . . and to be relaxed enough to do the Electric Slide."

"Oh Lord Have Mercy. I *forbade* Memphis from playing that nonsense!" Various generations and sizes of my family and family friends are now engaged in a lockstep version of this Hustle sequel. Someone must have convinced Memphis to play this unlikely crowd-pleaser as a détente measure. Or Daddy must have loaded up everyone's glasses with a refill of his truly toxic goo, because not only is no one fighting, but no one seems to care how ridiculous they look doing this silly dance. I even see Willie T. jumping into the line between Lou and Alma. When did he get here? All the old chickens of my life are coming home to roost, as towering behind Willie T., stepping and sliding in a row all by himself, is Curt, the massive Rebel lineman I had a major crush on in high school.

"Who's the Tom Selleck wannabe?" Davis asks with more genuine interest than irony.

Who? . . . Oh . . . that's Curt, Curt Dupree. You don't remember him from Lee?"

"You didn't remember me. It's a huge school, Jo."

"I guess that's true, but he was like a star linebacker, and he reminded all the girls of Fred Williamson. He had a big bushy moustache even back then."

"Whatever happened to the Burt Reynolds moustache, anyway?"

"Ronald Reagan," I respond. "We're children of the Reagan Revolution whether we like it or not. None of the people in the *Preppy Handbook* looked like Village People rejects, did they?

"Maybe that's why there's such a disconnect with the kids at school. We've still got madras and chinos in our brains as actual fashion, while they're all imitating hip-hop stars and wearing do-rags and ill-fitting pants. It's always something."

As we look out at the crowd, I notice that Mommy has moved on from assaulting her nephew. She is smiling again and striding arm-in-arm with Daddy. Her cropped locks are intentionally tousled in a way that adds softness to her angular features, and she appears youthful and energetic. Her guests reflect her energy as she greets them, radiating in the sunny disposition that seems to burn brightest on social occasions. She is so involved in her mixing and mingling that she doesn't notice her grandson streak across her path with a cup full of Daddy's margarita juice in his hand. Green slime sprays and splatters every which way as Trey darts back and forth, with Ann Marie in hot pursuit behind him. She finally nabs him, crouching her statuesque figure down to kids-eye level to wrest the cup from his hand. All three of her boys suddenly converge on her and drape themselves around her shoulders like a prayer shawl, squeezing her face with their small hands and smothering her with kisses.

"You know, there are too many things that terrify me about her life to mention. But sometimes I look at my sister, and I get the funny feeling that maybe I need more of a purpose in life. Though I don't know what to do about it, because if I had to have a real job and live on a cul-de-sac, I might end up killing myself with Mommy's cactus knife."

"Maybe it's best you run away again. Peace and quiet? That we've got. Purpose in life? You may need to get out of Midland."

"Well, I certainly try to get away. But it keeps pulling me back. Where else can I contemplate the meaning of life while snacking on jalapeno-stuffed cheese puffs made by my mother's loving hands? Or at least purchased by my mother from Sam's and placed really nice-like on a tray?"

"I guess frozen Mexican food from Sam's is a pretty irresistible draw." Davis winks at me. "But I've had a lot of your Dad's margaritas, so you could tell me anything and I'd probably believe it."

Poor Davis doesn't know the half of it. I watch his tall figure stroll away to refresh his cocktail again. On the way to the margarita machine, Davis opens the sliding glass door for Aunt Lula and extends a hand to help her into the kitchen. She's probably tired from the heat. More likely she's had enough of socializing and is ready to get back to her TV shows. Like me, Aunt Lula is addicted to television. Her favorites seem to be game shows and small screen jurists, as Mommy successfully kicked her from a really dreadful televangelist habit. She also loves talk shows, particularly *Oprah*. She much prefers to watch other people chat than to engage in conversation herself.

In his most recent daily gossip recap, Rudy shared that Danielle was gunning to be interviewed by Oprah. But "sources" say that Britney and Jamie Lynn Spears' breakdowns and birth announcements bumped Danielle from the running. I hope my story is getting stale in the press. If anyone here at the "cocktail barbecue" has seen or read anything, they are keeping it to themselves. Probably not for my sake, of course, but to save my long-suffering parents the embarrassment.

I feel a tap on my shoulder and kiss on the cheek.

"You look nice." Willie T.'s smile is so warm and genuine-looking that I almost believe him.

"So you find oversized peasant blouses covered with multicolored parrots and palm trees sexy, do you?"

"On some people, yes," he says with a wink.

"Hmmm," I murmur. "That's very kinky of you, Mr. Undertaker."

Willie T. laughs loud and long. He stretches his arm out in front of him to keep from spilling his margarita onto his crisp linen shirt. It's nice, watching him laugh. It's nice having him smile at me. Though it reminds me of how much I miss Ravi.

"What's on your mind?" Willie T. asks.

"If I shared what's on my mind, I might have to shoot you."

"Whoa," he says. He backs away from me but is still smiling. "How about I bring you a margarita and we talk about it."

"If I start spilling my soul, Willie T., then *you* will probably be the one needing a margarita, not the other way around. By the way, are your folks here?"

"Well," he says. His smile fades a bit. "Dad's here. You know, my mom passed seven years ago. Cancer."

I'm such a jerk. Our families are close. I've made out with this guy. I let him get to second base, for God's sake. How could I not know that his mother died? I'm sure it's one of those things that Mommy told me about that I was too absorbed in my own life to really hear.

"Jesus, Willie T., I'm sorry." What else is there to say?

"It's OK, Jo Ella. You've been gone a long time. She'd be glad we're reconnecting now, though. She always loved you. She used to call you 'Goofy,' you made her laugh so much."

"That's me," I sigh. "The goofball."

"And Dad's here. Sittin' over there with your Uncle Buddy."

Holy shit. I saw a white-haired man in a wheelchair talking to Uncle Buddy, but I didn't recognize him.

"He had a stroke not long after Mama died. He got most of his speech back, but he can't walk so well without a walker. That's when I took over the business and started looking after him. You wanna talk to him? I'll meet you over there—I told him and your Uncle that I'd find them some pound cake."

"Oh, Mommy's stashed it in a secret hiding place until dessert time. I'll sneak some over to them. You want a piece?"

"Not yet. I'm gonna grab a few of those ribs first."

Willie T. pats my shoulder and leaves me for the oil drum-turned-BBQ smoker. I stroll across the yard to the kitchen door and struggle to slide it open. The track is a bit stiff today—so many people milling in and out have pulled it off track. Aunt Lula is sitting very close to the blaring TV. She doesn't hear me come in. All of a sudden I see my face on the screen. My hair is long and wild, and my eyes have a fanatical gleam as I hover in a hedge of fake evergreens clutching a large kitchen knife. Then the image shifts from my soap opera scene to split screen shots of me, Ravi, and Danielle.

I lurch toward the set and press the power button. I hit it with far too much force, exerting so much pressure with my thumb that I not only kill the picture but effectively shove the entire television set off the counter altogether, the cord snapping out of the socket as the TV crashes onto the lemon yellow tile. Shards of grey-tinted glass and jagged pieces of dark, hard plastic spray every which way.

Davis appears out of nowhere. He ignores the cloud of glass dust collecting on his shoes and grabs the back of Aunt Lula's swiveling kitchen seat, rolling her clear of the danger zone.

"*Lord help me!*" Aunt Lula screeches.

"*Jo Ella!* What on earth is going on here?"

Mommy is standing in the doorway, beaming her brilliant, wicked smile in my direction as a small crowd gathers around her, fingers pointing in the direction of the fracas everyone rightly assumes was all my doing.

"I, uh . . . I thought I saw a yellow jacket, and I, um, uh . . ."

"Oh, Mrs. Randolph, Jo was trying to protect Miss Lula, here, and she accidentally knocked over the television." Davis suppresses a smile, but only just barely.

"I think she's drunk again," Aunt Lula mutters.

"I'm sorry. I, I, I'll get the broom."

"No, no, Jo Ella, you've done enough. Daddy and Memphis will clean this up. *Everyone, follow me for dessert.*"

The crowd dutifully follows Mommy like the Pied Piper. No one ever argues with her. It doesn't hurt that she makes the most wicked pies and pound cake in Midland. Even the most seditty of our friends and family have been known to hide Ziploc bags in their handbags in anticipation of raiding her dessert table.

"Come on." Rather than doing what's good for him and running in the opposite direction, Davis stifles a snicker and casually wraps his arm around my shoulders. "Why don't we go outside? There doesn't appear to be any electronic equipment to destroy out there, other than the boom box."

My head drops and my torso slumps forward, like Charlie Brown's slouch after being punked by Lucy at football.

"Come on, buckaroo, it's not so bad." Davis urges me away from the holy mess I made of the television and my life in general. "Hey, you can introduce me to Fred Williamson. Wasn't he in *Enter the Dragon*?"

The mention of movies perks me up a little bit.

"That was Jim Kelly. No moustache."

CHAPTER 8 ♡

My parents may be the perkiest people on Earth. By 6:00 A.M. they are scrubbed, dressed and well into their second cup of Maxwell House and the morning news. Even in retirement, they haven't given up their morning rituals.

They seem to like their new television set. Rather than church, I spent a good part of my Sunday comparing televisions in big box electronics stores with my cousin, Memphis. The twenty-inch flat screen I finally selected sits on a sleek little pedestal and adds a jazzy, *Jetsons* quality to my parents' sunny, '70s-era kitchen. Daddy tries to change the channel to *Sports Center* while Mommy's making toast. She snatches the remote out of his hand, returning the TV screen to *Good Morning Midland!*

"Morning, darlin'," Mommy greets me, her voice as chipper as her kitchen décor. "Want some coffee?"

"Sure," I grunt.

"Jo Ella, did you hear? President Bush is supposed to come home to Midland for a visit. He's gonna give a speech about education in the Lee auditorium."

"Really?" I couldn't be less interested, but I'm trying not to take out my sleep deprivation on Mommy. My late night TV marathons have been replaced with late night cramming sessions for my teaching gig.

"They just talked about it on the news, but Daddy and I heard about it last night on that Air America program we listen to. I almost strangled your father when he ordered that satellite radio thing off the TV." Mommy smiles in Daddy's direction as he hides behind his newspaper. "But I really like it now. You can't trust the TV news people anymore. Especially since they got rid of Dan Rather."

"Watch out, Mommy. You're starting to sound as paranoid as Uncle Harvey."

Mommy's smile is unforced for a change. "Well, it's hard not to these days."

Daddy finally looks up from his newspaper. "Now you watch out, Jo Ella. I bet those folks over at Lee try to trick you into being the token. Bush is on his way out of office, so I think he's just here trying to reform his image instead of education. He needs to raise money for his library, and these crazy Midland oil folks are the only people that still like him."

"Don't worry, Daddy." I accept the steaming mug of coffee Mommy hands me. I cradle the warm ceramic in my hands and inhale before taking a sip.

"I worry, baby, because they're tricky. Trickier than Nixon, even."

"Now you both sound like Uncle Harvey," I tease. I grab an apple from the crisper. "I better get back to work."

Mommy so far has heeded the *Ne pas déranger* sign I hung on my bedroom door. As a result, my room resembles that of a teenage girl. A heap of clothes spills out of my open suitcase, and fashion mags are strewn about the small, narrow space. Books I loved in my youth are tossed across the bed, their absence from my particleboard bookshelves causing the books left behind to lean and fall over in untidy clumps. My Blondie and Material Girl posters are still tacked up on the light turquoise walls next to a shirt-less Simon LeBon. I've added a makeshift collage of more recent photos to remind me of my other life. Jen and Rudy beam back at me from Bali, Tokyo, Athens, Sydney, Costa Rica, Iceland and our other exotic escapades over the years. My sari-ed silhouette in the shadow of a Keralan temple is half-covered by a postcard from Provence to remove Ravi's face from view, since I couldn't bring myself to rip him out of the picture.

My Blackberry vibrates from a new message. Jen may be the only person I know that rises earlier than my parents. At almost 5:00 A.M.

LA time, she's probably pulling on her workout pants to get to the gym before 5:30.

JenPhen: Saw Ravi @ Whole Foods last nite.

JoMaMa: Groceries? I doubt he's ever shopped for food in his life. How did he look?

JenPhen: Totally Hell-Ay. Buying groceries in unisex boots & $600 ripped jeans & skull tshirt. Wifey was w/him. As if a woman with household staff goes to the supermarket. Their jeans matched.

JoMaMa: He keeps calling me.

JenPhen: U talk to him?

JoMaMa: No. Just listen 2 messages.

JenPhen: D must've changed her mind. U should change your number. BTW—pics of them in Life & Style.

JoMaMa: Assholes.

I slam my coffee mug down on my desk. I almost knock over the framed photo of myself wearing a form-fitting, sparkly borrowed gown at the Daytime Emmy awards that's wedged between a stack of world music CDs and my little bronze Buddha. Ravi had a framed copy of the Emmy photo at the beach house. How did he pull that off? Did he set it out when he knew I was coming over and then replace it with a photo of his wife? Nothing makes sense anymore. I should meditate. I haven't meditated or done a single yoga pose since I've been in Texas. Why is it that we only do yoga when we're already serene and our lives are in order? When we're in crisis, we drink, not chant. At least that's what we do here in Texas. My yoga mat is rolled up in the corner near the closet and hasn't been unfurled since I took it out of my suitcase. I ignore it, as usual.

I settle into my molded plastic desk chair and open a dog-eared copy of *A Portrait of the Artist as a Young Man* to the Epigraph. The quote from Ovid. *Et ignotas animum dimittit in artes.* ("And he turned his mind to unknown arts."). I don't care what Mrs. Hightower says. We're not just going to memorize multiple-choice questions. We're reading Joyce. Mrs. Hightower means well, and I know we don't have a lot of time to get these students ready for State tests in the fall. There is only so much we can expect of them during the short summer session. "We can't do it all," she said when I flooded her with my ideas for summer reading assignments, her tone suggesting more resignation than conviction. But I'm going to try to sneak in some books. Or at least some short stories. Maybe a little Shakespeare?

I seek out another folded corner and flip to that page.

> *His throat ached with a desire to cry aloud, the cry of a hawk or eagle on high, to cry piercingly of his deliverance to the winds. This was the call of life to his soul not the dull gross voice of the world of duties and despair, not the inhuman voice that had called him to the pale service of the altar. An instant of wild flight had delivered him and the cry of triumph which his lips withheld cleft his brain.*

Can I teach lessons I haven't learned myself? My Afro-American Literature professor at Dartmouth used to say, "I'm a guide, not a know-it-all." So maybe there's hope. Though the state of my life makes me suspect as a guide. I'm surprised Midland, Texas, is willing to entrust young minds to a harlot, heathen Hollywood type like myself. Either Mommy and Daddy have something on the Superintendent, or the school district really is desperate.

Come on baby, come on baby, do the Conga . . .

Ravi's round of phone calls are starting earlier than usual today.

"Oh, Jo, darling, *thank God!* I have been *craaazy* wanting to talk to you."

I don't know what to say.

"Where did you run off to, Jo? I've been calling and emailing and texting . . . I *muust* see you."

All I have wanted is to see Ravi again. But to hear him say it, to hear him voice my inner desires real-time, where I have to respond for real and outside of my head, throws me off-balance.

"Jo, are you still there?"

I can't speak for a while. "What makes you think I want to see you?" I finally ask. "I mean, after everything that's happened, Ravi . . . And how does your wife feel about you wanting to see me?"

"Jo, darling, it's not what it looks like, I . . ."

"Well, you're still married, aren't you? And from what I hear, you're out shopping together and having your picture taken all over the place. So what am I missing, Ravi?"

"It's *reeeally* complicated, Jo. If I could just see you and . . . "

"Ravi, why didn't you just tell me you weren't getting divorced? Were you even broken up in the first place?" I can barely hold the phone steady my hand is trembling so much.

"Jo, I . . ."

"And how is it that a married man has a house his wife doesn't live in? *What the hell is going on?!*"

"Let me explain . . ."

"Just stop calling me, Ravi. If you have something to say to me, call my agent. Or my lawyer. Just leave me alone!"

I cut off the call and drop the phone. But I can't shut off my thoughts. Thoughts of my life before the mayhem. Thoughts of my future. I try to turn my attention back to Stephen Dedalus, Joyce's artist as a young man. The myth of Daedalus and Icarus. Daedalus, the artist and innovator whose creativity enabled him to be free. Icarus, the child too wrapped up in the thrill of it all to heed his father's warnings about flying too close to the sun. Too many metaphors for me to handle right now. I toss the book onto the floor.

Snap out of it, Jo. I haven't had a drink since Saturday, so why am I hallucinating? I slither out of the armholes of my P Funk All Stars "One Nation Under A Groove" T-shirt and slip on a bra without pulling my shirt over my head. I roll on some deodorant, then lean down and sniff my black leggings for anything offensive. I pull on a Dallas Cowboys cap and a pair of dark sunglasses, and I give my lips a swipe of gloss.

Mommy won't approve, but this will have to do. I grab my purse and stride to the kitchen.

"I'll be right back," I say to Mommy and Daddy. I race out of the door before they can ask me any questions.

Chugging through the commercial district just beyond my parents' subdivision in my barely-moving old Beemer, I seek out the public library. The library I used to frequent from the time Mommy helped me write my name in four-year old scrawl on my first library card all the way through high school. It used to be safe enough for me to ride my bike there alone. I pass a long stretch of strip malls, 7-Elevens, fast food joints and dollar stores. I've driven too far. I circle back, looking for familiar landmarks. The library, the blue and white-striped awning of the Polar Bear ice cream parlor, the red neon sign fronting Mister Moody's fried catfish place, the Esso gas station where they kept a huge jar of dill pickles next to the cash register. These were the points on my neighborhood compass growing up. But they all seem to be gone.

I spot a Fiesta supermarket in the vicinity of where I think the library used to be. I pull into the expansive, nearly empty parking lot and find a space near the entrance. Inside, I scan the magazine racks near the check-out counters, fingering through titles such as *People en Español, Vanidades* and *Cosmopolitan en Español,* until I craft a collection of *US Weekly, Star, Enquirer, Globe, National Examiner, OK!, In Touch, Life & Style, Soap Opera Digest* and, for a substantive touch, *People.*

Back home I shove aside the classics and stack up the slender weeklies. The bold typeface and bright colors of the headlines jump off the pages and wrap me in a chokehold. Huge grainy photographs of cellulite and surgically altered expressions are awful and irresistible all at once. I breathe a sigh of relief as I toss *People, US Weekly, Soap Opera Digest,* and *In Touch* on the floor. Luckily we didn't make the cut of the "good" ones. At least not this week. I carefully skim the pages of *Life & Style* but don't catch a glimpse of Ravi and Danielle. Though our weeklies aren't refreshed as quickly in Midland as they are on the coasts. So it's possible they're in next week's stash.

I scan the *National Enquirer* and suddenly stop.

"Where is Jo Randolph?"

There I am, black-clad, buzz-cut and bespectacled in my oversized dark shades. It's a bit fuzzy and distant—obviously a camera phone shot. But you can't miss me. I stand out. I don't know if it's the hair, the dark duds or something else. It's subtle, but there's definitely a sense of the "One of These Things (Is Not Like the Others)."

> *"The B-List Actress, best known for her role as Celeste, the scheming, backstabbing nurse on Young and the Restless, has been MIA since May. Until this week, she was last spotted on the set of the film, Obsessions. She was reportedly carried off the set by security after a fistfight with romance novelist Danielle Coleman. Randolph is rumored to have been involved with Obsessions director, forty-year-old Ravi Mehra, the sixty-something Ms. Coleman's husband. Sources say Randolph thought the couple was divorcing and was blindsided by their reconciliation. In an Enquirer exclusive, film producer, Regan Coleman, is quoted as saying: 'She's a real professional and did great work. I hope to work with her again. This thing isn't Jo's fault. I think she got caught in the middle of my mother and Ravi's ups and downs.' Randolph was unavailable for comment. Randolph's agent has canceled all the actress' appearances, but Randolph was spotted recently attending church with her family."*

I'm B-List? Jen is good. Even if she weren't one of my best friends, she would be worth every penny I pay her. She obviously had my publicist plant this bit to give the *Enquirer* a "story" to go along with the bootleg photo. Genius. But sleazy. Even though Danielle went racial on me and called me a "nappy, Black bitch," it's still lame that the mere mention of her age in the *Enquirer* will cause clucking and eye-rolling across the gossipsphere.

I shut the magazine and toss the lot into the waste bin. The thought of what lies ahead sours my stomach. Whatever happens will likely be ugly for all of us, no matter what spin we place on it.

CHAPTER 9 ♡

The Eyes of Texas are upon you, all the livelong day . . .

Since when did the University of Texas anthem replace "The Star-Spangled Banner" at assembly? Did we ever sing "The Star-Spangled Banner" at assembly? I don't remember. I also don't remember reciting a pledge to the Texas State Flag instead of the Pledge of Allegiance. I guess the Texas flag flying higher than the stars and stripes in the front of the school should be a clue that I'm not in California anymore.

I'm not sure I'm still in the US. According to Daddy's *Midland Reporter-Telegram*, there's a group of guys lobbying for the Republic of Texas to emancipate itself from the rest of the US. Most Midlanders the reporter interviewed don't find it wacky that out of shape, middle-aged men spend their weekends in fatigues and green face paint going through some sort of paramilitary shenanigans out in the woods. They're considered quaint in a Norman Rockwall kind of way, despite the group's secessionist, borderline xenophobic web rantings.

I scan the auditorium. Everyone seems caught up in the rapture of the State song, even the kids. At least they're enthusiastic about something other than the vapid pop culture from which I earn my living. Though just being Texan can be a pop culture exercise. The Lone Star flag and State silhouette are emblazoned on everything from nail clippers to running shorts around here.

My stomach is doing double herkies. I have an English degree from Dartmouth, but I don't know that it actually qualifies me to teach it to other people. I've never taught anything other than Urban Funk

Yogilates at the Sports Club/L.A. As soon as assembly is over, I head straight to the teachers' lounge for my third jolt of java for the day. Perhaps I should switch to herbal tea. Or vodka.

I glance down at my black cotton shirt with the three-quarter sleeves and slightly cinched waist, my off-white boot-cut slacks, and the wedge-heeled sandals that raised Mommy's perfectly arched brows in church. I carefully arranged this conservative (for L.A.), modestly hip (for Midland) outfit to convey confidence and competence and, to be honest, to be accepted. Forty-one years old, and I'm still trying to be accepted in high school.

Davis seemed to like my look. He treated me to a Starbucks this morning before school and greeted me with a whistle. "Make sure you have somebody with you when you meet with the boys. Or keep your door open so you don't find rumors about yourself online!" He was laughing when he said it, but I'm not certain he was kidding. Are my pants too tight? Maybe I should have passed on the nacho deluxe platter at El Camino's last night. I don't resemble one of those crazy teacher temptresses do I? I'm not quite pale or platinum or pouty enough, I don't think. Maybe I should wear flats in the future.

As I brood over my Midland PTA coffee mug, I'm roused by the squishing sound of Mrs. Hightower's Rockports against the linoleum floor. She has a pleasant face and demeanor that belong in a Reynolds Wrap commercial. She's holding a paper plate of Toll House chocolate chip cookies.

"Ready for your first day? I thought a little sweets might put you in the right frame of mind!"

"Thank you, Mrs. Hightower." I can't bring myself to call her Pat. She reminds me too much of Aunt Bea to address her so informally. It was a sweet gesture, though I'm sure the mix of sugar with the excess levels of caffeine I've ingested may convert my anxiety to mania by the time I reach the classroom. I down three cookies and take one more to save for my inevitable sugar crash later.

"Now, you have your outline and everything?"

"Oh yes, of course." Mrs. Hightower speaks to me as if I'm a child, making sure I haven't forgotten my books or lesson plans or yellow highlighters, even though I prefer pink. Davis explained that she used to teach kindergarten before moving to Lee High and still speaks to everyone under the age of sixty like a five year old. But I'm still suspect.

I finally pull myself out of my seat and over to Room 1-D. No one seems to notice my arrival. The students execute a flawless imitation of being not the least bit curious about my presence. It's as if a telepathic signal was transmitted the instant I entered the room, alerting them all that it was now time to act bored and disinterested. A few girls flip the tops of their cell phones, other girls giggle or smirk in little packs, and boys sit on their friends' desks with their backs turned to the board.

I'm dying to chomp on my already-distressed nails, but I remind myself that tackling this classroom is no less intimidating than being a thirtysomething at a casting call for a "sexy twentysomething" to play the part of a forty-year old. Or the sideways glances that size you up whenever you enter a party or restaurant or anyplace else in L.A. These teens can't be any more annoying or insecure than the trendoids back in La La Land. So I return their feigned indifference, turning my back on the class and writing my name on the chalkboard: "Ms. Randolph." Seems strange. But it doesn't matter. They'll all call me "miss" instead of "*mizz*," a foreign word in this Republic.

I write captions below a series of photos pinned across the top of the blackboard. Underneath a dolled-up RuPaul: *Cross-Dressers!* Underneath a preening Paris Hilton: *Heiresses*! Donald Trump: *Greed!* Tupac & Biggie: *Tragedy!* George Bush and Dick Cheney: *Treachery!* Owen Wilson and Vince Vaughn: *Comedy!* A big-toothed Jessica Simpson cheesing with former newlywed Nick Lachey: *True Love?* I end with a challenge in bold caps: *WHAT DO ALL OF THESE HAVE IN COMMON?*

I turn and scan the room, eyebrow raised Spock-style. The teens stop talking to each other and smirk in my general direction, slumping into their chairs with a malaise that matches their rumpled clothes. Maybe this is why my mother begs me to iron.

"So, who can tell me what these people have in common?"

Silence.

"Anyone?"

"They've all been on TV?"

I smile. "True, but not the answer."

"They're all in *People* magazine?"

"True, but no."

"They're all richer than me."

"I don't know that to be true, but in any event, it's not the answer."

Silence.

"It's not the people themselves that necessarily have anything in common, it's the themes they represent. None of these modern-day themes are anything new. We can find the same themes, the same personalities in stories written by the same author more than four centuries ago. Who can tell me who that is?"

A slight young woman with soft brown curls, gilt-framed glasses that repeatedly slide down her nose and a powder-puff pink Hello Kitty T-shirt raises her hand.

"Is it Shakespeare?"

"Yes!" I smile at the room, though Hello Kitty is the only one who returns it. "We all can connect with a really good story, whether that story is a year old or over a hundred years old, and whether the characters are white, black, male, female, American, Chinese, whatever. So, we're going to read some Shakespeare as well as some other writers: old, new, foreign, Texan, all kinds. I think you'll be surprised at how much you'll relate to them all on some level."

A rangy, redheaded kid in baggy jeans and a tilted baseball cap interrupts me without raising his hand. "I thought we were supposed to learn how to pass that State test, not read a bunch 'a books."

I grab one of the stapled sets of worksheets stacked on my desk and throw it in the direction of the slouchy redhead. "*Look,* know-it-all. I could just sit here and spoon-feed you a bunch of BS. But that's not doing you any good, is it?"

The redhead's face now matches his hair color. I suddenly realize that my voice is shrill, and I am shaking my finger in the kid's direction. I drop my hand.

"How likely is it that you're gonna spend your summer memorizing this crap? Let's get a show of hands here." No hands rise in response. "Trust me, I'll make sure to go over the test questions with you before the session's out. But if I teach you how to read and analyze literature, you'll be able to pass the test regardless of whether you memorize a bunch of multiple-choice questions that may or may not even appear on the test. And you might even enjoy it. What a concept! I promise you that what you read will be much better than what you typically see on cable."

"I've seen you on cable," sniggers a pimply-faced kid in an oversized Metallica T-shirt. The other kids trade glances, covering their mouths with their hands to hide their giggles.

"My point exactly," I retort. "I myself wouldn't pay good money to see half the films I've made. Now can anyone tell me a single interesting thing that happened on television last night?"

"The Cowboys beat the Eagles in that exhibition game."

"I said *interesting*, not predictable."

"Whitney Houston talked about 'doodie bubbles.'"

"OK, *gross*, but not that interesting."

"There was this special about sharks. It was kinda' educational-like."

"You mean someone over the age of seven and under the age of fifty other than me actually watches PBS?"

"What's that?"

"I'll pretend I didn't hear that," I sigh. "I'll admit there are some things worth watching on TV. Not necessarily anything *I've* done, but TV can be good. I even watch stuff other than *Masterpiece Theater*, like *Making the Band*. But you see my point."

I don't know that I have them convinced, but at least I have them curious, or perhaps shocked enough to give me the time of day. No one asks any more questions, however, other than Hello Kitty. One young black woman maintains eye contact, though she never dares to say anything. She is wearing a Cleopatra Jones T-shirt very similar to one I wore in high school, though this one is filled out more than any T-shirt I've ever worn.

I end the class with a mock game show where I divide the class into teams and have them guess the literary sources of popular movies and TV shows. I'm surprised that no one knows *Clueless* was based on *Emma*. I'm more surprised that many haven't even heard of *Clueless*. Most have seen reruns of the original *Star Trek*, so I'm able to surprise them that a host of *Star Trek* episodes are based on Shakespearean plays. They don't know that a recent Keira Knightley movie was an adaptation of *Pride and Prejudice*, none of them having even heard of Jane Austen other than Cleopatra Jones and Hello Kitty. I really should learn the kids' names. I run out of time today, but I'll do some sort of introduction exercise tomorrow to help me get to know them better.

I have a short break before my next class, so I duck into the teachers' lounge to enjoy the meatloaf sandwich and apple that Mommy packed for me in a neatly folded, brown paper bag with my name scribbled in her elongated cursive. Unfortunately Davis is still in class. I think. I try to call him but get his voicemail. So I pick a small, empty table in the far corner of the room and bury my head in the *New York Times*. Like the shy kids in my new class, I'm not ready to venture over to the long tables and worn woven sofas occupied by the big teachers on campus. Though I catch glimpses of them sneaking glances my way, so it's possible that they're equally afraid to speak to the "star."

My next English class doesn't run as smoothly as the first. I have to do all of the talking, though I finally succeed in bringing most eyes to the front of the room instead of toward each other or the magazines not-so-hidden on denim-clad laps or the bluish glow of cell phone screens being not-so-secretly scanned or the insides of closed eyelids. I even notice some white iPod earbuds and a Game Boy or two. I should start confiscating stuff and auctioning it on eBay. How does a kid who flunked eleventh grade get his parents to buy him a $300 video iPod that just came out two weeks ago? I made straight As, and I never earned a TV in my room, not even the rabbit-eared old black and white

TV gathering cobwebs in the garage. At least I have no rebellions to quell in class today, and I don't have to correct malapropisms or "you know what I'm sayin's," since most of the students aren't sayin' much of anything, at least not to me.

The Drama program doesn't begin until mid-week, so I'm done for the day. I'm not sure if it's OK to leave, so I call Davis. I get his voicemail again, so I take a stroll to Davis' classroom. It's empty, so I head back to my own classroom and close the door. I start to call Willie T., but I really want to chat with Davis about school. Maybe I'll leave him a message to call me about the summer musical, since he's directing the music.

"Hello."

I'm surprised to hear Davis' real voice and not the recorded version. He sounds deeper and duskier than usual, almost drugged, as if he has been smoking or engaging in something lurid.

"Hey, Davis. Are you still at school?"

"No."

Maybe calling Davis wasn't such a good idea.

"Uh, if it's a bad time, I can call back."

"No. No, it's OK. Jo?"

"Oh, yeah, it's Jo. I just . . ." I run out of words. "I, uh, I mean, I wanted to talk to you earlier and didn't talk to you, or missed you. I mean, you weren't at lunch, and, uh, I thought, um, just, uh, I would check in before I leave."

"I had to leave early." Davis sounds almost annoyed, but not quite. I can't pinpoint what's wrong, but it definitely seems like a mistake to have called him.

"Hello? Jo? You still there?"

"Oh, yeah, I'm still here." I feel stupid. "We can chat later, Davis. I didn't mean to bother you at home. Just . . . "

"Hold on," he says. I clench my fist to keep from chewing my fingernails.

"Sorry, Jo. I'm sorting through some shit here. Wanna meet for coffee again in the morning?"

"Oh, sure, let's do that." I try to sound chipper. "Same time?"

"Yep."

"OK."

"See you, Jo."

"Bye."

Oh, Lord have mercy. Maybe I misread things, which wouldn't be a first. Maybe I'm forcing Davis to replace Jen and Rudy and become my new best friend, when he's got a life and friends and probably a girl-friend, even. Or a fiancé. Or a boyfriend! Maybe he's not straight. He does dress pretty hip and listen to jazz music. And he's always wearing sandals. Maybe I make him uncomfortable because it seems like I'm hitting on him. I guess it is pretty desperate of me to invite him to a barbecue after knowing him for two seconds and then stalk him all day at school. What is wrong with me?

I drag myself out of the building to the parking lot. I wonder why Davis was so weird, and why I am acting like a stalker when I'm really a nice, non-stalker kind of person. I think. The longer I'm in Texas, the more I feel like high school. I'm as confused and incoherent and para-noid as I was at fifteen.

Chugging home in my little car, I tune into some frothy, '60s surf-inspired melodies on the radio. I've got to look on the bright side, to use one of Mommy's clichés. I've made it through another day with-out being sent to prison. I've felt the sun on my face and the sweetness of freshly laundered sheets. I've eaten farm eggs and bought fresh fruit from a little stand near the school. I've caught up with the first guy I kissed, who's still as handsome as when we snuck behind the Dairy Queen to smooch as teenagers. I've shared laughs with a fellow artist over gargantuan espresso drinks. I haven't even thought of Ravi once today. Until now.

Maybe getting away from L.A. and coming home for a bit was a good idea after all. And maybe this teaching thing won't be so bad. Maybe I'll be like Liz McIntyre, the groovy guidance counselor that Denise Nicholas played on *Room 222*. As a kid I loved how cool she was with the kids while looking fabulous in those fly suede jackets and flared pants. Maybe my summer students will go from failing to scoring off the charts. Then maybe I'll be on *60 Minutes* and write a memoir, and they'll do one of those heartwarming "teacher in the hood," *Mister Tibbs* kinds of movies based on my life. Maybe I'll pitch a present-day remake of *Room 222*. Maybe I have a future to look forward to after all.

CHAPTER 10 ♡

I'm seated in a high-backed wooden chair at a strip-mall Starbucks near the freeway. I'm totally wired as I sip my second venti soy sugar-free vanilla latte in a row. I can barely sit still. My ass—the one I was so proud of until I started broadening it with butterfat—is bouncing up and down in my seat, perhaps a reflection of its newfound buoyancy. When I'm not bouncing, I'm biting my nails. Jen would shout if she saw me, though she would also drag me to the nearest nail parlor. God, I miss her.

I try to pull off a jagged, dangling piece of nail that I have partially torn off with my teeth. Suddenly a once-familiar, cheerful voice greets me.

"Hey, good-lookin'!"

Does Davis possess as many Sybil-like personalities as I do? Davis's lanky limbs are draped in cuffed, baggy chinos, a faded Nirvana T-shirt and a slightly wrinkled, sailcloth blazer. He seats himself across from me and swigs from a venti-sized something-or-other. His ash-blond hair is still damp, pieces pointing upward and outward in haphazard spikes. Other than a bit of redeye, he appears to be in the pink, though I have a sudden urge to buy him an Egg McMuffin.

"So, how was the first day? You quit yet?" Davis's tone is chipper.

"It wasn't so bad," I respond. "I didn't throw up. I know it's a low bar, but my expectations weren't too high."

"Congratulations on repressing the urge to hurl. Maybe this means you'll grace us with your presence for a little longer?"

"I don't know about that." I try to mimic Davis's chipper tone, but

I don't have it in me. "Especially since my parents keep reminding me that we're hosting a party for W."

Davis frowns, "Your parents are Republicans?"

"Not my parents, Davis, the school! I hear he's coming to Lee." The thought of my parents as Republicans makes me laugh so hard that I have to set down my coffee.

"That doesn't surprise me," Davis smirks. "As long as I don't have to be around him, then I could care less. Eight years of that dude is enough. Speaking of nonsense, have you thought of any ideas for the summer production? The arts program starts tomorrow, so Hardy's gonna start bugging us about it."

"I have no earthly idea what to do." The Davis I first met is back, and I'm relieved. "How about *Oklahoma*? Though Texans hate Okies, so maybe we should do *Grease*. I know that musical pretty much by heart all ready."

"It doesn't matter," Davis responds. "As long as there are no gays or hippies in it, you could set the alphabet to music, and folks around here would love it."

"So *Hair* and *Rent* are out of the question? Hey, I sat up watching *North Dallas Forty* last night. Maybe we can set that to music," I joke. "It's got football, it's set in Texas, it's perfect!'

"I love that movie." Davis doesn't appear to be joking.

"I thought you hated football."

"I hated high school football players when I was in high school with them. But I love football."

"You know, I never really hated the football players or the cheer-leaders. I envied them, though. The popular kids were always able to be as shallow or as stupid as they wanted. And they got away with it! My people were oppressed, so as much as some of us try to be superficial, there's too much guilt and fear of letting down the race for it to work for us."

"Have you watched reality TV lately?" Davis asks. "Those women catfightin' over Flava Flav?"

I take a long drag from my coffee cup.

"The whole world is just high school to the tenth power," Davis continues. "Most folks are too self-centered or too insecure to feel for anybody outside their circle."

"And how did you escape that fate?" I ask.

"I had an ugly phase," Davis deadpans. "When you're young, ugly is like leprosy. If you don't kill yourself first, you develop a lot of empathy." Davis drains his huge, paper coffee cup. "Can I get you something else?" Davis rises and fumbles through his trouser pockets to retrieve some crumpled, loose bills.

"No. This is my second one of these. If I have anymore, I may shoot someone."

"Well, I actually may need to shoot someone, so I'll be right back."

I watch Davis stride in the direction of the barrista counter. He has the build of a distance runner, the lean muscles of his arms and shoulders apparent, despite the loose-fitting slouch of his clothes.

My purse vibrates, and I reach inside to pull out my phone.

HiFiNY:	What U doing?
JoMaMa:	Coffee. What U doing so early AM?
HiFiNY:	I'm back in NYC. Have launch party for G-NYUS 2nite.
JoMaMa:	Who?
HiFiNY:	G-NYUS. My new act. Don't U listen 2 radio?
JoMaMa:	Pronounce?
HiFiNY:	Like "Genius." U know, smart? G's from NY n the US, get it?
JoMaMa:	Yawn.
HiFiNY:	BTW, Jen saw X-Man.
JoMaMa:	I know.
HiFiNY:	U haven't called him, have U?
JoMaMa:	No.
HiFiNY:	Email?
JoMaMa:	No.
HiFiNY:	Western Union?

JoMaMa:	NO! NO! NO!
HiFiNY:	Good Girl. Had 2 check. Gotta go. Chat later?
JoMaMa:	Please.
HiFiNY:	Ciao, bella.

Why did I lie to Rudy? OK, it wasn't exactly a lie because Ravi called me, not the other way around. But it's still misleading. Rudy and Jen expect me to say or do something stupid if I talk to Ravi. They're so worried about me that, as usual, I feel ashamed. Despite demanding careers and personal lives of their own, they still care about my pitiful existence. I'm not sure what I would do without them.

"Everything OK?"

I don't realize that my eyes are still lowered, back curved and shoulders hunched in the direction of my lap. I straighten at the sound of Davis' voice.

"Oh, yeah, Davis, everything's . . . um, I'm OK." I take a deep breath and try to start over. "My best friends text me all the time to make sure I'm behaving down here." With much effort, I attempt an effortless-looking grin.

"Are you staying out of trouble?" Davis also appears to be exerting effort to throw his typically unforced, carefree smile my way.

"Do I have a choice? It's not like there's much trouble to get into around here."

"Well, don't feel bad." Davis sets his new venti coffee cup and a bagel wrapped in brown paper on the table between us. "This is Midland, you know," he continues. "We try our best, but we can't compete with the coasts. Actually, I take that back. We don't even try."

I cock my head to the side, like a curious pup, and examine Davis a bit more carefully.

"How about you? Are you OK?"

Davis takes a moment to answer. He glances out beyond the vision of the mermaid painted on the glass storefront. "Been better," he says. "But I'm OK."

"You didn't sound OK when I called you yesterday."

"I'm fine." He takes a sip of his enormous cappuccino and moves his long legs out from underneath the table in order to cross them. "Don't you hate these dried out things? This is no bagel," Davis scowls and bites into the round, chewy roll. He doesn't return my brazen stare as he reads the little quote on the side of his coffee cup and chews slowly, with some difficulty.

"Come on Davis," I needle, poking his forearm with my finger. "What's *really* bugging you?"

Davis looks exasperated, lines appearing between his eyebrows and a smirk sliding across his lips. He speaks very slowly to me, as if talking to a really dumb child.

"I've got issues with my ex," is all he says before taking another large bite out of what the pastry case labels a bagel but which is really a thick glob of dough.

"Is this ex a she or a he?" I press on, undeterred.

"She's a she," he mumbles as he chomps the mass in his mouth. If he's phased by my confusion about his sexual orientation, he doesn't show it. "A she-devil's more like it," he adds before taking in another mouthful.

"She-devil, eh? You know, Davis, exes have a way of creeping back into your life. If she's that bad . . . you should probably watch your back." What am I saying?

"I'm fine," he murmurs and stares out the window again.

"I didn't ask how you looked, Davis, I asked how you felt!"

Rather than baring his soul, Davis begins to laugh. His eyes soften and crinkle at the corners. "Ha! Why didn't I meet up with you ten years ago or so?"

I'm now more self-conscious than curious. "Um, ten years ago? I think I was in Vienna."

"Vienna?"

"Don't ask. That was a big mistake. A Black girl from the desert doing dinner theater in the Alps? *Fuhgeddaboudit.*"

"Oil and water?"

"Exactly. I don't know why I rearrange my life on such crazy whims.

I've had a million crazy, weird experiences, and I can't say I've learned a single thing from any of them."

"I guess you better just go ahead and shoot yourself now," Davis teases. "How about another venti coffee?"

"Let's get out of here, Davis, before you give me any more self-destructive ideas. And I thought you were my friend."

"Unfortunately for you, that advice may be the nicest thing you'll hear from anybody around here. Remember *Blue Velvet*?"

"You're not making this transition easy, Davis. Remind me to call the Midland Chamber of Commerce and tell them to never hire you, if they know what's good for them."

Davis laughs again and rises out of his chair. He extends his hand and helps heave me and my generous booty out of my chair. As we head for school, the Beemer putt putts to keep up with Davis's purring Mini Cooper. Though we drive the smallest cars in the entire lot, we have a hard time finding places to park. More than half the school parking lot is taken up by two huge, camouflage-covered trailers with GO ARMY emblazoned in bold letters on either side.

We're barely in the building when we catch sight of Principal Hardy hustling down the hallway to greet us. He's wearing white, rubber-soled shoes that squeak against the linoleum as he jogs toward us. His white shoes match his white, short-sleeved button-down shirt, which is crisp and free of wrinkles, despite the withering heat outdoors. His sleek, shiny hair is parted to the side, and not a strand strays out of place.

"Davis, Jo, just the people I wanted to see. Got a minute?"

As he is the man responsible for our schedules this summer, he knows, of course, that neither of us has a first period class today. We say nothing in response, nor does he wait for one. He turns and walks back to his office while the two of us trail behind him.

As we settle into our seats, Principal Hardy can barely contain himself. "We have great news!" He beams and clasps his hands together on top of his desk, as if about to engage in prayer. "The President is coming to Midland, and you won't believe what he's going to do while he's in town."

The look on the principal's face is so pure and so euphoric, that I can't bring myself to burst his bubble. I gasp and lean toward him, widening my eyes in a pretend display of bated breath.

"He's coming to Lee," Davis says flatly and slouches in his seat.

If Principal Hardy is disappointed at his failure to surprise us, it's not at all evident. He breaks into a wide, toothy grin and claps his hands like a game show contestant. "Isn't it wonderful?" he gushes as I bob my head up and down. Davis stares vacantly in Hardy's direction.

"We're so honored that he chose to visit *our* school on his last trip to Midland as President."

"Isn't this his *only* trip to Midland as president? His term's almost up, so I doubt . . ." I glare at Davis to shut him up, but it makes no difference. Principal Hardy is paying him no mind. His eyes squint up at the fluorescent lights overhead, and he nods and moves his lips, as if immersed in a trance or a daydream.

"You know, the media will probably televise the event," he says softly without lowering his eyes from the lamp. "So we should put on a grand performance to honor our President. Something patriotic and powerful that will show him the high esteem that we, that the world holds him in."

"Are you kidding me?" Davis scowls.

"We're gonna show the world what Midland, Texas, is made of." Hardy's eyes return from the heavens and finally focus on the mere mortals seated before him. "Now you're both such fine artists, I know you can come up with something for the students to perform that will honor the magnitude of this great occasion."

"What the . . ."

"Principal Hardy," I interrupt before Davis can say something we all regret. "You know, I'm new here, so I'm not really sure . . ."

"And I can't believe our *amazing* good fortune to have a professional actress of your stature with us this summer," he says as he beams at me. I assume he didn't see me in *Camp Chainsaw.*

"With your knowledge of theatrical matters, Jo, I know you'll come up with something extraordinary. Now I *love* hearing the words to *Proud to be an American* read aloud, but I'm not the artist here. I'll just let you work your magic. And Davis here is a mighty fine musical talent. So Lord knows the two of you'll create something really spectacular, praise Him."

I glance at Davis and notice that his expression has shifted from annoyance to subtle amusement. "How much time do we have to create this spectacle of spectacular-ness?" he asks, his eyes glimmering almost as much as the principal's.

"Oh, about two weeks, give or take a day."

My eyes widen for real this time, not for show. I am not at all tickled by the prospect of suspending what little life I have to speak of right now to devote myself to the praise of a president I actively dislike. Particularly not such a public tribute, when the last thing I need is to draw that level of attention to myself. An interview for the "Arts" section of the local paper is one thing. An appearance with the President of the United States is another thing altogether.

"Principal Hardy," I say with as much saccharin in my voice as I can stomach. "For a special event like this one, you might want to consider having the school chorus sing something really beautiful for the President. I hear that Mrs. Tyler worked really hard with those students all school year, and they're already used to performing together. She could probably . . ."

"Yes, yes, I thought of that," Principal Hardy says. "But everyone does that sort of thing. I would like to do something really unique and dramatic, especially since we have a famous actress on the faculty this summer. Something really inspirational, like those beautiful scripture readings the young people do on the Christian Broadcasting Network. Those readings always bring a tear to my eye."

"You know, Tom, Jo doesn't know this, but I actually saw her do Shakespeare in Central Park one summer. She has a fine sense for the dramatic. You couldn't have asked for a better person to work on this." A now-gleeful Davis grins and winks at me, but I don't grin back. This summer teaching experience was not supposed to be strenuous. I expected to skim a few books I've already read and then grade a few unremarkable essays. My spare time was to be spent moping and feeling sorry for myself and mixing margaritas with Uncle Buddy until it's finally safe for me to return to L.A.

"We'll get to work on it right away," Davis offers.

"Wonderful!" Principal Hardy gushes. He and Davis stand and shake hands. I rise to my feet, though I don't actually feel myself move. I feel numb as I plod toward the door. I need to get out of here, but my body is not cooperating fast enough. My hand slowly reaches for the doorknob, but before I can grasp it, Principal Hardy calls out, "Oh, Jo, just one other thing before you leave." Still smiling, he asks, "do you have any ideas for the summer show?"

"Well, sir," I stutter, "um, well, I'm still thinking . . ."

"Oh yes, sir," Davis interrupts. "Jo has this great idea." My eyes narrow as I try to focus on where Davis is going with this. "Now, Jo, don't be modest. She told me all about it, Tom."

Principal Hardy's doughy face retains its sweet smile, and an eager spark appears in his eyes.

"Get this," Davis continues as he pats Principal Hardy on the arm for emphasis. "*North Dallas Forty*–the Musical!"

I am too stunned to speak. What kind of damn fool is Davis, anyway?

Principal Hardy's brow furrows, and his smile shrivels. Davis and I stare at him as he raises his eyes to the heavens again and holds them there for a few moments. Suddenly, his eyes meet ours again with a gaze that is intense and serious. He flashes all of his teeth in a beaming, wide-mouthed grin and belts out a hearty belly laugh. He places a hand on his stomach, as if attempting to squelch an ache.

"Why, why, that's *brilliant!*" Hardy gives Davis a hug and then rushes past us. He throws open his office door, calling out to the secretaries in the front office.

"Doreen! Girls, you gotta hear this. This is just brilliant . . ."

"Don't thank me." Davis winks again and follows Hardy out the door.

It was a funny idea at breakfast. But there is no humor in this situation. First I'm roped into producing an extravaganza to honor a man I don't admire. Now Davis has committed me to write some fool-ass musical from scratch. I easily could have dusted off my old copy of *Grease* that Mommy stuck in a scrapbook after I played a Pink Lady on Broadway. I could do *Grease* in my sleep. Can this summer get any worse?

At least it's not prison. I trudge down the wide, sterile corridor to my first class. The fluorescent lights are brash and unforgiving, the walls lifeless. The kids mill around in small, slouchy groups, oozing boredom and disaffection. But the corridors of Lee are idyllic compared to Lynwood.

Unfortunately most of my students in my first class have failed to prepare the short, simple writing assignment I gave them yesterday. I asked them to write a single paragraph that answers the question, "My name is _____, and if I was a character in a movie I would be _____ because _____." Easy, right? I also thought they'd enjoy it, and I was looking forward to see what they wrote.

"Miss Randolph, I don't understand what you mean by these lines here."

"Miss Randolph, I can't tell if you want us to write a sentence or a paragraph. This don't make no sense."

"Miss Randolph, I hurt my finger in football practice, so I couldn't write nothin' last night."

"Miss Randolph, my computer's broke."

"Miss Randolph, I ain't got no computer, and the library's closed on Monday."

Almost every kid has an excuse, each one lamer than the proverbial dog-eaten homework. My next class is a bit more creative. They decide to spend the time and energy they could have used to knock out the same one paragraph to instead orchestrate a vast, high school conspiracy; ganging together to assert that they thought the assignment was due *next* Tuesday, not today.

In degree of difficulty, this assignment was the equivalent of the "How I Spent My Summer Vacation" theses we scribbled with number-two pencils on wide-lined notebook paper back in third grade. If I can't motivate these kids to do something this simple, how on earth am

I going to get them to compare and contrast Tolstoy and Dostoevsky or appreciate James Joyce? Of course, when I ask what was interesting on television last night, everyone has a distinct, well-articulated opinion on the subject.

I'm disgusted. I don't try to catch up with Davis at the end of the day. I race out of the door as soon as the bell rings. I want to peel out of the parking lot as fast as possible, but I have to sit and wait for my engine to stop stammering from the stress of starting up in 108 degree heat. Suddenly, my cell phone begins to *Conga*.

"Did you find me a job somewhere on the other side of the world yet?" I ask before Jen can even begin to speak.

"I'm working on it," she says. "Class didn't go so great?"

"No," I groan. I fan myself with the few student papers I collected in class. "Most of these kids are zombies. They don't want to work, and they don't seem to be interested in anything but TV. And to top it off, I not only have to write a musical from scratch, cast it, direct it and have these morons perform it before the end of the summer, but I also have to put together some sort of dramatic doo-hickey for President Bush when he comes to town in a week or two. I did not sign up for this shit."

"OK, so you agreed to teach English and run a summer drama program, and you're accepting a salary to do these things, but you're mad because you have to do actual work at the job they're paying you to do? Who's the zombie here?"

"Something told me that I shouldn't have answered the phone," I grumble. "Speaking of zombies, Rudy told me the other day that Oprah finally agreed to interview Danielle, and that it would air on Saturday, but Oprah doesn't air on the weekends. Where is he getting all this crazy stuff from?"

"Oprah is the least of your worries right now, Jo."

"I know, I know. I need to move on from Ravi and focus on getting my career back."

"Well, that too, but that's not what I'm talking about. Some sort of investigator called me, Jo."

"*What?!*"

"I don't think he's a police detective. Or at least I hope not. I didn't take time to find out. I stopped talking to him when I heard the sort of questions he was asking."

I gasp and gulp down a large dose of desert air from my open car window. My nostrils fill with dust. Coughing to clear my sinuses, I'm barely able to speak. "But I thought they dropped the whole thing," I rasp. "What about all those papers I signed?"

"He didn't ask me about the fight on the set, Jo. He asked about where you were later that day. He wanted to know when you left town, where you went, the whole bit. He called Rudy too."

"*Lord, help me.*"

"I don't know what's going on. One minute Danielle's a suspect and hiding from the world. Then all of a sudden, she's talking to the press, and she's prancing around town with Ravi again. Then these people start asking questions, and . . . look, Jo, I think you need a lawyer."

"But Rudy's lawyer . . ."

"Rudy's lawyer negotiates music royalties and concert tour agreements and crap like that. He can handle stupid stuff like, you know, the cops finding a little weed in the backseat or a fender bender on La Brea. But this has gone a bit *beyond*, don't you think? I mean, he hasn't really been able to find out anything or advise you on what to do since he got you out of Lynwood. Rudy trusts him, but I think you need a real criminal lawyer, Jo."

I can't speak. I don't know what to say or do. I sit in my sputtering car, staring across the parking lot at the rows of mega-SUVs and pickup trucks. They're not the rusty, scrappy trucks and vans of my youth. They're imposing, cruise missile-like monstrosities in shimmering shades of plum, blue and steel grey.

"Don't your parents know any lawyers, Jo?" I almost forgot that Jen was still on the line. "Rudy and I can ask around, but everybody here blabs everything to everyone. It's hard to keep stuff quiet if we do it. We'll get you somebody if push comes to shove, but as Plan A, you might want to ask around down there for someone, so it's more on the down low."

"Who the hell do I know in Midland that could help me? Especially since I'm not sure what I need help with!"

"You're one of those Jack & Jill kids that grew up around all the Black doctor and lawyer types. And with all the corporate scandals that go on in your State, it should be ripe with lawyers who know how to get people out of jams. Why don't you ask your sister?"

"Why don't I lie down in traffic?"

"Suit yourself."

"Why haven't they called me? Maybe they're insurance investigators?"

"I don't know, Jo. I'm sure it's just a matter of time before they call you. And if it's an insurance company, then it's probably just a matter of time before the police start poking around. So it wouldn't hurt for you to talk to someone."

I know she's right. But I'm not ready to face it. I'm not ready to face anything. I don't know if I say good-bye to Jen before I hang up the phone. I toss my cell onto the worn leather passenger seat and press on the gas pedal to push myself home.

CHAPTER 11 ♡

My phone is starting to annoy me. Another call comes in as I pull into my parents' driveway. It's at a Midland number I don't recognize.

"Hey, girl, what you doin' this weekend?" My childhood friend, Lou, is as perky on the phone as she is in person. "I'm treating Paula to a manicure and one of those hot stone massages on Saturday. Have you ever tried one?"

I start to answer, but Lou doesn't wait for a response. "You wouldn't know it to see her now, but Paula lost a whole lot of weight, girl. She lost fifty pounds, and she didn't even join Jenny Craig or nothing. Can you believe that?"

A trickle of sweat runs down the side of my neck as I sit in my sun-soaked car. "Hey, Lou, I'm in my folks' driveway, so . . ."

"You know, the church is always celebrating stuff with a whole bunch of food. But I had to tell Pastor Maples that we need to stop stuffin' our folks to death. The Willing Workers got kinda upset with me, but I told 'em if they don't start servin' up some salads instead of all that fried chicken and stuff, we're all gonna end up a bunch 'a diabetics."

"Can I . . ."

"Anyway, girl, Paula's been so good about walkin' and cookin' with olive oil and stuff, like Rachel Ray does on TV. I'm so proud of her! I wanna give her a different kind of treat than food. There's a new day spa over by the Baskin-Robbins, and I'm gonna take her there to celebrate. And we're gonna have lunch at that sushi place across the street. Do you eat sushi? We're gonna try it and then head over to Dillard's to pick out some new outfits for Paula's new figure."

I am stunned at the thought of eating raw fish in a desert town that's probably a thousand miles from the nearest sea, but I don't say so.

"Girl, you should come with us! After a week with all those teenagers, you're gonna need some pampering."

I can't help but smile. "You know, Lou, I don't think Paula's ever forgiven me for teasing her so much in carpool. She might punch me in the eye again if I tag along."

Lou giggles so loudly that I have to hold the phone away from my ear. "Girl, I had forgotten all about that fight y'all had in your mom's car. You are crazy!"

I'm at a loss for words. I'm actually longing to spend my Saturday with Lou and Paula at a day spa that's situated in a strip mall next to a Baskin-Robbins. I'm dying to dine on desert sushi with my elementary school carpool companions, one of which gave me such a shiner in third grade that everyone called me 'Pete-y the Dog' until damn near high school. I look down at my stack of school papers and the *Great American Oratories* and *Historic American Documents* resting on my passenger seat, and my day feels dark again.

"I'd love to go, Lou. But Principal Hardy just dumped two big projects on me this morning."

"Girl, it's the summertime! Those folks shouldn't be workin' you so hard! You know, you could come to the spa with us in the morning. And then you can just play it by ear."

"I think that'll work." I brighten up a bit. "Yes, I'll do it."

"Oooh, girl!" Lou squeals. "I can't wait!"

I hang up with Lou and scan my missed calls as I head into the house. Ravi, Davis, Ravi, Ravi, Willie T., Ravi. There's also a number I don't recognize. I don't even recognize the area code. Goose bumps appear on my bare forearm, though my reaction has nothing to do with the chill of the air conditioning. I head into the kitchen, which is always warmer than the rest of the house.

"Domino!" Uncle Buddy declares as he raises an ivory-colored tile in the air and slams it down hard on the kitchen table.

Memphis is seated across from Uncle Buddy. He shakes his head side to side and dominoes spill from his hands onto the tabletop. "I can't believe you beat me again, old man. Hey, Jo Ella! Uncle Buddy's killin' me over here."

"Memphis, you know better. In forty years have you ever seen Uncle Buddy lose at dominoes?"

"Uncle Buddy puckers his lips in the air to kiss me as I pass him. Mommy is stirring a large pot on the stove, and the kitchen smells of cumin.

"That chili smells good, Aunt Ella!" Memphis calls out from his chair.

"Well, it won't be ready for a couple of hours," Mommy frowns. "I took Aunt Lula to the eye doctor this afternoon, so I got a late start."

"That's OK," Memphis says as he strolls over to the refrigerator. "Long as you don't run out of beer, Aunt Ella, then I kin wait."

"Memphis, do you ever eat at home?" I ask. I extend a hand for him to place a beer into it.

"Nope," Memphis answers. "I kin fix just about anything, but I can't cook a lick. Ever since Mama died, Daddy's been eatin' Arby's every day. Too much of that stuff'll clog your colon. So here I am, baby!" Memphis grabs my outstretched hand and starts to jitterbug. He waves his beer in the air and swings me around the kitchen.

Mommy shakes a wooden spoon at us. "Will you two take this party somewhere else, please?" She tries to look stern, but she can't conceal her amusement.

"Okey-doke," Memphis releases my hand and opens the refrigerator again. "Here you go, Jo Ella," he says and hands me a beer. "Want one, Uncle Buddy?"

Uncle Buddy swirls the ice cubes in his tumbler of whiskey in response.

"By the way, Jo Ella, I got a modem and one of them wireless routers set up in your room so you kin use your laptop all around the house. You don't have to use Aunt Ella's computer no more."

"Wow," I stammer. "Thanks, Memphis. You didn't have to . . ."

"Aw, Jo Ella, it wasn't nothin'. You know my boy, Boo, works down there at the cable company, so he hooked me up with the stuff. I see you hunched up here in the kitchen all the time on that slow, old thang. Now you kin work wherever you want to.'"

Memphis smiles and starts out of the room to join Daddy and ESPN in the den. Uncle Buddy pipes up to taunt him. "Now that you've had your whupin', boy, you better go on and get out of here," Uncle Buddy chuckles. He turns to me and says, "you wanna play dominoes, baby?"

I gaze at the lines in his warm, weather-beaten face and feel sad. "I'm sorry, Uncle Buddy, but I've got papers to grade. Maybe after dinner?"

"Sure, sugar." Uncle Buddy's wide, crooked grin lifts my spirits. I head to my bedroom and dump my books and papers and beer bottle amongst the mess on my desk. I shove some cosmetics to the side to clear a space and take a red felt-tip pen out of my bag to grade the few essays I collected.

My male students don't make much effort to quash stereotypes. James Bond is widely admired for his hot cars and hot women. Bruce Lee, Batman, and any character played by Will Smith are also popular choices, as is Tony Montana from *Scarface*. The boys seem to appreciate kicking butt and taking no stuff as exemplary human qualities, whether or not these attributes are used for good. One kid chooses the Stiffler character from *American Pie*. I can't quite decipher the reason, but it has something to do with being a first-rate smart-ass.

A number of girls desire to kick butt and take control of their environments as well, choosing superheroes and superwomen as their favorite characters: Storm from *X-Men*, Catwoman, Charlie's Angels, Angelina Jolie's Lara Croft. Anything with Angelina Jolie, actually. Though I asked for role models from movies, not TV, many girls select Carrie Bradshaw from *Sex and the City* for her lavish wardrobe, extravagant lifestyle, and rich boyfriend. No one mentions the fact that her character is a writer. I'm concerned, but I have no standing to judge. I'm also surprised, because I doubt that Mommy would have let me watch that show in high school. I'm most intrigued by the student that cites Princess Jasmine from *Aladdin* as her heroine because this Disney Princess is independent and brave, and she follows her heart, even though it leads her to a pauper.

The grammar in these essays isn't great, but I go easy on the kids who at least made an effort to turn off *The Hills* and complete the assignment. I put them away and reach for the volume of *Great American Oratories*. I stretch out on my twin-sized bed and skim the pages for inspiration for the Bush event—Lincoln, Kennedy, King, Lincoln, Kennedy, FDR, Malcolm X, Kennedy, King again. Slavery, war, civil rights—nothing really on education, unless I use something from the New Deal or the Great Society. But quoting Democrats like FDR and LBJ might not go over so well with the current president, particularly since he's not quite as eloquent as his Democratic predecessors. Perhaps I should try something from Ronald Reagan. I find snippets from speeches here and there that I could use, but the overall tone just doesn't feel right. Federally funded education programs weren't really his cup of tea. I toss the *Oratories* on the floor and move on to *Historic American Documents*.

The Declaration of Independence is too obvious, but it's feeling good to me. It's not really on point with the education theme, but there's something perfect and powerful about it.

A Prince, whose character is thus marked by every act which
may define a Tyrant, is unfit to be the ruler of a free people . . .

The doorbell rings, but I keep reading. A few minutes later, it rings again. A house full of men watching TV, and no one can answer the door? I head to the foyer and swing open the front door without peeking through the peephole or asking who it is.

"Since I've probably ruined your summer, I brought you a peace offering." Davis wears a sheepish grin as he towers over me. He's clutching a large paper bag adorned with a large grease stain in one hand, and a case of Coronas in the other.

"Tacos?" I absorb the aroma of marinated meat as I wrest the bag out of his grasp.

"And this," he says as he pulls a Blockbuster DVD case out of the top of the taco bag. "*North Dallas Forty*. If you're not busy, I thought we might get to work."

"And if I am busy?"

"Then I'll take a taco to go." His eyes drop to his feet. "I apologize for just dropping in like this. I guess all my old Midland ways have come back."

"It's OK," I say. I take hold of his forearm and guide him into the house. "If there are some extras in this bag, you'll make my starving cousin extremely happy. And since he drank up all our Coronas, these reinforcements will keep him from starting in on Daddy's Coors. You may have saved us from another domestic disturbance."

"Considering the way your mother was swinging that knife around at the party, I would've thought that your cousin would tread lightly around here."

"I don't think that's possible in my family."

My family seems genuinely impressed by Davis's peace offering. Mommy is happy to transfer her chili to a crockpot and worry about it tomorrow. And she is thrilled that Davis has provided earth-killing, disposable plates and utensils that will spare her from ruining her manicure over the dishes.

"Davis, this was just lovely!" Mommy dabs taco sauce from the corner of her mouth with her dinner napkin. "Now I want you to make yourself comfortable while I thaw out a pie." She touches Davis's arm and winks at him as she rises from the table.

"Oh, ma'am, you don't have to . . ."

Mommy ignores Davis and opens the freezer. She examines the labels on a stack of carefully wrapped pie pans. "What's your favorite, Davis? Apple? Peach? Sweet Potato?"

"I'll let Mr. McElroy choose." Davis nods and raises his beer bottle to Uncle Buddy.

"Sweet potato," Uncle Buddy says and lifts his glass in Davis's direction. "Son, grab that bottle over there, would you?"

Mommy snatches the liter of Jack Daniel's from the counter. "Haven't you had enough, Buddy?"

The creases in Uncle Buddy's face deepen. "Now, Ella, I'm think I'm old enough to decide what's what. At my age, what's the worse thing that could happen, sugar?"

Mommy says nothing and sets the bottle in the center of the table in a huff. She returns to the sweet potato pie she removed from the freezer and carefully peels away layers of tautly stretched plastic wrap and foil and then gently lifts the frozen pastry out of its small, tin pan with the tips of her fingers.

"Davis, you wanna come watch the Rangers game with us?" Daddy offers as he rises from his chair.

"Thank you, sir, but I think Jo and I had better get to work. We've got to work on this school musical thing, and the Principal wants us to prepare something for the kids to do for the President when he comes to town in a couple of weeks."

Daddy frowns at me. "Baby, why in holy hell do those folks have *you* working on something for that rascal, with all the conservatives running around that place? I don't like it one bit!"

"Well, Daddy, I am the drama teacher, so . . ."

"There are plenty of folks over there that would be happy to roll out the red carpet for him, Jo Ella. Praising that man is not part of your job description." Mommy shuts the microwave door with a loud "snap" for emphasis.

"But, I thought I had to . . ."

"I'll be in the den," Daddy grumbles as he leaves the room with Memphis in tow.

"Oops," Davis whispers under his breath.

"I guess we won't be using the DVD player," I whisper back. " We can watch it on my laptop, if you don't mind the screen being kind of small."

"Jo Ella," Mommy interrupts. "We put one of those TVs with the built-in DVD in Ann Marie's old room." Mommy's back is turned, and she is pressing her index finger against the pie she just defrosted in the microwave.

I shrug my shoulders and gesture for Davis to follow me toward the bedrooms. No boy has ever invaded the inner sanctum of our childhood bedrooms before, as far as I know. My folks must think Davis is gay.

Like mine, Ann Marie's room is frozen in time, though hers resembles a *Good Housekeeping* article from 1983, instead of a cesspool. The walls are a salmon color. Framed posters of Judith Jamison dancing in *Cry* and a pink pointe shoe balancing atop an egg are symmetrically hung on either side of her white, mirrored vanity. Atop the vanity are crystal atomizers and a silver brush with matching comb. Her tall, white bookcase houses neatly shelved volumes of Edith Wharton, Toni Morrison and the *Preppy Handbook*, alongside her tennis trophies, model horses and an autographed photo of Dallas Cowboys legend, Tony Dorsett, in an intricate silver-toned frame. A ribbon-laced corkboard hangs above her white desk that matches the style of the vanity and her headboard, on which are tacked preserved homecoming chrysanthemums with flowing maroon and white streamers, pictures from proms and sorority life, and a laminated copy of her *Seventeen* cover.

Davis appears uncomfortable. Hands stuffed in his pockets, he looks at everything in the room other than the generous, queen-sized bed with its pink, green and gold paisley comforter and scallop-edged, monogrammed throw pillows. He sits very straight on the extreme edge of the bed, as the television has been placed atop the only chair in the room. I slide the DVD into the machine and sit primly on the corner of the bed opposite Davis.

I hear a tinkling noise and suddenly Uncle Buddy appears in the room, cocktail glass clinking. He totters in without his walker and seats himself right between me and Davis. "What we watchin'?" he asks, staring intensely at Davis from a few inches away.

Davis stifles a cough. "*North Dallas Forty*, sir."

"Parts of it are kind of racy, Uncle Buddy. We've got to figure out how to make it appropriate for the kids. I don't know if you . . ."

"I have HBO, sugar." Uncle Buddy takes a long, silent sip from his glass.

Davis and I say nothing else and take uncomfortable drags from our beer bottles as we stare straight ahead at the screen and not at Uncle Buddy or each other. It is immediately apparent that marijuana, alcohol and painkillers are essential supporting characters in the film. Other than Nick Nolte's interaction with a disco-haired girl, the male-female interplay consists mainly of molestation. As Mac Davis drapes his arm around two jersey-clad women and jokes about his boner, I know that there's no way we can turn this into a high school musical for the Bible Belt-set.

I peer around Uncle Buddy to glance at Davis. He's struggling to restrain the Dennis Quaid grin. Uncle Buddy's back is straight and his long fingers gently cradle the cocktail glass atop his lap. His eyes are closed. I set my beer bottle on the floor and remove the glass from his hands. I carefully maneuver Uncle Buddy onto his back, and he begins to snore softly, his mouth slightly agape.

"You know you got us into this mess," I say as I drape a maroon Rebels-stadium blanket over Uncle Buddy.

"I think this is gonna be great. Want another beer?"

"Yeah, really great. This is what they spend half the movie doing." I turn up my beer bottle and drain it. I hand my empty longneck to Davis as he rises and returns to the kitchen. A big hulk of a guy picks up a girl and throws her over his shoulder on screen. There's absolutely nothing PG-13 about this movie.

But there's something underlying all the debauchery that rings true. Something I can relate to because it's so fabulous and yet so empty, all at the same time. Kind of like my life. These guys reach the highest level of their sport and turn their talents into the kind of career that most other guys envy. They love what they do, or at least they loved it until it became just a business. A circus, actually, in which the players are mere sideshow acts performing for treats instead of the love of the game. And they can lose it all in an instant. One mistake, one injury can mean the end of their livelihoods and their lives as they know it.

"You know, the pressure on these pro players to win isn't so different from what high school players go through," I say as Davis reenters the room with two beers and a large slice of pie. "They have to play hurt, they can't buck the system, they have people fawning over them one minute and cutting them down the next. Their entire future can come down to one game or one injury. Everybody can relate to that kind of pressure on some level, can't they?"

Davis offers me one of the beers, but I continue to focus on the screen. "We could do this from a high school perspective. We can show

how important it is to the whole school for the team to win, and how the players' lives depend on their doing well at football. Kind of like *Friday Night Lights*, but we'll make it campy and funny."

I finally take my eyes away from the TV and look at Davis. He is staring at me, dessert fork dangling from his lips. "Go on," he mumbles.

"OK, like we can have this evil coach character who tries to push the kids to use steroids so they can win the state championships. But they refuse because they're such principled, all-American kids. You know, President Bush talked more about steroids in baseball than Hurricane Katrina in his State of the Union speech. So the steroids thing could be like the dark element behind all the asinine high-kicking and singing and dancing and crap we put into the show."

"The boosters and coaches might take offense, but that's actually pretty good."

"And we can have the star quarterback who does what he's told because he needs to get a scholarship to go to college because his family can't afford it, and he doesn't want to work in an oilfield or something like that. And then there's the Nick Nolte character who rebels against it all."

"But what are we gonna do about all the drugs and date rape?" Davis prods as he picks up the last bit of his pie with his fingers and shoves it into his mouth.

"You picked the drug and date rape story, remember? We'll just have to make up some wholesome song-type crap in place of all the NC-17 stuff. Whenever they snort coke or jump into bed with someone in the movie, we can have them break into song instead. Besides, there are a few Bible study-type players in the movie. We can have a little chorus of them who sing peppy little gospel songs to their teammates to keep them on the straight and narrow. What do you think?"

"I think you may be as twisted as I am." Davis grins wickedly. "You know that scene in the beginning where the coked-up teammates drag Nick Nolte hunting and keep talkin' about how they just want to 'kill a little somethin'?"

I nod my head.

"I've got this crazy opening song in my head," Davis continues. "It's like '*I wanna kill a little somethin*',' but in our song, they're talking about killing the other team on the field, not shootin' up somebody's livestock while they're f-ed up."

"And maybe we can turn that big party scene into a pep rally or something. Instead of football players flipping girls over their shoulders, we can have male cheerleaders flipping girls over their shoulders." I smile at Davis and turn back to the TV screen. We say little else until the movie is over. When the film ends, we are nearly as bleary-eyed as the ball players. Davis stands and stretches his arms in the air, his mouth open in a wide yawn.

"Are you gonna be OK driving home?" I ask. "You'll have to sleep with Uncle Buddy, but you can always crash here in the pink and green palace if you need to."

"Jo, I'm a musician. I used to drink beer like it was Dr. Pepper."

"I almost forgot," I laugh. I follow Davis out of the room as he strides steadily down the hallway. He stops in the doorway of Daddy's den. The television is blaring, and everyone in the room is asleep. Empty beer bottles are scattered across the coffee table.

"They're just gonna have to pick up after themselves." Mommy enters the den from the kitchen and walks across the room to where we are standing in the opposite doorway. "I'm going to bed." Mommy sighs and kisses both of us on the cheek before heading down the hallway.

I look up at Davis. "Well, I guess we made some progress. Even though I still have no clue what to do about President Bush."

"Hey, I'm teaching the band the *Battle Hymn of the Republic* for the Fourth of July. Why don't you just have them recite the words to that?"

Without thinking, I kiss Davis on the cheek and hold the door open for him to leave. He hesitates for a moment but doesn't try to kiss me back. Instead, he turns to leave, and I close the door gently behind him.

CHAPTER 12 ♡

I had the weirdest dream last night. Davis was dressed up like a drum major and was out on the football field with one of those big sticks, marching the band around while they played the *Battle Hymn of the Republic*. Though the football field looked the same, the bleachers weren't really bleachers. There was a soundstage with a studio audience, like the one we had when I did that TV pilot about a wacky, Hawaiian hotel that was never picked up by a network. I came out onto the playing field from my dressing room wearing my Gunne Sax junior prom dress and my old wavy-heeled Famolare platforms, with Ann Marie's homecoming princess crown pinned on top of my head and her satin princess sash draped diagonally across my torso. My fist was raised in the air as I stepped up onto one of those Olympic medal ceremony stands. When I reached the top, I lowered my fist and then pressed my palms together in front of my body, as if about to take communion. I shouted in my largest stage voice, as the band continued to play and march around in formations behind me. *We adore our freedom! We will defend our right to be free! Our forefathers shattered the shackles of slavery and the tyranny of monarchy, and the bombs and terrible acts of those that would destroy us. And still, our democracy endures, our freedom rings, our nation serves as the beacon the world follows through the storms of ignorance and injustice. Glory, glory halleluiah . . .*

I should stop drinking so much. I didn't count the number of beers I had last night, but my hallucinations and my nagging headache suggest one too many. My weird dream notwithstanding, I've decided that my drama students' first assignment today will be to memorize the words to the *Battle Hymn of the Republic*.

I stop at the row of doors that open into the auditorium. Why am I so nervous? I should finally be in my element. I have cottonmouth, and my palms are sweaty. I send a quick text to Rudy. In his frantic way, his words always calm me down before a performance. Today feels like an opening night on Broadway.

JoMaMa:	1st drama class. Stagefright!
HiFiNY:	Kids probably more scared 2 meet U.
JoMaMa:	Maybe. BTW, I have to plan a welcome home thing 4 Bush.
HiFiNY:	WTF? U need to find the North Star & RUN, Kunta! There's a reason black folks left the south, remember?
JoMaMa:	This is TX, not the South.
HiFiNY:	It's all the same BS. If U give a Texan an enema, U can bury him in a matchbox.
JoMaMa:	Just rub my nose in the doodoo, why don't U?

I shut off my phone and enter the auditorium. There's an eclectic group of the most dissimilar, oddball collection of kids I've encountered at the Big House so far. But somehow this room feels more in sync than any of the others. I notice Hello Kitty and Cleopatra Jones sitting together and smiling. Two young black men with sparkling stud earrings and long logo T-shirts grin at me as they settle into their seats. A beaming young man with braces and a thin moustache joins them, the word "Latino" emblazoned across his T-shirt in large, curvy script. All smiles are good-natured, not the sarcastic smirks I've become accustomed to around here.

I pull my attendance sheet out of my bag. "Tomás Martinez." The T-shirted kid waves at me and flashes his braces.

"Tyrone Jackson." One of the ear-ringed kids reveals enormous dimples as he smiles and gives me a thumbs up. I smile back and break into a warbly imitation of Erykah Badu's "I think ya better call Tyrone," which causes the entire class to laugh.

Once the giggles subside, I call for "Clance Crawford." A pale young man raises his hand in the air, his black duds, spiky hair, and black nail polish at odds with Midland's mainstream, red, white and blue sensibilities. Did his parents intend Clarence? Did their Texan twangs or an illiterate hospital record keeper mangle his name into something else? I don't ask. He can always change it when he moves, which I'm sure is an inevitable part of his future, based on his appearance.

"Gerald McDougal."

"*Riiight* here, ma'am," drawls a round-faced kid with dark, shaggy bangs.

"I had a classmate named Gerald McDougal."

"That's ma Dad."

What time does happy hour begin around here? Maybe if I dig deep enough into my bag, I can scrounge up one of Uncle Buddy's eighty-proof confections.

I make it through the attendance roll and belt out to the room, "Hey, everybody, I'm Jo Randolph. Like all of you, I went to Lee and grew up here in Midland. And I'm a professional actress." The group breaks into boisterous applause. I smile but can't help but wonder if I can still claim that identity. Well, whether I work again or not, that's who I am, for better or worse. I gesture with my hands to subside the kids' clapping. "Obviously you guys haven't seen any of my movies, or you wouldn't be clapping like that. Now, come up here on the stage. Let's form a circle."

Most are so eager that they jump and hoist themselves up onto the raised stage, instead of taking the stairs.

"So before we get into it," I continue, "the first thing we're gonna do—the first thing we always do in acting classes and before performances—is a round of warm-up exercises. Now they're gonna look and feel silly. But if you're too uncomfortable or embarrassed to do them, then acting is not gonna be your thing. You will have to let go of all your shame in this class, how about that?" Most of the kids squirm and wiggle like over-stimulated toddlers—they seem excited and ready for whatever I throw their way. "These exercises are really important to you as an actor. They loosen your body, loosen your vocal chords, and clear your mind. They relax you and help you perform in a more natural, fluid way.

"Acting involves a lot of physical movement." I lunge out of my place in the circle like a fencer, thrusting my right arm out in Tyrone's direction as if holding a sword. "Even beyond sword fights and fist fights, think of the gestures we make with our hands when we talk, the way we move around a room, the way we greet others or make contact with them when we speak to them." Moving into the circle, I primly pat Kiley on the shoulder. I stroll over to Clance and give him a bro' hug and a soul shake. "Who your character is, her personality, background, the setting—all of these things affect the way you move. Are you at an office or a barbecue? You have to be loose so your movements will flow naturally, and your performance will be authentic."

I rejoin the circle. "OK, just do what I do." I lead the class through a series of stretching, breathing, and vocal exercises. My students screw up their faces, jump up and down, wiggle their bodies frenetically, and yell tongue twisters faster and faster until they are yelling gibberish. They complete all of my silly-looking exercises without a single smirk or snicker and seem eager for more.

"Now that you're warmed up, I know you're ready to jump right into it, aren't you?"

"Yeah!" Tomás shouts. He jumps and pumps his fist in the air.

"OK! Then let's all sit on the floor here, and I'll tell you what you to expect this summer."

Everyone drops to the floor and sits cross-legged. "I'll try to make sure to explain the purpose of everything we do. If I don't, then *stop me!* Ask questions!"

Clance's silver biker bracelets jangle as he waves his hand to get my attention. "I really liked that movie *The Departed* that won the Best Picture. What makes those actors like Leonardo DiCaprio and Matt Damon so good? Are they just, like, naturally good, or is there something people can learn to be like them?"

"Well, a lot of what makes those actors so great is that they're well prepared and work really hard. They do a lot of research before they even show up for work and start rehearsing. And they think about the character and who he is and what motivates him. They pay attention to details and are good listeners. And actors like that know their lines so well that the dialogue becomes second nature. They can improv and be very natural because they don't have to think about what to say next.

"Ma dad says most actors end up waitin' tables," Gerald drawls.

"Well, it's a tough business and sometimes you go long stretches between jobs. Actors need flexible hours so they can go on auditions. I work pretty steadily, but sometimes I teach yoga classes so I don't have to dip into my savings too much between jobs. It's hard to get used to, but there's a lot of rejection in this business. But you have to realize that not getting a certain job doesn't mean you're not talented and just keep auditioning. You also have to learn to take criticism."

"What kind of criticism have you gotten, Ms. Randolph?" Kiley asks.

"Let me see . . . I've received a lot of it. It started when I was in high school here at Lee. My drama teacher, Mrs. Hoffman, told me, 'Honey!'" I stand and shift my weight to one leg and place my hand on my hip, like Mrs. Hoffman used to do. "'You're a born actress. You want to emote all the time, every minute of the day. When you get on stage, you have all this pent-up energy that you *throw* at us all at once.'" I leap and throw my hands out in front of me and shake them frantically, which makes the class laugh. "'The problem is, honey, if I can tell that you're acting, then it's bad acting.'

"That was the best advice I ever received. I thought that's *what you had to do as an actor*," I say in a faux British accent. "Think of all the people who overact on TV and in movies, (cough), *rappers*." The kids laugh in response. "We'll work on that. We'll do exercises that will help you with that. And, don't worry, we'll be doing scenes very soon. And at the end of the summer, we'll put on a performance for the community."

The auditorium resonates with whoops and cheers. "We'll have auditions to pick people for specific roles, but everyone will have a part."

The room buzzes, and the kids exchange smiles and hushed comments to each other as I tell them about the summer production and the upcoming presidential visit. I still don't know if we'll definitely do it, but I tell them to memorize the "Battle Hymn of the Republic," just in case.

At the end of class, it takes me a while to leave the auditorium. I chat with most of the kids one-on-one and already remember their names. I finally exit and notice Davis coming out of the nearby music room. He's chatting with a frizzy-haired, Napoleon Dynamite look-alike carrying an oboe case. I linger and wait for him to finish his conversation.

"So, how were the drama queens?" he asks as he waves good-bye to his student.

"Great, actually. Except one of them is the son of one of our old classmates. I need a martini."

"Join the club."

"Want to grab a drink or dinner somewhere? We can talk about the Bush thing. I think I'm gonna take you up on the 'Battle Hymn.'"

"Damn, I would love to go out, but I can't do it today. I gotta deal with some folks that would make a hornet look cuddly. They beat you senseless then tell God you fell off a horse. So I won't be too cool to hang around tonight. How about Friday? Oh, hell, that doesn't work either. I gotta go to Austin." He smiles weakly. "Rain check?"

I try not to look disappointed, or confused by Davis' strange animal metaphors. "Well, uh, hope you stay on your horse." What am I saying? "I'll take you up on that rain check."

"Cool." Davis tucks a stack of sheet music under his arm and saunters away. I need to head in the same direction, but I deliberately walk the other way. I take a long, circuitous, out-of-the-way route to the parking lot, rather than walking the fifty paces from where I was standing with Davis.

I exit out of the front door of the school and follow the sidewalk that leads to the back of the building. Hello Kitty and Cleopatra Jones, I mean Kiley and Qiana, are huddled together at the bus stop, intently eyeing an unfolded piece of paper. As I close in on the girls, I realize they are trying to decipher a city bus schedule.

"Looks like you can take the 5 bus to over here near this park, and then walk over and catch this bus here. My mama used to take that bus when she worked near where you live."

"Hi, girls, how's it going?"

"Hi, Miss Randolph," they chime in unison. Hello Kitty pushes her schoolboy glasses up her nose and smiles at me. "Qiana's tryin' to help me figure out how to get home on the bus. My brother forgot to pick me up again. I was here 'til 6:00 yesterday!"

"You girls need a ride? I can drive you home, if you don't mind that my A/C's not working."

They both grin gorgeous little girl smiles. As quick as it appeared, Qiana's smile fades. "I live south, and Kiley lives north 'a here. I already have a bus pass, if you wanna just drop her off."

"Don't be silly. I live south too, so we'll drop Kiley off first, and then I'll drop you off on my way home."

The prospect of a bus ride must be pretty dreadful, because both girls beam as they sink themselves into the worn interior of my creaky old BMW and situate themselves among the discarded diet soda cans and magazines and books scattered about the floor and the back seat. Qiana scoots forward and dislodges my "vintage" Adidas track jacket from underneath her rear.

"Just throw it anywhere, Qiana." I admire the image of Angela Davis on Qiana's T-shirt. "I had T-shirts just like yours in high school. That was my way of rebelling back then."

Qiana's eyelids drop and she doesn't respond. Kiley chimes in, "I told her those old shirts are soooo cool. Like, the celebrities in *Life & Style* wear cool T-shirts like that and stuff."

"My mama got 'em from somewhere. I don't know," Qiana responds flatly.

"Miss Randolph," Kiley continues, "I am soooo excited you're teachin' us actin'. I saw you in *Swamp Sisters*. It is soooo cool that you're like a real celebrity and stuff!"

I'm taken aback that this freckled-faced, Midland kid in slip-on Pro Keds and Harry Potter glasses thinks I'm a real celebrity. I don't know if it's a tribute to my career or an indictment of her taste in movies. "That's sweet, Kiley, I appreciate it. Though you may be one of the only people who saw that movie. I'm glad I chose acting because I love it, rather than for fame and fortune. Otherwise I might have been pretty disappointed." I sound like my old self back in college, before I moved to L.A.

"How'd you get into the movies, Miss Randolph? Did you win a contest or somethin'?"

"No, Qiana. I studied drama in college and graduate school. My schools had a lot of contacts in New York, so after graduation I moved to New York City and started going on auditions. I did plays and some commercials. I moved to L.A. after I got a part in a soap opera."

"You don't have to go to college to be a movie star, do you?"

I laugh as I struggle to shift gears. "I'm a working actress, girls, not a movie star. And, no, you don't need a degree to do what I do. But for every Demi Moore who made it big without a degree or family connections, there are twenty people who made it because they had friends or family in the business or a rich Daddy who could buy them a career. And even Demi went to high school with some Hollywood folks."

"Is that the lady that married Ashton Kutcher?"

"Um," I stutter, "yea, that's her."

"But what about Britney Spears? She's a big star."

I take a deep breath before answering. "It's not impossible for people on the outside to break into the business. Obviously, I did it, and I grew up here in Midland, which is about as removed from the movie business as you can get. But my parents taught me that it's good to have an education or skill you can fall back on. I don't know how Britney got where she is, and I'm not sure I would recommend that path anyway, considering how her life has turned out. But even people who make it don't usually stay on top for very long—five years if they're lucky. So if they don't have something to fall back on, they have a hard time adjusting when their star fades and their money runs out."

I peer at Kylie's face through my rearview mirror. I have doused all of her spark. Qiana appears equally dejected. "Hey, girls, there are a thousand channels on cable these days. So there's a place for everyone, right?

Still, don't discount the school thing. College wasn't just job training for me. It was the best time of my life. And it exposed me to so many things and people outside of life here in Midland. In one of my first roles, I played a girl from Brooklyn. I had college friends from New York, so it wasn't foreign to me. I was able to persuade the casting people that I was that girl from Brooklyn."

"College is expensive," Qiana shrugs. "Plus, you gotta have good grades."

"You can turn right up there, Miss Randolph," Kiley leans forward from the back seat and points at an upcoming intersection.

"Is this still Lee's district?" I ask as I pull in front of a tidy brick ranch house. A faded blue Chrysler LeBaron is parked in the driveway.

"No, ma'am. My Dad lives in our old house near Lee, and we use his address for me to go to school. My folks say the people are better over at Lee. Thanks for the ride!"

"No problem, Kiley. If you get stuck again, look out for me. But, before you go, I have to ask you girls something. It's probably none of my business, but it's driving me nuts."

The girls' eyes widen.

"I don't mean to scare you," I laugh. "I just want to know why two nice, smart girls like you are in summer school." I haven't spent enough time with them to know for sure, but I have a feeling that something is amiss. That it wouldn't take much effort for these girls to do well. They stare at me with strange expressions, as if no one had ever asked them that question before. Their reaction shocks me, because that would have been the first question I heard if I ever flunked classes and had to go to summer school. I bite my lip, realizing that it was probably impertinent for me to pry.

"I'm . . . I'm gonna try to do better," Kiley stutters a bit. "Sometimes I get kinda bored in school." Her face brightens as she pulls down the handle and opens the car door. "But I really like your classes, Miss Randolph."

I smile back at her. "I'm glad. See you tomorrow."

As soon as Kiley is safely inside the house, I make a U-turn and head back to the 'hood. Qiana and I don't speak, and I almost forget that she's next to me, as I lose myself in a top-forty monster mix on the radio. Rows of unpretentious brick homes give way to smaller, wood-frame houses with simple porches. Some of them have upgraded their wood planks to white or putty-colored aluminum siding.

The longer I drive, the more wear and tear I notice. The houses have wood siding with signs of rot. Old folks sit on lawn chairs or rusty metal swings on dog-eared porches. Small children peek through screened front doors and watch each new car pass down the narrow streets. The neglect soon moves from the homes to the streets themselves. Potholes and worn patches of asphalt appear, and many of the side streets are unpaved. A young man in a grown person's body steers a child's two-wheeler from a dusty side lane onto the main road, his baseball cap casually tilted to the side.

"Hey, Qiana . . . you know, you don't have to be rich to go to college. There are scholarships, and you can always take out student loans. Most schools, if they really want you there, will do what they can to help you afford it."

She responds in a small voice I can barely hear over the radio, "I don't want a bunch of loans. Maybe if I work and save money, I can go later."

"People say that, but then they get into a rut, or get used to making money, and they never go back. Folks have no problem taking out a car loan as soon as they get their first job, but they get their panties in a bunch over low-interest student loans. College is like an investment in yourself that not only helps you get better, higher-paying jobs, but also helps you become a more well-rounded person."

"That there's my house," Qiana whispers. She points at a weathered, wood frame cottage that is missing part of its porch railing. She drops her eyes into her lap and examines the backs of her hands.

"I'm sorry, Qiana." I lower the volume of my voice. "You know, I've got a really big mouth. And I'm always butting into things that aren't my business." Qiana raises her head and dares to look at me. "I just want you to know you have options, that's all. Don't sell yourself . . ." I hesitate a moment. "Just don't sell yourself short."

"Thanks, Miss Randolph. I'll see you tomorrow." The shy smile returns briefly as she closes the door behind her.

I face the full onslaught of the still-intense afternoon heat as I sputter home, resting my arm on the edge of my open window. I switch the radio to lite rock, where the Eagles are crooning "Take it Easy." That's easy for them to say. Don Henley may have been born in Texas, but he's probably chillin' in Santa Monica right now. But that's OK. At least today has been pretty easy for me in Midland.

CHAPTER 13 ♡

I stayed up too late last night watching that stupid *North Dallas Forty* over and over again. Damn you, Davis! I'm so tired, I'm thinking of calling in sick. I can barely lift my eyelids. And I'm hot! My cotton pajamas are so damp that the fabric hangs from my body in clumps like folds of Shar Pei skin. Despite the heat, I roll onto my side and pull the covers over my head to block out the sunlight streaming in through the sheers.

Ravi had this big, cushioned platform on wheels that we used to roll out onto the deck to sleep in the moist, sea breeze. The unfiltered sunrays never bothered me as they do now, when they rudely rouse me out of my bed and off to the Big House. I feel as hazy and unclear as the California sun this morning. I pull my cell phone from beneath my pillow and dial a familiar number.

My breaths are shallow as the phone rings and rings until I finally hear the lilt of Ravi's voice. The message beep shakes me out of my stupor enough to shut down the call before I start drawling how much I miss him, even though I hate him.

The harsh streaks of sunlight grow more inconsiderate. I press my pillow over my head, but the veins at my temples keep pounding my brain to wake up. Suddenly, Mommy barges into my room. She noisily rummages around, opening and closing the closet and bureaus repeatedly.

"Jo Ella," Mommy singsongs. "It's time to get up, darlin.' Want some coffee?"

"I'm sick," I muffle from underneath the bedspread. "I'm not going to work today."

Mommy pulls back the coverlet and places her slim fingers on my forehead.

"You feel just fine, Jo Ella. Come and have some coffee and say hi to Ann Marie. She brought me a new coffee maker!"

I groan in response. Mommy ignores me and opens my closet door again. She forages through the large, plastic storage bins stuffed in the back of my closet. "I'm dropping off some clothes and food at the church today."

"Why?"

"Oh, we run a soup kitchen, and we donate items to the families we help. A lot of folks lost their jobs when that big petroleum products plant closed the other year. Is there anything you don't want?"

"No." I peek down at her partially filled shopping bags and notice some very nice cotton blouses and a number of Daddy's dress shirts, neatly folded and wrapped in plastic shirt pouches from the cleaners. A sharp pain shoots through my forehead, but I drag myself out of bed and lumber over to one of my suitcases. I pluck out two pairs of jeans, a faded polo shirt that probably no longer fits over my BBQ belly, a few sundresses, and a short stack of snarky T-shirts from my vast collection.

"Here you go, Mommy. I need to get in the shower, but I can look around for some more stuff later, if you need it."

Mommy's eyes soften as she accepts my peace offering. She doesn't say a word but kisses me on my cheek and tweaks my nose like she did when I was small. I grab my bathrobe off of the floor. I momentarily forget my heat stroke as I figure out what to wear.

"Mommy, have you seen any of my old T-shirts from high school? I used to have an Angela Davis one and . . ."

"Oh, Jo Ella, those things were in the back of the closet for so long that I thought you'd forgotten about them. I already gave them to the church. I can see if they've given 'em out yet, if you want."

"No, no, that's OK. I don't need them."

I leave Mommy to collect more clothing from the closet while I collect a cup of coffee. I enter the kitchen and see my sister pulling a drip coffee maker out of the manufacturer's box. There is a sealed bag of ground coffee on the counter along with a box of raw sugar and a small carton of half and half. She's dressed for work, in a taupe silk shift and bone leather slingbacks. Only Ann Marie can make coffee in light-colored, non-washable fabrics without incident.

"Real coffee!" I exclaim. "I must have done something right to deserve this."

"Mommy asked me to help her pack up things for the church this morning, since I don't have any patients until ten. I refused to do it unless she gave me something other than instant coffee and powdered milk. Have a seat." Ann Marie places the glass carafe under the faucet and fills it with water.

My sister is taller than I am and blessed with long, extraordinarily shapely legs, just like Mommy. We have the same eyes, though. Large, inquisitive and dreamy, just like Daddy's. Ann Marie has been enhancing and bringing the best out of her quite lovely assets for so long now that it's second nature, like breathing. I have to hand it to her. She always looks great, regal and composed, even when her life is whirling around her like a tornado. She smiles and dresses and carries herself ever so appropriately and prettily as she breezes through her obligations to family, patients, clubs and Mommy's endless meetings and greetings, to which she has continued to drag Ann Marie long after we both embarked upon our own independent lives. Even if Ann Marie doesn't have it all together, she always looks and acts as if she does.

"There we go," she says. "It says here, that we should have eight cups of coffee in four minutes. I told Mommy that it doesn't take much effort to make real coffee." Ann Marie takes a seat across from me at Mommy's round kitchen table.

Ann Marie and I don't speak. We stay inside our heads and listen to the best of the eighties from the ancient clock radio on the kitchen counter. The eighties were a good decade for Ann Marie. She had big, beauty queen hair, and everybody said she looked just like Jayne Kennedy. I no longer remember why Jayne Kennedy was famous, but I remember that all the boys desired her, just like they all desired Ann Marie. I, on the other hand, streaked and crimped my hair to look like my idol, Madonna, but I ended up looking bizarre. Maybe I should have been more Jayne Kennedy, more conventional, like Ann Marie. Maybe I'd be married with a bunch of bad, beautiful kids that I love more than life itself. Maybe I'd have a home to share with someone I love, no matter how much he annoys me from time to time. Maybe I wouldn't feel so alone.

I try to imagine myself with a normal life. With Ann Marie's life. I try to imagine myself living in Midland day-in and day-out. I just can't do it, even though I'm sitting right here in the midst of it. Even though I knew nothing different for the first eighteen years of my life.

"I don't know how you work out at home, Jo Ella." I jump in my seat. I almost forgot that Ann Marie was sitting there.

"You should join a gym for the summer," she says. "That way you can meet people. All the doctors and professionals go to The Grind."

"That sounds pornographic," I grumble. "It's too hot to work out, anyway."

Ann Marie rolls her perfectly shadowed eyes. How does a woman with three rowdy kids and a demanding medical practice find time for perfect makeup? I guess I've been away from Texas too long. "I'm just saying, Jo Ella, you're not getting any younger. Lots of nice guys like Willie T. work out there. You might hook up with someone suitable for a change. I mean, if that's what you want."

I start to retort but decide not to say anything. I can tell she's trying really hard not to tell me what to do, though that's exactly what she's doing. I shrug my shoulders and rise to retrieve coffee cups and spoons from the cupboard. I pour coffee for both of us and add cream and sugar. As Ann Marie has remained in Midland all these years, I assume her tastes have not changed.

"Thanks," she says, as I hand her a mug of coffee.

I sit and glance at my sister as we sip from our steaming mugs. Silky strands of her long, straightened hair fall in neat layers around her face. There's nothing dowdy about her appearance or hairdo, as Ann Marie still hops on Southwest Airlines once every six weeks to have it cut and colored by the same Oak Lawn stylist she's been seeing in Dallas since her Southwestern Medical School days. With her expertly applied makeup, sophisticated 'do, and tasteful attire, she could easily pass for a Brentwood or Beverly Hills girl. As I observe her, it occurs to me that my sister isn't peppering me with questions that have me ducking and weaving to avoid her punches and my inevitable knockout. Something must be wrong.

"You OK?" I prod.

"Yep."

"You sure?" I ask.

"Yep. Well, no. I mean, I'm just a little disappointed is all." Ann Marie sips her coffee without leaving a trace of lipstick on her cup.

"And?"

"It's nothing, Jo Ella."

"Nothing? It takes a whole lot of something for you not to badger me to death. What gives?"

Ann Marie sighs and sets down her mug. "Well, I was supposed to go to Dallas for a girls' weekend with my Sorors from college. We booked rooms at the Mansion and were gonna shop and get spa treatments and drink champagne. And now, well, I'm not going."

Her sultry eyes are sullen, her lips pursed.

"Do you need me to babysit?" I ask.

"No."

"Then why can't you go?"

"It's complicated."

"Contrary to popular belief, Ann Marie, I can handle complex thoughts."

Her expression reminds me of the tight tension in Mommy's face when she told me she was worried about my future. "Well, Claude's been traveling a lot, and he's leaving town again for a week to work on a new car franchise for Big Claude. He's upset that the family's always apart, and that I'm leaving on the one weekend in over a month that he'll be home. Now I planned *my* trip ages ago, and he knows how much I want to do this, but . . ." her voice trails off.

"Why don't you just go anyway?"

"Jo Ella, I have to live with Claude day-in, day-out, not my girl-friends. Missing this is disappointing, but I can't deal with bad moods and guilt trips for weeks on end. I don't need the extra stress. It's hard enough keeping it all together as it is."

I don't know what to say. I always thought of my sharp, sophis-ticated sister as invincible. Cool as ice and capable of mastering every situation, just like Mommy. But this ice princess seems shattered.

"Maybe it's a good thing that I can't keep a man," I finally say to her.

Her smile surprises me. "Oh, you could if you wanted to, Jo Ella. You'd just rather be with a fantasy man than deal with a real one. Real relationships aren't movies. They're like what Uncle Buddy always says: you gotta have a little salty with your sweet."

"Ann Marie, he was talking about slapping a slice of ham on a piece of pound cake when he said that."

"You know what I mean, Jo Ella. Claude can be moody and needy sometimes, but he's a good father, and he's a decent guy. It's not like he's abusive or some ne'er-do-well."

"Those are your choices?" I shout. "Ann Marie, you work like a dog, take care of three young boys, take care of Mommy & Daddy, keep up a huge, spotless house, volunteer, everything. Why can't you have one weekend away? I can't believe that you of all people have to beg Little Claude for permission to do something that you really want to do that doesn't hurt or inconvenience anybody else and that you're able to pay for yourself. It's just one weekend out of a lifetime, for God's sake, and—"

Ann Marie cuts me off. "Jo Ella, I know I'm failing the cause of all women on Earth by not standing my ground. It's weak-minded, but I just don't have the energy to fight every single battle to the death anymore. After a while, you start to feel beaten down, and you just do what you have to do to get through each day with as much peace as you can."

I've never seen Ann Marie this vanquished, even when Blair Bean beat her out for Homecoming Queen and she had to settle for Princess.

"What happened, Ann Marie? Ever since high school, you guys always seemed like the perfect couple with the perfect life. Unlike your dysfunctional sister and all my weird relationships. Other than Willie T., I don't think I've ever dated anyone that Mommy and Daddy would approve of."

Ann Marie smiles a little bit. "What's perfect anyway?"

"I don't know what the dictionary definition of perfect is," I respond. "But you and Mommy might be it."

"Hardly." Ann Marie loses her smile and stands to retrieve the coffee carafe. "Claude and I have always done what was expected of us. That's just the way we are, and it makes us compatible in a lot of ways. You're different. You're creative, and you don't like to be confined. You need someone who will let you be you and won't keep you in a box. Sometimes I wish I had had the courage to do what you did and have adventures and experience more of the world before I settled down. I don't have as much flexibility to do that anymore, because I have kids, and Claude isn't as interested in that sort of thing as I am. But, you know, we have to be true to who we are. And at the end of the day, all I ever wanted to do was be a doctor. I love being a parent, having a family. Jo Ella, you've made Mommy and Daddy proud enough by doing so well in school and working so hard and becoming so successful at this crazy career you chose for yourself, which scared the bejesus out of the rest of us when you started down this path. Just remember that they don't have to live with whoever you choose to love; *you* do."

Did I hear my sister say that I have courage? And that I, of all people, should just be myself? She must really be miserable. "So why are you so sad, Ann Marie, if you're where you want to be?"

"I don't know, Jo Ella. I got married right after I graduated from med school. I don't know what it was like in L.A. and New York, but here in Texas, the next big goal after you check degrees off your list is getting married and having the big, beautiful wedding. And of course, with me and Claude being everyone's 'dream couple' for some reason, we had to lead the pack."

"Well," I say in between sips of coffee, "y'all did look good. Nobody else we knew had a reception in the sculpture garden at the Museum of the Southwest. At least nobody Black."

Ann Marie smiles for a second. "You know Mommy had to be bigger and better than the rest of the Links and AKAs! It *was* really beautiful, and I thought that I had 'made it' after that wedding." Her smile fades. "But we all change as we grow up, and those changes can be stressful on a marriage. I think we're in one of those transition periods, because Claude is kind of frustrated professionally. He mopes around and isn't much fun to be around anymore. And I'm stretched so thin, that I don't really have the time or patience to try to make him feel better, especially since he doesn't seem motivated to do anything to change his life. I've got enough jobs and people to take care of as it is. I guess it's a rut."

Ann Marie's expression is sullen. She pours another cup of coffee for both of us and takes a few sips. All of a sudden she seems to snap out of it. "Enough about me and my nonsense," she says as she focuses on me again. "What about you? I want to know what's really going on with you. Why are you here this summer?"

"You know why. I broke up with my boyfriend, and I lost my job, Ann Marie. Isn't that enough?"

"That's bullshit." Ann Marie has a way of making swearing seem ladylike. "Are you in some kind of trouble?"

"Why do you think I'm in trouble?" I try to control the tremble in my voice.

"It just doesn't make sense. You've had a million breakups and projects that got cut short or whatever. But somehow this time you've come home to Midland to teach school for the summer?"

"Look, Ann Marie, I didn't come home to teach school. I just came to visit and Mommy and Daddy bullied me into it. I'm not in trouble, and nothing's wrong with me, OK?!" I fight the urge to burst into tears.

"Give me a break, Jo Ella, I know—" Ann Marie abruptly stops speaking. Her lips move, and she appears to be silently counting to ten. "I'm not trying to beat you up or anything. I just know that there's a lot you're not telling me. Breakup or no, it's completely bizarre for you to come home like this. We can barely get you to stay for more than a day at Christmas, and now you're staying for the whole summer? Something's not right."

I bite my lip and bat my eyelashes to prevent tears from forming. I reach for my coffee mug, but Ann Marie gently grasps my hand before I can pick it up.

"Come on JoJo," she says softly. She hasn't called me that since we were kids. "What's the matter? What happened back in L.A.?"

I raise a paper napkin to my face with my free hand and wipe the tears I can no longer contain. "I gotta go," I sniffle and rise from the table. I race to my bedroom, wiping my face all the way. Ann Marie doesn't follow me. I grab the first clean shirt and pair of jeans that I see. I flee the house before I have to talk to anyone or explain anything else to anybody. I blast punchy pop music all the way to work. Spunky and soulless, it distracts me from my troubles.

Luckily, work is uneventful until lunchtime. Principal Hardy highjacks our lunch hour to talk to the faculty about the upcoming Bush rally. The president and first lady will only make a short visit to Lee to receive some love before they head off to a private fundraiser open only to folks with big wallets. Those of us with smaller pocketbooks must ensure that everything runs like clockwork, so that the first family can stay on schedule.

Our principal looks proud as punch and primped to perfection as he strides onto the auditorium stage to address his employees. His hair is shellacked to a fine sheen, his rounded figure distinguished in a brass-buttoned navy blazer, crisp blue button-down shirt and sharply creased tan slacks. "Now, we have Agent Brooks from the Secret Service and Mr. White from the president's advance team here with us today. These good folks are going to review all of the procedures we will need to abide by when the president visits us."

As Mr. White approaches the podium, Principal Hardy extends his arms to display the horizon of the auditorium chairs, where all of his employees are gathered to be put through our paces in anticipation of the big event. "Mr. White, Agent Brooks, this here is our first-rate faculty and staff, and we're all honored to have you with us today. We'll work as hard as we can to make sure our Commander-in-Chief's visit runs as smooth as possible."

My Drama class' dramatic interpretation of the lyrics to "The Battle Hymn of the Republic" will serve as the springboard for the president to announce his "Phonics for Freedom" educational initiative. Never mind that Lee is a high school and our kids (hopefully) mastered phonics ten or more years ago. The first lady's alma mater will provide the perfect backdrop for the self-proclaimed "Education President" to redeem his legacy for about thirty minutes, before he heads to a series of big-donor fundraisers for his presidential library.

Though I intend to start rehearsing the "Battle Hymn" today, I haven't given up my lobbying efforts with Principal Hardy to let the chorus just *sing* the damn song instead. Principal Hardy insists that Mrs. Tyler's hardworking chorus is not quite ready for primetime, in spite of Mrs. Tyler's intense lobbying efforts to the contrary and my lackluster enthusiasm about the whole thing. Poor Mrs. Tyler is almost frothing at the mouth to perform this important function for the man she loves and admires with a fervor that borders on frightening. I glance across the auditorium at her and notice her hanging on every word that comes out of the speakers' mouths, her "W" baseball cap pulled snugly over her short bob. She wears that thing so often that I can't recall her hair color. I guess I understand her disappointment, if not her ardor, as I would be equally frustrated if Principal Hardy invited Denzel Washington to school only to draft Mrs. Tyler to direct him in a musical.

The atmosphere at Lee, and in Midland in general, is heady in anticipation of the arrival of the town's most prominent native son, by way of Connecticut. Mrs. Hightower has pulled out her most notorious cookie recipe, hoping to bribe the Secret Service into allowing her a bit closer to her hero. Flags are flying, and the entire town has swathed itself in a sea of red, white, and blue. The school facilities are being scrubbed and buffed and polished to a dull sheen, the lawns roped off and carefully tended and watered daily, bright new flowers peeking out of the pots and planters scattered around the grounds.

Every inch of the school is being scanned and searched for signs of potential peril. Black-booted cops lead dogs on leashes to sniff every nook and cranny of the building and surrounding area. Dark-suited dudes in Ray-Bans are circling the neighborhood and learning the lay of our land. They are weeding the crabgrass from the event guest list and lining up all of Lee's chosen ones for fingerprinting. It seems a bit dramatic for a thirty-minute photo op. But I don't think much of it until Principal Hardy calls me into his office after the faculty meeting for a little chat with Agent Brooks.

"You've got quite the passport young lady. Brazil, Tanzania, Argentina, Greece, Italy, 'Nam, Montenegro, India . . . you teach geography or something?"

"Um, no sir, um, I'm teaching English. I studied English. I, uh, I like visiting places I've read about. Kind of makes them come alive . . ." unwilling to let him see me bite my nails, I tear the edges of my cuticles under the table.

The agent pulls his shirtsleeves out of hiding from beneath the cuffs of his suit jacket. He doesn't smile as he flips through a manila folder.

"Um, also, sir, I'm an actress? I often have to travel for film roles."

"Hmmm. What's the last thing you were in?"

"The last thing?" Oh shit. "Well, the last movie I finished was a movie called *Swamp Sisters*. But, um, I was working on another movie for the Lifetime Channel before I came home for the summer. I didn't finish that one, so, um, I guess that's it."

"Didn't finish? Why?"

"Why? Well, um, I didn't get along, I mean, I stopped getting along with the director. It didn't really work out, so I didn't keep working on that one."

"Why didn't you get along with him?"

"Did I say it was a him?"

The stone-faced Secret Serviceman doesn't appear amused by my question. Though this is not a change in demeanor for him. I, however, change my tune and soften my tone pronto quick. "Well, sir, Hollywood is a difficult place. Difficult people. I mean, they're not always on the up and up with you, and . . ."

"Why'd you start teaching all of a sudden?"

"Why?" Having moved off the subject I want to avoid, I'm able to speak without stuttering. "Well, sir, actors have to catch as catch can. You often go for long periods where you're not working, and you have to do other things to pay the bills between projects. My parents are good friends with the superintendent, who mentioned to them that they were kind of desperate for summer school teachers. I think he was trying to get my mom to come out of retirement for the summer, but she has no desire to do that, let me tell you. So my folks thought, we all thought that since I specialized in English in college—did I mention I went to Dartmouth College and was valedictorian here at Lee? Anyway, we thought this might be a good way for me to have a nice, steady job for the summer and help out a family friend at the same time."

"Have you ever been arrested?"

"What? Arrested?" Oh, shit. They've got me. I'm destined for skunk stripes for sure. "Well, sir, I had an argument with a woman on the set of a movie I was working on, the Lifetime movie, and, we kind of got into a fight. She started it, but then she called the police, and I had to go to the police station. But she didn't press charges or anything. I don't know if I was really arrested, or if I was just questioned, or what you call it, sir, but, um, I did, sir, have to go in and talk to the police about it."

"Where was this?'

"Los Angeles. Los Angeles, sir. Not so long ago. But other than that, I've never been arrested. And I've never had a fistfight before, sir, I swear. Well, a classmate punched me in the eye in third grade, but I don't know if that counts since I didn't hit back or anything. Um, yeah, I mean, yes sir."

After a litany of questions, the man who never smiles finally releases me. My hands are shaking, and I'm shivering all over, though the temperature's hot as blazes. I'm too nervous to face the teacher's lounge, so I head out to the parking lot and the searing summer sun. I pace back and forth and bite what's left of my ragged fingernails until the start of my afternoon class saves me from suffering a heat stroke. I ditch the "Battle Hymn" for the day. Though I told the Drama kids we would wait until next week to do scenes, I run them through a frenetic set of scenes from *Streetcar Named Desire* that I happen to know by heart. The ranting renditions of Stanley and Blanche I demonstrate for the class are borderline scary and probable examples of the sort of overacting I want them to avoid, but the students seem to like them. Soon all of them are screeching senselessly as well.

The day can't end fast enough. As soon as class ends, I race to my car. As I exit the lot, I notice Qiana leaning against the worn, green paint of the bus stop signpost. She stares down the road, her large backpack lying at her feet. I stick my hand out of my window and motion for her to get in. She smiles at the sight of me, or perhaps just the sight of my car.

"Thanks, Miss Randolph," she says as she slides into the passenger seat. I smile at her, and she looks down at her feet. Qiana was not much livelier than this during class. She seemed uncomfortable during our *Streetcar* screeches. Though she mouthed the words along with her classmates, she didn't shout them. While the others flailed their arms and pushed the drama of the scenes even farther than Tennessee Williams called for, Qiana never let go. I turn down the volume on the car radio to talk to her.

"So, Qiana, what made you interested in my class? You don't seem like the drama queen type." She raises her head in response, her expression stricken. "That's not meant as a criticism at all," I backpedal. "My sister always says I have an attention-*seeking* disorder, which is why I became an actress. You seem more well-adjusted than I am and less comfortable acting out for no good reason."

"I don't know," she shrugs. "I like movies. Maybe I can get outta Midland and be in movies like you." Her eyes return to the floor.

"Oh." I don't know what to say. "Well, I hope you enjoy it, is all."

"I like it," she says without raising her head.

"Good."

After a long silence, I say, "I'm sure you'll have fun when we do the summer play."

Qiana doesn't say anything in response. To avoid putting my foot in my mouth any further, I shut up and concentrate on the road ahead of me. I find the "urban" station and bop my head along to a series of southern rap songs I don't recognize. As I wait for a light to change, I glance over at Qiana and notice that she is staring at a book on the floor.

"That's Elaine Brown's book. She was the only female head of the Black Panther Party."

She raises the book to her lap and begins to flip through it, examining the center set of photos and scanning the text of the book jacket. We say nothing else for the rest of the trip. As I approach her house, I notice that her head is still buried in the book.

"Why don't you take that with you? I've already read it three times. I would love to make a film about her. Actually, I'd like to know what you think about it."

The little girl grin returns, and Qiana folds the book jacket over the page she was reading. She presses the book against her chest while exiting the car.

"Thanks, Miss Randolph."

After dropping Qiana off, I don't head straight home. I shut down my phone and drive to the nice part of town. I cruise past golf greens and grand houses. I hum and tap my fingers to the beat of the tunes on the radio. I relax as I watch orange, gray, and purple streaks appear across the sky.

I'm suddenly enveloped in a cloud of dust. I can barely see anything through my windshield. I cough from the spray of sand flooding though my open window and flowing into my mouth and nostrils. I squeeze my steering wheel and press the brake pedal, praying that no one rear-ends me.

I hate all this dust. I hate this fucking heat. I hate the drab, parched ground, so absent of color and life. L.A. is another town where dreamers and prospectors funneled in water, turning an arid wilderness into their very own Shangri-La. I prefer L.A.'s ocean-view wasteland to my native desert, but I can't stand either one right now.

The dust subsides as suddenly as it started. I wipe a layer off my dashboard with my palm then grasp the steering wheel with both hands to turn toward home.

CHAPTER 14 ♡

Saturday morning. I wake and find myself covered with white sheets of computer paper instead of bed sheets. The only upside of my nonexistent social life is that I've become extremely productive. Rudy had one of his interns scrounge up a copy of the *North Dallas Forty* script and scan it into a Word file for me. So I spent Friday evening adapting the script into a campy, sanitized stage version. I hope to make enough progress to feed some draft pages to Davis on Monday so he can start work on the songs.

My cell phone pounds out the beat of the latest Jay-Z tune. Memphis took it upon himself to change my ringtone for me last night, as the constant *Conga*-ing was driving everyone crazy.

"Jo?"

"Davis?"

"I hope I'm not interrupting your weekend . . ."

I start to say "no, of course not," but I keep my mouth shut. It won't make me feel better to remind myself of my less than thrilling weekend while Davis is in Austin, where there are bars and clubs and stuff to do other than write warped high school plays and watch re-runs of sitcoms that didn't offer me parts.

"I'm still in Austin, but I was thinking about you. I was wondering if we could have that rain check for dinner or drinks after rehearsal on Monday."

"Well, you know it's tough managing my hectic schedule here, but . . ."

"It's OK if you have plans," he interrupts. "We can do it whenever you're free. It's just . . . I'd enjoy the company. I've had a shit week, so it would be nice to have something to look forward to when I get back."

"Well, I might have to reschedule George Clooney and Brad Pitt, but I think I can make time for you on Monday," I deadpan. It's a good thing Davis can only hear my voice and not see my face, because the goofy smile creeping across my lips would spoil my attempt at biting, dry wit.

I'm still smiling as I steer my car into a parking space near the entrance of the St. Tropez Spa. As I enter the door, the scents of sandalwood and sage alarm my senses, which have become accustomed to inhaling dust. The décor is over-the-top Mediterranean, with tall plaster columns, wide white candles on iron prods, and walls sponge-painted to appear like marble. The Zen Riviera décor is confusing, but the overstuffed, off-white seating is inviting, and the dim light, soft scents, and New Age music create a soothing effect. I was so anxious to arrive that I made it here twenty minutes early. I wrap myself in a plush white robe and prop my feet on a tufted stool. I indulge in some tea and tranquil thoughts. This being St. Tropez, I close my eyes and try to recall whether there is a French word for Zen.

"Jo Ella!" My eyes fly open as my sister's mother-in-law, Alma McKlintock, bellows my name over the wind chime-y music.

"Midland must be treatin' you right, Jo Ella!" Big Claude enters the spa lounge behind his wife. They are wearing white robes that match my own, but they haven't removed their jewelry. Big Claude's gold link bracelets jingle as he strolls over to sit next to me. A diamond-studded anklet sparkles above Alma's large, pedicured feet.

"Hi, Mr. McKlintock. I'm waiting for Lou and Paula. They're letting me join in on their spa day."

"Well, darlin', I hope you're having the mud wrap," Alma says as she sits on my other side. "Me and Claude are addicted! Aren't we, baby?"

"Yes, Lord. They sure do a good mud wrap." I want to ask Big Claude how he manages to keep his elaborate hairdo intact during the mud wrap, but my thoughts are interrupted by Lou's squeal.

"Now isn't this a coincidence!" she yelps as she shuffles over to us in her robe and slippers with Paula in tow. Paula acknowledges the McKlintocks and then finds a seat as far away from us as possible. She buries her head in *Shape* magazine as Lou and the McKlintocks converse about the pros and cons of paraffin wax pedicures. I hope no one else enters the lounge, as the volume of the discussion may cause patrons who don't know us to complain.

A petite bottle-blonde with bird-like features and a cheery voice calls my name. I follow her lab-coated figure down a narrow hallway to the last door before the exit sign. "And how are you to-day-ay," smiles the bird lady. "Anything special you want me to focus 'awn, Miss Randolph?"

"Everything," I tell the bird lady. I don't wait for her to leave the room before I remove my robe and slide under the slim sheet.

"Oh, my! Sounds like you need some re-laxin,'" chirps the bird lady. "I have just the thing to relieve that ol' Hollywood stress." She rubs oil in her hands, and I detect a whiff of lavender.

I disappear into my massage. As the masseuse's slender fingers work out my kinks, I'm no longer in Midland. I'm not in Los Angeles either. I'm somewhere else; someplace where I'm able to breathe deeply and easily. Someplace where I can let go of my aches and pains and painful thoughts. I emerge refreshed, my mind still cloudy but calm, my thoughts no longer needling.

Even Lou is at a loss for words when we meet in the locker room and change into our street clothes. Paula is smiling, in spite of my presence, as we leave the lobby for the stark singe of the climate outside.

"Well, look-a-here! If it ain't Curt's Angels!"

The sultry sound of Curt Dupree's voice rouses all three of us out of our trances. Curt and Willie T., the two old Rebel teammates and sometime rivals, approach us toting small Radio Shack shopping bags. I can't help but notice what appears to be a Super Bowl ring on Curt's left hand where a wedding ring would normally be. An enormous, diamond-encrusted thing. Willie T. is back in the '80s. The collar of his pink polo shirt is turned up, tassled loafers adorn his sockless feet, and his Levi's are neatly pressed. His chestnut face is unblemished. He has prominent cheekbones and a distinct jawline that narrows to a well-defined, chiseled chin. Maybe my Go-Go's era choice of Willie T. over the infinitely popular Curt as my prom date made sense.

"What are you fine things up to this morning?" Curt drawls.

Paula doesn't speak but displays the happiest expression I've ever seen light up her face. Lou speaks for all of us, as usual.

"Hey, y'all! We're havin' a girls' day. We just got massages and now we're goin' to lunch."

"Sounds like you ladies know how to treat yourselves," Willie T. says as he grins at me.

"You know ol' Curt here coulda' given all y'all the massages of your lives. For free!"

"Free?" I tease. "I doubt you wouldn't want *something* for your trouble, Curt."

"No trouble at all," Curt says with a wink. "Now why don't you let us treat you PYT's to lunch. How 'bout some desert dogs!"

Lou, Paula, and I glance at each other with raised eyebrows. This concoction of wieners, raw onions, and jalapeños that Curt is touting sounds like a sure-fire Maalox moment. "OK, big spender," Lou says. "But we're plannin' to have sushi, not some gassy hot dogs. So I hope you're up for it."

"Girl, Curt is up for ev-er-y-thang!"

The sushi place is actually a Japanese steakhouse, which is perfect for our large new lunch companion. A petite Hispanic hostess escorts us to a u-shaped banquette. We pile in with me in the middle flanked by Curt and Willie T., and Lou and Paula at the perimeter.

Curt winks at me. I hide my head behind my plastic-coated menu and scan what the desert has to offer. I decide to live dangerously and order the chef's sashimi platter. Lou and Paula share an assortment of sushi rolls, and Curt orders an enormous slab of beef, grilled medium well, and a side order of shrimp fried rice. Willie T. favors the tempura platter. Curt takes it upon himself to order for everyone from the elaborate bar menu of complicated concoctions. He orders a round of "Lotus

Blossoms," a combination of sake, Triple Sec, and Sprite. They arrive in bulbous hurricane glasses and are topped off with a pineapple slice and a pale-colored orchid bloom.

The lunchtime crowd is sparse, but the restaurant is noisy. A group of middle-schoolers are celebrating the birthday of a pert, ponytailed ten year old. The kids are seated around a large hibachi in the middle of the room, and they cheer and clap as the grill master juggles knives and sauce dispensers and tosses bits of shrimp and chicken into their open mouths, like a seal act at Sea World.

I take my eyes off the flying food and steal a quick glance at Curt. Curt's high school wardrobe of Wranglers, cowboy boots, and too-tight T-shirts hasn't changed in twenty-some-odd years. Today, he has dressed up his denim and boots with an oxford shirt. It's an unusual combination of Tattersall and chest hair, as Curt has left a few too many buttons of his starched shirt unbuttoned. He's not my type from a style perspective, with his disco-era duds and facial hair. But he's interesting in an endangered species kind of way. He seems to have this effect on everyone. Paula smiles shyly in his direction, but he turns and grins at me instead.

"Look at you, Miss Randolph. You haven't changed a bit, except the hair." He touches my frizzy locks and frowns beneath his lush moustache. "Girl, you used to have good hair. You haven't become one of those feminists, have you?"

"Well, my mother's a feminist too, so what do you mean?"

"You a lesbian or something?"

His peaked eyebrows and gleaming smile beneath the porn star moustache suggest that he might be disappointed if I tell him I'm not a lesbian. By the look on Curt's face, I realize that he's one of those guys that defines "lesbians" as "women with whom Curt might have a threesome."

"No, I'm not a lesbian, Curt. You should wipe that grin off your face, because there will be no Playboy Channel threesomes for you tonight. And you call yourself a Christian?"

"Well, that threesome would be a blessing, now wouldn't it?"

I can't help but laugh. I know it's the hair. Nappy hair is hip again on the coasts, like those $100 Che Guevara T-shirts. But people still make assumptions about me when my hair is too "ethnic." Either I'm really authentic, I'm really wild, or I'm really threatening, when my truth is much simpler and shallower than the perception.

Willie T. smiles at me. "I like your hair, Jo Ella. I'm glad you're back. This is like old times."

"I hope it's not too much like the old days when she hung out with your scrawny behind," Curt taunts while jabbing Paula with his elbow. Paula's face brightens, but Willie T. rolls his eyes.

"If she didn't like the young version, what makes you think she'll change her mind now about your old ass?"

"Trust me, boy, this ass can still show her a thing or two."

"How is it possible that you two are friends?" I ask.

"I ask myself that all the time," Willie T. shrugs. "So, Jo Ella, when's that movie coming out? I can't wait to tell everybody that I kissed a movie star back in the day."

"Now I'm jealous." Curt leans forward, bringing his face quite close to my own. "I wanna kiss the movie star." Paula's eyes widen for a moment and then lower to examine the contents of her glass. She appears as if she will melt into the table, her creamy, chocolate skin dissolving, Terminator-style, into the rustic wooden slats of the table-top. I, on the other hand, lean back, forward, and then to the right, bobbing and weaving to avoid the onslaught of Curt's rapid advance in the direction of my lips.

"Don't be . . . I mean . . . I'm not sure it's actually gonna be released. You know how sometimes studios and networks drop projects? Well, this one doesn't look too hopeful."

"Hush, Jo Ella," Curt says. "I bet it ends up on DVD at least. You know, one of those 'straight-to-video' kinds of things."

"Like that DMX movie," Willie T. offers.

"Yeah, man," Curt agrees. "I love that movie."

I breathe a sigh of relief as Willie T. and Curt lose interest in my failed film career and shift their focus to the merits of various rappers' performances in less-than-meritorious movies. My respite from the limelight doesn't last long, however, as Lou brings it up again.

"Jo Ella, you gotta tell us more about this movie. Girl, that is so exciting! Even if they don't do it or just make it a DVD or somethin.' How'd you get picked for it? I always wondered how you actors get parts in stuff."

I take a large swig from my Lotus Blossum, downing my cocktail so fast that it causes a brain freeze. I crumple and pinch my forehead in an attempt to relieve my headache and figure out how to talk my way out of this mess. I speak rapidly, in a manic, uncontrollable chatter without punctuation or any end in sight.

"Well, um, one of my best friends, Jen, is an agent. You know, she like helps actors get auditions and parts in films and TV shows. So, I went with Jen to this cocktail party for this actor she knows, who, like, was on a reality show and gets a lot of work on TV. Like he's often the guy who gets killed on *Law & Order* and *CSI* and stuff. Anyway, this guy had switched from acting to film directing. Actually he was a music video director, but he was trying to get into doing feature-length films and stuff, which are, you know, like the two-hour movies you see in the theaters and on cable. Anyway, I told him I was an actress, and then he told me he was doing this movie, and it sounded interesting, since he was trying to do a hip-like, soap opera-y movie with a music video kind of look. With, you know, all the silly, over-the-top soap opera drama. Not that there's anything wrong with soap operas because, like, I used to be on one. But crazy drama with a hipper video vibe. Like MTV, or more like MTV2, since the regular MTV doesn't show videos anymore. And I told him—the director, I mean—that I thought it was a great idea and really interesting and stuff and that I'd like to look at the script. And then I auditioned—well, I didn't really audition like a normal audition, you know, but I kept talking to him about it, after the party, I mean. And, um, I ended up getting, like, the lead part."

All of the time and energy and expense that Mommy and Daddy and Dartmouth and Yale spent transforming my Texan teenager speech into proper English has just flown out the window. Maybe it's the brain freeze that's causing me to be so incoherent. Lou is following me, however. She leans forward, her hands clasped tightly on the tabletop, her eyes flashing and her smile widening with every word. Both Willie T. and Curt have ditched their DMX discussion and are in rapt attention.

"Girl, I *love* soap operas," Lou squeals. "This sounds like one of those Lifetime movies! I love those too. Paula, girl, you remember that movie about that lady whose husband turned out to be a serial killer and she didn't even know it?"

Paula shakes her head. Even she is paying attention to my rambling Valley Girl tale, though she doesn't appear too happy about it.

"Oh, girl, yes you do. That movie was deep! I had to pray over it because, oh, Lord, I don't want that kind of thing to happen to me. So, Jo Ella, what happened next? Tell me about what goes on when you're filming a movie and stuff. Is it like that Universal theme park? Have y'all been to Universal?"

"I went to the one in Florida a couple of years ago," Willie T. responds, never turning to look at Lou as he speaks, his torso and eyes positioned to directly face me. My friends' gazes are not withering like Mommy's crazy stares, Paula's excepted. But I'm still melting faster than the crushed ice dissolving rapidly in my humongous cocktail.

"So, Jo Ella, tell us what it's like to be an actress. How do you remember all of those lines? Do you have to memorize them, or do you have those big cards that tell you what to say like those people on the game shows? I was never so good at memorizing stuff," Curt confides.

"I know. I remember you trying to look over my shoulder during many a history exam," Willie T. laughs.

"It was easy, too, since you're pretty low to the ground. Good thing we were on the same team and you didn't have me rushing you, boy, or you wouldn't be here today."

Willie T. snickers as Curt leans across me to place himself more squarely in Willie T.'s face and personal space. His broad shoulder presses into the center of my chest as he bends forward, squashing me against the burgundy vinyl seat.

"You know it's true, you punk. Jo Ella, what'd you ever see in this little dude anyway?"

Curt breaks his spell of restaurant rage long enough to notice me again. He smiles, and the tip of his nose veers so close to my own that he practically Eskimo kisses me.

"Step off her, man!" Willie T.'s voice is low and even. Curt leans back and leers at him, eyes narrowing. Willie T. doesn't back down. "Give the woman some space. She didn't come to lunch with us to get molested."

Curt says nothing. He takes several long slurps from his Lotus Blossom without removing the flower. He stares at me for a moment and then smiles again.

"So, Jo Ella, how many TV shows've you been on anyway?" Willie T. and the Lotus Blossom seem to have diffused Curt's fire, at least for the time being.

"Including walk-on parts and one-time jobs? I couldn't even tell you." Though the thought of the number of gigs I've done makes me weary, the same thought causes Curt to gleam behind his cocktail glass. "I'm no star, Curt. I'm out there hustling for a living just like everybody else."

"Girl, I saw you play the cruise director on that remake of the *Love Boat*," Lou interjects. "How come they didn't do more than one episode of that? You and that bartender were too funny! We were gonna do *Love Boat* parties every week to watch you, and then the show never came back."

"Willie T. made some mean cocktails at that party. We got issues, but this boy sure can mix a drink," Curt adds.

I don't know what to say. My throat closes and my eyelids fill.

"Girl, are you OK?" Lou touches my hand. Paula's eyes soften as they stare at me over the top of her hurricane glass.

I take a deep breath and then take a sip of my flower-filled drink. "I'm OK," is all I'm able to scratch out. I take another sip and say, "I'm sorry. I just . . . I didn't know anybody noticed or cared about all the silly stuff I do."

"Course we do! How many folks can say they have a friend who's a big Hollywood movie star?" Curt's eyes glimmer as they intently fix on my face.

"It may not be true, but your life at least seems a lot more exciting that the day-to-day of most ordinary folks trying to make a living around here." These are the first words I've heard Paula speak in decades. Unlike her gazes at Curt, she views me soberly.

"Nonsense," I say, forcing myself to smile. "That's the trick about Hollywood. We just make people feel like their lives aren't as big so that they'll pay to watch ours. Or at least the lives of the characters we play. It's a big, corporate conspiracy, you know."

"Girl, I love me some movies, but I wouldn't give up my job to be on TV unless they paid me some Donald Trump money."

"What do you do?" I realize that I have no idea what Lou or anyone else I grew up with does for a living, other than Willie T. and my brother-in-law. And that's only because they work for their fathers' businesses, which were fixtures in our community growing up.

"I work in human resources at Dillard's."

"I didn't know you worked at Dillard's," I say as I stick a soybean in my mouth and suck in the salt, drawing the beans out of the pod with my teeth.

"Oh, girl, yes. I've been there over ten years. I just got promoted to head up human resources for all the West Texas stores, and I just love it. It's the best job in the world."

"That's really great." I've never heard any of my friends on the coasts call their jobs the best jobs in the world, not even the rich ones.

"Well, you know I love people, Jo Ella. And I also love to shop, so I guess I got the best of both worlds. But I don't spend all my money, now. I save too. Girl, I couldn't have a bunch 'a shoes and no closet to put 'em in!"

"I bet you have some nice shoes, Jo Ella. Like them *Girlfriends* girls. I saw that episode where you were that lawyer from Joan's job that was after her man." I pretend not to hear Curt. Our entrées arrive just in time for me not to respond. I tear the paper wrapping off of my chopsticks as Curt raises his fork and knife and tears into his steak. Willie T. raises a fried shrimp with the tips of his fingers and dips it into a little bowl of sauce. Paula cradles her chopsticks between her fingers and deftly lifts a spicy tuna roll with the slender bamboo sticks.

"Girl, you gotta show me how to do that," Lou cries as she fumbles with her chopsticks. "Where'd you learn that?"

"I spent a semester in Japan, you know," Paula states blandly without ever raising her eyes from her tiny sushi plate.

"Did you ever go to Nikko?" I shout over the din of the restaurant. "I shot this over-the-top, karate movie in Tokyo, and we drank too much sake after shooting all night one night. We got the director's driver to take us to see the temples at, like, five in the morning, and . . ."

"I didn't go there," Paula responds flatly.

Another Lotus Blossom arrives in front of me just in time to save my lips from flapping more nonsense in Paula's direction.

"So, Jo Ella, does this teaching thing mean you've come back for good?" Willie T. asks.

"Oh God, no!" I say a little too fast and a little too forcefully. "I mean, I haven't given up on my career. I plan to keep acting. I just needed a break from the whole L.A. scene for a little while."

"Baby, you know you could make Midland your home base. Get you one of them big new houses like your sister and fly out to work on your movies and stuff. You know, my new house'll have plenty of room for your Oscar awards and stuff." Curt winks at me and devours a large slice of steak. I ignore this invitation, but I can't ignore the sullen look on Paula's face.

"You know, Curt, with all the smart, beautiful Midland women like Paula and Lou here, you don't need me for a roommate."

"Yeah, but you know, Curt's got an image to maintain. I'm a football star. I need me a movie star in my kitchen."

I have no response for that remark. I take a long sip of my drink and don't dare turn my head to see Paula's reaction.

Willie T. rolls his eyes. "Curt, you rode the bench one season with the Cowboys a million years ago. Give me a damn break."

Lou chimes in as well. "Curt, you need to go somewhere with all that nonsense. That's why nobody takes you seriously. You know, Jo Ella, Curt's got a nice little construction business and is building a nice house for himself. But he's gotta stop that sexist stuff. Girl, we're in the twenty-first century now! Nobody's *ever* gonna step into his house, much less his kitchen, unless he cuts that stuff out. Ooh! I think I finally got the hang of this!"

Lou appears as happy as the Fourth of July as she dips a California roll into her soy sauce bowl with her chopsticks. The birthday party kids begin to sing, and the rest of the restaurant joins in. As I look around, I notice that the restaurant has finally filled up with a jovial crowd of Texans enjoying their flying shrimp and the challenge of eating with small bamboo sticks. A middle-aged lady with a tall bouffant and appliqués all over her sleeveless denim shirt admires the shoji screens near our table and leans over to share with us that she just bought a set for her screened porch. A thin young man with a thin blond beard reaches across his table to hold his date's hand as their waiter tells them the seafood specials of the day.

Though I've been to the best, from Matsuhisa to Nobu, I'm pleased with my meal and my day overall. I decline Lou's offer to join them at Dillard's and give hugs all around as we exit the restaurant. Curt ducks into the men's room before we step out, and Lou and Paula head for their car, leaving me and Willie T. alone at the entrance.

"Let me walk you to your car," he says and places a casual hand on my back.

"I know you've probably had enough of us for one day," Willie T. continues as we walk across the parking lot. "But I'm not doing anything tonight. Wanna grab a bite somewhere?"

Though he's not quite as tall as Curt, who's pushing 6'5", I still have to look up to see his face. He smiles down at me and says, "No desert dogs, I promise."

I smile back. "I'd love to, but I have loads of work to do tonight."

His smile fades. I'm not sure he believes me.

"I have to write a stupid musical from scratch and help the school prep for this Bush visit. A lot more than I thought I was signing up for this summer. Can I get a rain check?" I offer. "I'll be disappointed if you say no." I give his arm a squeeze.

"Of course," he says. He reaches for the door of my car and opens it for me. My car's not valuable enough to lock, and it's too hot to keep my windows rolled up. He waits for me to get settled and then closes the door. "See you later," he says with a wave.

"Soon, I hope," I say and wave back at him.

As soon as I arrive home, my phone begins to rap.

"Hey, sexy girl. You know, today's your lucky day."

"To what do I owe this stroke of good luck, Mr. Dupree?"

"I been thinkin' about us. How 'bout you and me get some enchiladas at Cactus Juan's tonight. You play your cards right, and I just might buy you some champagne." Curt's voice is low and synthetic, like a late-night disc jockey. I can't take him seriously, though I'm sure he's dead serious.

"Champagne, Cactus Juan's, and Curt Dupree? How can a girl refuse an offer like that?" I shouldn't play along, but I can't help myself. Curt is a piece of work.

"You can't refuse. It's alright though, baby, you can't help yourself."

"Well, Mr. Irresistible, I'm not sure that I can handle so much Curt Dupree in one day. Besides, I have to get back to work. All play and no work makes Jo Ella Randolph a very unemployed girl."

"Aw, come on now. People like us don't stay home on Saturday nights. Just think 'a what folks'll be talkin' about on Sunday when they see the two of us out on the town Saturday night—the movie star and the football star. Curt's got big plans for you and me. We're gonna run Midland, Texas, baby."

"That may be too much for even me to absorb. Seriously, Curt, I have tons of work to do. Principal Hardy unloaded two big projects on me at the last minute, so I think I've played enough hooky for one day. Besides, you know Paula . . ."

"Alright then, lady," Curt interrupts. "You're gonna miss out on me driving up in my carriage and doing the whole chivalarity thing and all. But I get it. You're one of them independent career women. Curt digs that."

I laugh a good-bye as I set down my bag on the kitchen table.

"Good day?" Mommy asks. I didn't notice her standing by the sink.

"Pretty good," I respond. I peek at my phone and notice no nagging messages or unknown callers from the West Coast. I'm still smiling as I head to my room and start back to work.

CHAPTER 15 ♡

"Hey, sexy girl, what you up to?"

"Up to?" I'm so groggy that I can't recall how my phone came to be pressed against my ear. "I wasn't up at all. *Jesus,* Curt! It's three in the morning!"

"Jesus don't wear no wristwatch, baby girl. Where you sleepin'? Your old room? I shoulda' pitched a ladder up to that window back in the day."

"Well," I yawn, "that would have been pretty weird, as we don't have a second floor."

"You mean I coulda' just stepped right in? Damn! Oops. Sorry, Lord. Now, I know it's nice to be home 'n' all, but baby you'd be a lot more comfortable right 'chere in the palace. I got some nice satin sheets. Black. I know you sophisticated girls like black. Yeah, you'd be REAL comfortable in the love palace, alright. What you wearin'?"

"Curt, why don't we both go back to sleep and pretend this was just a bad dream before I have to report you as a stalker."

"Ha ha ha HA HA HA HA HA! Woo, you are funny as hell . . . 'scuse me, Lord. Well, you sleep tight now, sexy girl. Try not to keep yourself up thinkin' of me."

"Sure thing, stalker boy."

I was sleeping soundly for a change, before Curt's interruption. I'm no longer able to rest. My Monday is bleary-eyed and bleak. When I finally see Davis at our first Bush rehearsal, he looks as disheveled as I feel. His dark red polo shirt is faded, and there is a prominent run in the knee of his jeans that threatens to pull apart and form a huge hole. "This is bullshit," is all he says to me before settling into a seat. I hope he's in a better mood by dinnertime.

Tired as I am, I don't feel cynical, for a change. It's a big deal for a kid to perform for the president of the United States. I push my predilections about this president to the side and attempt to prepare my Drama kids to make a good impression.

The kids recite endless rounds of the "Battle Hymn". I stage their movements and the theatrics around them—dry ice, laser lights, color guard, sparklers, baton twirlers, flag wavers. I think it would be a nice effect for us to get the baton girls to set the tips of their batons on fire and spin them around, like the Watch-Fires of A Hundred Circling Camps. The A/V manager is trying to talk me out of it. He also has reservations about my idea to have the captain of the rodeo team ride his horse behind the narrators while dressed like George Washington. I finally leave the stage and sit down next to Davis to watch what I've created. I shake the sweat glow from my embroidered cotton top and sit up straight in my chair, careful to keep the back of my shirt from sticking to my skin.

I watch the color guard swish their flags and march in formation as the band strikes up another chorus of the "Battle Hymn". I rock back and forth in my auditorium seat, somewhat in syncopation with the cadence of the song. "So, where do you want to go this evening?" I whisper without taking my eyes off the stage.

Davis doesn't answer me. I glance over my shoulder to look at him. He is slumped over in his seat, the tattered collar of his polo shirt turned up on one side. His flip-flopped feet are resting on top of the seat in front of him, and a bit of pale, second-day stubble dots his chin. He appears to be sleeping.

Davis has looked increasingly bedraggled and besieged of late. He has become less Beach Boy and more beach bum with each passing day. I don't know whether to be concerned or scared out of my wits. I'm beginning to worry about him. He really looks like a troubled soul, not a serial killer, but, given my track record with men, I can't honestly say that I know how to tell the difference.

"*Wake up little rosebud, wake up . . .*" I whisper in a croaky voice, like Popeye.

Davis finally drags one eye open. "Did I miss anything?"

"Only the entire song you're supposed to be listening to. You're lucky your kids already learned this song, otherwise you'd be in trouble, my friend."

"*Do it again!*" Davis yells in the direction of his students. "*Keep going! I'll tell you when to stop!*"

Davis allows his head to drop back, elongating his neck in a manner that resembles either a stretch or a seizure. His hair sticks close to his scalp rather than falling in the direction of his leaden head, suggesting to me that he hasn't washed it in a while.

"What is wrong with you?" I blurt.

"Nothing," he snaps. "It's just . . . look, Jo, I just haven't been getting a lot of sleep lately, OK?"

I don't say anything, but my face must be saying a great deal, because Davis's eyes narrow, and his frown recedes into a tense, straight line. He grasps my hand, despite the fact that we are seated directly in front of and in full view of all of our students.

"Hey, I'm sorry."

"Don't worry about it," I say, my eyes focused straight ahead on the kids onstage, not at the man sitting next to me. I reclaim my hand and move away from Davis, taking a seat a few rows in front of him. I shout for the kids to start the whole routine from the top, though my mind is no longer on the show in front of me. My thoughts are consumed by the show that has become my life. I have become a character in my own, personal soap opera that's as crazy as the one I played on TV. Jen keeps telling me that I should stop seeking an audience and spend more time with myself. Maybe I should take her advice.

"Mizz Randolph, do I gotta hold this up the whole time?"

Poor Kylie is straining to hold a pale green Styrofoam torch above her head like the Statue of Liberty's beacon of freedom. She has dropped the English textbook that is substituting for her tablet of justice, for the time being, and is using her spare arm to prop up her warbling torch.

"OK, maybe the whole Lady Liberty thing isn't such a good idea after all," I laugh. I rise and hoist myself onto the stage to relieve her of her foam baton. "I thought this would be better than the Uncle Sam costume I found in the prop closet, but maybe not."

Perhaps the display of Americana I have conceived for the president's visit is a bit too kitsch, particularly for a cynical resident of West L.A. like myself. But perhaps it's just right. The other night, I stumbled upon *The Music Man* on one of those classic movie channels. I became inspired by the colorful, buoyant energy of the Fourth of July parade scene. It's easy to become wrapped up in the heady optimism of marching bands and bunting and sparklers and suspend one's politics for a moment to enjoy the party.

I smile at Kiley, "Just hold it in your hand like this," as I demonstrate a bridesmaid bouquet-like grip. "You can wait to lift it up after Gerald says his last line. Actually, I want to re-block this thing and have you stand over here instead." Grasping Lady Liberty by the shoulders and moving her to the opposite side of the stage, I rearrange the kids' positions and have them practice a new entrance a few times before I remember my annoyance with Davis. Maybe he's just having a bad day, and we can have a nice dinner and forget about it.

"That's a wrap, amigos," I shout to my students. "Same bat time, same bat channel tomorrow." The kids completely miss my reference to Adam West's *Batman* re-runs I used to watch on TV as a kid, but I don't stop to explain. I hop off the stage to collect my belongings and talk to Davis about our dinner plans. But where is Davis? I don't recall him leaving. Perhaps he's just in the men's room or stepped out to take a call. I wait for the kids to leave the auditorium and continue to sit for another five minutes or so, but still no Davis. I leave the auditorium and head out to the parking lot, but his car isn't there. Strange. I scan my phone, but I see no calls or texts from Davis or anyone else.

"This is Davis. Leave a message."

He's not picking up his cell either. I start to call Jen or Rudy to complain that I've been stood up, but I have second thoughts. I'm not up to examining or explaining anything to them right now. I shut down my phone and head home.

"I thought you were going out to dinner with Davis," Mommy says as I stroll into the kitchen.

"Spending a lot of time with that boy, ain't you sugar?" Uncle Buddy asks. I was so absorbed in my thoughts that I didn't notice Uncle Buddy, Uncle Harvey, and Aunt Lula sitting with Daddy at the kitchen table. Uncle Buddy's "HUNT COON!" trucker cap is cocked a bit to the side, and he's wearing his favorite baby blue Sears coveralls. Aunt Lula is wearing a bright, floral housedress and is casually perusing a copy of *O: Oprah* magazine. Her smooth, silver hair is parted in the middle and plaited in two long braids that she has pinned across the top of her head like Heidi. She appears oblivious to the goings on around her.

"You're not seeing that white boy from the party?" Uncle Harvey says in a low, leery voice.

"We're working together on these two big projects for school," I say wearily. I drop my bags on the kitchen floor and open the fridge. I have no idea what I'm looking for.

Uncle Harvey shakes his head. "I thought we taught you better than that, Jo Ella. With everything those people did to us?"

"Now, Harvey," Daddy interjects, "this is a new century. Davis had nothing to do with anything that happened sixty, seventy years ago. Besides, they have to write a play."

Uncle Buddy removes a flask from the breast pocket of his coveralls. He gestures for me to come closer and bend down so that he can whisper something in my ear. "Get me a glass there, sugar."

Mommy gasps, "Uncle Buddy! You're not still making moonshine, are you? Now I begged you to let José haul that old still to the dump!"

"And just give them garbage folks all my hard work? No ma'am. You kin throw it away when I pass on." Uncle Buddy leans toward me and whispers, "you know, Jo Ella, I left my still to my neighbor, José, in my will, cuz I knew he'd take care of it. But since you're back now, I kin leave it to you if you want it. I'm gonna call my lawyer tomorrow."

Uncle Buddy winks knowingly in my direction. Aunt Lula rises slowly and takes her magazine into the den to read in peace.

I take Aunt Lula's seat and scoot closer to Uncle Buddy. I grasp his long, bony fingers in my own. "Uncle Buddy, you have a lawyer?" I whisper.

"Oh sure, sugar," he announces a bit louder than I had hoped. "That fella down on Main Street. I bought my house from his daddy cuz, you know, Jewish folks was the only ones that'd sell to us colored folks back then. When those ol' cracker cousins of ours stole the home-place, I don't know what we'd a done if Mister Kahn hadn't held paper for me 'til I got that situation worked out."

I rarely see Uncle Buddy angry or even annoyed. Until he starts talking about the 'cracker cousins,' that is. His forehead is now pinched, and his lips are pursed. He tells me the story I've heard a million times before.

"You know, your grandmother, Gun, was visiting from Californie, and she wasn't doin' so well when those folks showed up at the old house. I wish I'd 'a been home. If she'd 'a been herself, she wouldn't 'a signed them papers. Colored folks couldn't take white folks to court around here back then, but old man Kahn helped us. He got 'em to pay to keep us from tellin' the whole town that a congressman had a bunch 'a colored cousins."

I decide to ask a taboo question. "Uncle Buddy, doesn't just about every white Southerner have some Black folks in their family tree somewhere?"

"Yeah, sugar, but they didn't talk about it in public back then," Uncle Harvey interjects. "Still don't. Them white men love invadin' our women so long as nobody sees 'em doin' it." Uncle Harvey pauses and stares at me intently. "And they wanna have their fun and then have nothin' else to do with us. Can't tell ya how often I've seen Black women struggling to raise kids on their own, when the daddies live across town in nice houses with good jobs, taking their white children on vacation and sending 'em to college."

"Well, we wasn't gone let them take advantage of us and go away quiet," Uncle Buddy continues. "You know, that politician cousin of ours was havin' a hard time gettin' reelected over some oil contracts he handed out to his friends and his white family. The fella runnin' against him could 'a used us to knock him down a peg. They was all crooked, so at least we got something for us out of them no good white folks. But we lost our land. That was good land, oil land that our grandpa left us. Wrote it down on paper . . ."

Mommy walks over to the table and pats Uncle Buddy's shoulder. "Buddy, try not to get yourself so worked up. It's just not worth it to worry yourself like that. Now let's eat, everyone."

With that comment, Mommy closes the door on the discussion, but not my thoughts. While I was submerged in my Hollywood bubble, all the old tensions and inequities and resentments back home were still simmering on the surface of day-to-day life. Not that racism isn't present in Los Angeles. Far from it. But multi-ethnic groupings of friends and colleagues are so common these days that they don't generate a second glance. But whether it's laughing over coffee at Starbucks or chatting in the faculty lounge, time I spend with Davis definitely draws folks' attention and seems to make a statement.

I'm not trying to make a statement. I'm just lonesome. I miss my friends. I miss being part of a creative community, though it's debatable whether Hollywood qualifies as such. I don't want my family to think I've turned a blind eye to their struggles, but does going for coffee or dinner with Davis rise to that level?

No longer hungry, I skip out on dinner and retire to my bedroom to work on the play. I ignore my phone until the morning. When I finally turn it on, I see three messages from Davis and two from Curt. I don't listen to them. I also have a message from an unfamiliar number with a strange area code. I don't text Jen and Rudy, and I don't call anyone back. I plow through my morning classes and avoid the teacher's lounge. The lunch bell rings, and I head outside into the blazing heat of the midday sun. I sit by myself on the hard edge of a massive, stone planter on the perimeter of the school courtyard, partially shaded by a small mesquite tree. I ignore my lunch and watch freshly planted impatiens wave to and fro in the warm, dry wind.

I'm lonely. I know that I'm lucky to have my family, not to mention my personal freedom. But there's still something missing that I can't describe. The crazy thrill I feel when I'm around people I enjoy. The operative word being "joy." I've had glimmers of it since I've been home. But I fear that "joy" will not be a constant presence in my future. Unfortunately, Davis now feels like part of my problem, not my salvation. Curt's over-the-top come-ons prevent us from even having a simple conversation, in spite of the fact that he calls me five or six times a day. I pull my cell phone out of my pocket and dial Willie T.

"Hey, you, whatcha' doin' this evening?" I ask.

"Jo Ella?"

"Yeah, silly. Who did you think it was? Want to have dinner or see a movie or something tonight?"

"I thought you were busy working on the play. But . . . yeah! Why don't you let me make dinner for you? Come over after work."

"Great!"

This apparently has been too sudden for Willie T. He sounds like he doesn't quite trust it. "Just you, or are you bringing Lou or anybody else . . . uh, so I can know how many to cook for?"

"No, just me and whoever you invite yourself."

"OK, then. Just you and me. OK! I guess I'll see you . . ."

"I should leave school at about 7, 7:30. These rehearsals are crazy. Luckily, my mother has been making sandwiches and snacks for me to bring to the kids, so they aren't just ravenous by the time we release them. Everyone around here has lost their damn minds. They're so caught up over Bush that they're not thinking about the fact that these are kids we're shuffling around like puppets."

"You know, it's probably more the TV cameras they're focused on than Mr. Bush. I think folks are more interested in being on TV than anything else. Everybody wants to be on TV these days. Look at all those stupid reality shows."

"Willie T., you don't know the half of it."

"You can call me Bill, actually."

"When you start calling me Jo, instead of Jo Ella. All right, *Bill!* I'll see you this evening."

"OK. Bye, Jo Ella. I mean, Jo."

As soon as I end my call, I notice Davis approaching me from the other side of the courtyard. His gait is casual and his smile is warm, though his clothes are a bit rumpled. His black, Bob Marley T-shirt is frayed around the hem, and there is a large extra crease running down the front of his trousers.

"Hey, Jo. Did you get my messages?" I don't say anything in response.

"I am so sorry," he says as he sits next to me on the planter. "I'm such a moron. I call you up and ask you out to dinner, and then I completely space out about it."

This looks and sounds like the old Davis, but I can't be sure. I sit silently and stare at his face. His eyes are stricken and he begins to frown. "I've been so out of it recently. Something came up yesterday that kind of threw me off-guard, and I was so preoccupied that I forgot all about our plans. You've been nothing but nice to me, and I've repaid you by being a moody son of a bitch who stands you up. I'm so sorry."

"And they criticize women for being PMS-y." I try to sound cool, but my defenses are breaking down. There is warmth in Davis's voice and his eyes are soft and kind.

"Can I make it up to you? I just got a few cases of some really good wine I ordered from Napa. Really exceptional stuff, actually. And I'm pretty wicked on the grill. So, why don't you come over this evening and hang out?"

"I don't think so, Davis."

Davis initiates the full court press. The sly smile returns, almost buffing up his tarnished appearance, though his outfit still screams for a steam press. "Now I don't invite just anybody to share my wine with me. You're the first person, actually. You may be the only person around here who would appreciate it. Or a lot of things."

I tear my eyes away from Davis's. I notice Mrs. Tyler and Midge Hauser, the social studies teacher, standing next to a planter directly across the quad from the one that Davis and I are sharing. They are staring straight at us, of course.

"Davis, are you trying to make my life difficult, or am I just lucky that way?"

Davis's smile fades.

"You know Sue Ann and Midge are standing right over there pretending not to look at us," I continue.

Davis flashes me his widest grin and wraps his arms around my shoulders with a force that knocks both of us into the gritty soil and pebbles of the planter. Mrs. Tyler and Midge scurry away, their open mouths rumor-bound and wide enough to attract flying insects.

"Davis, are you on drugs or something? Because you're definitely tripping!" I try to express outrage, but I find this whole thing outrageously funny. I shake the dust and leaves from my hair and blouse as I rise and extend an arm to Davis. I can't stay mad at him. I don't know if I can tolerate this school or the rest of this summer without his friendship.

"So are we on for tonight?"

"No, Davis, I have plans tonight. This time I'm the one who'll have to take a rain check."

"My loss," Davis sighs.

"You better save some of that exceptional stuff for me though, brother. You owe me, now that you've made me the subject of all kinds of torrid, tawdry gossip that's being spread while we speak."

"I'll make it up to you. Scout's honor." Davis raises two fingers and places his other hand over his heart. Though for some reason, I doubt he's such a boy scout.

"I certainly hope so, since you've turned me into the faculty's resident harlot strumpet of Babylon without any of the benefits that go along with that title." I really have to watch my mouth sometimes, as I can be a tremendous flirt. My sister would say it's further evidence of my attention-seeking disorder that is the basis of my acting career. But, married or no, I've seen Ann Marie flirt in her cool, "I'm-too-good-for-you-so-adore-me" way as well. And then there's Mommy's obsessive winking and Uncle Buddy's "baby's" and "sugars". This thing must be genetic. I really want to share a nice glass of Napa and some laughs with Davis sometime, but I need to cut out the snake charming, lest I get myself into trouble again.

I may have already let the cobra out of the basket. "OK," Davis drawls. "But don't keep me and the good stuff waiting too long." Davis places a hand on my dusty back, though he removes it right away. "I may end up drinking the whole lot myself and look even more crazy and hung over than I have been recently."

"Don't worry, I won't," I reply with a wink and a squeeze of the arm, even. *Stop it, Jo.* "As you can see from my desperate attempts at charm, I've really been in need of a good cocktail and conversation of late. Maybe I won't take you up on that offer and just head my butt over to AA instead."

"And miss rehearsal? Death, disease, football. Those are all suitable reasons to miss rehearsal around here. Rehab? No deal."

"You're right, I'll see you at rehearsal."

"I'll try not to sleep."

"That would be a better example to show your students than snoring through their sonatas."

"I can't make any promises, but I'll try."

"See you then," I wave as Davis strolls away.

Boy, am I the popular girl today. I should call Ann Marie. I now have a desperate need to show off instead of a desperate need to hide.

"What?!" Ann Marie shouts through the phone.

"I told you, Ann Marie, I'm having dinner with Willie T. tonight. Oh, don't tell Mommy." I know that telling Ann Marie is the equivalent of telling Mommy and the entire population of Midland and its environs, but self-control has never been my strong suit.

"Jo Ella, you live with her. You really expect Mommy and Daddy not to wait up for you? Why do you think I got married so quick after school?"

"Oh, because you had your wedding planned out down to the last salmon pink dye-able pump by the time you turned seven, maybe?"

"Well, that may be true, but that's not the reason," Ann Marie continues with no apparent humor or sense of irony. "No. Even after

I came home from med school and got my own apartment, Daddy would call me & leave messages every hour on the hour to make sure I didn't end up dead on a road somewhere when I went out, or worse."

"Worse?"

"Yeah, lying in some guy's king-size somewhere."

I'm still not used to talking to my sister like this. "So why'd you tell him?"

"Might as well. This is Midland, Jo Ella. There are no secrets here. Everybody knows everything. By the way, you've got to tell me what's going on with you and that ski bum-looking teacher friend of yours."

"Already?!" I shout back at Ann Marie. "That just happened, like, five minutes ago!"

"What just happened five minutes ago?"

"Oh, never mind. Why do you think something's going on with us?"

"You mean other than the whole family thinks you're dating him? Or the fact that you practically threw him on the ground and mounted him in the middle of Mommy's backyard?"

"Did not!" I screech.

"Did so. You were cuddled up with him the entire time at Mommy's barbecue."

"Nuh-uh!" This conversation feels like a déjà vu reenactment of every conversation I had with Ann Marie growing up.

"Anyway," Ann Marie continues, "everyone's been saying since Day One that they think something's going on between you and this Davis guy."

"Lord, help me!" I groan.

"Though I'll admit that he seemed nice at the party. He's not bad looking, actually, in a slacker kind of way. I never dated a white guy. There was this guy in college who used to call me all the time. But I think he had some kind of exotica complex thing going on that creeped me out. You know, the whole slave master sneaking out back kind of thing . . ."

I never realized my sister sounded so much like me. Or maybe I just forgot. I got so used to her ignoring me in our youth and criticizing me in our young adulthood that I usually just argue with her as a reflex instead of really talking to her. "Not that there would be anything wrong with it, Ann Marie, but Davis and I are *not* dating. He's just the only person on the faculty here that I can relate to. And he's really funny. But, we're just friends, OK?"

"If you say so." She doesn't sound convinced. "Actually, it's probably for the best. You know, when these guys reach forty or so and they're not married, they're probably just out to play you. If they're not gay, that is." I have no quick response to Ann Marie's assessment of the situation. Kind of like a self-help book, it sounds right on the surface, but when you dig deeper, there's no there there. "So maybe I shouldn't have dinner with Willie T., then."

I seem to have stumped her. I'm not sure this has ever happened before. "What do I know?" she finally says. "I've been married a million years. I have no idea what it's like to be single anymore. Anyway, Willie T. will be relieved you're not dating Davis. He has a huge crush on you."

"Yeah, but he's always smiling at me. I like it, and he's fine and all, but it's a little weird."

"Jo Ella, he's just shy. No, I take that back. Shy's not the right world. *Reserved.* That's it. He's reserved. He doesn't blab on and on about stuff the way everyone else does around here. And sometimes people smile a lot or have facial tics or whatever because they don't know what to say. Besides, he probably has his guard up. Even though he likes you, he probably thinks you have a thing against brothers."

"What?"

"Sometimes it seems that way, you know. You were sparkling with conversation with that Davis character at the party, but you barely spoke to Willie T. or Curt. You always seem to clam up when you're with the brothers around here. And you're no clam, sister. I've seen you in action. Remember that Spanish guitarist we met after that show when I visited you in New York that time?"

I had forgotten all about that. "Ann Marie, one, that's not true. You were too busy chasing your alcoholic six year old at the party to notice the fact that I talked to Willie T. for a long time. Two, if I'm comfortable around Davis, maybe it's because I'm not dating Davis, and I'm not under constant pressure to date Davis. Like pressure from my *family!* Maybe I can even be a bit reserved myself sometimes."

"Well, then, maybe you and Willie T. are made for each other. Gotta run. I've got a waiting room full of females frantic for Botox. Can you believe how popular this stuff has become? I mean, I'm shooting botulism into people's faces, but I practically have to shoo patients away with a stick, they want it so bad. Pays the bills, though."

"I'm glad someone is paying bills around here. See you later."

"Let me know how the thing with Willie T. goes. By the way, Jo Ella, don't wear any of that batik crap, OK?"

I look down at my Indian print shirt and drawstring linen slacks and smile. "OK, bye."

I guess that Ann Marie and I possibly are related. We're like that old *Star Trek* episode with the people in the parallel black and white universes that are the same but polar opposites. I really watch too much TV.

I glance at my watch. Lunch hour is almost over, and I need to hang a sign-up sheet for the *North Dallas Forty* auditions on the school bulletin board. I still have quite a bit of work to do to finish the script, but I've done enough to get the ball rolling once we get through this Bush visit. I pull the sign-up sheet out of my bag and start to stroll back inside the building. Before I reach the door, I see Qiana coming out of it. Her large backpack is slung over one shoulder, and there are tears in her eyes.

"Hey, Qiana, you OK?"

Her eyes grow wide and she stops short, as if I startled her. She hurriedly wipes her face with the back of her hand. "I'm OK," she sniffles.

"You sure?" I approach her and put a hand on her shoulder.

She nods and drops her head to stare at the ground. I remove my hand from her shoulder and place my arm around her back and squeeze.

"Well, you can always come and talk to me if you need to. Sometimes having somebody who's not in your situation to talk to—someone who's not judging you—can help."

"OK," she whispers. "Thanks, Miss Randolph." She turns and heads back into the building. I wonder if I kept her from ditching the rest of the day. I don't know, but I hope she allows me to find out.

CHAPTER 16 ♡

I squint the sun out of my eyes as I try to decipher the directions I hastily scribbled in too-small print on the back of a Texaco receipt while simultaneously driving, looking out for where I'm supposed to turn, and applying lip gloss and mascara during red lights. I'm surprised at how relaxed I am about this dinner with Willie T. I bop along to Donna Summer, whom I can secretly enjoy in the privacy of my battered Beemer. I like the "Lite" radio station. This, of course, reveals my secret, inner un-hipness and will probably disqualify me from the Authentic African-American Society. Ann Marie also likes Lite radio, but I expect that sort of thing from her. There's something uncomplicated, airy, and mildly intoxicating about a Lite station, like a cool glass of white wine on a hot summer day.

A dark cloud hovers in the twilight sky. I lose Donna's synthesized disco beat to some sad sack Bread song. As another testament to my un-Blackness, I can actually identify a Bread song, though I never really dug this one. Is Ann Marie right about me? Am I what Uncle Harvey calls a " self-hating handkerchief head?" When I was growing up, you could have white friends and socialize with white folks. But not too many. And if you dated across racial lines or were too chummy with too many white folks, you were suspect. These boundaries were pretty straightforward when I was a teenager in Midland. But everything feels murky and uncertain these days.

I take a deep breath as I pull into Willie T.'s driveway. His home is a well-maintained, renovated ranch, not too far from the neighborhood where we grew up and a very short drive from the funeral home he has run since his father's illness forced him to retire. According to Ann Marie, this career move has been a lot more lucrative than his stint as an oil and gas loan officer. Since he grew up in the funeral business, I guess it's not as scary for him as it is for me. Just like dissecting frogs and the smell of formaldehyde didn't phase any of the doctors' kids other than me in biology class. Or Willie T., for that matter.

As I approach the columned porch with my housewarming gift of a very warm bottle of white wine, the front door swings open. Willie T. comes out to greet me and gives me a polite peck on the cheek. The Lacoste shirt is navy blue this time, and he's wearing khakis—flat front, I'm impressed to say—and polished cordovan loafers with no socks. But for the crocodile placed where the golden fleece should be, he could easily be mistaken for the random Black guy in the Brooks Brothers ads.

Stepping into Willie T.'s home, I immediately realize that this is not the low-ceilinged collection of formal, compact rooms of my parents' ranch house. Willie T. has raised his ceiling and removed the walls that separated his living, dining and kitchen areas, inserting skylights, triangular arched beams and unadorned, slender columns to create an airy loft-like space. In spite of his '80s attire, there is no *Miami Vice* influence on his décor. The color palette and furnishings are neutral and modestly tasteful, like a Pottery Barn store. There is not a hint of black lacquer or flamingo pink anywhere in view.

The kitchen is sleek and organic all at once with stainless steel appliances, Shaker-style cabinets and bluish-gray slate counters and floors. A slender island is the only barrier between the kitchen and the vast living/dining area, with its wall of floor-to-ceiling sliders leading to the flagstone patio. I am overwhelmed.

"You like it?" Willie T. smiles, knowing my answer already.

"This is fantastic! I would expect to see this house in someplace like Seattle or Austin, not Midland. Did you come up with all of this yourself?"

"Well, me and HGTV. I'm addicted to those home improvement shows. The big stuff I hired people to do, but a lot of it I've done myself. Your cousin, Memphis, helps me out. Last week he came over here and helped me haul and lay out all that stone on the patio and around the pool. That stone is hot as hell in this heat, but it looks real nice, so I couldn't resist." Willie T. averts his eyes, seeming self-conscious after exposing his inner sanctum. "Well, I guess you can see what I do with most of my time around here. When I'm not working, I mean."

"Well, it's fabulous. But are you afraid of over-improving it? I mean, our neighborhood is nice, but it's still 'the 'hood.' It's not like the white folks that get approved for bank loans are knocking each other over to live here."

"I don't worry so much about that. This is my home, Jo Ella. Unlike you, I'm not going anywhere. I'm doing this stuff for me."

"OK," I pause. I look at him as if for the first time. "OK, Willie T., there's one question that's eating me up right now. How the hell do you keep this place so neat?"

Willie T. laughs heartily. He obviously remembers my high school locker. One kid taped over the front of it with bright yellow crime scene tape, it was such a holy mess.

"What's so funny, mister? Hey! You may have as many books as I do." I glance at the wall of built-in bookshelves opposite the row of sliding glass doors, where reams of books are neatly arranged. I bet they're categorized via Dewey Decimal System or something equally organized and anal.

"You hungry?" Willie T. asks. "You can help me set stuff out on the table outside. Everything's ready, but I wanted to wait 'til you got here to put the fish on. Want a drink?"

"You needed to ask? Oh, I almost forgot. This is for you." I hand over my peace offering.

"Let's open this," he smiles as he slides the wine bottle out of its shiny cellophane wrapper. "Oh, I guess it's not so cold. I'll put it in the fridge, and we can open it later."

Willie T. places the wine in his tall, narrow Sub-Zero wine storage unit with the glass door that allows me to peek inside at all the goodies. He removes a Pyrex dish of marinated salmon from the other glass-front refrigerator.

"I can't get over this," I gush. "How on earth do you keep your refrigerator neat enough to have glass doors?"

"Because I care. Can you grab that corkscrew and those glasses over there? You can open this while I put the fish on the grill."

We step outside where covered glass serving bowls of mixed greens, some sort of rice salad and fresh tomato slices are already set out on the weathered teak table.

"Willie T., I have to admit something to you." I pull the cork out of the bottle with a cheery pop and begin to pour generously. "I expected you to either live in a big, white 'Crockett and Tubbs" kind of house or some gated community McMansion like my sister. I didn't expect anything so, so . . ."

"Not tacky?"

"No! You're not tacky at all. I've never thought that. You're just kind of retro. You're the same guy with the same haircut and the same wardrobe that I knew in high school. That's not a *bad* thing, mind you, because you were The Man back then . . ."

"Please," Willie T. smirks. "I thought Curt was The Man."

"Well, Curt was the big jock who was more outgoing. But you were the good-looking student-athlete that a girl's parents would let her leave the house with. Plus, you always had the best Ralph Lauren stuff shipped from your cousin in Houston before any of us bumpkins had seen it."

Willie T.'s belly laughs begin. He clutches his side with one hand as he shakily turns the salmon with the large metal spatula in his other hand.

"Girl, once you open your mouth, you are a complete nut."

"I know. Sorry." I take a large sip from my wine glass.

"No, no, I like that about you," he offers. "Everybody does."

"Really?"

"Oh, yeah, for sure."

"You gotta get, that, dirt off your shoulder, You gotta get, that . . ."

"What the hell is that?"

"I'm sorry, Willie T. I thought I had turned off my phone." I pick up the phone to turn off the rapper, but Jay-Z starts up again.

"Hey, Curt, I . . ."

"Hey, baby girl. Where you been? I must-a called you a million times."

"Oh, Curt, I've been really busy with . . ."

"I'm not far from your house. I'll swing by to pick you up."

"But . . ."

"And before I forget, I need you to get me into the Bush thing. Pastor Maples is going, but he must've forgot to invite me. You think them Hollywood reporters'll be there? They got a star planning an event for the President, so . . ."

"*Curt!*" I scream into my cell phone. Willie T.'s eyes remain focused on the fish he is grilling. His posture pretends not to be concerned with my chatting with his less-than-friendly rival in the middle of our dinner date. "Look, I'll get you on the list for the Bush thing. But you've got to stop calling me, OK? I've got work to do, and . . ."

"You know, Curt gets you career girls. I don't want to mess up your job situation or nothin'. I forgot you been rehearsin' and stuff. What time you want me to pick you up at the school?"

"*No,* Curt. I've already . . . look, I'm having dinner with Willie T. I can't talk to you right now. But I'll make sure to put your name on the list for the rally."

I shut down my phone before I have to deal with Curt any further. "I'm sorry," I say to Willie T.'s bowed head. "That guy won't take a hint. I don't know how he gets any work done, he calls me so much."

"No big deal, Jo Ella," he says flatly.

"No, really, I apologize for picking up. I just can't seem to shake that guy. Curt must call me ten times a day."

"Here, this is ready." Willie T. ignores my remarks about Curt. He slides the salmon on a ceramic platter resembling Spanish Majorca pottery and brings it over to the table. He pulls out one of the teak armchairs for me, lights a few hurricane lanterns with his grill lighter, and then seats himself.

"So, Jo Ella, I have to ask. What made you call me today?"

I take extra time chewing my salad to contemplate my response.

"I don't know, Willie T. I didn't really think about the whys of it. I thought it might be fun to get together, so I called you."

"I wasn't sure you were interested," he says.

"Really? I thought I came across as over-interested."

Willie T. takes a sip of wine. "You're hot and cold," he says.

That's a critique I don't usually hear. Most people think I'm too "hot" all the time. "Maybe I'm avoiding relationships with anybody that seems too rooted here in Midland and isn't a transient like myself, even if I'm interested. How's that for pop psychology?"

"But all your roots are here, Jo Ella."

"And that appears to be my problem."

Willie T. examines me quizzically. "What are you running from?"

Hmmm. The question. "I haven't figured that out. I keep thinking I'll know what I'm looking for when I see it, so I keep running around trying to find it. But I don't know that I've ever found it, at least not until it was too late to go back and get it."

Willie T. stares at me for a moment. Then he starts to laugh. "Jo Ella, what the hell did you just say?"

"I told you it was pop psychology. You've watched Dr. Phil, haven't you?"

"Just don't try to write any self-help books. Because that didn't make a lick of sense."

"And people wonder why I do all the nonsensical things I do. What's your view, since mine is so senseless?"

"I think you're bored," Willie T. responds, his laughter having settled down into a soft smile.

"Really? I've always thought of myself as the opposite of bored."

"No," Willie T. continues. "You're the opposite of boring. But you seem pretty bored, Jo Ella. Growing up, you spent all your time with your head in a book wanting to be someplace else more exciting. Or on a stage pretending you were someone else more exciting. But life's not necessarily where you go, it's what you make of it. I mean, look at me. I keep up with stuff and read and get out of this redneck town when I need to. But I have a home I can come back to that also makes me happy."

"I'm not so bored, Willie T. I just like experiences. I don't like doing and being the same thing all the time. Maybe that's why I became an actress. Didn't you ever want to be someone else?"

"Yeah, I wanted to be Tony Dorsett and run touchdowns for the Dallas Cowboys. But, unlike Curt, I got over it. I'm happy with who I am."

"Willie T., I'm not unhappy. I'm just, just . . ."

"Bored."

"OK," I laugh. "If I have to go on the couch this evening, so do you. Why aren't you married yet?"

"Why aren't you married?" Willie T. retorts.

"Because I'm a crazy, basket case attention hog that does tabloid-worthy stuff all the time, that's why. Now what's your excuse?"

"No excuse. No reason, really," he shrugs.

"You have to have a reason. This is the Bible Belt. Everybody's supposed to be married before the age of twenty-five, whether they like it or not."

"I just . . . I don't know. I don't have anything against it. If I meet somebody I want to marry who wants to marry me too, then I'll get married. But I'm not in a rush."

"You're not in a rush? You're damn near eligible for an AARP card! What are you talking about?"

"I don't want to get married until I feel like I'm with the right person. I want to have something like what Claude and your sister have."

Willie T. and my brother-in-law are close, so I don't bring up my sister's recent revelations. Willie T. helps himself to more salmon and pours more wine for both of us. I watch him as he cuts a tomato into small, even pieces. He cuts and chews very slowly and methodically. "Willie T., I can't quite figure you out."

"What's to figure out?" he replies, never looking up from his plate.

"Well, you're not married, you're neat, you cook food other than steak and chili, and you have taste. Now this wouldn't be such a big deal in Manhattan or California, but this is West Texas. You're not one of those down-low brothers, are you?"

His large, puppy dog eyes meet mine before he rolls them upward in exasperation. "Jo Ella, not every unmarried Black man is gay or some kind of dog that runs around with a bunch of women."

"Well, that's what all the Black women who write books these days say. You have any of those 'chocolate love' books on your shelves in there?"

He stands and begins to clear the dinner dishes. I don't think he found my joke amusing. "You want some dessert?"

"Changing the subject, eh? Yes, I will have some dessert, please." The sky is turning blue-black, clouds obscuring our view of the stars. The patio begins to glow from the candlelight and the outdoor beams that automatically turned on at sunset.

Willie T. returns with two bowls of vanilla ice cream topped with strawberries, but his expression has not changed.

"Besides, rumor has it you're not really in the Black man market these days, so how would you know?"

I'm not going to take the bait. No good can come of it. "So what am I doing here?" Oops.

"I don't know."

"And if you think I like Davis . . ."

"Who?"

"Davis, the white elephant that seems to be standing in every room I walk into these days. If you think I'm into this white dude, why did you keep asking me out?"

"Jo Ella, I'm a guy. Unless a girl is married or going out with a friend of mine, I'm at least gonna try. Guys let you make the decision to say no; we don't make it for you."

"So, *Bill,* if nothing else, at least I've learned a valuable lesson about the male psyche tonight."

"Who said anything about anybody's psyche? I don't think that's what makes us act the way we do."

I stretch my arms into the air, extend my legs straight in front of me and yawn, curving my back like a cat while still seated in my arm-chair. I forget that I used to teach yoga and am pretty limber. Based on Willie T.'s facial expression, I probably shouldn't do these kinds of things on a first date. But I'm stuffed and sleepy and a little bit high. I really have to head home now, if I'm actually going to make it home, so I curl myself out of my chair and begin to pick up the dessert bowls and spoons.

"Don't worry about that. Why don't you just relax yourself?" Willie T. motions in the direction of the sofa as he begins to blow out candles and clear the patio area of other dinner detritus.

"Oh, man, if I become any more relaxed, I'll be snoring on that sofa over there. Actually, I better get going. This was really lovely, but I have to be up early and work fairly late tomorrow. The big day with the Bush folks is coming up, you know."

"Oh, yeah, I almost forgot. I may stop through. They invited a few folks from St. Luke's, I think so they can get some voting-age, colored faces out there for the cameras. Most people don't want to go, but I might just run through to see what he says."

"You better wear a cross around your neck or something so they won't suspect you for a protester. They try to weed out those folks. The only way my bohemian butt is getting in is that I work there. Principal Hardy must have reminded me twenty times to bring my faculty ID with me on Thursday."

"Ha ha. Good advice. Can I make you some coffee at least?" Willie T. throws me an Oscar-worthy, Denzel-like grin. Maybe I underestimated him.

"No, that's OK. I don't have far to go." I retrieve my bag from the back of one of Willie T.'s armchairs. Chloé. I remember when snagging the latest Chloé bag months before it made it to stores meant something. I casually sling an arm through the handles and toss it over my shoulder.

"Nice bag," he remarks.

"You sure you're not a down-low brother?"

He doesn't answer me. At least not verbally. I think he's had a little bit of practice with women since high school.

"OK, maybe not. Let me get out of here before I'm tempted to stay."

Willie T.'s eyebrows rise expectantly. "You don't have to leave, you know."

I place a palm on his lovely cheek and sigh. "Yes I do. One, my father will show up with a posse of his boys from the golf course to get me; Two, my Uncle Buddy will shoot you with that old rusty pistol of his, if he doesn't accidentally shoot himself first; and Three, I think I need to slow down before I throw myself into something else . . . it's a long story for another day that will require you to open up two or three of those bottles in that neat little refrigerator of yours. I need to reign in my fast behind and figure some stuff out before any more nice people get hurt."

"OK, I didn't hear a 'never' or a 'get the hell away from me' in there, so that's hopeful." Willie T. winks at me and shrugs his shoulders.

"Springs eternal, doesn't it?"

"I never knew what that saying meant."

I have to laugh because that sounds exactly like something I would say. "Me neither."

As I stroll out onto the porch and head for my car, I wave and blow a kiss at Willie T. He waits for me to get in safely, lock my door and start the engine—no small thing in my thirtysomething vehicle.

Well, that was interesting.

I just can't bring myself to call him "Bill."

CHAPTER 17 ♡

The Bush event is rapidly shrinking, to Principal Hardy's chagrin. His hopes for a large, flag-waving rally have been dashed in favor of a brief hand-shaking session in front of the school, followed by a few remarks about education by the President on the front steps before a small, pre-selected crowd of reporters, supporters and students. Before he speaks, my kids will do their dramatic reading, without all the bells, whistles, sparklers and colonial horsemen. They'll take a quick photo with the President, and then he's off to collect checks.

The big day finally arrives, and my kids are nervous. I try to break the tension by wisecracking about their bright red and blue t-shirts emblazoned with "Phonics for Freedom" in large white diagonal letters with a sketch of an eagle soaring in the background. They also have been forced to wear boxy white pants, which do not go over very well.

"Miss Randolph, I look like a dork," Kiley whines.

"Yeah, these pants are whack!" Tyrone complains.

"Yo, Miss Randolph, we're gonna be on TV, right?" Tomás inquires hopefully.

"If all the TV news vans and people with cameras camped outside are any indication, then I think so. You guys better shine so that people notice you and your skills, not those ugly outfits you're wearing," I tease.

"Miss Randolph, do you ever get nervous before you go on stage?"

I tweak Kiley's nose like Mommy does mine. "Every single time, kiddo. But once you get out there and start doing your thing, I promise you, it's the best feeling in the world." I scan my kids' hopeful, nervous faces. "I appreciate y'all working so hard. The whole school does. I'm really proud of you because you've acted like real professionals. More professional than most of the crazy adults around here. So, break a leg!"

They all begin to high five and slap each other on the back. They're nervous, but they're performers, so deep down I know they love this. I count heads and do a mental roll call and see that everyone is here except Qiana. Though it's time for us to leave my classroom and make our way to the front of the school, I hold back for a few minutes. Five minutes pass, then ten, then fifteen, and still no Qiana. We'll have to go ahead without her.

I round up my herd and shuttle them outside. We've already gone through the multiple layers of security the president's advance team has set up in and around the school to protect him. We presented our photo ids, our names were checked off of pre-approved invitee lists, our fingerprints were scanned, and each one of us was searched every which way for weapons and such. Of course, Ravi tried to call me as I was preparing to place my cell phone in the x-ray conveyer belt and step through the metal detector. It's a good thing that the detector only screens for weapons, and not evil thoughts or intentions; otherwise I might have been bound and gagged. When my phone and I were cleared as non-dangerous, for the president at least, I shut off the ringer and shoved it into the pocket of my mushroom-colored, linen jacket.

Once outside, the kids huddle together and mumble to one another in hushed, reverential tones as we catch sight of the Presidential Seal on the podium, which has been set up on the school steps. They seem shocked and awed by the return of the bomb-sniffing German Shepherds and the suits with white earpieces moving around in stone-faced solemnity. Maybe, like me, they're easily influenced by their surroundings. Like the impact of Ravi's serene, seaside vista on my senses the night we met. Why else would I have fallen so fast and so hard for a guy like Ravi that I knew so little about and spent so little time subjecting to proper due diligence? Jen and Rudy always had an uneasy feeling about him, like the queasiness I'm feeling right now as we await the arrival of the motorcade and my students' stint in the spotlight. It's the same pit in my stomach that I always feel before I perform or when I think about Ravi.

Are my friends right about me? Am I really such an attention hog, that I always need an audience or a guy to fawn over me? That may be part of the explanation, but I don't think it explains everything. My relationship with Ravi felt real. It *was* real. He listened to my dreams and crazy ramblings about everything and nothing. He confided in me and encouraged me. It wasn't perfect, but what is? It felt like real love. The only thing missing from my love story by the shore was a soundtrack, or so it seemed.

The real-life band strikes up the first in a litany of Sousa-style marches, which means the President is on his way, and which, I'm sure, is annoying Davis to no end. His back is turned to face his band, so I can't see his expression. But he visibly gritted his teeth through all of our rehearsals and the meetings we held with our dear principal and the Parent-Teacher Presidential Preparations Committee regarding this event. He agreed to play Sousa, but he stopped them from making the kids march round and round in full band regalia in the hundred+ degree heat, convincing the committee that it would create a homeland security risk.

We wait on the school steps with Principal Hardy and an assortment of security people. Photographers and reporters are clustered in a pack in front of us, with a small gathering of invited onlookers behind them. I notice Willie T. in the back of the crowd, and I wave in his direction, though he doesn't see me. I wonder if he took my suggestion to wear a cross or something Christian. It appears that Curt got the message, even though I haven't spoken to him since my date with Willie T. I notice him approaching Willie T. wearing a church T-shirt and an enormous gold crucifix that I can see clearly from across the lawn.

I now screen all my calls so that I don't have to talk to Curt, and I've taken to parking in my parents' garage so that he won't see my car in the driveway if he cruises by the house. He left me eight voicemails yesterday and five or six today. He sounded pretty anxious on the messages, but I ignored them. That nervy kind of pushiness is part of his style and the means he uses to get what he wants. Rumor has it that Curt was selected the team MVP back in the day over Willie T. and Kelly Sanders, the popular Rebel quarterback, only because he worried the coaches so relentlessly about it that they gave him the title just so he would leave them alone.

Curt is annoying, but he's also humorous, in a Steve Harvey kind of way. However we have very little in common, other than jokes, and I fear that any outings or overtures on my part will convince him that I'm looking for a night at the "love palace," no matter what I tell him to the contrary. Curt's come-ons have me perplexed, given his recent religious conversion. In one breath he cracks a joke about cleavage, and in the next breath he quotes Scripture. I doubt I'll have to dodge his come-ons and attempts to convert me much longer, however. My recollection is that Curt's attention span for women is short and shifting, and I will end up a passing fad like so many lovelorn cheerleaders and pom-pom girls back in the day.

The band begins to pound out "The Stars and Stripes Forever," and the earpiece guys plant their feet in strategic locations. The not-so-subtle presence of machine-gun slingers in riot gear and Army fatigues heightens the drama of this little visit. Principal Hardy approaches me and gives me a pat on the back. A rousing cheer and rounds of applause burst from the crowd as the motorcade enters the school driveway, and the limousine bearing the Presidential insignia pulls in front of the school. Cameras begin to roll, and the hodgepodge of reporters, wilting from the long wait in the insidious southwestern heat, raise their microphones and put on their game faces. Secret service men and women converge on the limousine, and a stoic man in dark glasses opens the door of the Cadillac. The first man and lady stride toward us, all waves, winks, and grins at the outrageous outpouring of true love and enthusiasm from the crowd.

They are an attractive couple, and I find myself smiling in their direction, though just this morning I was cursing them over coffee with Mommy and Daddy and Air America. I can't stop smiling, actually. This weird Cheshire cat grin that I can't seem to wipe off my face, even as I find myself being pulled toward the podium by Principal Hardy, who urges not only my students, but me as well to join in the jamboree for local and national media.

Wait! What am I doing on camera?

I shake hands with the first couple and somehow find myself wedged right between President Bush and Principal Hardy. There is no escape. Maybe this is what it's like to be Condoleezza Rice. Still grinning, I gesture for my kids to begin their production and nod approvingly as they perform their parts without a hitch. Though Davis is busy directing his band, he glances at me a few times with an amused grin at what I am sure is my absolutely absurd expression. Being around Mommy so much has now transformed me into the Joker.

Mommy's watching this on TV! Lord, help me!

I continue to grin like an idiot as first Tomás, then Kiley, then each of my other students steps forward to recite a line of the "Battle Hymn" while gesturing at the flagpole and going through all kinds of ridiculous hand and body motions that were the only things I could come up with for them to do after I had to forego the fog machine and the sparkling laser lights mimicking cannon fire and the twirlers leaping with flaming batons while wearing tri-corner hats.

Oh shit! I'm the token! Everyone in America can see me up here pickin' and grinnin' with the president like some kind of sellout!

Though my feeble attempt to lay low and be incognito is now a complete and utter failure, at least the performance is a success. The crowd goes wild with cheers as the students complete their act. The President places his arm around my shoulders and gives me an approving squeeze while simultaneously saluting and waving at the crowd, the kids and the cameras. Wow, he's a bit taller than I realized. Am I still smiling?

The president grins and continues to hug my shoulders as Principal Hardy steps forward to make a few opening remarks. To compensate for the din of the crowd, and being pretty worked into a frenzy himself, Principal Hardy begins to shout a flourish of almost incoherent tributes to our guest. He is red-faced and so excited that he begins to jump up and down like a kid entering the Magic Kingdom for the first time.

"He's the *leader!* The *free world! Glory!!! Glory* to the U S OF A!!!"

Principal Hardy is so worked up that he starts to pump his fist like Arsenio Hall, chanting "USA, USA" over and over again with the crowd. Laura Bush's smile is frozen on her face. The president's grin is beginning to resemble a smirk. Principal Hardy finally winds down a little bit, not from diminished enthusiasm, but to avoid heat stroke. "And *now*," he shouts. "I have the *high* privilege and *dis-tinct* honor to present to you *Midland's* president of the *U-nited* States of America, *George W. Bush!!!*"

Screams overcome us like a tidal wave, and I hold my hands over my ears. The crowd goes hand-clapping, foot-stomping, whoop-whoop wild.

"And Robert E. Lee High School's *own*, First Lady *Laura Bush!*"

I am now in a hallucinatory bubble, where I hear nothing and do nothing but smile and nod my head like a bobbling doll. I pay no attention to what the *leader* of the *free world* is saying right next to me, until I hear him drawl my name.

"Now, look at Jo, here." The president squeezes my shoulders again as cameras snap and flash. "Jo could be out there in Holly Woood."

"*Boooo!*" the crowd hisses.

"But Jo knows what's really important. She's here with *real* Americans. Hard-working Americans. Teaching our kids here the phonics and things they need to succeed. Helpin' to educate our young people, not corrupt them, like those folks out there in Hollywood."

Luckily my high schoolers have moved beyond phonics, but who am I to correct the president of the *USA, USA!* He finishes his remarks and then grabs both Laura's hand and mine and leads us to the rope line, where reporters hold out microphones for sound bites, and admirers hold out hands for handshakes. It's similar to a premiere, with the blinding flicker of bright white flashes and strangers with microphones and cameras shouting my name. I raise my hand to shield my eyes. Through my fingers, I notice Curt surrounded by reporters, and then I lose sight of him as well wishers push forward to meet their man.

All of a sudden, there is a scuffle and shuffling of bodies in the back of the crowd. It's hard to tell exactly what's going on amongst the multitude of limbs and suits and blurred faces scrambling around back there.

"Bastard!"

"Get off me, man! Leave me alone!"

"You punk! This is what you get for tryin' to mack on my girl!"

"Yo, man . . . if she's your girl, what was Jo Ella doing at my place?!"

"Fuck you!"

That voice sounds familiar. Actually both voices sound familiar. My plastic grin is transformed into a virtual *Scream* mask as I realize the familiar voices and faces being tackled by the Secret Service belong to Curt and Willie T. It's official. My life has become an episode of *Jerry Springer*.

I am now clutching the First White Man even tighter than my tackle of Davis during Mommy's Tex-Mex shindig. I embrace the chief executive as if he was my lover, not the leader of the free world, all live and in color for the network news cameras. What am I doing? I voted for Howard Dean! I wore a McGovern button to kindergarten, for God's sake! White earpiece guys yell into little mics and race toward us from every direction, swarming us and whisking the president and first lady away before I can blink. The swarm of Secret Service is replaced by a swarm of reporters that close in on me from every direction.

"Miss Randolph, why did you leave L.A.?"

"Jo, is it true you had an affair with Danielle Coleman's husband?"

"Are you still seeing him?

"Have you given up acting for good?"

I duck my head and pull the lapels of my jacket over my face. I make a dash toward the front door of the school, photographers nipping at my heels. Someone grabs my hand, and I try to yank it back.

"Jo, come this way," Davis says. He wraps an arm around my shoulder and bum rushes me through the throng into the school building. School security guards and local cops barricade the doors after our entrance, preventing the mob from invading the school building. In contrast to the crushing din outside, the hallways inside the school building are empty and quiet. Our footsteps echo as we shuffle down the main corridor.

My cell phone vibrates in my pocket, and for some reason I decide to answer it.

"I saw it on the local L.A. news," Jen announces breathlessly.

"It's on the national news too," Rudy adds via conference. Rudy has the same frantic, near-hysterical tone in his voice that he has had in almost every crisis we have endured together, starting with the time he tried to make me throw away my *Flashdance* sweatshirt in college. "Anderson Cooper was just talking about it on CNN."

"Oh, here's Fox," Jen continues. "They've got a caption that says, *'Bush breaks up boyfriend brawl.'* Hey, Jo, that's you! That's a nice jacket."

"I'll have to talk to you guys later."

"You need an intervention!" Rudy shrieks. "We're coming down there."

I drop the phone back into my pocket.

"Let's get out of here," Davis says in a calm, low voice. I had almost forgotten that he was standing there, propping me up. Suddenly, the dam breaks. Whatever I have been holding back or holding in or trying to squelch or sort out all comes crashing down at once and spews out of me at gale force. So many tears stream so rapidly down my cheeks that they all blur together, turning my face into a veritable creek bed. Damp spots pop up here and there on the front of my shirt and blazer. I lean against Davis and cover my face with my hands. I can't stop sobbing, even as the tears fill my palms.

I hear footsteps and clutch Davis' shirt, expecting to see more photographers. Instead, I see Willie T. and a few folks from church and school, also seeking asylum from the madness outside.

"Willie T., are you OK?" I mumble through my tears. Willie T. turns his gaze away from me with an expression of disgust. I release Davis's shirt and walk toward Willie T. "I'm so sorry. I shouldn't have invited Curt. I didn't know . . ."

"I'm not a punk, Jo Ella," he says in a calm voice lined with steel. "I don't need this shit," he says as he turns on his heel and walks away. He strides down the corridor toward the school entrance.

My sobs resume, and Davis pulls me into a hug, wrapping his lean arms around my shoulders.

"Wanna get out of here?" he whispers into my hair. He can't reach my ear, as I have buried my face into his chest, leaving a large damp spot in the center of his shirt. He holds me a bit longer and then grabs my watery palm and leads me down a side corridor and through a service entrance to the rear parking lot. Blanketed by the warmth of the early evening air, I blindly follow his lead to his little car and crouch down in the seat so as not to be seen as we speed away.

CHAPTER 18 ♡

I am a complete mess. My eyes are burning and my cheeks are streaked with salt. I would be suspicious of Davis's motives if I didn't feel so puffy and unsightly that even the wino that hangs out by the neighborhood liquor store wouldn't whistle at me if he saw me in this state. The ragtop of Davis's midnight blue Mini is down, and the lukewarm air is moist and musty, slapping me in the face like a damp rag.

We drive down peaceful streets lined with large pecan and live oak trees, and it dawns on me that we are approaching the country club. We turn onto a curvy, shaded lane bordering one edge of the golf course, with spacious homes facing the greens on the opposite side of the road. Though most are larger versions of the ubiquitous, traditional ranch, there are also colonial, Spanish and craftsman styles scattered amongst the low-rises, with a "Tara" or two thrown in for good measure.

Davis turns into the driveway of a substantial, stucco Spaniard with a broad, lush lawn and a red tile roof. There's a hearty, second story balcony that runs the length of the front of the house and is decked with a strong, wrought iron balustrade. Davis hurries out of the car and strides around to my side, opening my door for me and extending a steady arm in my shaky direction. Though I'm clearly just neurotic, not invalid, he holds my arm and walks me slowly across the front lawn to the carved wooden door. As we enter the house, I am struck with the same sense of airiness and light that I felt when I stepped into Willie T.'s renovated ranch. The huge sunken living room runs almost the entire length of the first floor, accented by a Mexican ceramic tile floor, a high wood-beamed ceiling, and an enormous fireplace at one end.

We pass but don't enter the generous living room. Davis leads me into the kitchen, where he drops his keys onto a large, weathered farm table in the breakfast area. He starts opening pine cabinets, one of which conceals the refrigerator. He begins to gather and spread out glasses, cheese, salami, olives, and all sorts of picnic fare.

"Go have a seat and make yourself at home in the den there." Davis gestures behind him, as his head remains embedded in the refrigerator. "The remote's on the table, if you're interested."

I saunter into the pine-paneled den, which is lined with bookcases and also includes a fireplace. A modern addition, a slender, high-definition television, is mounted on the wall above the fireplace. There is a long, spare area of wall that hosts another modern touch — neatly aligned rows of framed black and white photos featuring austere profiles of elderly blues musicians, gnarly oil workers and somber church ladies. The gallery includes a few playful images to counterbalance the stark severity of the adults, with three shots of an adorable child in denim overalls clutching a fistful of wildflowers. I'm not sure if it's a boy or girl, but the toddler has an angelic, heart-shaped face, large floppy curls and a bemused grin.

"These are fantastic! Did you collect these, or are they your Mom's?"

"I did them." Davis sets a few small bowls on the coffee table.

"You took these pictures?" I gasp. "These are, like, museum-quality."

"I like to keep a record of my journeys. Maybe I'll learn something from them sometime."

"Does it work?"

"No, not yet. I'm still a work in progress." Davis flashes me a child-like grin.

"Taken any recently? I'm curious what parts of this Midland journey you decide to log in your records."

"You wanna have your picture taken?"

"Are you kidding me?" I screech. "Those old guys in the oil fields there are a right better sight than I am right now. Besides, where would you put me, with the seniors or the children?"

"You'd be in a category all by yourself."

"Good answer! Probably a lie to spare my ego, but a good answer."

"I'll be right back," Davis says before disappearing into the kitchen again.

I shift my focus from the photo gallery to the extra-wide, leather sectional sofa that is inviting me to sink into its hefty cushions. I am prone and half-asleep when Davis finally emerges. He doesn't say a word as he sets the rest of his Mediterranean fare on the coffee table and positions a generous glass of pinot noir directly in front of me. He sinks into the sofa, props his long legs on the end of the table that is not covered with food and drink, and clicks on the television.

"Is that for me?"

"Of course."

"Thanks. I guess we're finally checking that rain. Where did the term 'rain check' come from anyway?"

Davis's shoulders shake a bit before the sound of his laughter actually emerges.

"Welcome back, Ms. Randolph. Here's to feeling better."

"Amen to that." I mimic Davis' propped posture as I sip my beautiful glass of wine and slowly begin to revel in the change of scenery. These lovely new surroundings lift me out of my funk a bit, providing a peaceful, much-needed distraction from the carnival that has become my life. I would like to sit right here in this spot for eternity, but that would probably be an imposition.

Glancing back at Davis's photo gallery, I become fixated by the images of the beautiful child. His or her smile is unforced and carefree, like the way I used to feel all the time.

"That's a gorgeous kid," I mention. "Boy or girl?"

"That's my son," Davis replies, his voice monotone. He points the remote at the television and starts scanning the channels. I am stunned, my mouth agape in such a large, round 'O' that my last sip of pinot threatens to escape and dribble down my chin.

"Davis!" I yell. "How can you drop a bomb like that and then act like it's no big deal? We see each other every damn day, and you never told me you had a child!"

Davis appears nonplussed. "It just never came up before, Jo."

"Never came up!!!" I screech. "I must've drilled you with a million questions about your life since I met you, and you never said anything about having a kid! What are you doing, hiding him in a closet or something?"

Davis laughs. "That's fair. I guess I . . . I'm not trying to hide anything from you, Jo. I'm going through a really bad breakup, and I just haven't felt like talking about it. It's bad enough having to live it." Davis sighs and sips his wine, his eyes drooping as they return their focus to the flickering television screen in front of us. I want to ask him more, but raise my glass to my lips instead.

We don't speak for a while. In true man-style, Davis surfs channels with aplomb. I never quite understood the frenetic yo-yoing between programs that inevitably seems to occur when a man holds a remote, but as the jumping around quite resembles the way in which I have lived my life for the last twenty years, I guess I shouldn't be judgmental.

Davis finally glances over at me cautiously. "So, I hope you're feeling better."

"Well, I don't know if I'm feeling better or just distracted from how I really feel."

Davis seems to be searching for something to say. He keeps throwing quick, sideways glances my way. He starts to speak then shuts up again and again.

"OK, I guess I've beat around the damn bush long enough," Davis finally blurts. "You're not in some scary love triangle situation where some weird dude is gonna be hiding out in my bushes with a machete or a machine gun or something, are you? I'm trying not to pry, but I am curious whether I need to be concerned for our personal safety right now."

I finally laugh for the first time in what feels like a very long time. "Don't worry about it. I hear the cops come pretty quick in this neighborhood."

"Yeah, but did you see how swift your Fred Williamson-looking friend moved in on your other friend with the Secret Service standing less than five feet away? Even on this street, I may not be able to round up the cavalry fast enough to save my scrawny behind from the likes of that guy."

I sink further into the seat cushions. "I think we're safe for now. Curt is pretty crazy, but he's probably had his fill of me for the time being."

Davis' eyebrows peak then turn toward the television.

"I guess that could be interpreted in a lewd sort of way."

"No, no. Hey, you can't help it if you're Midland's most wanted."

"Huh?" I almost spit up my last sip of wine.

"You know, the girl all the guys want," Davis comments blandly while skipping channels, eyes never leaving the TV screen.

"I'm sorry, you must be confusing me with someone who looks like my sister."

Davis finally glances back at me. "Jo, if your sister cut her hair short like yours and you put on a dress and some prissy heels, you two would look exactly alike. She wasn't the only beautiful Randolph girl who had a lot of guys interested in her in high school."

I am now rendered speechless by this revelation that I had "a lot" of admirers back in the day. Of course I had to wait twenty years to find out this fact. I'm also taken aback that Davis can use the word "beautiful" and my name in the same sentence when I look this frightening, not to mention compare me to Ann Marie in a way that's not "do" vs. "don't." I'm tempted to kiss him.

"You're being kind, Davis. I'm not convinced that I'm so popular. I'm probably just someone different from the women these guys see day in and day out around here. And there is this myth of me, the 'movie star.'" I gesture an air quote. "A myth that is pretty far removed from reality. Look, I've known both of these guys most of my life. And Willie T. and I dated in high school and are starting to reconnect. But neither of them is my boyfriend or anything. If the tabloids are right, I have enough boyfriends as it is."

"Hey, I'm . . . you don't have to explain anything to me." Davis says. "I'm the last person that needs to press you for details when I haven't exactly revealed too much to you either. Or so you've pointed out to me." He smiles faintly.

"Well, my explanations for stuff may not make any sense anyway. They're just the best ideas I can come up with in the moment. Tell me—do you think you hang out with me because of my sparkling wit, magnetic personality, and breathtaking beauty? Or am I just someone new and unusual to break up the boredom."

Davis laughs. "I'm pretty sure boredom's not the reason. My personal life is anything but boring right now." His smile starts to fade again. "I don't really analyze stuff, Jo. I just like being able to hang out with someone that makes me feel good for a change, rather than having to constantly wade through shit all the time."

Davis appears relaxed and within reach. I scoot a little closer to him on the sofa. "Well, Davis, you still haven't told me if you've locked your kid in one of these closets here, but it's OK."

The melody in Davis' laughter is back, and it's a pleasure to hear. "My kid's not in a closet, Jo. He's with his mother, which is the biggest part of my problem right now. I'd like for him to come live with me here, since she's on the road all the time, but it hasn't happened yet. One minute she says it's OK and she's bringing him here to stay with me, and the next minute she won't let me see him. Like this week . . ." Davis stops and takes a sip from his wine glass, his face a frown again. "Anyway, he's not here yet. So I can bring all kinds of wanton Babylonian women over here and let them talk endlessly about themselves." He winks at me, and a bit of the smile returns.

"So this is all just a ploy to get sex, eh Davis?"

Davis' long, low laugh returns again. "No, Jo, I'm not that lucky these days. Actually, I'm just glad to have someone to talk to who's not calling me a dumb motherfucker over and over again. And you remind me of my old life. At least the good parts – the parts I miss."

Davis stares directly into my eyes, and all I can do is babble. "I'm probably the dumb m-f'er, to tell the truth. Everything that happened today is my fault. Curt and Willie T. have had this ridiculous competitive thing going on ever since we were preschoolers. I should have known Curt would get jealous when he found out I had dinner with Willie T., but it's not like I ever agreed to date Curt or anything. I just talked to him on the phone a lot. He was the one who always called me, and . . ."

"So you've been dating the other guy, Curt's friend, and he got jealous because he thought you liked him instead because you were leading him on."

"No, it's not that . . . well, maybe it is. Lord, help me." I plop my head back against one of the weighty leather pillows. "Maybe I really am the resident harlot strumpet of Babylon."

"Without any of the benefits, huh?"

"Exactly. So maybe I should piss you off as well, so I'll be three-for-three this evening."

"Well, your love triangle did touch a nerve or two."

I try to suppress a smile. "I've gotten pretty good at pissing people off. I guess I can add this evening to my long list of embarrassments and disappointments of late."

Davis swivels in his seat to better focus on me. "Do tell."

"Oh, Jesus, I don't even know where to begin. Losing my job. Finding out my boyfriend wasn't getting divorced. Breaking his wife's nose. Trashing my ex's house. Jail . . ."

"Jail?"

"I spent the night in the county lockup. It's a long story."

"We're deep in the heart of Midland, Texas. I've got nothin' but time." There's a wicked twinkle in Davis' eye.

I take a long sip from my wineglass. "Well, as the tabloids wont let me forget, I was dating the director of this movie I was shooting. We were on set about to shoot a scene, and then this crazy woman, his ex-wife, appeared out of nowhere and jumped me. Or at least I thought she was his ex. I thought they were separated. I mean, they didn't live together anymore. Anyway, she went *gangster* on me and tried to punch me out on the set. When did white people stop being afraid of Black people anyway? I bet she wouldn't show up talking trash and jumping in people's faces and calling them 'nappy Black bitches' in Watts or Crenshaw or anyplace like that . . ."

The corners of Davis's mouth are straining not to turn up. He has a whimsical grimace as he struggles not to smile at my descent into ranting lunacy.

"*Davis!* It's not funny. It's ridiculous. Two grown-ass, educated women with careers had a knock down, drag out, roll on the ground fight in front of a boatload of people. Over a GUY! How degrading is that?"

He can no longer control himself. The laughter peals out slowly, then rapidly, like water streaming through a broken dam. "I'm sorry," Davis snorts. "Ha ha ha ha ha ha ha ha ha ha ha . . . " Davis laughs so hard that he begins to hiccup. He reaches for his glass of wine and drains it while dabbing his eyes with his forefinger.

"Ha ha very funny, Davis. I find out that the man I was head over heels for is lying to me, and I lose my job, and it's hilarious. She's not just any wife, mind you, but a rich, well-connected wife that can crush my career and completely ruin my life if she wants to. If she hasn't done it already."

Davis' belly laughs finally slow down to a snicker, and then settle into silence. He appears to be about to say something, but he refills his glass and takes a drink instead.

"Actually, I deserve to be laughed at," I go on. "I went from being what I thought was a smart, independent actress with a solid career to being some Hollywood loser's cheap mistress. I haven't read his wife's books, and I really didn't know much about her. I didn't follow up and make sure that what he was telling me about their breaking up was true. I guess I was too goo-goo eyed and caught up in the fact that I was dating this beautiful, creative man who seemed to have this amazing life. I didn't exercise any common sense. Then this whole thing happens tonight, and it's like another crazy fight to show me how stupid and out of control my life has become. Ai yai yai."

"Don't be hard on yourself," Davis says in a soft voice. "This kind of thing happens to the best of us."

"Maybe this kind of thing happens to those people that go on *Montel* or the *Rickie Lake Show*. But it's not supposed to happen to people with fancy educations whose mothers start book clubs and belong to sororities and taught their daughters to know better and have a little bit more self-respect."

"Jo, this type of thing happens to everybody. Look, my wife went out and . . ."

"Your *what?* You have a *wife!* Oh, hell, not again!" I drop my head to my lap and cover my eyes with my hands. Davis leans over to try to look at me, but I continue to cover my face. I feel his long, slender fingers rubbing my back, but I don't move.

"Jo? Hey, Jo, you OK? Look, we're not together anymore. I'm separated. I'm not exactly a shining example of how well things work out in the end, but I'm sure it'll all be OK. We'll both be OK. This shit just takes time."

I finally lift my head from my hands. As soon as I face Davis, my tears begin to overflow and run rapidly down my cheeks. "I'm such an idiot," I squeak. I try to say more, but only wails, not words, come out.

"Don't feel bad, Jo." Davis takes my hand and gives it a squeeze. "Like I said, this love triangle thing is not so unusual. Neither is punching somebody in the face or breaking a bottle of Wild Turkey over somebody's head over it." A pained version of Davis's famous grin returns.

I wipe the corners of my eyes with my hand. "You mean, it wasn't so weird for me to break Danielle Coleman's nose and then spend the night in county jail for assault?"

Davis smiles faintly. "I guess we have even more in common than we thought." He takes another long sip of wine before he speaks. "I found out that my wife was screwing one of the guys in my band—a guy that was in our wedding. That's the main reason I broke up the group and didn't go back to Austin after my mom died. A few months ago, I ran into them when I was back in Austin for the weekend to see my kid. It was in this club, and I was pretty wasted when I saw them, so I just let loose on the guy. We got into this huge bar fight, and I ended up having to spend the night in lockup. It was all pretty ugly." Davis shakes his head. "I think that was the thing that made me realize that I better change the direction of my life, especially since I have a kid. If a night in jail wasn't a red flag for me to get my shit together, then I really am a dumb motherfucker."

Davis drains his glass and scoots closer to me. "Hey, come on, jailbird. I think we could both use another drink." Davis fills both our glasses and then wraps his arm around my shoulders. I want to say more to him. I want to tell him everything that's wrong with my life, not just the stuff that can't get me arrested. I don't speak and just slump my sluggish body against his. Neither of us speaks for a very long time. We just lean against each other and stare at the TV screen, though I'm not paying attention to what we're watching. I nestle comfortably in the crook of my co-worker's arm and forget the rest of the world and everyone in it except for the two of us and the peace and quiet of our surroundings.

I'm so relaxed that I could sleep. But there's still one question burning in my brain. It's as if text messages from Rudy and Jen are popping up in my head, prodding me to find out at least this one thing.

"Hey, Davis?"

"Yep," he answers quietly.

"Was it your wife or your bandmate that you whacked with a liquor bottle?"

Davis laughs and the relaxed, musical tone returns to his voice. "Don't worry, Jo, it was the guy. I feel like breaking a bottle over Rita's head most of the time, but I was raised better than that. I typically try to be a man of peace. Though I gave up weed a long time ago to save my vocal chords, so it's harder to stay peaceful. Wine helps, though."

"Cheers." I clink his glass with my own. "By the way, I'm sorry for all my blubbering before."

"It's OK."

"No, no it's not. I mean, I'm not the victim here. And unlike you, I was the adulterer, or adulteress, or whatever you call it. I didn't know Ravi and Danielle were still together until she showed up on the set. But I still behaved badly. I don't know what got into me, but . . ." I move out of Davis's casual embrace and sit up straight. I look directly into his eyes and don't turn away, even though I'm tempted to cover my eyes in shame.

"Davis, I've got this big problem, and only my two best friends and their lawyer back in LA know about it. I don't know if anything will happen because of it, but the anxiety is killing me. I don't know what to do about it."

Davis stares at me, his eyes riveted by my unwavering gaze.

"I'll understand if you kick me out of your house and decide you don't want to come within five hundred miles of me after I tell you this."

"You kill somebody?"

"If only it was that simple. Then I'd *know* I was in trouble. No. After the fight with Danielle on the set, I drove down to Ravi's beach house, and I . . . I trashed it. I spilled wine all over the place and tore up the underwear drawer. And I wrecked his clothes and . . . and stuff like that."

Davis squints at me as if he didn't hear me correctly. "Hmmm. Woman scorned stuff? Well, that's not so unusual. Every guy's had at least one crazy girlfriend episode."

"That's not all, Davis. I . . . I might be in trouble."

I feel I can trust him. But I'm not sure I should trust my feelings these days. I'm not sure of anything anymore. But Davis's eyes are locked on mine and won't give me an easy out.

"I . . . I mean, there was a fire at my boyfriend's house right after we broke up. There's an investigator asking questions. I haven't talked to him yet. But I'm afraid he thinks I set the house on fire or something since, you know, I had this fight with Ravi's wife." Davis's narrowed eyes search mine for more answers, so I'm forced to go on. "But I know Ravi was having financial problems on the movie and didn't want to ask Danielle for more money, so . . . so he might be out for insurance money. It's all kind of suspicious."

My voice becomes very quiet, like that of a little girl. "But there's also a chance they might try to blame me for it. I could go to jail for, like, years! Decades!"

Davis stares at me slit-eyed and stern-mouthed. Not sure what to do, I don't do anything at all and wait for him to come to his senses and call the police. I didn't quite tell him the whole truth and nothing but the truth, so help me God, but even my half-truth is pretty ugly.

Davis grasps my hand and sits as upright as he can, considering the amount of wine he has consumed. "Do you have a lawyer?"

I shake my head. "I have an entertainment lawyer that helped me get out of my night in county lockup without anything on my record. But my best friends think I should talk to a real criminal lawyer about the other stuff. Some kind of investigator called both of them, and now he's left me a message too. They say I should talk to someone before calling him back. Someone down here, so I can keep it off the radar screen back in L.A. But I don't know who to call, and I can't exactly ask my folks."

Davis isn't smiling, but he isn't reaching for the phone either. Nor is he pushing me out the door and bolting the lock behind him. I can't look at him anymore. I drop my head and try to retrieve my hand from his, but he wraps both of his hands around mine and interlocks our fingers. "There's a woman, she went to Lee actually, who helped my younger cousin out with a meth bust. She's helped a lot of the Lee kids, and Lee alums for that matter, with all kinds of stuff. I can put you in touch with her if you like."

I nod my head in Davis's direction, but I don't raise my eyes.

"You might know her, actually. Paula, Paula Harris."

My eyes flash up to meet Davis's.

"I think she was in our class."

I slink back into the seat cushions and stare vacantly at the television.

"She's really great," he goes on. "Remind me to give you her number before you leave. I . . . I wish I had better advice for you, but . . . damn, Jo!" He shakes his head.

I don't respond, other than to take a very long, slow sip from my wine glass with the hand that Davis isn't clutching. Davis releases one of his hands from mine and joins me in my sipping. We sit holding hands without speaking for a long time. The room is still and soundless other than the clamor of whatever's going on on the screen in front of us. I need a change of focus from TV. From my life.

"Hey, Davis."

"Hmmm."

"I guess I see why you didn't go back to Austin after everything happened with your wife. But why stay here in Midland? What about your career? Your music?"

"Well," he drawls, "for one thing, being back in Midland made me realize that my music and my career were two different things. I had kind of lost sight of that distinction."

"I don't get you."

Davis's eyes are soft and pensive. "I was getting paid to play music. Paid pretty well, actually. But I wasn't creating anything anymore. You're an artist, Jo. You know how it is when your brain and every nerve in your body just gets flooded with, I don't know what it is. You just gotta get it out? Like that rush when you can't stop thinking and creating and thinking about creating. I hadn't felt like that in a long time. I hadn't written a single song in, like, two years, until I came home and slowed down my life and started pushing some of the more negative stuff out of it."

I recognize what he's talking about. "I hate to admit it, but when we were watching that video at my house, and when I was working on that stupid spectacle for the Bushes, all these weird, crazy ideas kept popping in my head, and I couldn't shut them off. I finished a big chunk of the first *North Dallas Forty* draft in one weekend. It was kind of like when I used to do stage work, and when I first started working in movies and TV. I took every part so seriously. These days, I can pretty much phone it in. But I used to dive into every character like it was Shakespeare, even if I was just an extra."

"See?"

"But can't you be creative someplace other than Midland?"

Davis shrugs. "I guess so. But I also needed some time and space to work on my life overall, not just the creative part of it. I needed something different than being on the road all the time and partying 'til all hours of the night and having all kinds of crazy drama day-in and day-out. I have a job with great hours here, and Mama left me a pretty nice house, so I don't have to start from scratch in Midland. Haven't you ever thought about it? Normal life, I mean?"

"What's normal anyway?" I respond. "What I find normal may be crazy for someone else and vice versa."

"You know, normal? Working and coming home before dark and

kissing your kid and grilling a big slab of steer in the backyard and making love to your wife. Not hanging out all night after a gig and then waking up at two in the afternoon and dumping your kid on your mother-in-law and never seeing him because you're on the road, and having big, drunken fights with your girl. You know what I mean?"

"I've never thought about having a wife." I take another sip of my wine. "Besides, from what I've been told, married people don't make love."

"Some of them do. Though I guess if my life is any indication, it may mean they're headed for divorce. But, I guess what I'm trying to say is that I'm tired of my life being so volatile. It takes too much out of me. My ex wants to stay on the road and live that life, but I can't do that anymore. And my son deserves better than that."

Davis leans his head on my shoulder. The pace of his wine consumption has exceeded mine practically three-fold, and he's having trouble balancing his head atop his body. I wrap an arm around his shoulders and his head settles against the base of my throat. I crook my neck to look down at his face. His eyes are closed. I lean forward and touch his lips with my own.

What the hell am I doing? I pull back and struggle to slide my arm from behind Davis's head. I should not be doing this. Rudy and Jen are right. I should stop slipping and sliding from man to man and concentrate on getting my head together. Getting my life together.

Davis grabs my hand to keep me from pulling away. He draws me close again and presses his lips very softly against mine. We wrap our arms around each other, and I slide back against the sofa as Davis shifts his body above mine.

I should stop right here, if I know what's good for me. I should leave, if I know what's good for Davis. But I really don't want to go.

CHAPTER 19 ♡

I am cotton-mouthed and bleary-eyed. I'm inexplicably clad in a large Dallas Cowboys football jersey and no pants, lying on my stomach on the wide, soft sofa with one arm dangling over the side. Davis is laid out flat as a pancake on the floor, his Texas Longhorn-boxered butt the first thing I notice when my eyes resume focus.

Lord help me, I'm hell-bound for sure. This is a clue that I *must* stop drinking.

I slowly rise to a sitting position, blinking hard at the bright sunlight streaming through the French doors. Oh God, I've been here all night! What will Mommy say? I have to get to work!

I scramble around to find my clothes. How did I get into this getup anyway? I accidentally trip over Davis and fall flat on my face, narrowly missing the edge of the coffee table. Davis finally stirs, but he's unable to sit up straight or even lift his head.

"Hmmm . . . what?" he mumbles.

"Davis, *get up!* It's like, oh hell I don't know what time it is, but we have to get to work!" I glance down at my watch and scramble to my feet, my panic turning to hysteria as I realize that my first class begins in forty-five minutes.

"Oh, no! Oh shit!" I run back and forth without direction, like a caged gerbil. "I guess I'll just have to wear the same clothes I had on yesterday. And I can't find my underwear. This is too awful!"

"Hey, calm down." Davis props himself up on one elbow and rubs his eyes with his fist. "Want some coffee?"

"*Coffee?!* Davis! How can you even think of coffee at a time like this? Get up!"

"Jo, I live like ten minutes away from Lee," he yawns. "You can shower upstairs and wear one of my shirts. I'll make us some coffee and we can drive in together."

"No, this won't cause any controversy. Owww, my head hurts."

Davis grins, "Considering what happened yesterday, I don't think you can shock anybody with anything else. Besides, everybody already thinks we're sleeping together. You know, it's like Bonnie Raitt said '*let's give 'em somethin' to talk about,*'" he croons. Davis grabs my ankle and one of my wrists and pulls me down on the ground with him. He kisses my neck, and I can't help but reciprocate. I clutch his face in my hands and draw his lips up to meet mine. I suddenly snap out of it. A vision of Principal Hardy's dippity 'do pops into my mind just in time to spoil all my fun and remind me that I'm in deep doo doo.

I shove Davis and scramble back onto my feet. I race around the room, gathering random articles of clothing in my arms. Davis ignores my mania and continues to sing as he props his back against the coffee table, despite the fact that he's late to work and surely hung over as hell. "Davis! Listen, this is not funny. We're gonna get fired!!!"

Davis rolls back onto the floor, chuckling and snorting as I start to pace again and gnaw at my nails. "Go on, Jo. Try to get yourself together, if it makes you feel better. The bathroom's up the steps, first door on the left. My room is the messy one across the hall. Just help yourself to whatever's in there that's clean."

Forty-five minutes later, Davis and I approach the school in his Mini Cooper. I notice a few photographers on the sidewalk, barred by a few of Midland's finest from getting any closer to the school entrance. I duck down in my seat, and Davis proceeds down the drive toward the parking lot. He parks behind one of the huge Go Army trailers, and we hurry toward the janitor's entrance from which we made our escape last night.

I'm a bit more composed now, I think. Though baggy, my borrowed shirt is relatively crisp and clean, tucked neatly into yesterday's slacks. I leave my jacket, the one that was so prominently displayed on the evening news, in the car. I'm showered and scrubbed and sober, though a vein in my left temple is throbbing in a subtle but insistent manner. I'll go to the nurse to get a pain reliever or two or three before class. Though I can't stop thinking about last night, I try to push it out of my mind for the time being. Davis and I present a composed, united front as we stroll down the school's main corridor. My calm, cool and collection shatters at once, however, as Principal Hardy steps out of his office to greet us.

"Oh, you're just the two I was looking for. You have a minute?"

Like guilty school kids without a hall pass, Davis and I skulk behind Principal Hardy, ducking our heads to avoid greeting the secretary and assorted other beings in the waiting room as we walk into his office, and he closes the door behind us.

"Have a seat, have a seat. Want some coffee? Doreen makes the best coffee. *Doreen!* Doreen, honey, can you bring us some coffee?" Principal Hardy bellows into his intercom machine.

As Doreen hands us our large ceramic mugs of steaming black Maxwell House, both Davis and I sit and stare at the wall behind Hardy's head, like a couple of teenage truants. We sip our coffee in silence as we await our sentences.

"Now first I want to thank both of you for all your hard work with the students to get them ready to perform for our president."

"Thank you, Principal Hardy," I croak in my smallest, meekest voice. "Though it was the kids. They really came through for us." I glance over at Davis for confirmation, but he continues to stare straight ahead, mute as a mummy.

"Now, Jo, Davis, please don't take this the wrong way, because I really am pleased with the work you both have been doing around here. I really am. And I really like you a lot, but . . ."

"But?" Davis sneers at Principal Hardy. Of course Davis can be cocky and sarcastic. He's a white male in America who lives next to a country club. I, on the other hand, cannot afford to be so confident. I'm bound to be fired for sure. I don't know why I suddenly care so much about keeping this job, but I'm scared to death.

Principal Hardy rolls his eyes wearily. He doesn't seem quite ready for the revolution, particularly when it's being waged by a blond-haired, blue-eyed member of the ruling class. "I think it would be best for everybody if you would keep your romances under wraps and to yourselves. Yesterday was a lot more excitement than we needed around here on that day of all days. It wasn't necessarily the best example for Lee High, or Midland for that matter, to present to the president of the United States. Not to mention the rest of the world. We made our home, the president's home, the laughing stock of the country. Just look at some of these headlines." Principal Hardy begins tossing papers and printouts from a pile on his desk in our direction. The "boyfriend brawl" is featured on the front page of Midland's daily newspaper, right alongside a short piece on the death of a Midland teenager in Iraq and a photo and longer story covering the Rebel-red pantsuit the first lady donned at yesterday's rally.

"And, I mean, we're talkin' about school kids here. Minors. What kind of example are we setting for them? We want to make sure we're not sending them the, you know, the wrong kind of messages . . ."

"What do you mean by 'wrong kind of messages?'" Davis retorts.

"I mean, you know, with teachers bringin' their personal lives into the school building and causing all kinds of violence." Principal Hardy takes a long drag of his Maxwell House, seemingly unphased by the scorching hot temperature. "And then there's the romances among the faculty members and all. And with the two of you in particular, I mean, well, Davis, I don't want to judge y'all. That's the Lord's job, praise Him. But we don't want to have the wrong sort of influence on the kids here." Principal Hardy again raises his coffee cup to his lips, and his eyes meet Davis's stare down. I, on the other hand, decide to carefully examine the coarse coffee grounds settled in the bottom of my mug.

"Tom, with all due respect, there are 'faculty romances' all over this place. I mean, Harlan and May have been screwing for as long as anybody can remember. Everyone here knows it, including all the students. Including everybody in Midland, for that matter. Everybody other than their spouses, when that's the real threat to the kids. You ever see the gun rack on the back of May's husband's truck? So I'm not quite sure what you're getting at."

"Well, there was all that ruckus yesterday."

"How do you know that fight had anything to do with Jo anyway? Are you just making assumptions because it was a couple of Black men fighting?"

"No, Davis, I'm assuming it was about Jo because Curt Dupree was yelling 'that bitch, Jo Ella' at the top of his lungs for over an hour for everyone and their children and grandparents to hear, that's why. And then there's the two of you carousing all over the place. Like I said, I don't want to judge y'all. That's for the Lord Almighty to do. But I do have to keep order in my school and try to set a good example for these young people we're tryin' to teach here. It's hard enough tryin' to keep them on the straight and narrow without our teachers havin' such a liberal attitude about their own behavior. Now, I know you two have been away in more, well, flexible places, but we're just good ol', traditional, God-lovin' folks here in Midland, and . . ."

"Tom, that's a bunch of crap, and you know it!" The volume rises in Davis's voice, and his face turns from slightly tan to cherry red. Rather than becoming shrill or frenetic, a solid, stronger bass note emerges in Davis's speech as his tone becomes more forceful. "We all know what this is really about, don't we? It's just plain offensive."

We all stare at each other for a few moments that feel monstrously long. I try to think of what Mommy would say in this situation, but there is no pixie smiling on my shoulder today. Of course, Mommy would never get herself into such a pickle.

"Uh-hmm." I steer my stutter into a fumbled cough and pick at a loose thread in the cuff of the oversized oxford Davis lent me.

"Well, then," Principal Hardy exhales. "Point taken with Harlan and May. I'll speak to them. But you gotta understand, Davis, that even though this just happened yesterday, there are already a bunch of folks pressing me to get rid of Jo over this."

My eyes widen, and I almost tip over my coffee cup.

"Actually, there are people who've just been waitin' for an opportunity to serve up both your heads on a platter just because they don't like you, and they don't like the two of you bein' friends. Look, it's not that I don't value the two of you, because I do. I know you mean well, and, hey, we're all sinners. I'm not gonna fire Jo for this incident last night or anything, but for me to be able to keep her here, to keep both of you here, you gotta help me out and be more discreet about your business. Just, folks, let's just keep our personal lives personal, OK?"

"But," I finally find my voice, "but, we're . . ."

"Like I said, I don't want you to think I don't appreciate what you two're doin' and all. This whole year I kept hearing how much the students like you, Davis, even though there are folks on the faculty, and I won't name names, who think you bring a little bit too much of the hippie influence to our kids here. But I don't agree with 'em. You bring out somethin' real nice in the kids you teach. And my instincts told me that you were gonna really be good with our kids too, Jo. That you might reach 'em in a way that Tyler or Hightower or a lot of the other teachers wouldn't be able to do. Like you made them understand how important last night was in a way the other folks preachin' at 'em can't do, even though I know you don't quite share the same amount of affection for Mr. Bush that the rest of us do here." He glances over at Davis. "Or at least most of us. Now, don't get me wrong. Tyler's a good woman, a good teacher, and her heart's in the right place. But the young people don't relate to her as well, even though you're the same age."

I'm the same age as Sue Ann Tyler! *Lord* help me!

"Thank you, sir. But . . ."

Principal Hardy rises from his seat to end the meeting.

"So I think we're done here. Keep me posted on the play. I can't wait to see it."

I don't wait for Davis or even turn to see his reaction. I slam my mug on the desktop and rush out of the room. I am sweating and my heart is pounding hard and fast. A wave of anxiety rushes over me. I don't know why, but I hurry down the hall to get out of reach and out of sight before Davis can catch up with me. I wade my way through the crush of students toward my classroom. I can't shake Davis, however. He is suddenly strolling leisurely beside me. He doesn't appear rattled at all by what just happened.

"Well, that was weird," he drawls. "You OK?"

I shake my head. "Look, Davis, I need some space, OK? Can you just leave me alone?"

The playful glint in Davis' eyes loses its glimmer, and his lids narrow as he tries to read my face.

"Yea. OK, Jo." Davis stops walking and allows me to continue down this path alone. I turn and glance back at him. He isn't moving. His hands are stuffed in his pockets and his head is cocked to the side as he watches me walk past my classroom toward the computer lab, which is obviously not where I intend to go.

My cell phone vibrates in my pants pocket. The word "Mommy" is lit up on the screen, and I realize that I finally have to face the music.

"Jo Ella?"

Like she has done throughout my life, Mommy artfully turns my name into a million questions that demand to be answered.

"Oh, Mommy, I'm sorry, I . . ."

"Jo Ella, we were worried sick about you."

"I'm sorry. I should have called, I . . ."

"Yes, you certainly should have called us. For all we knew, you were in a ditch by the side of the road or something."

"No, Mommy, I was with Davis. I . . . we . . ."

"I know. We saw you with him on TV last night."

"Oh. I . . . I know I should have called. But I drank too much wine, and I . . . I guess I fell asleep. The next thing I knew, it was morning and I was still on Davis's sofa."

"Well. In the future, why don't you call us *before* you go out drinking with some man so your parents won't be up all night worrying and thinking you're dead."

"OK."

"And, Jo Ella, some man called here asking for you?"

"Man?" I stop walking.

"A Mister Hanks? He said it was urgent?"

Lord help me. "I don't know who that is. I . . ."

"So you'll need his number so you can find out?"

Though she's not in view, I can feel Mommy smiling wickedly, expecting answers I'm not prepared to give her. "No, no . . . I will get it later. I'm walking and don't—"

"So I'll see you this evening?" she interrupts.

"Yes." My voice is very small.

I click off my phone and turn back to see if Davis is still there, but he's gone. My head is pounding. I trudge down the hallway to my classroom and shut the door behind me. Of course I have no Tylenol. I drop into my desk chair and turn my phone back on.

"Hey, Willie T., I'm really sorry for everything. I don't want to leave things like . . . like we did last night. Can we talk?" I don't know what else to say to his voicemail, so I hang up. Why did he react like that? I guess I don't have standing to judge. Willie T. is a good guy who doesn't deserve and probably doesn't have the patience for this level of crazy.

And Davis . . . what is wrong with me? Why was I such a bitch? I owe him an apology as well. My temples are throbbing. I shut my eyes and rub the sides of my head. But there's no relief. I should see the nurse. Perhaps she can at least help my head, even though I have no idea what to do about everything else that ails me.

CHAPTER 20 ♡

"Y'all better get on away from here!" I hear Uncle Buddy yell. Mommy and I race to the foyer. The door is open, and Uncle Buddy is on the front porch, waving a pistol at the scattering of photographers parked across the street from my parents' house.

"Buddy, get yourself inside of this house this instant!" Mommy hisses. She grabs the strap of his overalls and pulls him into the foyer, shoving the door closed with her elbow. I turn the deadlock, while Mommy disarms Uncle Buddy. She points the barrel of the pistol away from us and expertly removes the bullets from the chamber. Suddenly the phone starts to ring.

"Oh . . . sugar!" Mommy exclaims and stomps into the kitchen. "Oh sugar!" is the closest Mommy comes to swearing. Uncle Buddy and I silently follow her. We both know better than to cross her right now. Mommy tosses the bullets into the garbage can and places the pistol on the counter.

"Randolph residence," she says into the phone receiver. Suddenly she extends the phone to me."

"Who is it?" I whisper.

"It's Mister Hanks again, Jo Ella."

"He's probably from the tabloids, Mommy. Just tell him I can't talk to him. Tell him to call my agent instead."

Mommy doesn't move a muscle. She stares at me, phone still extended in my direction.

"Please, Mommy. I promise I will talk to him. I just need to talk to Jen and my publicist first."

Mommy doesn't move for a few moments. "Mister Hanks, you will have to call her agent if you need something from her or want to arrange to speak to her. Now please don't disturb my household again, sir. Thank you."

Mommy slams the phone down, grabs Uncle Buddy's pistol and storms out of the kitchen.

"Sugar, can you hand me a glass?" Uncle Buddy asks. He looks shell-shocked.

"Sure, Uncle Buddy. I think I could use one of those myself."

I'm having a rough week. I don't know who Mister Hanks is, but I'm not ready to find out. I'm still ducking photographers. And Willie T. never called me back. Also, I haven't spoken to Davis. I've started to call him a million times, but I can't go through with it. I don't know what to say, because whenever I open my mouth, I seem to stick my foot into it.

Mommy has said fewer than five sentences to me since she called me at school Friday morning. Daddy ducks behind his newspaper whenever I walk into the room. And to add to my general sense of shame about my life, I'm ashamed about staying out all night. This is the longest stretch I've spent at home since college. So none of us knows how to deal with the reality that I am now a middle-aged woman who spends the night with men instead of the girl who spent all her nights in her teenage bedroom, where the photos of my teen idols remain tacked on the walls to this day.

I throw on a bikini and tie a sarong around my waist. I retire to the pool with my iPod and my writing tablet. I drag a lounger under the picnic umbrella to keep from burning to a crisp and stretch out like a slug. I don't know how long I lie there, motionless, listening to a mix of world music and techno. Suddenly a shadow looms over me, and I notice the lean figure of my sister staring down at me.

"So I hear you didn't come home the other night," she hisses.

"I don't want to talk about it, Ann Marie."

Ann Marie grabs a patio chair and drags it under my umbrella. "Willie T., Curt, Davis? Jo Ella, do you know what you're doing? One day you're with Willie T., and he's calling Claude to tell him what a great time you guys had. And then a couple of days later, you're sleeping with Davis? Willie T. really likes you!"

I start to retort, but Ann Marie cuts me off. "I'm not trying to be a bitch, Jo Ella. I know you're not heartless and wouldn't hurt Willie T. on purpose. I'm just not sure you think about the stuff you do before you do it."

I stare at my sister's lovely face. Typically, I'm able to get mad at her even when I know she's right. Sometimes *especially* because I know she's right. But I can't do it today.

"I'm sorry, Ann Marie. I'm not really sure what I feel. And by the time I figure it out, the summer will be over, and I'll be heading back to L.A. Or at least I hope so. And then, what?"

"Well, I'm concerned about you," she says softly. "But Willie T. is our friend, so I can't help but be concerned about him too. I can't defend you when you lead him on and hurt his feelings."

I can't argue with her. "Willie T.'s a great guy, and I'm not trying to lead him on. I really like him. A lot. We're different, but I'm definitely attracted to him and had a good time with him at dinner. The problem is that I also have a good time with Davis. I'm starting to realize that I really like him too. We're more alike in a lot of ways. But, honestly, I don't know what I'm doing. I think I need to slow down. With everyone."

"I agree," she responds.

"But the problem is, someone like you can have a rational thought and then behave rationally. I'll have the rational thought, but that's as far as it goes."

"At least you finally acknowledge that fact," Ann Marie smiles. "That's progress!"

"Besides, you and Little Claude were like my Ken and Barbie fantasy of Black Love. If you two have problems, there's absolutely no hope for someone like me. Especially with someone as perfect as Willie T. He's got to have some flaw, Ann Marie. Like he secretly collects kewpie dolls as a hobby or kicks puppies when nobody's looking."

Ann Marie starts to laugh. I don't see her laugh too often anymore.

Her real laugh, as opposed to the fake one she affects to be polite. Her real laugh is totally out of character with the rest of her demeanor. She throws her head back with her mouth open and caws like a crow.

"You're out of your mind," she says as she rises and leaves.

I stick my ear buds back into my ears and return to my playlist and sloth. I loaf by the pool for the rest of the day, until the sun dips below the edge of Mommy's mid-rise, wooden fence. When the evening's mosquitoes shoo me from my chaise, I move inside and stretch out on my bed with my laptop.

I'm going to Google myself and my boyfriends through the years. I wonder if I'll discover some theme or pattern to my life that will reveal something greater and deeper than the flitting around of a flaky actress. Jen always wisecracks that I'm attracted to "anything with an accent," and as I scan the men of my life on the Internet, I realize that she may be right. There's Ravi, of course. Then there's the Cape Verdian soccer player, the Ghanaian PhD student, the South African painter, the Australian surfer, the Scottish/Nigerian drummer, and the Jamaican playwright I met in London. Even my college boyfriend had a Brooklyn accent, which is pretty foreign for a girl who grew up in West Texas. I learn that he now manages a venture capital firm in San Jose and was one of *Silicon Valley Magazine*'s top ten tech entrepreneurs of 2002. He's also married to a woman with highlighted hair who dresses like my sister and raises money for after-school arts programs. Rats.

I also look up Willie T. There are archived football articles from the *Reporter-Telegram* and the *Bryan/College Station Eagle*; a notice of a charity golf tournament hosted by his fraternity; and an elaborate website for his family's funeral home, featuring a handsome photo of Willie T. and his Dad at the door of the long, white-washed structure that serves as our community's way station between this world and the next one. There's not much else about him online that doesn't relate to football or funerals. When I Google myself, however, there's a litany of stories and photos of my triumphs and foibles, professional and personal, and the outfits I wore through all of them. His life is private and quiet, mine is loud and always on stage. How quickly would he get sick of me, after the high school nostalgia wore off? Who am I kidding? He's already sick of me! And can I blame him?

At about two in the morning, I Google Davis Farenthold. The website for Ionic Bond, an eclectic group of guys who met in the Lee High Chemistry Club, has not been updated to remove its guitarist and lead vocalist from the lineup. A sepia-toned photo of five guys and a girl outside an abandoned Esso station in the desert somewhere displays a Hispanic guy in Elvis Costello glasses and motorcycle boots, a pale, buzz-cut guy in a plaid shirt opened to reveal a Radiohead tee underneath, a bearded Black guy with waist-length dreadlocks holding a pair of drumsticks, and a Bono type with toned biceps and dark, curly hair in a short-sleeved dress shirt and a striped skinny tie. There is a woman, whom I presume to be Davis's wife. She's a beauty, with glowing bronze skin and large, dark eyes. I can't tell her ethnicity. She resembles a Brazilian swimsuit model, with tousled black curls and dark, dancer-like limbs. In the center of the group is a tousled, stubbled Davis. He's staring directly into the lens with a gaze that is as searing as the desert landscape that surrounds him.

There are lots of reviews—the *Austin Chronicle*, the *Dallas Observer*, the *Nashville Scene*, the *Village Voice*, *Blender*, *Billboard* —most of them good. Davis's performances are "blues-y and passionate," his voice described as "silken bits of Lyle Lovett laced with the gritty energy of a Pentecostal preacher." Ionic Bond brought down the house at South by Southwest when they ended their set of original songs with an improvised, funked-up medley of bandmember favorites as varied as Willie Nelson's "Bloody Mary Morning," the Kinks' "You Really Got Me," Bob Marley's "Stir it Up" and Devo's "Whip It." Rita Lewis is cited for her gutsy, gospel-inspired vocals on the band's cover of "Gimme Shelter" at the Aspen Music Festival.

I read posts scripted by the other band members about the breakup. I scan the fanzines and the music blog musings about the band's demise and hopeful reunion, now that Rita Lewis has left to sing backup for Bryan Adams. I read the lyrics to songs Davis wrote and watch video clips of his performances. I spin explanations and rationales and stories of his life from the bits I piece together from around the web, the way a fan gets to know their favorite star from the pages of *Star* and the *Enquirer*. It's filling but hollow, like a low-calorie snack food.

The next thing I know, it's almost noon. I'm lying on top of my bed, my arm draped over the keyboard of my laptop, which has joined me in sleep mode. The house is empty, a residue of sausage patties and coffee lingering in the air from my parents' pre-church breakfast. A sausage biscuit on a small plate is covered in Saran Wrap with a note penned in Mommy's elongated script. "*Jo Ella. We'll be back around 2.*" I pour a cup of cold coffee and munch my breakfast in silence. I don't turn on the television or look at the headlines of Daddy's neatly folded Sunday newspaper. Daddy must be really upset with me if he's willing to escort Mommy to church more than once a season. I wash my plate and return to my room to search for my cell phone among the rubble on my desk.

"Leave a message." Davis's voicemail greeting is short and sweet.

"Davis, I . . ." I don't know what message to leave, don't know the best way to say that I'm sorry and want to see him. So I just hang up.

I spend the rest of the day sifting through my script for *North Dallas Forty*. Willie T. never responds to my messages, nor does Davis respond to my lack of one. I assume that Davis recognizes my phone number when it pops up on his cell phone screen, but perhaps he doesn't. That's an easier explanation to swallow than the thought that he might not care. Luckily, Uncle Buddy and Aunt Lula come over for Sunday dinner and provide a welcome distraction from my angst-ridden thoughts and the awkward silences between me and my parents. I head to bed early, but I toss and turn the entire night.

I finally get out of bed and head out to the patio, since sleep is futile. I stretch out on my favorite lounger in the backyard and cradle my Blackberry in my hand. It's too early in the morning to call anyone in Midland and too late at night to call anyone in L.A.

I scroll through my texts and see Ravi's most recent message. *You can't run from me forever, Jo.* I stare at it until the light goes off on my screen, and Ravi's words turn black. Sleep-deprived and solitary in the murky hours before daybreak, my judgment is dim, and I don't have any of my sponsors around me to remind me why it's not a good idea to call Ravi. I'm sure he's either asleep or partying, so I won't have to talk to him directly and can just leave him a message.

"Jo?" I can't believe he picked up at this ungodly hour. "I've been trying to reach you for *aaages*." Ravi dispenses with formalities. There is no "hello" or "how have you been" to bridge the cavern that contains everything that has happened to each of us since we last saw each other.

I'm faintly relieved to hear his voice. The feeling passes as fast as the impulse that prompted me to dial his number. I don't have to feign annoyance with him to save face. "Ravi, I intentionally called you when I thought you were asleep so that I could tell you to leave me alone without ever having to speak to you again."

"I *caan't* leave you alone, Jo. I can't stop thinking about you. I'm just *sooo* sorry about everything, and I never got a chance to talk to you about what's gone on."

The soft lilt of his pleading voice normally turns me to mush. But the more he speaks, the more my brain takes over where my heart left off. "Yes, Ravi, you are sorry," I snap. "A sorry excuse for a human being if I ever met one."

"Come on, Jo, give me a *breeak*," he jeers, his lilt turning lecherous.

"Give you a *break?!* Are you kidding me?"

"No, no, I'm sorry," he backtracks. "I just have wanted to talk to you since, since, well, I haven't had a chance to explain . . ."

"What is there to explain?" My voice is calm and steady like the tone I've used in acting roles, never real life. "You're married. Not to me. What else is there to say?"

"Look!" Ravi's voice starts off urgent, but he catches himself. He slows and deepens his speech into the alluring tone he used to turn on when he was trying to seduce me. "I don't love Danielle anymore, Jo. I mean, I *caare* about her, but I'm not in love with her. I doubt I ever was. It's terrible, but true. I was a kid when I met her, and I was in awe of her. I was amazed that someone as accomplished as her actually took me seriously. She saw more than the stupid *Real World* guy."

"Ravi . . ."

"No, Jo, listen to me. You think you know everythin' but you don't. Danielle and I have lived separate lives for a while now. It was a mutual thing, so I misled you when I said she was the one who broke it off. We haven't divorced, but we haven't lived together for a while. I appreciate what Danielle's done for me, but I've grown up and moved on. I should have ended things with her before getting involved with anyone else, but then I met you and there's the movie, and . . ."

"Ravi," I cut him off, "that sounds worse than the soap opera we were shooting. Even if I accept that everything you say is true, it doesn't matter."

"But it does matter, Jo. I know I didn't tell you the complete truth, but I never lied about how I felt about you. I just wanted us to get through the movie before getting out of this situation with Danielle. That's probably selfish, but I *caan't* lose this opportunity."

My stomach begins to churn. This is wrong. "I don't want you to call me anymore, Ravi. Let's just move on with our lives, OK?"

"I *haave* to see you, Jo," he implores. "Just agree to see me. If you still feel the same way, then so be it. But we *caan't* stop having feelings for each other just because, because of some silly incident."

"Some silly incident?" At one time I would have screeched, but this time I laugh. "Like your wife assaulting me and getting me sacked from my job and thrown in jail? You mean, that incident? We all know I'm crazy, but do you think I'm stupid too? It may have taken us an extra couple of years longer than everybody else to find out that slavery was over here in Texas, but we eventually figured it out, you know?"

"I just . . ."

"Ravi, don't call me anymore," I say sternly and slowly, without drawing from any of my prior acting roles to tell me what to say or how to say it. "If you call me or text me again, I'm going to call the police."

"Shouldn't *yooou* be the one who's afraid that I'll call the police?" His tone is no longer meek or pleading. It's now ominous, like the sea pulling away from the shore just before the tsunami hits.

"What are you talking about?" Ravi's threat chips away at my new-found cool, the hot air of his rhetoric melting the edges of the glacier like so many greenhouse gasses. "Uh, your wife started the fight, right? Everyone saw that, right? I could have pressed charges against her instead of, instead of the other way around, you know?"

"But what about my house," Ravi continues nonplussed. "Weren't you the one who torched my house, Jo?"

"What do you mean?" I ask with relative calm, considering my racing pulse and the rat-a-tat of my heart.

"My house? The fire at the beach house?"

"What?! What happened?"

"There was a fire at the beach house the same day you and Danielle fought on the set. Now you're going to tell me you don't know anything about it?"

"Oh my God!" I gasp dramatically.

"Danielle told me to get my shit out of the beach house and followed me down there to *screeam* bloody murder while I was at it. The place was ablaze when we got there. Luckily the fire department made it there minutes after we did. They were able to put it out before it sacked the whole place or affected the neighbors, but there was still a lot of damage."

"That's awful, Ravi. I loved that place. Wait . . . I thought you bought that with your TV royalties. What was that big story you told me about sleeping on sofas doing appearances at malls and car shows to save money? The beach house was Danielle's?"

"Well, yah. I mean, it was an investment place, Jo. Danielle gave it to me to manage when we were first married."

"You take all of this from someone you don't even love? You're a son of a bitch, you know that?" I sneer. I can't help myself, though my taunt feels hollow. "Was anyone hurt in the fire?"

"No. No one was in the house, thank God," he continues. "There was a lot of damage, but no one was hurt. We lost some of the furniture and a few paintings. Other than a few art pieces, we didn't keep very many valuable things there. Luckily the firemen salvaged a lot of the valuables. It's quite *straange* that the neighbors weren't affected, since the houses are so close together. But these fires seem to have a mind of their own."

"Did anyone see anything?" I prod. "You know, that could help you figure out what happened?"

"No, nothing." The edge in his voice deflates. "You know people are only out at the beach on weekends, typically. We hoped the police would find leads by interviewing cleaning people and gardeners and such, but they've run into a spot of trouble."

"Trouble?"

"Well, no one wants to let on about the people they hire, because then they would have to admit they're all paying people under the table who might not have their proper papers. And all the places have been bought up by weekenders who are never around, so nobody saw anything."

"No one is around unless they're using the places to shack up with their mistresses, that is," I snipe.

"Hey, darling, it's not like you didn't get anything out of this whole thing. We had a good run, didn't we? There was the movie, the gifts, and the trips—India, Barcelona, Capri, the Maldives. Am I leaving anything out?"

"So, we're like you and Danielle? The value of our relationship is the cost of the trips and the *stuff* I got out of it, is that it?'

"That's not what I'm saying at all, Jo, and you know it."

I raise my eyes to the heavens and notice the sky has turned from midnight blue to bluish-grey. I search for the first points of light of the day, but they're not yet apparent. "Look, Ravi, we had a great time together while it lasted. But a sham like that couldn't go on forever. Haven't we been hurt enough and hurt enough people already? Why can't we just move on like adults and be done with it?"

"OK, Jo, I'm going to level with you." He pauses for quite a few moments before continuing. "I need you to come back to L.A. and finish the movie."

"Are you *kidding* me?"

"Regan took the rushes to Lifetime and they *loove* what they've seen so far. They're talking about green lighting not just the movie, but a full series based on it. A real soap opera, five days a week. They love the MTV/reality TV twist on the whole soap formula."

"So, you got what you wanted," I reply in a calm manner that surprises me. "Though the last time I saw you, you didn't want to be on TV. You called Regan a 'fucking moron' for suggesting a Lifetime pitch, if my memory serves me. Look, Ravi, why don't you just cut me out of the movie and do it with someone else? You can go and make a boatload of money and leave me alone for good."

"They won't buy the rights unless I finish the pilot and you're in it. They really like you, Jo. And even if they didn't, they won't give me the money to re-shoot the whole thing, since it's almost finished. And Danielle *def-in-i-tely* won't give me anymore money. Why do you think I've been doing so much to make amends with her and help her save face in the press? I need to finish the movie, and I can't do that without you at this point. I won't be able to get the network to buy in unless you commit to at least finishing the film and the first round of episodes."

"You've really got a lot of nerve, you know that? And how does Danielle feel about me coming back and working with you?"

"Well, she has to accept it because it's the only way she can . . . just let me worry about the wife, OK? I just need, I mean, I *waant* you to come back. I'll double what I agreed to pay you once we get the Lifetime funds. I'll take it out of my own cut if I have to."

I start to think about it, consider it just a little bit. Then I notice that pesky pixie fluttering near my nose. This time I don't swat Mommy away or try to ignore her.

"No."

"Come on, Jo, be reasonable. This could work out really well for both of us."

"No."

"You know you're still under contract. I'll sue you and make you do it."

"Your wife fired me, didn't she? And even if she didn't, you can't make me do anything. You can sue me for money, but you can't make me work, that much I know. So go ahead. Good luck squeezing blood out of this turnip."

"Then I'll just tell the cops that I think you're the one who set my house on fire."

"Fuck you! You can't prove that. Fuck you!"

"No, I think you're the one that's really going to be *fucked* if you don't come to your senses."

"I don't think so, Ravi! It's pretty obvious that you're overextended and trying to set me up. Big coincidence that your wife picks a fight with me on the same day that there's a fire at a house that I hear is insured for a lot more than it's worth. Yeah, Ravi, I have my sources. You say Danielle gave you that place to manage? Well you won't receive a nice, hefty check for damages, will you, if there's any question that you or Danielle were at fault."

"I'll take my chances." His voice is chilly. "I thought you didn't know anything about the fire, Jo."

"I didn't know any of the details, Ravi, only rumors. I haven't really been returning calls that relate to you these days, if you haven't noticed."

"Well, either way, why don't you think about it and get back to me. But I want to start shooting again within the next few weeks, so don't take too long. Ciao, *daarling*."

I hear the clatter of breakfast pots and pans somewhere in the distance. It must be five o'clock, if Mommy's up. I curl into a ball and pull my knees tight against my chest. I bury my face against my knees so that no one can see me cry, even though there is no one in sight.

CHAPTER 21 ♡

Maybe a little morning yoga will clear my mind of Ravi. I ditch the idea and decide to get to work early for a change. I slink into Davis's classroom and drop a revised draft of *North Dallas Forty – The Musical!* onto his desk. I notice the remnants of a lesson on the physical properties and phases of matter scribbled in Davis's erratic script across the blackboard. I press my finger in the chalk dust and follow the curves and lines he made with his hands.

"Jo?"

"Aaargh!" I scream with a start. Davis is standing at the opposite end of the room underneath a large mural of the periodic table. He is collating a set of papers on the long, low bookcase bordering the back wall of the classroom. A trace of darkness has settled underneath his eyes. Though he appears tired, the rest of his appearance is relatively tidy, the tail of his shirt tucked into new-ish jeans that do not yet appear to have been run through the rinse cycle a thousand times.

"You startled me, Davis. I didn't realize anyone was here."

He says nothing and just stares at me as he sits atop the credenza and sets down the sheets of paper he was holding in his hand before I interrupted him. I can't bring myself to look at him directly. I look down at the manuscript I just set on his desk.

"This is just, I mean, I just wanted to leave you an updated copy of the play. It needs some more editing, but . . ." my voice trails off.

"OK."

I glance up to find the same, stoic stare. There are a million things I want to say to him, but nothing I really feel, nothing meaningful will come forth from my lips. I drop my eyes and fill the void between us with rambling instead. "I guess we should think about tryouts and rehearsals and everything. I mean, if you still want to work on it. If not, I can maybe make up some stupid lyrics to some Top 40 songs and ask Sue Ann Tyler or somebody to help me with the instrumentation, or something like that."

"I'll read it," he responds flatly. "I've already done most of the music based on your earlier stuff."

"OK," I say and turn to leave. Davis doesn't respond or react to my departure.

I make my way to my own classroom, my gait sluggish and slow. I pass the bulletin board and check my sign-up sheet to see who is auditioning for the play. The list is so long that the names fill every space on the page and spill over onto the other side. I need more actors than my drama class can fill, so there are quite a few names I don't recognize. Every one of my drama kids has signed up. Everyone except Qiana.

Qiana hasn't been to school since Wednesday, and I don't see her in English or Drama class today. As I leave Drama, I see Davis coming out of the music room. His eyes waver uncertainly as he notices me barreling toward him.

"Hey, Davis," I call out. I jog toward Davis and grab his arm. "Did Qiana show up for chemistry today?"

Davis's eyes narrow. "No, she didn't. I was gonna ask the office if she called in sick. Is there a problem?"

"I don't know. I wouldn't necessarily worry if a kid missed a couple of classes. But she hasn't been to school since last Wednesday, and she didn't sign up for the play. She also missed the Bush thing."

"I'll walk with you to the office."

I'm not certain why I am so worried about Qiana, but some gut instinct tells me that something is wrong.

"No, her mother didn't call us," Doreen tells us as she scans the school roster. "She didn't call in sick or anything. I tried the house earlier today, but no one answered."

"I'll stop by her house on my way home," I say and hurry out of the office. I saw Qiana crying last week, but it's probably presumptuous for me to assume that something is seriously wrong. These kids are in summer school for a reason, so it's probably not out of the ordinary for any of them to skip school from time to time or to forget to call. But I seemed to be getting through to Qiana. She always came to class, always turned in her assignments on time. She seemed to be opening up more and shedding her shyness with each passing day. I've seen her toting books that I didn't assign her to read, and she seemed enthusiastic about the play. I loved it when she told me she might try out to be the over-bearing team booster, even though the part is scripted for a white male.

I swing open the door of my unlocked car and am startled to see Davis settling into my passenger seat. I didn't even notice him walk with me to my car.

"You know where she lives?" he asks as he pulls copies of *Entertainment Weekly* and *The Hollywood Reporter* from under his rear and tosses them onto the back seat.

"Yeah," I say as I start up the car. I hope this is not the wrong move. I don't want to offend Qiana or scare her by showing up on her door-step. But I'm not sure she would let me know if something was really wrong with her. There's a crack in the door, but it isn't fully open yet.

As I pull into the dirt-covered driveway in front of Qiana's wood-frame house, I realize that Davis and I have not spoken a word to each other the entire trip. I obsessed over him all weekend, but now that I have him captive in my car, I ignore him altogether. I don't dwell on it as I slow to a stop and step out of the car. The front door of the house is open behind a closed screen with a long tear in the mesh. Davis stands slightly behind me as I rap my knuckles against the wooden frame of the screen door.

We wait a number of minutes, but no one appears. I raise my fist to knock again, but I lower it as I notice movement in the darkness beyond the door. Qiana appears, toting a baby on her hip. The infant has only a few whisps of hair and is wearing a diaper and nothing else. Qiana's eyes grow wide, and she stops before us on the other side of the screen without opening it.

"Miss Randolph?"

"Hi, Qiana. I'm sorry to drop in like this. I was just . . . I was a bit worried, because you haven't been to school, and the office said you didn't call or anything. I just wanted to make sure you were OK."

The fear in her face reveals her youth. Qiana says nothing and drops her eyes as she bounces the baby up and down.

"Qiana, darlin', can you come out and talk to us a minute? We won't hold you up for long, I promise." Davis's voice is gentle. I turn to look at him, but his eyes are focused on Qiana. His gaze is soft and he smiles slightly.

Qiana steps out onto the porch and sits on a metal chair with a woven plastic seat the color of sunshine. I sit on a matching seat next to her, and Davis leans against the portion of the porch rail that is not loose or unhinged.

"What's his name?" Davis asks as he reaches out both hands toward the infant.

"Marcellus," she whispers.

"Like the Roman," I say.

"Or the musician," Davis offers. "Or Cassius Clay's middle name before he changed it. Can I hold him?"

Qiana appears apprehensive, but she hands over the child to Davis, who holds him in a soft hug against his chest. "I have a baby boy," he smiles as he pats the baby on the back. "He's not such a baby anymore, though. He's almost four."

"Is this your baby brother?" I ask.

Qiana shakes her head. Davis and I exchange looks. A flicker of worry appears in his eyes as he glances at me and then returns his gaze to Qiana.

"Did you have to babysit today? Is that why you had to miss school?" I prod.

Qiana nods her head and finally speaks. "My mama finally got a new job. So . . . so I have to stay home."

"Qiana, if I get you, I mean, your mother some information about childcare services, would you be able to come to school?" I place a hand on top of hers, which are clasped together in a tight grip.

"We can't afford nothing like that."

"Let me talk to some people. I might be able to get y'all some help. If I call you tonight, will I be able to get through on your home line?"

"Yes, ma'am. I'll answer it."

I lean over and give Qiana a hug. I feel her young, plump arms circle my back. I release her and rise to my feet as Davis leans down to hand the baby back to her.

"OK," I say as I pat her shoulder. "I'll talk to you this evening. And don't worry about your assignments. I'll give you an extension while we work this thing out."

"OK," she says. She stays on the porch and watches me and Davis return to my car. Davis waves his hand out the window at Qiana as I pull away from the drive. Steering with one hand and clutching my cell phone in the other, I pound out Ann Marie's number with my thumb.

"Hey," she answers.

"Ann Marie, I need a *huge* favor. I know you won't believe it, but I wouldn't ask you for something like this if it wasn't really important."

"What is it, Jo Ella?" The haste in her voice sounds like concern, not impatience.

"I know you have a full-time nanny that helps you out with the boys. You think I could impose on her to help out with some babysitting for a few days so that one of my students can come to school?"

"One of your students has a kid?"

"I think so. I just stopped by her house to see why she didn't show up for school, and she was home with a baby. I'm reading between the lines, but I get the sense that her mother may have been one of the folks laid off when that plant closed – the folks Mommy and the church have been trying to help. My guess is that her mom must have been taking care of the kid so that my student could come to school, but she can't do it anymore because she found a new job. This is a really bright, sweet girl, and I'd hate to have her fall through the cracks. I'm gonna check out whether there's any social services help that she can tap into, but in the meantime, I want to get her back in school before she gets too far behind and loses her momentum."

"Yeah, Jo Ella. If it's temporary. I mean, my boys are a handful, so I can't lay that extra work on Carmen for too long a stretch. But I'll help you out short-term."

"Oh, God, Ann Marie, I appreciate it. And I'll pay Carmen whatever extra money you think she needs for her trouble."

"Don't worry about it, Jo Ella. And talk to Mommy. They have a daycare center at the church, and they do a lot of counseling and outreach to teens. I think they even do parenting classes."

"I forgot that they have a daycare center."

"So, what time is she gonna drop off this child tomorrow? Carmen usually comes at 8:30, so I need to know whether to ask her to come earlier."

"Oh, hell. I forgot all about that. School starts at 8:30. I'll ask her if her mother can drop him off at 8:30. Otherwise, I may have to pick her up and bring the baby to your house at about eight, to give us enough time to get to school."

"Well, I'll have Carmen be here at eight, just in case."

"OK. Thanks, Ann Marie. I owe you."

"Always," she laughs as she hangs up the phone.

I pull to a stop in my parents' driveway.

"Is this an invitation?"

I'm startled by the sound of Davis's voice.

"Oh, hell. Davis, I'm sorry. I completely forgot to drop you off at school."

Davis leans his head against the headrest and smiles at me.

"Wanna have dinner with us? Maybe this is some kind of karmic hint that you and I need to work on the play tonight."

"Or something," he says. "Sure, I'd love dinner."

Unable to resist, I touch his cheek and then lean forward and give him a long, slow kiss. Though he doesn't reach out for me, he doesn't pull away.

"I would say that I'm not as big a flake as I seem, but I'm not sure that I would be telling the truth," I mumble, my lips still slightly touching his.

"I probably wouldn't believe you if you tried," he says as he starts to stroke my hair. "But you've got heart, Randolph. That goes a long way."

CHAPTER 22 ♡

Davis and I stride into the kitchen. On sight of Mommy and Daddy, Davis turns red as a radish. Daddy clears his throat before he speaks.

"Davis." Daddy peers at Davis over the rim of his reading glasses.

"Mr. Randolph," Davis extends his hand. "Good to see you again, sir." Daddy ignores Davis's hand and returns to reading his newspaper.

Mommy smiles wickedly and walks over to kiss Davis on the cheek. "Oh, Davis. How lovely to see you. Would you like to stay for dinner?"

"Thank you, uh, ma'am. I . . ."

I interrupt Davis's stuttering. "I invited Davis to dinner, Mommy. We're gonna work on the play tonight."

"Y'all seem to be working awful hard," Daddy sniffs from behind his newspaper. Davis opens his mouth to speak, but I pinch the back of his thigh and shake my head to shut him up.

"Well, have a seat, Davis. Dinner's about ready. Jo Ella, grab an extra place setting, will you?"

Davis sits next to Daddy and carefully examines his cuticles. Daddy lowers his newspaper and carefully examines Davis. Mommy sets a pot roast in the middle of the kitchen table, and we both take a seat.

"This looks delicious, Mrs. Randolph," Davis says in a manner reminiscent of Eddie Haskell. He grins at me and I can't help but grin back. I take my eyes away from his and meet the probing stares of both my parents. I think they're beginning to regret having me back at home.

"Am I late?" I have never been happier to see Memphis. "Hey there, Davis. You a brave man, son, showing up here after keeping Jo Ella out all night." Memphis laughs and offers Davis a soul shake before grabbing a plate from the cabinet and pulling a chair up to the table. "Girl, you either a bold so-and-so, or you just in love." Memphis blows kisses in my direction before diving into a hefty slab of pot roast without saying grace.

Davis takes a large sip of sweetened iced tea to stifle his laughter. I start to do the same but I no longer care. I laugh hysterically, setting down my fork to wipe the tears from my eyes as Memphis starts to smooch at me again. Mommy and Daddy do not appear amused.

"OK, Memphis. *Enough!*" I giggle. "I actually have something serious I have to talk to Mommy and Daddy about, and you're not helping."

"Hmmm. Somethin' y'all wanna say? Dum dum da dum . . ." Memphis hums a few off-key bars of the wedding march.

"Hush, Memphis. No. I actually have an issue with one of my students."

"What kind of issue, Jo Ella?" Mommy appears relieved at the change in subject.

"I think that one of my students has a baby. I think it's why she fell behind in school. She needs a babysitter, or else she won't be able to come to class and finish summer school, or high school for that matter. She's a really bright girl and a hard worker, and I think she has become more motivated over this summer . . ."

"Thanks to you," Davis offers.

"That's sweet, Davis, but I'm not so sure about that. Anyway, I was wondering if you knew of any social services agencies or organizations that help teen mothers with that kind of thing. Or maybe the church?"

Mommy smiles at me. A genuine, sweet smile, not the scary one that shelters her from things she finds unpleasant. "We have a daycare center at the church. I could talk to Mae Etta—you know, my soror, Mae Etta? She directs the day care center. I'm sure we could work out something to help this young lady." Mommy pauses a moment. "But you know, Jo Ella, it will probably work best if it's not just charity."

"But she doesn't have any money," I protest.

"That's not what your mother means, Jo Ella," Daddy interjects. "I'm sure this young lady will appreciate the help, but for her sake it's probably best if there's somethin' at stake for her. If she has to do something in return."

"What do you suggest, sir?" Davis asks. Daddy narrows his eyes at the sound of Davis's voice, but Davis doesn't back down. "Jo has gotten to know this young lady better than I have, but from my experience with her, she seems to be a kid that wants to do the right thing."

"Well, Davis, it may be as simple as telling her that this help will be available to her as long as she has good attendance and keeps her grades at a certain level." Daddy stares at Davis for a second, though his expression is a bit less severe. "Something like that. So that she doesn't let herself get distracted or just coast along. So she has to work for it herself. She might not always have folks like you and Jo Ella there to watch over her and motivate her to do what's best for her."

"I'll call Mae Etta after dinner." Mommy smiles softly

"Thanks, Mommy. I . . ."

"Don't thank me, Jo Ella. That's what being a good teacher is all about." Mommy pats my hand before returning to her pot roast.

"I'm sure she had a great role model, Mrs. Randolph," Davis offers in the Eddie Haskell voice. Mommy beams from the compliment, but Daddy rolls his eyes.

"So, Davis, I guess we'll be seeing a lot of you around here?" Memphis teases.

"Um . . ." Davis's eyes flicker in my direction.

I rise from the table to end the conversation. "Memphis, leave Davis alone." I pick up my plate and begin to gather up other plates from the table. Davis rises and joins me in collecting glasses and forks and serving bowls.

"Thank you Mrs. Randolph, Mr. Randolph. I appreciate dinner," Davis says as he joins me at the dishwasher and helps me load it with dinner dishes. "Can I wash these for you?" Davis points at the pots in the sink.

"No, no, darlin', you and Jo Ella better get to work before it gets too late," Mommy responds.

Though it's not yet six o'clock, I don't mention this fact. I grab Davis's hand and pull him out of the room.

"Shit," is all Davis says as he wipes his brow.

"Welcome to my life," I respond. "And you wonder why I'm so screwed up in the head."

I lead Davis into the living room and offer him a seat on the sofa. I pull my copy of *North Dallas Forty – The Musical!* out of my bag and drop it onto his lap. "Take a look at this. Want a cocktail?"

"Please," he pleads.

Davis flips pages as I pour bourbon and bitters and a splash of grenadine into a cocktail shaker. "*Memphis!*" I yell. "Bring me some ice, please!"

Memphis appears with a plastic pitcher full of ice cubes and a highball glass. "What you makin'?" He places his chin on my shoulder and peers down at my mixture. "Some love potion for your man here?" Memphis cracks himself up again. He laughs and strolls over to Davis with his palm raised to invite a high five. "I might need some of that myself," he jokes as he extends his empty glass in my direction. "I might get lucky tonight!" Memphis sits next to Davis and pokes him in the ribs with his elbow.

"The way Mr. Randolph was staring me down during dinner, I don't think my luck will be so good." Davis winks at Memphis and accepts the tall glass I offer to him.

"Naw, man. He likes you. He's just gotta give you a hard time. These girls are his heart, podner."

"I understand that," Davis says softly as he sips my version of an Old Fashioned. "Wow! This'll set you free." He clinks glasses with Memphis.

"I don't think she ever learned to cook nothin', but Jo Ella sure can mix a drink. If you're fond of bourbon, you might have to marry her."

"Too many of these, and I'll be on my knees before the night's out," Davis grins.

Memphis bursts into laughter again. "Boy, you better watch what you say!" he yells. "That could be taken the wrong way, son. Whew, you are alright, Davis."

"OK, Giggles. We have to get some work done here." I step over Davis's legs and try to scoot myself between him and Memphis on the sofa.

"I can take a hint!" Memphis howls. "Tryin' to get rid of me, huh, Jo Ella?"

As Memphis leaves the room, Davis sets his drink on a coaster. "Listen to this," he says. He strides over to Mommy's upright piano and pulls out the seat. He lifts the lid and begins to pound out a boogie-woogie beat. He sings a silly song called the "Steroid Shuffle." A funny, wacky kind of tune that might appear in one of those off-Broadway satirical revues. He plucks out a few lively numbers, each more offbeat than the previous, and then moves on to a ballad he's still working on for the lead character.

When Davis finishes playing, he turns to me. "What do you think?"

"You may be as twisted as I am. The music is perfect."

Davis turns back to the piano. "We need at least one group song that's a bit slower and sleepier. Something with more of a drawl to it, but not too twang-y." Davis starts to play Fleetwood Mac's "Dreams", which takes on a life of its own and morphs into something more meandering and Middle Eastern. I take another sip of my Old Fashioned and close my eyes.

I'm back at the beach. I'm standing on Ravi's deck, watching small flames morph into a bonfire before my eyes. Sparks flicker onto the long slats and wooden planks of the deck as the house goes up in flames. First splinters, then jagged pieces then entire panels burn faster than I can process what's going on right in front of me. Then the flames engulf me. I reach out, call out, but no one comes to my rescue.

"Jo?"

The sound of Davis's voice jolts me awake like a defibrillator.

"Oh! What? I'm sorry."

"The music was that exciting, huh?" Davis deadpans.

"No. I mean, yeah, it was great. I just . . . I must have fallen asleep. I didn't get much sleep this weekend."

"No worries." Davis rises from the piano bench. "You look exhausted. And I guess I should be going anyway."

"OK. I'll get my keys." I'm fuzzy, and I stagger a bit as I rise to my feet.

"I'll drive," Davis says. He approaches me and places an arm around my shoulder. I wrap my arms around his waist and press my face against his torso.

"Jo Ella," Mommy chimes from the doorway.

Davis and I separate faster than a couple of teenagers caught necking.

"Oh, Mommy," I mumble, "I, um, need to drive Davis to pick up his car . . . "

"I left Mae Etta's number on the kitchen table," she says, her tone more stern than singsong. "Just call her tomorrow, and she'll arrange everything. Good night, Davis."

"Good night, Mrs. Randolph."

As soon as Mommy is out of sight, Davis sighs. "I can't seem to win for losing, can I? There's something about your house that makes me feel like I'm fifteen."

"Speaking of teenagers, give me a minute. I just want to call Qiana before we leave."

"It'll probably take me a few minutes to start up your car anyway," Davis responds. "I'll meet you outside."

I call Qiana, who must have been sitting by the phone, because I don't even hear it ring before she picks up. I arrange to pick her up in the morning, and then I meet Davis outside at the car. It's strange not to sit in the driver's seat. I close my eyes again as soon as we start to move.

"Jo, we're here. You gonna be OK driving home?" Davis asks. He touches my arm to rouse me awake. "Wanna come home with me?"

"Are you kidding me?" I slur as I rub my eyes.

"No."

I start to laugh but stop as the blur clears from my eyes, and I'm finally able to focus on Davis, who's neither laughing nor smiling.

"Come on, Jo, who are we kidding," he asks as he grabs my hand. "Everybody knows the deal now—the school, your family, everyone. So what's holding you back? Is it Willie T.?"

"No. I don't know. Maybe. Either way, it doesn't matter, because he refuses to speak to me."

Davis looks stricken.

"Davis, to be honest, Willie T.'s not the reason I'm hesitating. *I'm* the reason I'm hesitating."

"Well, do you want to come with me or not?"

I nod but don't look at Davis. He turns my face toward his.

"Then why are we acting like a couple of kids, Jo? Just call your folks and tell them you're coming home with me. You're a grownup. You don't need their permission anymore. You just need to make sure they're not sitting around worrying about where you are."

"I know. I'm not afraid of my folks, Davis. OK, I take that back. I *am* afraid of them, but that's not it. It's just . . ."

Davis says nothing. He merely waits for me to go on. I open my mouth to tell him that he's the one who should be cautious, not the other way around. But I still can't form the words.

"Never mind," I say. "Let's go."

CHAPTER 23 ♡

If Qiana is surprised to see me show up with Davis in the Mini to pick her up, she doesn't let on. Davis dusted off his son's old infant seat and spent a good deal of time making sure it was secure in the backseat, while I looked on from the garage step, sipping coffee from a large *Don't Mess With Texas* mug. Qiana is already sitting on the porch holding Marcellus in her arms when we pull into the driveway. There is a plastic-coated, mint green diaper bag with sketches of teddy bears on the seat next to hers, and Qiana is dressed in indigo-colored jeans and a lightweight cotton top, with an armful of colored metal bangles and a subtle swipe of lip gloss on her lips.

Each morning we pick Qiana up at the same time, and each morning she is ready and waiting for us on the front porch when we arrive. Each evening we pick up Marcellus at Ann Marie's and drop them off at home on our way back to Davis's house. I avoid the phone, friends, interview requests, investigators, unknown extensions. As Willie T. never returned any of my calls, I avoid thoughts him as well. I avoid thoughts of anything deeper than our production of *North Dallas Forty*. Davis and I avoid talk of exes or personal issues. We talk films and music, however. We talk books, politics, weird news, trivial pursuits, food, our favorite destinations and the places we still desire to explore. The only real-world intrusion into our cocoon is Davis's angst about his son. He misses him and is desperate to bring him to Midland to live. His ex won't allow him to see his son because she's holding out for more money. She can have all the money if he can have their son.

The only exception to my no call rule is my daily attempt to call my parents. They no longer return my calls to tell them I'm not coming home or come out to talk to me when I stop by to pick up fresh clothes. They hold their tongues for almost two weeks before Mommy finally breaks her silence. I'm surprised to see "Mommy" on my screen while lounging on Davis's patio with a large glass of Cabernet. "Hi, Mommy," I say as I watch Davis struggle to figure out how to turn on his new gas grill, as he's more accustomed to charcoal.

"Jo Ella, you know your friends are coming in on Friday."

"I know, Mommy."

"Will you be home, or will your Daddy and I have to entertain them ourselves?"

"I'll be home. I'm gonna pick them up from the airport after school."

"Well, alright then. Dinner is at six," she says and hangs up abruptly.

I set down my phone and focus back on Davis. "I guess we can go back to our old routine next week. My mother's friend told me the church has a minivan that picks up some of the seniors. She's gonna talk to Qiana about arranging something for Marcellus."

"No more carpool?" Davis says as he turns a little wheel on the top of the propane tank.

"No. You don't have to drive the school bus anymore. I appreciate you helping out with Qiana, though."

"That's not the part of the carpool I was talking about." Davis holds his hand slightly above the grate of the grill to test for warmth and then closes the lid and turns to look at me.

"I don't know, Davis. I haven't really thought that far ahead. Why don't we see if we're still speaking to each other after the tryouts tomorrow before we make plans."

He laughs and then strolls into the kitchen to fetch the steaks.

"Do you need me to do anything?" I yell in the direction of the house.

"No," he yells back.

I'm afraid to think any further ahead than dinner. The past couple of weeks have been like floating in a bubble, where I've focused only on what's right in my life right now. No Ravi, no Danielle, no fire, no investigators, no worries about my life or my career other than to pull off the play, which I've enjoyed much more than my last few acting roles. I look forward to piling into Davis's little car and heading to his house to hide from the rest of the world. We shut out the rest of the world and just exist, which is nice for a change.

Davis has become a lot less disheveled of late. By the Friday of the tryouts, he's almost conservative. He puts on what appears to be a new orange polo shirt and neatly pressed khaki trousers with actual shoes instead of sandals. His hair is a little long, but it's clean and neatly combed, and he gets up early to shave before we head to school.

He still appears fairly crisp as we sit across the aisle from one another in the auditorium Friday afternoon. Davis winks in my direction before turning back to stare at the latest sorry excuse for a singer on the stage. This one doesn't actually sing. She screeches a loud, scratchy version of Kelis' "I Hate You So Much Right Now" that is downright frightening. There aren't too many of these tryouts left, which is a good thing, since I have to pick up Jen and Rudy from the airport at five. My plight must be serious for them to fly down to a place with no nice boutiques or chic eateries or beautiful people to see or be seen with just to check on me.

As yet another young woman sings yet another Alicia Keyes song, I start to pack my scattered belongings into my satchel, preparing to tear out the door as soon as this last contestant ends our agony. I shouldn't be so hard on everyone, as quite a few of the kids are not bad at all. Except we're ending with a bang, as our last crooner squeezes her eyelids shut and belts out a long, last note, which happens to be two or three notes off-key. She has pipes, I'll give her that, but no pitch whatsoever. Davis appears stunned as the girl takes a bow and her friends in the front row clap heartily. He is still seated in an apparent state of shock as I rush past him down the aisle in order to make it to the airport on time. Waving good-bye, I yell, "Thanks everyone! Y'all are great! We'll get back with you after the weekend!"

As I push my shoulder against the heavy metal door leading to the parking lot, Davis easily presses it open with his hand.

"So, your mom tells me that we won't have dinner 'til about 7:30, but I should come by at 6 for cocktails." Davis flashes me a winning smile. I have no idea what he's talking about.

"What?"

"Dinner," he says slowly with a wink. "This evening. For your friends . . ."

I feel my brow wrinkling, belying my confusion. My mind races, perplexed by these plans that I do not recall whatsoever.

"Wait, you don't know what I'm talking about, do you?"

"Uh, no? I mean, I don't remember . . ."

"And you didn't ask your Mom to invite me to dinner?" Davis's smile fades fast.

I shake my head as a faint recollection of the conversation with Mommy that I ignored while lounging around at Davis's house starts to come back to me.

"You know, Jo, this whole 'acting like we barely know each other' shit is kind of ridiculous," Davis says, his voice growing deeper and more stern, like a scolding parent. "Are you ashamed of me or something?"

"What?" Where is the English language, not to mention my memory, when I need it?

"Really, Jo, what the hell are we doing?"

This is beginning to sound like countless conversations coming out of nowhere that I have had with countless men and boys over the years, only in reverse. A conversation that, in this instance, I am not ready to have, given the tenuous state of my life. I have been content to just coast along in limbo, enjoying the moment and avoiding the ugliness of my recent past and the uncertainty of my indeterminate future.

"Jo, are you listening to me?"

"Davis, I think you need to get a grip. I forget that my mom is making dinner, and it becomes some kind of referendum?"

"You haven't even talked to them about me, have you?" Davis's voice grows deeper and meaner.

I feel flush, and my heart is racing. "Maybe this shit is cultural, Davis. Black folks don't just go on and on, spilling their guts about every damn thing going on in their personal life with their families, like some bleeding heart hippies."

"Spare me the 'it's a Black thing you wouldn't understand' shit, Jo. You know this has nothing to do with that. It didn't even occur to you to include me in something important to you." Davis' formerly carefree grin is now a contorted scowl bearing more of a resemblance to Lon Cheney than Dennis Quaid. His face is as red as the sunbaked plains that surround our hometown. "Goddammit, my SON is Black," he shouts in an atypically un-cool fashion for the likes of Davis. "My ex is Black and Hispanic!"

"So now you're an expert on what it means to be Black?" I snap. "At least you've met my family, and just about everybody else I know in Midland, for that matter. But have I met your son or any of your family? Or any of your friends? I didn't even *know* you had a kid until I saw his picture at your house, when you were trying to fuck me!"

"That is so fuckin' . . . I . . . I . . . oh, *to hell with it!*"

Davis strides swiftly ahead of me in a huff, his long gait impossible for me to keep up with without breaking into a sprint. I don't bother.

"Maybe your ex was onto something when she was calling you a dumb motherfucker over and over again," I yell at his back as he continues to move swiftly toward his car. His shoulders cringe but he never turns around or breaks stride. Annoyed, I turn my back on Davis and see Qiana, Kiley, and a handful of my students are standing in the doorway of the school, staring straight at us. The stricken, sorrowful expressions on their faces are more devastating than any words Davis or any other man in my life might utter.

"Guys, I'm so sorry. I'm sorry that you had to see that," I say as I search their disappointed eyes for some flicker of the hope that was present when we were all inside the auditorium moments ago. "You know, even the best of friends can say awful things to one another sometimes. Everything will be OK," I assure them, though they don't appear convinced.

"Davis, *wait up*," I shout in Davis's direction. Davis doesn't turn around and continues to march in the direction of his Mini. I sprint after him and, with some effort, catch up to him. I swing open the passenger door of his car and jump in as he revs up the engine. Thank God we don't often lock doors down here in Midland, otherwise I would have had to do something drastic and stupid, like throw myself in front of his moving car to get his attention. I don't think he would have stopped for anything less.

"Davis, I'm sorry. I'm really sorry. I shouldn't have said those things. And I honestly didn't remember anything about a dinner party. I barely listen to anything my mother says to me, which is probably part of my problem." I smile and reach out for his arm, but he flinches at my touch.

"This is so fuckin' juvenile, Jo. What have we been doing the last few weeks? I guess I assumed too much. You know, I gave up . . . oh, never mind!" Davis glares out the window, the engine of his little car chugging and sputtering as it strains to keep us cool in the 100-degree heat as we silently sit in place. I cover my eyes to block out the sun and concentrate on why Davis is so upset with me. He can't believe that I deliberately didn't invite him? He has never introduced me to anyone in his world, but I never assumed that it was deliberate. At least not until now. What the hell did he have to "give up" to spend time with me that's any more important than anything I might have to give up in my own life to spend time with him? I used to think that talking to Davis was like talking to myself, but perhaps I don't know him at all. Maybe I don't know myself as well as I think I do.

I uncover my eyes and turn to gaze at Davis instead of the insides of my hands. He's so tall that he has to slump forward in order to sit in his car. With nothing else to say to him, I say the first thing that pops into my head.

"Davis, why would someone as tall as you buy such a tiny car?"

He glances at me, his expression revealing that he's not at all amused by my irreverence. "Cody picked it out," he replies dispassionately.

"Cody?"

"My son, Cody. I was finally gonna get a chance to see him in Austin this weekend, but . . . would you mind terribly if I didn't open the door for you?"

My mouth opens, but nothing comes out. I robotically press down on the door handle and slide myself out of the car. Davis continues to sit and slump and stare ahead through the windshield, the top of his head leaning against his driver's side window. I slowly drag myself to the Beemer. It's a good thing I drove my car today to pick up Jen and Rudy, otherwise I might have been left stranded here in the faculty parking lot.

My body feels numb, but it's moving anyway. I fumble for my car keys in the depths of my handbag and creak open the door of my ancient little vehicle. My brain is so flooded with emotions and feelings that it shuts down altogether, operating in a sleep mode that enables me to mechanically turn the keys in the ignition and, hopefully, haul myself to the airport in time to pick up Rudy and Jen, but disallows me from doing anything that requires an iota of thought or thoughtfulness. I turn the key again and again, thinking no further ahead than the right turn I have to make at the end of the road. It finally dawns on me after several attempts at turning the engine over that my car is not moving anywhere. My ability to process anything still too slow to do anything constructive about my situation, I moronically keep turning the key in the ignition and listening to the dying churtle-churtle-chug-chug that fails to ever turn into the noisy drone that proves that I'm actually moving.

A car pulls perpendicular to the rear of my immobile mobile, and I hear the buzz of the automatic window rolling down, a feature that I don't possess. I don't turn around, continuing to twist my key back and forth, as if repeating this monotonous motion often enough will miraculously produce some new result.

"Jo, why don't you just hop in. I'll take you home."

My window is wide open, as I still haven't purchased an air conditioner. I stick my head out to view Davis's weary expression, no emotions readily apparent on the surface other than fatigue and, perhaps, annoyance.

"It's OK. You go ahead. I have to go to the airport anyway. I'll just call . . ."

"Come on. Just get in."

Still in robot mode, I abandon my car, not even bothering to roll up the window as I gather my bag and trudge over to Davis's car.

"But . . ."

"I'll take you to the airport. Just come on."

We speed silently down the expressway. Davis deftly weaves in and out of traffic in much the same way that those Minis tackled those European roads and rotaries in that movie I can't quite name right now since, as usual, my brain is not quite functioning as it should. We approach the airport entrance, and I glance down at my watch. 5:20. Just as we glide in front of the American Airlines terminal, I notice a couple of colorful, somewhat out of place characters strutting through the glass double doors that lead outside.

Rudy's tailored silk blazer is slung over his arm, the collar of his custom white shirt already unbuttoned in anticipation of the onslaught of boiling hot temperatures. Jen's face is barely visible behind her enormous tortoise shell glasses, her asymmetrically hemmed Helmut Lang dress confusing but cool, her choice of white linen well thought out and appropriate for the roasting she's about to face. They are both pulling monogrammed Goyard roller cases from Paris, Rudy's in royal blue and gold, Jen's in crimson and green.

Though I've been longing to see my best friends in the flesh, I have to haul myself out of the car, lacking much enthusiasm or excitement about much of anything. Suddenly Jen, peeking over the top of her humongous sunglasses, notices me dragging my feet in her direction, and she stretches out her arms and screams. She drops the handle of her stylish suitcase and jumps up and down repeatedly, in spite of the danger this entails due to the very high, geometrically-shaped heel of her otherwise casual espadrilles.

"Jo! Jo! Over here! Jo!"

"Girl, get yourself together. She sees us."

I can't help but smile. I wave and gesture them in the direction of the car. I almost forget that Davis is waiting behind the wheel until he raises himself out of the car and walks around to open the trunk.

Jen and Rudy stop dead in their tracks. Sly, inquisitive smiles spread across their faces. As they slowly resume their approach, Davis pays no heed to the million unanswered questions raised by my friends' curious, wide-eyed expressions. He coolly and courteously introduces himself while grabbing each of their suitcases and hoisting them into the tiny trunk.

Jen and Rudy don't exactly hide what they're thinking. They slant their eyes back and forth from Davis to me to each other and back to Davis again. As we arrive at my folks' house, Davis pushes a button to pop open the trunk, and Jen and Rudy jump out, seemingly oblivious to the uncomfortable silence between me and Davis or our uncharacteristically stiff body language. I hastily place a hand on Davis's arm before he can step out of the car to help my friends with their luggage.

"Davis," I whisper, "there's a lot I want to talk about but," I cut my eyes side-to-side to avoid eavesdroppers. "I mean, this isn't the best time. Won't you at least come in and have dinner with us?"

His eyes are soft, though his lips remain stern and straight. I start to babble rapidly, getting in as many words as I possibly can before he can turn me down.

"Please, Davis. We'd really, I mean, I would really like for you to come in and have dinner with us. Just come in for a drink, maybe. I really want you here. I wasn't trying to exclude you. I just wasn't giving it much thought one way or the other. A bad habit of mine. Just come inside for a little bit. You can at least have a cocktail and a nice meal, since I screwed up your weekend plans with your son, and . . ."

"Why Davis, darlin', I'm so glad you could make it!"

The vision of Mommy's outlandish smile and Jen and Rudy's gargantuan grins through the windshield cut short my decidedly desperate pleading. To my relief, Davis stares straight into my mother's smile and returns it warmly. A glimpse of his old grin from the time before Jo Ella turned it into a grimace breaks through as he steps out of the car and kisses my mother on the cheek.

"I wouldn't have missed it, Mrs. Randolph."

Mommy grasps both Davis and Rudy by their elbows and escorts them towards the porch, leaving me and Jen to trail behind them toting all of the luggage and my belongings from school.

"Not bad, Jo. Not bad at all," Jen whispers in my ear as she raises her eyebrows up and down. "Why didn't you *tell* me? I thought Davis was just some goober you talked to on your coffee breaks because he was the only person at work that wasn't a complete redneck. Damn, Jo, you're holding back on me!"

"There's nothing to tell, Jen." There's actually a whole lot to tell her. It suddenly dawns on me that I've told my two best friends very little about what has been going on with me over the past few weeks.

"Mm hmm. Right. Now I see that night you spent at his place in a brand new light. Lover's quarrel?" As usual, Jen sees right through me, as if I was one of those Baccarat crystal vases she collects and lines up on her mantel.

I glare at her and grab the handle of her bag, as she's about to break her ankle trying to carry it while wobbling in her funky, four-inch espadrilles and simultaneously whispering in my ear instead of paying attention to where she's stepping in the dry, patchy grass.

Daddy greets our guests heartily and grabs the bags, placing Jen's suitcase in my room and Rudy's in Ann Marie's old room. Unmarried boys and girls do not sleep in the same room in the Randolph household, even if the boys have no romantic interest whatsoever in said girls.

Sleeping arrangements settled, Daddy starts mixing and handing over heady cocktails in rapid succession, which we all down in rapid succession. Though my friends' visit was initially intended as an intervention, Mommy has turned it into a cocktail party.

"So, Davis, Jo told us about you, but evidently not *all* about you." I glare at Jen as she giggles over her old-fashioned glass.

"That's probably best." Davis's mouth attempts a smile but twists into a wry expression resembling a sneer. "Otherwise, you might not want to have dinner with me."

"I doubt that. Jo not speaking about something speaks volumes, if you know what I mean." Jen studies Davis carefully from behind her cocktail glass, sizing him up and taking down notes in her mental memo pad.

"But . . ." I try to speak, but no one's listening. Even my beloved Daddy is now talking to Davis like I'm not in the room

"So, Davis, we appreciate you helping Jo Ella out and driving her to the airport. I sent Memphis over there to look at her car. I keep telling Jo Ella to stop driving that raggedy ol' thing, but she can be kinda' hard-headed."

"I'm learning. I'm glad I could help, sir. But you give me too much credit. It's not like I had anything better to do this afternoon." Did Davis cut his eyes at me?

"My Lord. It's Friday! You know, Davis, I usually pull out the grill on Fridays. If you ever want to join us, come on over." For the past couple of weeks, Daddy has been treating Davis like he has leprosy. Now Mommy's inviting him to dinner, and Daddy's acting like he's his new best friend. What is going on with these people?

"A regular Friday night barbecue. Isn't that convenient?" Jen smirks.

Davis' response is serious and a bit stern. "That's very nice of you, sir. I usually try to get to Austin on weekends, but I appreciate it."

"Girlfriend? *Ouch!*" Channeling my nephew, I kick Jen in the ankle.

A scant smile passes across Davis's face. "My little boy, my son lives in Austin. At least for now. I'm trying to bring him here to live with me full-time."

"You have a little boy?" Mommy is passing through the den with a large platter of cheeses and little jalapeño biscuits.

"Yes, ma'am," Davis lifts a biscuit off the tray Mommy holds in front of him. "I'm in the middle of a divorce. A nasty one, I'm afraid. I'm trying to get custody of my son."

"Oh my Lord, Davis," Mommy drops onto the sofa next to Davis as Daddy, Rudy and Jen all lean in to listen. I try to get someone to pass me the biscuit tray, but it's a lost cause.

"Well, ma'am, you know I'm a musician, and I used to travel an awful lot. But I've been trying to settle down here and set up something more stable for him so hopefully they'll let him live with me. The courts, I mean."

"That must be so difficult for you. Is his mother in Austin?"

Mommy can always get away with asking the most personal questions without ever seeming inappropriate.

"Well, yes, sometimes. She's a backup singer for a rock band, and she's on the road most of the time. But her mother lives in Austin, and my son's staying with his grandmother right now. Sometimes my ex takes Cody with her on the road, but I don't think, I mean, it's just not the best environment for him. And he's almost school age, so I think he needs to be in one place, with one of his parents."

"I understand it's not easy for men to get custody of their children." Mommy grasps Davis's hand, and Jen shifts to an armchair closer to where Davis is seated. "Do you have any family around here that can help you with him?"

"No, not really." Davis' eyes dim, and he takes a sip of his cocktail. "I mean, I have people around here. But my family's not close. And most of 'em aren't so nice anyway. I only talk to them when I have to, and I wouldn't want to bring Cody up around any of them. Actually, I think I would have an easier time with this custody thing if my family was more like yours."

"Except we're Black people," I say and take another long drag from my cocktail glass. "Courts would rather give custody to white serial killers than us."

Mommy strokes Davis' hand and glares at me. "Davis, darlin', do you have a picture of your little boy?" she asks.

Everyone other than me surrounds Davis and oohs and aahs over a small photo he produces from his wallet. Mommy continues to man-handle Davis, grabbing his face and squeezing his cheeks. "Oh, Davis, you poor thing. How can you bear to be away from this beautiful child?"

"It's not easy, ma'am," Davis muffles through Mommy's vice-like clench.

"Here, son, let me refill your glass there." Daddy pats Davis on the shoulder.

I stroll in the direction of the hors d'oeuvres and peek over Rudy's shoulder to get a glimpse of the floppy-haired child from Davis's gallery. This image is in color and is set in a swimming pool instead of a field of flowers. The child has a tawny glow that wasn't so apparent in black and white, and Davis is holding him in his arms in the unnaturally aquamarine water. Their cheeks are pressed against each other's as they both make fish faces for the camera.

Why are my parents treating me like a pariah, but all of a sudden embracing Davis like a long-lost relative? Why did Mommy call Davis without telling me? I don't get what's going on. But whatever it is, it's really annoying. I pour myself another cocktail and grab a biscuit off the tray. "You know that baby's Black," I slur.

Everyone turns and stares at me in apparent horror. Everyone except Davis, who laughs and smiles at me for the first time since we left school.

The doorbell rings insistently, as if someone is leaning against the button. Before Daddy can rise to answer it, the front door lock clicks and a whirlwind of noisy voices and footsteps roll into the house. It's Ann Marie and Little Claude and their brood, with Uncle Buddy, Aunt Lula and, *Lord help me*, Willie T. in tow. They trundle into the den, and the room becomes a cacophonous crowd of Texans I didn't intend to talk to this weekend.

Mommy and Ann Marie exchange pained, plastered-on smiles. Someone must have missed a memo. They whisper rapidly through tightly clenched teeth, like a couple of Long Island Lockjaws. Mommy drags Ann Marie into the kitchen, leaving an awkward Willie T. and Little Claude standing in the middle of the room surrounded by Davis and his adoring public.

"I'm Davis. I think we met at the barbecue . . ." Davis breaks the ice by standing and extending his hand to Little Claude then Willie T. Willie T. reciprocates, turning his back to me while greeting Daddy and everyone other than me. The big boys chat about the weather, while the little ones, my nephews, crawl all over my lap.

"Auntie Jo, is that one your boyfriend, or that one over there? Or is it Uncle Bill?"

The sideways glances being thrown in my direction do not go unnoticed.

"*You* are my boyfriend, you little cutie!" I tickle Trey, who protests but giggles uncontrollably. Mitchell and Martin climb onto my back and shoulders to join in the ticklefest.

As I pull my nephews off of my back, Jen slides next to me on the love seat. She leans toward me and comes precariously close to ejecting the contents of her overfilled martini glass all over Mommy's upholstery and my lap.

"Oh my *god*, Jo! *That's* the Willie T. you've been talking down all this time? You have *really* been holding out on me. He is *fine!* Maybe I should stay a bit longer. What other men are you hoarding for yourself down here? I thought we were best friends!"

"You think?"

"Girl are you *blind?!* Why didn't you tell me all the good men are hiding out in Middle America? Maybe I misjudged the South. These guys don't seem at all dull or stupid. And they're cute! They're really cute! You know how much actors pay people to try to look that cute? I need to scout out this territory."

"OK, Lewis & Clark. For your information, this is Texas, not the South, but whatever. Do what you gotta do." I glance past Jen to peek at Willie T. He's wearing a crisp white shirt with his ever-present khakis. He has a fresh, close haircut, which shows off his chiseled features. Willie T. is the perfect gentleman with nice manners from a nice Negro family like my own. I watch his attractive face as he chats warmly with my family and friends. My every fault and flaw feel more exposed than ever. I take another long drag from my cocktail and turn back to Jen. "Why don't you go over and talk to Willie T. I'm not getting anywhere with him."

Jen pops up from the sofa. She sidles up to Willie T., who doesn't shy away from the attention. He seems pleased, actually. Everyone has found someone nice to talk to, other than me. Perhaps I will shrivel up and shrink into the sofa cushions. I don't think anyone would notice. I'm not sure I'd be worthy of attention even if my head started spinning, and I spewed pea soup and swore at everyone in a Damien voice. Everyone pays attention to Mommy's dinner bell, however. They hasten into the dining room, leaving me alone on the couch contemplating my abundant faults and need for an exorcism.

The multiple bottles of wine consumed during our multiple courses of tortilla soup, green salad, and baked chicken with mashed potatoes and green bean casserole dissolve the dinner conversation into rounds of my family's "what's your fantasy" game—a game we used to play when there were no playground politics or political parties to discuss at the dinner table. As Mommy and Ann Marie have produced diametrically divergent fantasies for me this evening, this game may prove dangerous.

"Willie T., if you could live anywhere in the world, where would you live? What's your fantasy place?" Mommy leans her slender chin against her palm.

"Ummm, Miami."

"Dallas," Ann Marie chimes in, to no one's surprise.

"San Francisco," Little Claude blurts to everyone's surprise. Ann Marie seems particularly surprised, setting down her wine glass and staring at her husband, who appears too self-conscious to stare back. They spent half their honeymoon in San Francisco, and she has always described it as the best time they ever had together.

Mommy whispers the point of the game into Aunt Lula's good ear. "Oh, I saw a pretty house over there on Maple, right across from the church."

"Disney World!" Trey, Mitchell and Martin chime in unison.

"Rio, sugar." Uncle Buddy takes a long drag of his Jack Daniel's, having declined the dinner wine in favor of his favorite beverage.

Mommy raises her eyebrows but doesn't stop smiling. "Rudy? Jennifer?"

"St. Barth's," Rudy responds.

"St. Barth's," Jen echoes. "What about you, Mr. Randolph?"

"Right here with Mommy and my girls. How 'bout you, Ella?"

"Paris. But only if you came with me. Davis?"

"Sydney. Sydney, Australia," Davis responds. "Or maybe Harlem, since it's been suggested that I might have certain cultural preferences."

Everyone other than me bursts out laughing. Even Aunt Lula, who dabs her eyes with her linen napkin.

All of a sudden, all eyes are on me.

"Jo Ella?" Ann Marie raises an eyebrow at me, expectantly.

"I don't know." My eyes drop into my glass.

"What about the beach?" Ann Marie presses. "You love the beach, don't you? Didn't your boyfriend back in L.A. live at the beach?"

I glare at my sister and grasp my head in agony. Why is she choosing this of all occasions to torture me, especially when we've been getting along of late. The twinkling prisms of light sparkling down from Mommy's chandelier combined with the sulfites in the wine are making my head ache. "Why don't you give it a rest, Ann Marie? Why do we have to play this stupid game anyway?"

"Come on, Jo Ella . . ."

"Shut up, Ann Marie! *Just shut the hell up!* Jesus Christ!"

"*Lord, help me,*" Aunt Lula mutters into her wineglass. Ann Marie's eyes narrow, but she doesn't respond.

Jen hastens to come up with a new challenge, her boisterous rasp charming and distracting everyone from my crow-like squawking at my sister. Everyone except Davis, who looks at me like he doesn't know me at all.

"OK, everybody," Jen calls out to the table. "*Who* is your ultimate fantasy? It doesn't have to be a real person."

"Mommy," smiles Daddy.

"Sidney Poitier," Mommy grins. I don't think Daddy was expecting that one. "If I was a widow, of course." Daddy's smile fades entirely.

"Pocahontas!" shrieks Trey.

"That nice-looking guy on the food channel that helps people with the dishes they keep messing up. Could you imagine coming home to a cute guy cooking you a gourmet meal every night?" Ann Marie says, reaching across Little Claude to grab the neck of the wine bottle. I'm not sure what's going on with them this evening, but I hope that Ann Marie stops taking it out on me. I have enough to deal with right now.

Everyone sips and stares at their dinner plates until Little Claude breaks the silence. "If I had to do it over again, I'd still pick Ann Marie," he mumbles. Ann Marie averts her gaze, in a shy motion I'm not accustomed to seeing. She pours more red wine into the bulb of her wine glass, filling it to the brim.

"I'd pick Dorothy Dandridge," Uncle Buddy chimes in. What a surprise. Every Black man over the age of sixty has a thing for Dorothy Dandridge.

"Adam Clayton Powell," Aunt Lula adds cheerily. This is the most animated I've seen her in a long time. Though I've noticed her down at least two large glasses of wine this evening, so that may have something to do with it. "What a fine man he was. And a reverend too!" She raises her glass as if to toast, spilling half of her wine on Mommy's Irish linen tablecloth.

"Aunt Lula, that's enough wine for you." Mommy grins as she delicately dabs the tablecloth with a dampened napkin. "Besides, what would Reverend Bumpers say?"

"Now, Ella Lynn, what do you think that Jesus drank?"

"Well, until Jesus appears at my dinner table to pour you some more wine, I think you should put down your glass. Rudy, darlin', why don't you tell us who you fancy."

"I think it would be a combination of Brad Pitt, Richard Roundtree and Prince," Rudy wishes. Mommy's smile grows severe, and she passes the potatoes and green beans around the table, even though no one has asked for seconds.

"Rudy, how is that even possible? For me it would be some combination of the chairman of Goldman Sachs and Denzel Washington, with a little Tiger Woods and Michael Jordan thrown in for good measure." Jen is nothing if not predictable. Stock portfolios and strong physiques still tend to rank higher than fidelity or affection on her relationship wish list. A couple of months ago, one could say the same thing about me.

"How about you, Bill?" Jen says as she leans closer to Willie T. He doesn't seem to mind, despite her exposing her predilections so explicitly. Mommy and Ann Marie trade steely stares again.

Willie T. clears his throat. "I guess some combination of Diahnn Carroll and Beyoncé would be my fantasy." Willie T. glances at Jen, who bats her eyelashes and flips her new, blond, Beyoncé-like hair extensions in response. Am I that obvious a flirt?

Ann Marie shrugs her shoulders and turns her attention to Davis. "What about you, Davis?"

"I don't know," he says in a soft, low voice. "I guess a combination of Amelia Earhardt, because she was fearless, Angelina Jolie, well, for obvious reasons, and . . . I guess someone like Jo." Everyone at the table takes another sip from their glasses. No one says a word. Davis' expression is sad, and he drops his eyes down toward his glass.

Suddenly, twenty-six silent eyes are staring directly at me. I sit frozen like the Anastasia ice sculpture Daddy purchased for my Winter Palace-themed debutante ball.

"I told you, I don't want to play this game."

"Come on, Jo Ella, there's gotta be someone," Ann Marie pesters. Her words slur a bit as she speaks.

This doesn't feel like a game. It doesn't feel fun. It's not fun to put my feelings and Davis' feelings and Willie T.'s feelings on display like this when there's so much we need to talk about first. When there are so many amends I need to make to both of them. When I need to tell Davis what I now realize I feel about him.

"Jo Ella?" Ann Marie prods again.

"OK, Leif Garrett." I blurt without thinking.

"Who?" Mommy looks puzzled.

"Leif Garrett. The *Tiger Beat* teen idol from when I was a kid."

"You never liked Leif Garrett, Jo Ella," Ann Marie drains her glass. "You liked that curly-haired guy from *Family.*"

"How would you know? Oh, I forgot, you used to read my diary."

"It was some blond white boy, same difference," Ann Marie snaps. "What is wrong with you tonight, Jo Ella?!"

"*What's wrong with you, Ann Marie?* Why can't you leave me the *fuck* alone?!!!" I have no recollection of rising up from the table. But I'm standing with my fists clenched, yelling like a foul-mouthed five year old. As fast as my temper flared, my regret begins to roil. Everyone must think I'm a crazy, immature ass. And they're right. I practically stomped my feet and spat at my sister at the dinner table like an errant preschooler. It's obvious she's drunk and annoyed about something that has nothing to do with me. Why can't I make nice and play along like normal people? Why am I so terrible? I drop my head and drop my butt back into my chair.

"*Girls!*" Mommy's voice is stern and a last straw. Ann Marie's expression goes from simmer to boil, but she dares not speak. Her eyes narrow to dagger-like slits. I've lost the fury to frown back at her.

"I think we've had enough of this game. How would everyone like some peach cobbler?" Mommy's request is a command, not a question.

Mommy stands to emphasize her closure of the conversation while everyone else sits in stone-faced silence, muted either by too much wine or our flashback of an adolescent temper tantrum. Mommy begins to pick up serving dishes from the table and marches toward the kitchen. All of the boys—Daddy, Willie T., Davis, Rudy, Little Claude, and even Uncle Buddy—dutifully gather and carry dinner plates into the kitchen for her without waiting to be asked. When dessert arrives, I shun the sweets and pour myself another glass of wine. Willie T. continues to dote on Jen, and Davis broods in silence. He looks as if someone has told him there is no Santa Claus. His eyes are somewhere else, not at all focused on me or anyone else at the table. His shoulders stiffen, and he seems straighter and even taller than usual, though he's still seated.

The dinner conversation returns to politeness once I leave it, though the spark is entirely gone. I pricked the balloon, and it has floated down to lie flattened on the dining room table. Everyone appears tired and deflated, with the exception of Jen and Willie T., who have removed themselves from the general discussion to focus on one other, and Rudy, who is getting a tutorial on Jack Daniel's from Uncle Buddy. My nephews have already retreated to Mommy and Daddy's bedroom, where they are either being lulled to sleep or into a stupor by the Disney Channel. Ann Marie toys with her cobbler, while Little Claude wolfs his down with relish.

I retreat to the powder room. I return just in time to see Davis give his goodbyes to everyone and head out the front door.

"Davis, wait up!" I chug down the porch steps. "I want to talk to you a minute. I want to thank you for . . ."

"Look, Jo, I appreciate dinner and all. But I really don't see any of this working out anymore."

"But . . ."

Davis cuts me off. "I really like you, Jo. You know I do. But I really don't need any juvenile, high school shit in my life right now. I can't handle it."

"Davis, I . . ."

"I know you have issues because of all the shit that happened to you back in L.A. But I'm going through some major stuff too. I know I haven't told you all the details of what's going on in my life, and maybe I overreacted this afternoon. But I need something real in my life right now. Something solid that's not going to shift underneath my feet every five minutes. I can't deal with some crazy, childish relationship just because I have a stupid, kiddie crush."

"Davis, hold on," I grab his hand. "I think you're reading too much into everything. I'm not myself this evening. This is not me. Can you sit down for a minute? If you want a mature, real relationship, can we at least have a mature, real conversation? Maturity and reality aren't my strong suits, obviously, but I'd like to give it a go."

Davis nods wearily. We sit on the porch steps, and I place a hand on his knee. He doesn't remove it. "Davis, being with you has been great. But everything is moving so fast, that I don't know what to make of it."

"I know," he says. He doesn't smile, but his eyes are gentle. "Me neither."

"I've started thinking about the end of the summer. I keep wondering what will happen because . . . and I can't believe I'm saying this . . . I'm not sure I want to leave Midland. Or at least I'm not ready to leave you, and I don't know what to do about it."

Davis doesn't say anything. He places one of his hands on top of the hand I rested on his knee.

"But I might have to leave, Davis. There's so much going on with me that I haven't told you."

Davis's eyes narrow.

"Well, I've told you a lot of it. But not everything."

"So, you really did kill someone?" he deadpans.

"No," I smile, though it fades quickly. "But I did something awful. You know how I told you I trashed my ex's house?"

"Yeah."

"And that I thought he and his wife might blame me for a fire at their beach house?"

Davis nods.

"Well, the fire . . . the fire was kind of my fault."

Davis continues to squint at me. "What do you mean, it's kind of your fault?"

"I mean, I was sitting out on the deck trying to set fire to my exes' T-shirts. That's all I wanted to do. I just wanted to burn some stupid, overpriced t-shirts he used to make a big deal about. But what started out as a small fire in a container on the deck ended up spreading to the house. I didn't know what to do. I called the fire department right away, which is probably why they got there in time to contain the damage. But I didn't stick around."

"Shit, Jo."

"Yeah, some shit, huh? Anyway, my ex wants me to come back and finish the movie we were working on. Evidently, the studio really likes it. I didn't admit anything to him, but he said that he's gonna tell the police I set his house on fire if I don't come back. This is his big break as a director, so he needs to finish the movie so he can sell it to the network."

"So, your problem's solved," Davis says, his speech monotone. "You get your career back, and you're off the hook for torching the dude's house. Though it doesn't stop his wife from going after you, does it?" Davis spits the words out like bitter medicine.

"I don't know, Davis. I don't know. Either way, my life is pretty fucked up right now. It's my fault—I'm not blaming anybody else. But I don't want to go back. And I don't want to go to jail either." I try to hold them back, but the tears come anyway. "I'm scared to death," I whisper.

I place my head atop Davis' bent knees. He strokes my hair and lets me cry. I cry for what feels like an eternity. I finally lift myself up and wipe my nose with the back of my hand. Davis places his arm around my shoulders and gives me a slight squeeze.

"I want to be here for you, Jo. I really do." Davis kisses the top of my head. "So don't take this the wrong way, OK?"

My back stiffens. I feel as if the tears will stream again at any moment.

"I have to focus on this thing with my kid, Jo. My custody hearings start next week." Davis stares ahead at the street instead of down at me. "I love you, Jo. I really do. But I can't be in the middle of this. I have to be squeaky clean if I'm gonna get custody of Cody, and . . . I'm sorry, Jo."

I drop my head into my hands.

"I want this to work out for you. You're not a bad person, Jo. You behave badly sometimes, but you're a good person. I know you wouldn't intentionally hurt anyone. I just . . . I want to be here for you, but I can't do it. Not right now."

Davis kisses me on my cheek. The soft, sweet sort of kiss you give a child or a dotty old aunt. Davis stands and says nothing else. I watch his back as he strides down the driveway, hands shoved into his pants pockets. I follow his car with my eyes as it accelerates down the street I traveled a million times on my red Schwinn bicycle as a kid. I suck in a lungful of hot air, quickly releasing my breath and coughing coarsely. The air is crisp and dry, sparkling with static and completely lacking in moisture, like the fallen leaves of autumn that crunch underneath your feet. The atmosphere contains none of the soft moisture of spring, when all is possible and everything comes to life. I bring my knees to my chest and cover my head with my hands.

CHAPTER 24 ♡

I slowly drag myself into the house. My eyes are puffy and my vision is glazed. I step into the powder room and splash water on my face, but it's no use. There's no hope for me.

All the activity is centered in the kitchen, as usual. Rudy is setting up the coffee maker. Mommy is putting away the large platters and pots washed by Ann Marie and dried by Jen. Daddy is clearing barware and glasses from the living room, while Uncle Buddy caps the bourbon bottle and Little Claude wipes crumbs from the chair cushions. Aunt Lula is passed out on the sofa, snoring softly. Ann Marie and Jen move from the sink to collect the dinner linens. Willie T. loads the plates and glasses they didn't wash by hand into the dishwasher. I step beside him and start to reorganize his work to suit Mommy's unyielding dishwasher-loading specifications. Willie T. gets out of my way and takes to rinsing the cruddier of the dishes in the sink before handing them to me. "I'm surprised you came," I say softly.

"Why shouldn't I come? I like your family, Jo Ella. Besides, Ann Marie and Claude invited me. Claude's my best friend, you know."

"I'm glad you came, Willie T., even though you hate me. Though I'm not sure you *why* you hate me so much. Curt's the one who started the fight, not me."

Willie T. stops mid-rinse. The tap water splashes from his fingers onto the rim of the silver-lined plate he's holding under the spigot. "I don't have to put up with you brushing me off, Jo Ella."

"Brushing you off?" I feel the acid rising in my throat. "I wanted to see you again! I tried to call you a million times to apologize. I think I'm the one who got the brush-off, not you!"

"Didn't take you long to get over it," he says in a low, lethal voice. "How long did it take you to dive into that white boy's bed after being so broken up about me? An hour? Two?"

"Davis was trying to help me get out of that place. You just jumped to conclusions!" I shove a plate into a wire slot, which causes a clatter but luckily not a break.

"I don't really care about that Curt thing," he says, his gaze focused on the sink and not me. "Or, I don't *blame* you for the Curt thing, Jo Ella. I just don't like you playing us—me, Curt, this Davis fella—just because you're bored."

"That's not me! I'm not bored! Why do you keep saying that?! You don't know a thing about it or a thing about me, for that matter!"

Willie T. shakes his head as he passes a plate under the faucet, scraping off bits of dried potato with his nail. "One day you're with me, the next day I see you leaving with this dude. All you women talk about how no good brothers are, and then when you find a good one, you dump him for the first idiot or slacker that comes along."

I grab Willie T.'s chin with my wet hand and turn his face toward mine. I leave a scattered streak of dishwater droplets on the ridge of his jaw.

"Willie T., I had a million photographers sticking cameras in my face. I wasn't really in a rational state of mind when you saw me. I didn't know and, frankly, didn't care what it looked like. I just wanted to get out of there, and Davis helped me do it. Think about it. The five seconds of media attention you got when Curt jumped you wasn't so pleasant, was it? Well, welcome to my life!"

His eyes look past me as if he's focused on his thoughts and not me standing and screeching in front of him. "I know," he says. "I understand that. But the next thing I knew, it looked like you were living with the guy. I didn't think you cared about seeing me. I figured your calling me was just to get over your guilt about what happened."

"Willie T.," I say, a bit softer. "Why didn't you say that to my face instead of making assumptions and then coming to my parents' house and hitting on my best friend?"

His eyes meet mine again. "It's not like she was resisting the pitch, Jo Ella." He pauses. "Hey, I'm sorry. That was out of line. You're right. I should have talked to you about how I felt instead of making assumptions."

"So what now?" I ask.

"I don't know." Willie T. hands me the wet plate he was washing and shakes the water off his hands. "See you later, Jo," is all he says before he leaves. He remembered to call me Jo. I don't follow him or extend goodbyes to him or anyone else. I hunch over the dishwasher to arrange the last of the plates and pour cleaning powder into the little cup attached to the dishwasher door. Suddenly I feel two lanky arms wrap around me, and I turn to return Uncle Buddy's tight squeeze.

"What's the matter, sugar? Where's my sunshine?"

"Just a little sleepy, Uncle Buddy. Maybe I had a bit too much wine."

"That's why I stick to Jack Daniel's." Uncle Buddy kisses me on the top of my head. "That wine just makes me sleepy and gives me gas. See you later, sugar."

"Bye, Uncle Buddy." As he disappears through the kitchen door, I press the power button on the dishwasher and head straight to my room.

"What's wrong with you?" Rudy throws out the question like a dart as he marches into my room with Jen in tow.

"Everything." I sift through a pile of clothes on the floor for a t-shirt to sleep in.

"What's going on with you and Davis?" he prods.

"Nothing." I pull an old "Rebels" t-shirt over my head. "Not anymore."

"Oh, Lord. Don't say *another word* until I get back." Rudy races out of the room and scurries down the hallway.

Jen zips open her trolley bag. Suddenly, she starts to cry.

"I'm so sorry, Jo," she blubbers. "I'm horrible. I hit on my best friend's man. Am I that desperate?"

I give Jen a weary hug. "Don't beat up on yourself. You were kind of drunk. And with Davis there, I'm sure the whole thing was confusing."

"You're too good to me," she says and wipes her eyes.

"No I'm not," I say flatly.

Jen starts to sort through the perfectly folded clothes in her suitcase. She pulls a long embroidered caftan with shimmery sequins along the collar and hem out of her valise.

"Morocco?" I ask.

"Bahamas. Harbour Island has the best shops."

Whereas I typically choose my travel destinations from fiction, Jen selects hers from the pages of *Vogue* and *Tatler*. Jen sits cross-legged on the floor and pulls her burnished gold extensions back into a sleek ponytail, which she secures with a shell-encrusted clip.

Rudy reappears wearing a starched pajama set of royal blue and white-striped Sea Island cotton. He stretches his slender legs lengthwise across the bed and props himself on the floral pillow shams Mommy recently picked up on sale at J.C. Penney's.

"So," Rudy says. "Tell us all about what's going on with you and Davis, and don't leave out a single detail." Though his voice is *Flash-dance* frantic, Rudy looks quite relaxed as he lounges on my miniscule thread count bed linens bedecked with pastel petunias and pansies. Mommy always finds a way to make flowers bloom in the desert, even if she can't afford fancy sheets.

Jen jumps in. "You know, if you and Davis were trying to hide something from the rest of us, you weren't doing a very good job of it."

"I don't know where to start." I respond.

"From the beginning!" Rudy urges.

I open my mouth to speak, but I can't do it. I crumble. My limbs weaken and the tears flow. I don't think they'll ever stop. I spread out on the floor and bury my nose into the synthetic threads of the shag carpeting. I cry so hard that my chest heaves, and my body shakes.

Both Jen and Rudy have drop to their knees and rub my back to console me. But it's no use.

"Lord have mercy, girl!" Rudy exclaims. "What did that man do to you?"

"Nothin'," I rasp between sobs. "He . . . he didn't . . .my fault."

"You were a bit psycho this evening," Jen says. "But you weren't *that* bad. It'll all be better tomorrow. Just tell him you drank too much."

"N-not it," I stutter. " I . . . I drank a lot . . . b-but that's not it." I raise myself up and lean against the side of the bed. I have the sniffles, and Rudy hands me a tissue box from the mess on my desk.

"I screwed everything up," I say between nose blows. "Davis and I . . . I guess we got too close too fast."

"What do you mean by too close. We need details, Jo, *details!*" Rudy is in a frenzy.

"I really just thought of him as a good friend. Or I thought I did. I've been my usual, you know . . ."

"Self-centered celebrity?" Jen smiles.

"Pretty much," I nod. "I've been completely absorbed in all my own stuff—Ravi, the movie, the fire. Flirting with everyone. Then when all the shit hit the fan at the Bush rally, Davis was the person I needed and realized that I wanted. I've pretty much lived at his house the last couple of weeks."

"And Ella Randolph allowed that to happen under her watch?" Jen quips.

"She's barely spoken to me until tonight," I sigh. "I can't say I blame her. I'm a mess. And I keep stomping on everyone's feelings. Like with Willie T."

"Girl, you are wearing me out!" Rudy yells. "You create all those fireworks and love triangles back in L.A., then you start reliving your high school hots with Willie T., and the next day you're playing house with Davis. Are you sure you like Davis, or do you just like drama?"

I'm stumped. As always, my friends are my reality check. "I don't know, Rudy. I know I don't exactly have any credibility in this department, and I get carried away in my emotions sometimes . . ."

"All the time . . ." Jen adds.

"But I don't think that's it this time. I don't know how to describe it. Davis and I just chilled around each other. We weren't trying to get something from each other or use each other to get somewhere or just feeding each others' egos. We just *were,* you know?"

"I have no idea what you're talking about. But if you're this incoherent and unable to describe it, then it sounds pretty serious." Rudy
doesn't appear to be joking.

"I know," Jen agrees. "Every other man in your life you've been able
to pitch to us as if you were trying to sell us a script. So what happened?
Did you screw it up by trying to date everybody under the sun and
settle down with Davis at the same time?"

"Well, maybe at first. But we had finally zeroed in on each other.
Stuff started to go wrong this afternoon, and then it all snowballed. At
first his feelings were hurt because I didn't invite him to dinner tonight.
He thought it meant he wasn't important to me. It probably wouldn't
have been as big a deal if he hadn't skipped visiting his kid this weekend
to be here."

"Well, was it as important to you as it was to him?" Jen asks.

"Look, I didn't even remember that Mommy wanted to have this
dinner for y'all tonight. I figured I would take you out for tacos and
tequila and then come back here and pass out. Day-to-day, I haven't
been focused on anything but being with Davis and getting through
each day without being sent to jail. But, yes, he's important to me."

"So what's the big issue now?" Rudy appears confused. He sits back
on my bed and starts to fiddle with my old Malibu Barbie.

"Well, it didn't help that I acted like such a weirdo this evening.
Mommy and Daddy have been furious about me staying with Davis,
and then all of a sudden they're treating him like their son-in-law? And
I love my sister, but sometimes she gets under my skin. Ann Marie and
I were both stressed out, and we took it out on each other, as usual. So
I think Davis got kind of spooked. With everything he's going through
with his divorce and his custody fight, the last thing he needs is another
crazy, volatile woman in his life. But I think we could've gotten past
that too if it wasn't for all my other nonsense."

"What other nonsense?" Jen asks.

"When Davis was leaving tonight, I told him about all the crap back
in L.A. I had already told him most of it—all about Ravi and the fight
with Danielle and all that, even the prison part. He even suggested a

lawyer I should talk to, though I haven't called her yet. She's yet another person who hates me, so I haven't wanted to face her."

"Jo, you're killing me," Jen complains. "What the hell happened?!"

"Well, I told him . . . I told him that I torched Ravi's house."

"*What!*" Malibu Barbie falls from Rudy's hand and lands headfirst on the floor. Jen says nothing and simply stares at me.

"Jo!" Jen yells. "The one thing you've had going for you in this whole thing is that we are the only three people other than your lawyer who knows what happened! Even though Ravi and Danielle think they know, as long as you don't open your mouth, they have to prove it. The more people you talk to, the harder this is going to be. What if they make Davis testify about what he knows?"

"That's right," Rudy says. "This is not a Lisa 'Left-Eye' Lopes situation." Rudy picks up Malibu Barbie from the floor and shakes his head at her as he smooths the static from her hair.

"What are you talking about, Rudy?"

"That rapper girl from TLC that tried to burn that football player's shoes in the bathtub and set his house on fire. I don't think she did time. But the football player didn't want them to charge her with anything because they were still together. You don't have it like that."

I lie back down on the floor. I feel so sad that I can't even cry anymore.

"Come on, cha cha," Rudy says, his voice now calm. "Just give Davis some time. That's a bit of a shocker, wouldn't you say? That's a lot for the poor man to process. He seems like a good guy—how often have you heard me say that?"

"Never," I mumble.

"I talked to him for a while about music. He's funny, and he seemed really decent. And he definitely seemed ga-ga for you, so he might come around."

"No, he won't," I groan. "Even if he does, by the time it happens, I'll be back in L.A. Especially since Ravi threatened me."

"He threatened you? Should we call the cops?" Jen's eyes are wide and worried.

"It doesn't sound like he has any proof, but he said that he'll tell the cops I set his house on fire if I don't come back and finish the movie. He said the studio loves it. They love me, evidently."

"But that's great, isn't it?" Jen offers, though I catch a glimpse of Rudy shaking his head at her.

"We'll take this one step at a time, Jo," he says. "You get your stuff in order, and then work on Davis. He'll be more open to you once you get your shit in order. If not, then maybe you can make him jealous by going out with Willie T. again."

"Hell, no!" Jen interjects, though she laughs as she says it. "That's juvenile, Rudy, and our girl here is trying to have a mature relationship. Also, I think Bill is more my type than Jo's."

"Figures," I respond. I finally feel up to sitting up again. "It's mighty convenient for you to say that, you flirt. I don't think I've ever seen anybody bat their eyelashes that much in my whole life, other than in those old silent movies."

"Jo's got you there, girl," Rudy laughs. "I guess she better go ahead and release that man to you before you do this to her." Rudy starts a cat-fight between Malibu Barbie and a headless Chrissie doll. Even without a head, Chrissie kicks Barbie's ass.

I laugh and mimic Jen's cross-legged stance on the scratchy fibers of the green wall-to-wall carpet. Rudy waves Malibu Barbie in my direction. "You need to talk to this local lawyer person so that you can get back to having hot screaming sex with Davis again."

"Who am I kidding?" My humor fades again. "I'm a felon who can barely take care of a houseplant. Can you see me seriously involved with a guy who's got a kid?"

"Is that guy a tall, white guy from Texas named Davis? Then, yes I can," Rudy says.

"So, Jo, who's this lawyer Davis told you about?"

I raise my eyes to the ceiling bulb. The light is so harsh that I start to see spots. "Her name's Paula, and we grew up together. She's hated me since third grade."

Despite my serious expression, Rudy and Jen cackle and honk like a gaggle of geese.

"What," Rudy snorts. "You steal her man too?"

That comment is not at all funny, but they both seem to find the whole thing hilarious.

"You think I can look up some new best friends in the Yellow Pages?"

"No," Rudy hoots. That's what's MySpace is for!"

Jen sniffles and blows her nose into a tissue. "Jo, we're just kidding. You used to have a sense of humor before you became a criminal. You know what? It's not that late. You should call this Paula person right now."

"It's 11:00 on a Friday night. What if she's having hot, screaming sex?"

"Call her," Rudy presses.

"Maybe tomorrow. Or Monday, when she's in her office. What's the big rush?"

"Jo, darling girl. Even though we're laughing, this really isn't a joke. At some point you've got to face up to what you've done and figure out what to do about it. You need to sit down with somebody sane and figure out how you're going to get on with your life and what that life will look like going forward. Because the arsonist adultress thing is kind of old and not so attractive, you know?"

I don't say anything. I just close my eyes and lie back down on the carpet in a corpse pose like the one I used to do at the end of my yogilates classes.

"Jo, you might have a real chance for a really great relationship with Davis," Rudy continues. "Or if not with Davis, then with some-one else. Maybe you're finally ready for a real relationship in your life rather than whatever the hell you've been doing ever since I've known you. But you'll never know it if you don't resolve this other situation."

"And then there's the whole matter of your career," Jen adds. "I know you're distraught about Ravi, and you have mixed feelings about leaving Davis, but being 'forced' to finish a lead role in a movie at your age after everything you've done is nothing to turn down your nose at."

"You're my agent," I respond. "Of course you would say that. Espe-cially since Lifetime loves it and wants to turn it into a series after the pilot airs."

"What!" she screams. "And they didn't call me? And you're conflicted about it?!"

"Focus, Jenny girl," Rudy tells her.

"I'm not just saying this stuff as Jo's agent, Rudy, but as her friend. How many Black women do you see carrying scripted shows on TV these days? Ravi or no Ravi, this is a huge break for you, Jo, at this point in your career. It can also open doors for other people if you do a good job at it. Which you will—work is the one thing you're serious about. You can't take something like this for granted!"

I know she's right, but I don't say so. I say nothing and continue to lie on my back with my eyes closed.

"Come on, Jo, call Paula," Jen pleads.

"No!"

"Call her, Jo, or else I'm telling Mommy everything and letting her call this Paula person for you," Rudy snaps back at me.

On that note, I pick myself up off the floor and finally pick up the phone.

CHAPTER 25 ♡

I thought I would be the first one in the kitchen this morning. But the lights are on, and the percolator is gurgling cheerily.

Rudy pads into the kitchen in his pajamas holding his head with one hand. "I smell coffee," he says. His other hand is extended in front of him, as if he's searching for the coffee pot by touch instead of sight.

"It's not ready yet," I offer.

"What did you put in those drinks you made after we peeled you off the floor?" Rudy helps himself to a *World's Greatest Grandmother* mug from the cupboard and sits at the kitchen table.

"You don't want to know."

Mommy breezes into the kitchen in her belted satin robe and matching slippers. She drops a newspaper on the table next to Rudy's coffee cup.

"I brought in the paper if y'all want to look at it." Mommy clicks the television on to a local Saturday morning news/talk show. "You look a little green, Rudy," she says as she removes a carton of eggs from the refrigerator.

I try to concentrate on the summer fashion advice Midland's big-haired talking heads are cheerily offering on TV. But I can't do it. It all seems too trivial. And tame. If I wore Bermuda shorts and eyelet shifts like those in L.A., I'd be mistaken for someone's grandma. I walk out onto the patio to make a phone call.

"Paula, this is Jo. I sent you a text last night, so if you got that message already, you can ignore this one. I wanted to see if I could set up an appointment to talk to you next week, if that's OK. I have a prob . . . some legal questions I want to run by someone, and my . . . a friend recommended I call you. Anyway, you can call me back on this cell number whenever you get a chance. Thanks."

I stride back into the kitchen. "Mommy, can I borrow your keys?"

Mommy doesn't ask me any questions. She points in the direction of the opposite counter. "They're over there next to my purse."

I grab the keys and race out the front door. I'm in such a hurry that I don't have the time, or the dignity, to change out of my drawstring pajama pants stenciled with sketches of cocktail glasses and my ratty Rebels T-shirt from high school that hugs my frame too tightly to be appropriate for anything other than hiding out in the house by myself.

As I pull into Davis's driveway, I notice the garage door is open. Davis is bent over the open trunk of his Mini Cooper, tossing a leather duffle bag and a paper shopping bag into the hatch. His eyes widen, but he says nothing as he watches me leave Mommy's Cadillac and trudge across his carport in my tattered sleepwear.

"You don't have to say it, Davis. I know what you're thinking. 'It's bad enough that Jo tortures me with all her other craziness, but now she's torturing me with her looks too.'"

His grin is warm, and he doesn't stifle his impulse to laugh. "That's not exactly what I was thinking, no. But my mind was reeling a bit. Though I can't talk. If I wasn't on my way to Austin to try to convince people that my son is safer with me than his mother, I'd be wearing some cruddy sweats and T-shirts too."

"I know. I've seen them, remember?"

"I remember. At least mine don't have pictures of liquor all over them. I may be a drunk, but I try not to advertise it." Davis shuts the lid of his trunk and leans against it. "I'd ask you inside," he says, "but I have to leave in a few. I'm gonna try to catch the 10 A.M. on Southwest so I can spend some time with Cody." He crosses his arms across his chest, and his expression sobers, though it's not unfriendly.

"That's OK, Davis. I'm not staying. You think I want to burn this image of myself into your brain?"

"Probably not. So what's up?

Having nothing to lean on for support, I shift on my rubber san-daled feet in the middle of Davis's driveway. "I just wanted you to know that I understand why you can't, why we can't be together right now. It upset me, because it's the last thing I really want to happen. But, you've already been more than understanding and patient with me. And I know this thing with Cody is your biggest priority. And it should be. So I understand."

Davis drops his eyes. "I appreciate that. I was kinda' shell-shocked last night. But after I bolted, I felt really bad about leaving you like that." His eyes are cloudy as he looks up at me again. "If it makes you feel any better, I can guarantee you that I felt as awful as you seemed to feel about it. Maybe more so."

"Thanks, Davis. That does make me feel a bit better. Oh, shit! I didn't mean it like that!"

Davis smiles and wipes one eye. "I know what you meant, Jo."

"Oh." I sway from foot to foot, clasping my hands behind my back to keep them from shaking. "Anyway, Davis, I don't want to make you late, but I also wanted to tell you that I have no idea why I acted so weird last night. I knew I had to tell you the whole story about what I did back in L.A. The fact that I hadn't told you everything was eating away at me. And I felt so awful making you miss seeing your son yester-day. When my sister brought Willie T. over and then started meddling me at dinner, I guess I just melted down from the stress of it all. I mean, I never really resolved anything with Willie T. We just stopped talking. So it was awkward seeing him last night. I'm cuckoo and a hothead, but I hope I'm not as bad as I came across yesterday. That's not how I want you to think of me, because I would like to try to go on being friends, even if we can't . . . well, you know."

"I didn't know that we weren't still friends," Davis says softly.

"Davis, were you listening to yourself last night? I didn't come away with the impression that we were still friends. In fact, that's the opposite of what I believed when you left last night. That's why I came over here looking like I just escaped from the loony bin! Actually, that will probably be a headline, since I risked being photographed leaving the house like this – Jo Randolph Escapes From Asylum!"

Davis rises to his feet and walks toward me. I don't know what to do. I hold my breath. Davis wraps his arms around me and gives me a big, brotherly hug. It feels nice, even though it's pretty platonic.

Davis releases me and glances at his watch. "Jo, I gotta go. But I'm glad you came by. We can talk on Monday about the tryouts and the play. I'll have to go back to Austin mid-week and will probably have to skip out of town from time to time as this custody thing gets going. But at least we can pick the cast and get the kids started to work."

Davis pecks me on the cheek and turns away to walk back to his car. I don't want to do it, but I let him go. I return to Mommy's car and back it out of Davis's driveway. I sit idly, waving my hand out the window as he pulls his little car out of the garage and the driveway and then heads out of my sight.

Before I can get going, my cell phone starts up its hip-hop beat.

"So you want to torture me some more?" I say to my sister.

"Hey, Jo Ella. I wanted to apologize for yesterday."

I don't say anything.

"You there?" she asks. She sounds tired.

"Yeah, Ann Marie, I'm here." I can't stay mad at her. "We all have our bad days. Trust me, I know."

"Thanks." Her voice cracks, and she pauses for a moment. "I was annoyed at Claude yesterday . . ."

"Really?" I cut her off.

"Very funny, Jo Ella. Anyway, every day Claude talks about how Willie T. wants to call you up but is all conflicted about it. So after weeks of this crap, I invite him to come to dinner with us so that he'd be forced to talk to you and resolve things one way or another. And then Claude has the nerve to tell me to butt out of it! And then he gave me that 'I told you so' look when we saw Davis there, so that made me even more pissed off."

"The wine didn't help. You're an angry drunk, you know, Ann Marie."

"You're one to talk, sister dear."

"I know," I say. "It's OK, Ann Marie. It wasn't exactly the fun evening I was looking forward to having with Jen and Rudy. But a lot of stuff finally came out that I've been putting off dealing with. If you can get out of the house this week, I'll treat you to dinner and bend your ear about it."

"That would be good. Tuesday would be *especially* good, since it's a soccer night."

"OK," I laugh. "Pick a place that has good wine."

"Of course," she says and hangs up.

I slowly make my way back home. As I pull up, I notice an unfamiliar car parked behind mine in my parents' driveway. Another BMW, though this one is much newer than mine, with a nice coat of silver paint.

"Jo Ella, you won't believe who stopped by to see you," Mommy says as soon as I enter the kitchen.

"Who?"

"Paula. She's having coffee out on the patio with Rudy and Jennifer."

I peer out the sliding glass door and see Paula sitting at our umbrella table with Rudy and Jen. Rudy's lips are moving, and Paula is smiling, laughing even.

"There you are," Jen calls out to me as I step outside. "We've gotten your whole situation worked out for you already, so you can just pull up a chair and have some coffee."

"Hi, Jo Ella," Paula says quietly, though she continues to smile as she says it.

"Hi, Paula. Wow. I appreciate you coming over."

"It's OK. I went to the gym this morning, and I decided to drive by your house on the way home."

"We already spilled all the beans," Rudy says in his silky voice that returns when he's not under stress.

"So how screwed am I?" I sit in an empty chair between Rudy and Jen.

"Well, it depends. Your friends here tell me they don't have any real evidence against you yet, just circumstantial stuff."

"As far as I know."

"And it sounds like your friend must be pretty desperate to make this movie, if he's willing to blackmail you over it."

I shrug my shoulders. "I know he really wants to do it. I mean, this is like his big break into directing. And he'll get paid big-time if the network is serious about picking up the pilot. He won't have to depend on his wife for money anymore."

"Well, Jo Ella, the first question is, do *you* want to do this movie?" Paula's expression is calm, her demeanor patient. My friends' expressions are not so calm or patient.

"No. Not at all," I say, the words spilling out of me before I take the time to think about them. I watch my friends' expressions turn dark. "I mean, something like this is great for my career, particularly under the circumstances. And it's not like I couldn't use the money. It's rare for a Black actress or an actress my age to get a break like this one, and I know I shouldn't turn down good work at this stage of my career. But I honestly don't want to have to work with my ex day-in and day-out. And, though I can't believe I'm saying this, I really want to stay here. At least for the rest of the summer, so I can finish the play and my classes. The kids are depending on me."

Paula seems surprised. She studies my face for a while before responding. "I understand how you feel. But are you sure you're ready to give up your acting career and become a West Texas schoolteacher? Or risk going to jail?"

The answer is obvious, but I can't bring myself to say it.

"Well, if it's any consolation," Paula continues, "your ex seems desperate for you to come back and finish the movie. So I bet they'll wait a few weeks longer, 'til the end of the summer. It's not that much more time."

"What about the wife?" Jen asks. "How should Jo deal with her? I mean, it was the wife's house that was damaged."

"My guess is that she must really want to get this film done too. Now that things have calmed down a bit, she's probably now thinking about how she can get her money out of it or turn something painful into something that's at least profitable for her. That would be my guess. Otherwise, she probably would have gone after Jo Ella for the fire already." Paula focuses back on me. "If you go back and do the movie, there's no guarantee that they won't still go to the police or try to sue you unless we get them to sign a release. I can call your friend's lawyer on Monday and offer them a deal. I know you don't want to do this movie, but that may be your way out. I can tell 'em you'll come back and work on this movie and TV show if they let you start at the end of the summer and if both of them sign a release. So you get one of the things you want, which is to stay in Midland for the rest of the summer, and you'll have a good, well-paying acting job to go back to, even though you'll have to put up with seeing your ex. I mean, it's kind of a small price to pay, don't you think?"

Rudy and Jen trade worried glances.

"Paula, if getting paid to work on a movie keeps me out of jail, I would be stupid not to take that deal," I respond. "I may be a head case, but I know that if you're able to work out a solution like that, it would be a blessing. But if it's at all possible, could we just agree for me to do the movie and not tie me into the series too?"

"Really?" Paula seems taken aback. Jen looks like she might have a coronary. "You don't want them to guarantee you the TV series too? I thought that was the whole point of these things."

"Well, it is," I say in response. "But if this thing gets picked up as a soap series, it's a five-day-a-week deal that can go on for years, if the show does well. Crazy as it sounds, I'm not so sure anymore if that's what I want."

"Have you lost your mind?" Jen looks at me as if I have turned into an alien life form before her eyes. "You've worked your whole life for this type of opportunity."

"I know the series would be great money, Jen. This kind of job would normally be a dream come true for someone like me. It *was* my dream come true remember? But the more I think about it, the more I realize that it might not be such a great idea to keep Ravi in my life for that long, if I can help it. This whole situation has been pretty toxic for all of us, so maybe I should move on from this project and these people. I haven't given up on my career entirely, but I'm starting to realize that success for me may be something different than what I've pictured in my head all these years."

"Why cut off your nose to spite your face, Jo?" Jen asks. "Unless something magical happened while you were out just now, you don't have a relationship with Davis or Willie T. to keep you in Midland. And the school hasn't offered you a permanent job, as far as I know. Why would you walk away from locking in the kind of deal that not only keeps you out of jail, but could also fund your retirement? Even if the pilot gets picked up, realistically how long does the average television series stay on the air? With so many actors out of work, you can't just turn down your nose at a great opportunity to do what you love and make money doing it. Besides, I don't think you really have a choice to be so selective." Jen's expression is sober and serious.

"Jen may be right," Paula adds. "Legally, I mean. The more important you are to this movie and to any series that grows out of it, the less likely they will be to press charges against you or even bring the issue up to blackmail you in the future. And as much as you don't like these people, the reality is that you did burn down their house." Paula's words are blunt, but true. I can't run away from them. "I assume from what everyone has said," she continues, "that you can't afford to reimburse them for their loss. So this may be a way for you to do so."

They all stare at me in an odd sort of way, as if they are having trouble reading my face. For a change I haven't carefully crafted my expression for a particular effect, and I have no clue what my face is conveying.

Rudy breaks the tension. "You know good and well that you're too much of a mess to move in with me if you end up unemployed and out on the street. And if you and Davis really care about each other, you'll find a way to make it happen."

My gaze shifts from Rudy to Paula's wide, brown eyes. I see my conscience staring me in the face. Perhaps the reason I never got along with Paula in our youth is that my own inner ugliness is so clearly revealed in her quiet expressions. I'm so freakin' self-centered. It's a quality that has served me well as a performer and public persona, but it hasn't had such a positive effect on my soul. Or the people I care about. Even in my worst moments, I am always looking for the angle that benefits me. Perhaps Mommy's right when she says I would have made a good lawyer. Though this time it's less my ego than my heart that's guiding my emotions and actions. Like when I decided to turn my back on law school for an MFA and never looked back. I followed my heart to stage and screen and have never regretted a moment of it, despite my limited monetary success and accolades.

I smile at my friends over my coffee cup. "I know you're right." They all exchange relieved glances. "But you know me well enough to know that I can't admit you're right without trying your patience about it. So before I slink back to L.A. with my tail between my legs, maybe we can have the gall to ask for one concession? Can we try to make doing the series optional for me, in case I change my mind? Though *Lord help us* if I do change my mind."

Paula shrugs her shoulders. "I'll try it," she says.

"But if they reject that, *lock the girl into a contract!*" Rudy squeals. "She knows not what she does, trust me!"

Paula laughs and nods in response. "Don't worry. That's why people hire me."

"I have a question," Jen prods. "Isn't asking them to sign a release kind of an admission that Jo did this stuff? If they don't have a case, why act like they have one?"

"People settle stuff all the time, whether they're at fault or not. A lot of the time, all people are saying is, this is not worth it to me to have to pay lawyers to defend my interests or to have something like this drag on or be made public, so I'll reach a deal with you. Even if you're not at fault for something, there's always the risk that a judge or a jury won't see the facts in your favor, so it's a way to make the case go away before it gets to that point." Paula glances down at her watch. "I better get going. But, Jo Ella, I'll call you on Monday to talk some more before I call these people, OK?"

Paula turns to leave, and I reach out to grasp her forearm. "Hey, Paula, I can't thank you enough. And, I want you to know that I'm really sorry about the whole thing with Curt. I really didn't intend to lead him on. I didn't even realize how much I was leading him on. That's what I get for being so vain—I told you I was self-centered."

"Jo Ella, you haven't exactly cornered the market on vanity. Curt's pretty into himself too. But his heart's in the right place. Lou tells me all the time that I need to be more like you and her and just tell him I like him." Paula's eyes drop to the ground. "It's kind of hard to do," she says without lifting her head.

"Paula, I don't think you have to go that far. Just say 'hello' to him, and he'll think you're trying to reserve a room in his 'love palace.' Trust me."

Paula smiles and gives me a hug. I've known her most of my life, and I've never seen her smile so much. Maybe I'm making progress, because she's not even smiling at my expense. Though that changes quickly as Rudy pulls me away from Paula and points his index finger at me. "Now enough of that warm and fuzzy stuff. Girl, if you don't go right now and wipe the crust off your face and take off these ugly rags, then I might be the one who calls the police on your behind."

"Sorry, Rudy," I say and kiss him on the cheek. "There are no fashion police in Midland."

CHAPTER 26 ♡

Jen and Rudy are more excited about this musical than I am. Rudy in particular texts me multiple times a day with ideas about the production and offers to help.

HiFiNY:	Jones is coming!!!!
JoMaMa:	What?
JiFiNY:	Jones! My friend, the theater producer. I told him re: your wacko show & he luvs idea. He's also cute & possibly avail. I'm bringing him w/me to see your play!
JoMaMa:	Thx.
HiFiNY:	What's wrong, mama? No excite?
JoMaMa:	Mama sad. But glad U & Jen will be here.

I shove my phone into the pocket of my lightweight, loose-fitting yoga pants and take a seat on the worn floorboards of the auditorium stage. I'm the only one here; the kids won't show up for another twenty minutes. I feel the warm, weathered planks and pockmarks underneath my fingertips as I lean back on my hands and stretch my legs out in front of me. I lean forward and wrap my hands around my ankles, drawing my head to my knees. I move into a v-sit and sink into some long, ballet stretches. I've finally gotten around to stretching out my underworked limbs. I rouse myself out of bed at daybreak and roll out my yoga mat on the patio by our pool most days. I ritually dive into the pool when I get home from work and get in some laps before dinner. I even take the occasional spin class at The Grind. Despite Ann Marie's description of this gym as the hookup spot for Midland's miniscule Black bourgeoisie, my spottings of other Black folks are almost as rare as finding a registered Democrat among the Lee faculty. If Willie T. frequents that place, I've never seen him.

I finish my warm-up and cross my legs into Lotus Position. I close my eyes and take deep breaths, expanding my chest as I inhale. I try to clear my mind but I'm flooded with memories of my early days in New York City. I did Shakespeare in the Park and *Grease* and had small parts in a few other Broadway shows. But I mostly lived off and off-off Broadway, in small theaters seating a few hundred people or less, like Cherry Lane, The Public Theater, and La MaMa. I did indie productions, readings of playwrights' works in progress, and even an experimental revival of *Hair* where females played all the male characters and vice versa. I was both serious and excited about the work, just like my kids this summer. None of my performances have survived as more than mentions on my résumé or deeply buried credits on the theaters' websites. The masses can't readily rent these performances from Netflix or catch them late at night on Cinemax. But it's the work I'm most proud of.

I remember my evenings with Davis before the disaster dinner at my folks' house. Me stretched out on his patio chaise well after dark, the stars, the nearby strip malls and the street lamps the only breaks in the indigo sky, other then the amber glow of his patio lights. We shared stories of stages in those evening hours. I told him long, rambling sagas of my ramen noodle days doing experimental theater in East Village black boxes. He made my sides ache with hilarious tales of redneck bars and dives he crooned in on the road. And revealed the star-struck teen buried beneath my jaded L.A. exterior with his recants of studio sessions with the likes of Eric Clapton, Lenny Kravitz, and the White Stripes. We sipped wine, and he held my hand, and I felt the same sense of "I'm where I belong" that I felt during my early days in New York. The same feeling I experience working on this show for the kids. I don't know what it is, but if I could bottle it and sell it, I wouldn't have to work on soap operas anymore.

"Hey, Miss Randolph." I'm so lost in my thoughts that I don't even notice Tomás and Tyrone. The metal bar that opens the heavy auditorium door clatters as it's pressed over and over again by the stream of students entering the room behind them.

"Hey, guys, come up here and sit with me." I wave for them to join me. Soon we are all seated cross-legged in our warm-up circle.

"Before we warm-up and rehearse those new scenes I gave you, let's chat a little bit. The summer's moving pretty fast, and we're getting into the intense part of rehearsals. Before we lose ourselves in this show, and I turn into a raving lunatic, I wanted to take a moment to let you guys ask me any questions you have about the show or acting in general. Or to just talk about anything that's on your mind."

The kids exchange sideways glances. They seem to be afraid to look me in the eye. Kiley tentatively raises her hand.

"Miss Randolph, how come you came back to teach us? You don't wanna be an actress no more?"

"Yeah, Ms. Randolph," Clance interjects as he flicks his jet-black bangs out of his eyes. "If I got out of Midland and could live in New York and California and be an actor, I would never come back."

I scan their eager faces. All eyes are fixed on mine. "Well, my loves, I would be stretching the truth if I told you that I *willingly* came home to work with you guys this summer. But y'all probably know that already. Who's read the tabloids? Let's get a show of hands."

All of the kids raise their hands. A murmur of giggles ripples around our circle.

"So you *did* steal that old lady's husband?" Kiley gasps. "Did she run you out of town?"

I can't hold back my laughter. I laugh so hard that I can barely speak.

"I, whoo . . . it didn't exactly happen like that. Ha ha ha ha ha ha, hmm. Ok, maybe there's SOME truth to that story."

The kids smile and lean in.

"Look, y'all have to know that most of what you read in those magazines is garbage. But in the middle of the trashcan there may be a few kernels of truth. You're all super smart, so I'm not gonna treat you like idiots. I *did* become involved with someone that I honestly thought was getting a divorce. It was awful naïve of me, especially with everything I've been exposed to through the years, but I still believed it. We were working together, so when the truth came out, it became impossible for me to stay. I said and did a lot of really immature things. But the one smart thing I did in the heat of it all was listen to my two best friends. I have two levelheaded friends who always tell me the truth even when I don't want to hear it. No matter what you do in life or how successful you are, you should always keep close to your true friends who tell you the truth, and not what you want to hear.

"Anyway, I took my friends' advice to get out of Hollywood for a while to really think about what I was doing and where I wanted to go next. Most actors and people in the public eye are just as flawed and insecure as everyone else. Sometimes more so, especially if they got into the business at a young age. They make the same mistakes as everyone else, but their mistakes are magnified because they're in the public eye and many of them are dependent on the public's approval for their self-esteem."

My students remain in rapt attention. "As you can see from this summer, if you love theater or music and have a talent for it and get to do it for a living, even if it's not a big living, it can be the greatest thing in the world. But it's a hard and unforgiving and unfair business. It can make people so desperate that they do things that aren't true to who they really are inside. They'll act like people they're not, or they'll lie or turn on their friends or kiss up to people that they detest, just so they can keep working and doing the thing they love. They'll lie to themselves to get approval—even from people they don't even know."

"Sounds like high school," Qiana says. Others nod in agreement.

"It *is* like high school!" I respond. "And a lot of folks never grow up. Can you imagine? Anyway, to finally answer Kiley's question, I did leave L.A. because I got myself into a hot mess. I thought I was disappointed with my ex. But getting out of the limelight has made me realize that I'm most disappointed with myself. I put blinders on about the people I was associating with and the roles I was taking not just because it's my living and I need to make money, but also because I still wanted to believe in a Hollywood fairy tale life that doesn't really exist other than on film."

"So are you gonna stay here, Miss Randolph?" Tyrone asks.

My smile fades. I stare into their hopeful, sweet faces. "I don't know, Tyrone. I might. But I can't promise anything."

"Well," drawls Gerald McDougal, "could ya' stay long enough for all of us to graduate?"

My smile returns, "I can't tell you right now, but when I figure it out, y'all will be the first to know."

"What about Mr. Farenthold?" Gerald asks.

The kids exchange shocked glances. I pause for a moment. "Well, I expect he will be here. I know he has had to miss a lot of our rehearsals because of some personal business he is trying to settle back in Austin. But I know this is where he plans to be."

"So . . ." Tyrone hesitates. He frowns for a second and then shrugs. "Maybe if he stays, you'll stay too?"

A round of hushed giggles resumes.

"No comment," I deadpan. "I think that's enough questions for today." The kids all laugh in response.

"Miss Randolph, can I ask one more thing?" Qiana says softly.

"Sure, go ahead." I respond.

"You never wanted to have kids or get married or nothing?" She averts her eyes. "I'm sorry. That's personal."

"Qiana, look at me." She turns her head. "I've been joking around, but I want you guys to feel comfortable asking me anything. Ask me real questions. I want y'all to know that you should just walk into my office or email me whenever you want to talk about anything. I got out of Midland and have been able to live my life exactly as I've wanted to, for better and for worse. I have the feeling that a lot of you, whether you stay here in Midland or decide to leave, have things you want to do with your lives that you can't figure out how to achieve. So while you have me here as your old, wise one who has been through the ringer, you should take advantage of it!"

"So," Kiley says, "about Qiana's question?"

"Ha! OK, I was digressing," I say. "Honestly, I love kids, and I love being in love." The giggles resume. "But I also really love what I do. I kind of threw all of myself into it at a young age and let it take me wherever it was gonna take me. For most of my adult life, there were things that were a bigger priority to me than having kids. Now if in that time I had settled down and married one of my many boyfriends," I do a fake hair flip and bat my eyes, "then I'm sure that I would have had kids by now. But it was something I was never going to do on my own, at least not as a young woman running back and forth between auditions. I decided that as a young age. Not to say that my choice is the best, just the best one for me. With all the things I wanted to do and places I wanted to go, those things were always a bigger priority than settling down."

"Did you get proposed to?" Qiana asks, wide-eyed.

"Yeah, I did. But I wasn't ready to get married any of those times." Qiana's mouth drops open at my revelation of my multiple proposals. "All great guys, but we would have split because my head was always someplace else, and they would have taken a backseat. I'm self-centered and impulsive, but I had enough good home training to reign myself in before hurting someone else. At least in those situations."

My kids still appear stunned. Is it still so unusual in West Texas to be a willingly unmarried woman over the age of thirty?

"I finally realized I might be ready to get married after I turned forty. When I met someone I really connected with, I let myself get *so* wrapped up in happy ever after daydreams that I made a lot of mistakes. Big mistakes that landed me in the tabloids. A life lesson for everyone."

"But you can still have kids one day, right?" Kiley asks innocently.

"Of course," I respond. "It might be hard for me to have a child the natural way at my age, but I can always adopt if I feel I'm ready for it. I've never been hung up on the whole biological family thing as the only definition of 'family.' For me, family can also be the people you choose to make a part of your life. Actually, I've already adopted all of you, so I have, let's see, how many children?" I raise my index finger in the air and start counting heads. "I guess that's a cue that we should start our roll call. And I thought you were gonna ask me easy stuff like the best places to take acting lessons or how to find out about auditions! Y'all are a tough crowd!"

I take attendance, and we start our group warm-up. We rehearse and block the new scenes I gave them. We become so absorbed that when we finally take a break, we realize that rehearsal has run a half hour too long. I release the kids and head back to my office. As soon as I reach my desk, my cell phone calls out to me. I answer it without paying attention to the number of the caller.

"Ms. Randolph? Jo Randolph?" asks the deep voice on the other end of the line.

"Yes, who is this?" I answer.

"This is Miflin Hanks. Ms. Randolph, if you have a few minutes, I wanted to ask you some questions about an incident in May at the home of Ravi Mehra. Is this a good time? If not, maybe we can set up a time that's more convenient."

My body freezes. All of the de-stressing and relaxing exercises I did during drama class have lost their effect. "Who are you again? Who do you work for?"

"I'm Miflin Hanks. I apologize, Ms. Randolph. I'm an independent investigator . . . let's say I'm an *appraiser* looking into some losses suffered by Mr. Mehra and his wife at a residence they owned in Manhattan Beach. Your name came up as someone who might have some information you could share with me."

I scribble "Miflin Hanks" in pencil on the back of one of my English student's most recent disaster of an essay. "Uh, Mr. Hanks, I'm really not sure what this is about, and I don't really feel comfortable chatting with a complete stranger. You'll have to talk to my agent or my lawyer. If they say it's OK to talk to you about whatever it is you're talking about, then we can set something up."

"Oh, OK. Well, it will only take a few minutes. I really don't have much . . . "

"Mr. Hanks," I say, using all of my acting tricks to feign calm. "Let me give you the contact info for my agent and lawyer . . ."

CHAPTER 27 ♡

"So where did he say he worked again?" Paula asks. She is so nonchalant, I wonder if I just woke her up.

"He didn't!" I screech into my cell phone. "Why is this guy calling me? What does he want? I thought that this deal we're working on with Ravi and Danielle would settle everything. So why . . . "

"Jo," Paula says calmly. Is that a hint of annoyance in her voice? "You're gonna have to calm down. I'll check this guy out. He could be from the tabloids. He could be someone hired by Danielle and Ravi to scare you into signing a deal on their terms. Or he could be relaying information back to them. Or he could be from an insurance company investigating claims they made after the fire."

"How did he get my number?"

"Well," Paula says, "I don't know, but I presume your ex probably gave it to him."

Lord help me!

"Look, Jo, I will check him out. Whoever he is, even if he's police, you don't have to talk to him. You refer everyone to me. If he's an insurance investigator or some sort of PI, he can't legally force you to do or say anything. Ravi and Danielle are the only ones that have to answer to him. Just be patient."

"Oh, alright." I say.

"By the way, Jo," Paula continues. "I need to talk to you about these negotiations."

"OK . . ." something's wrong, I know it.

"They seem prepared to sign a release, but there's one big holdup. The fact that you want to be able to opt out of a series. They won't know for sure until the ratings for the broadcast of the movie come in, but it looks likely that the series will be picked up by Lifetime. And if it's successful, it helps them with the network if you're locked in."

I'm confused. "But that doesn't make sense. Usually for producers, the more freedom they have to replace me the better, right?"

"Jo, no one ever asks for *less* rights in these kinds of deals. They think the only reason you don't want to be committed to the series is so you can demand more money when the series is green lighted. You're the main character, and if the ratings are good, they think this is a strategy to make them pay an enormous amount to keep you."

"Didn't you tell them I just want flexibility, in case things don't go well? That I may want the freedom to come back here?"

"Not in those words, no. It doesn't benefit me, or you, to say that to them. Look, Jo, I made some arguments about our apprehension over working with Ravi and Danielle Coleman given everything that has happened. But as your lawyer, I have to be honest with you. I know this is what you think you want, but it's a mistake. It looks more like this will be a weekly series, not an every day of the week daytime soap opera. You'll go on hiatus. You won't be a slave to this series for the rest of your life. You can find ways to keep in touch with your students you've become so fond of. And if your personal stuff here is meant to work out then, well, you'll find a way to work it out. Why put yourself in the position of losing such a big opportunity when you don't have any others on the horizon? I talked to Jen, but her phone's not ringing with offers for you. And who can say that Ravi and Danielle won't spread ugly rumors about you or blackball you if you leave after the pilot?"

I know she's right, and I resent it.

"OK," I say. "I hear you, Paula. Do whatever you think is best."

I have a rough night. Neither laps in the pool, old movies at midnight, or several of Uncle Buddy's Jack Daniel's-laden concoctions help me get to sleep. By the time my eyelids start to drop, my alarm goes off.

I struggle through my English classes then retreat into my office to put my head down on my desk before drama begins.

"How's it going?"

I'm startled and accidentally bump my forehead on my desk. I raise my head and find Davis standing in my doorway. He walks in and shuts the door behind him.

"I'm exhausted!"

"Obviously," he deadpans. "Late night?"

"How about *no* night." I rub my eyes and smooth my hair. "I didn't get a wink of sleep."

"How were rehearsals?" he asks.

"Good," I answer. "You didn't miss much while you were out this time. My biggest problem is with the guys playing the dumb jocks. I think they're taking their parts a little too seriously, because they can't seem to remember their lines to save their lives, no matter how many times we go over them. They remember your songs, though. How about you? How was Austin?"

"I think it's going OK." Davis pulls a chair up to my desk and sits in it. "I'm afraid to get too optimistic about it, but my lawyer thinks we're doing pretty well. It should be ending pretty soon. My ex has missed a bunch of court dates because she got a new gig with the Rolling Stones, so that's worked in my favor, I think. And, as of yesterday, my divorce is finally done. So at least I got that part behind me."

"That's good news, then." I bend my neck from side to side to work out the kinks. I try rubbing the back of my neck, but I can't seem to knead out the stiffness. Davis leans toward me for a moment, but then sinks back into his chair.

"Actually, I was wondering how all your other stuff is going," he says. "We haven't really talked about too much other than the play in a while."

"I figured that was the best thing, to focus on work. Otherwise, I wouldn't be able to focus on work." I smile at Davis, and a glimpse of his old grin returns.

"You're right," he says sheepishly.

"Miracles never cease."

"But seriously, what's going on with you?" he asks again.

I close my script and set it on top of my desk. "I think we're pretty close to working it out. Paula's negotiating for them to sign a release that they won't sue me or anything. I'll have to go back to L.A. and finish the movie, though. But I'll be paid well for it, so I can't really complain. And I'll get to finish out the summer here."

Davis looks relieved, but it's hard to tell.

"But I'll probably have to commit to doing the series if the network picks it up," I continue. "It means I might have to deal with my ex a lot longer than I want to. I tried to get an option to quit the project when the movie's done, so I could leave L.A. sooner, if I wanted to. But it doesn't look like that's gonna happen."

"But isn't getting a series a good thing for you?"

"I used to think so," I respond. "Now I'm not so sure." My eyes hold Davis's.

Davis says nothing for a while. He seems to be calculating something in his head. Or maybe he just ran out of things to say. "Well, at least you'll get to stay here the rest of the summer," he finally offers. "I imagine you won't start shooting the series right away after you finish the movie, right?"

"That's right." I say. "The movie will have to air and they'll probably want to see the ratings before they green light it. So even if they decide to do the series, I should get some time off before we start up again."

Davis pauses again. "How long do you think it will take to finish the movie?" he finally asks.

"Three or four weeks, tops. I might have to go in to do some looping and stuff like that from time to time. And I'll have to be available to do publicity when they release it, but I should be free after about a month or so."

"A month? That's good to hear." Davis fixes his eyes on me and says nothing more. I feel self-conscious and find I can't look at him any longer. My eyes search the ceiling, and I try to think of something to say. But my mind is blank. I look back at Davis who is still staring intently in my direction.

"Well," Davis finally loosens the grip of his gaze. "I'll be back at rehearsal this afternoon. I'm sorry I've missed so much."

"It's OK, Davis."

"No, it's not. Dealing with this custody thing, I couldn't avoid. But I didn't have to deal with us the way that I did. I blamed you for flaking out on me, and then I did the same thing to you. I feel like maybe I overreacted. And now I've missed out on most of the summer that we could have spent together."

"Artists are entitled to be flaky, Farenthold."

"That sounds like a rationalization, Randolph."

"It is. My sister calls me out on that one all the time, but I figure if I say it often enough, maybe somebody will let me to get away with it."

"I'll tell you one thing, though. This being a parent deal can make you crazy. You do the weirdest things out of fear for your kids that you would never do in any other situation."

I reach over and grasp Davis' hand. "I don't have kids, Davis. So what's my excuse?"

Davis smiles and kisses the top of my hand. "I better get out of here before the kids walk in." He stands up and starts for the door. "Or even worse, Hardy'll walk in and start calling us a couple of heathen sinners destined for Hell again."

"OK." I'm finally able to smile. "I'll see you later. You know, you might be able to persuade me to grab a drink or a taco or something after rehearsal. If you ask me nicely, that is."

"I think I can do that." Davis winks and strolls out the door.

Rehearsals are proving difficult. Especially dress rehearsals. "Miss Randolph, these pants don't fit no more!" Pearce Calhoun, a huge freckled-faced teen of about 6'5", 280 lbs. with the voice of a mockingbird lumbers over to me from the dance studio that serves as our dressing room. His beefy fingers struggle to fasten the front of his football pants. Kiley tries to help him tug on the straps and tie them together, her small, slender hands being better suited for that sort of thing. But nothing works. As these are the pants he actually wears to actual football practice, this is as much a problem for Coach Buck as it is for me.

"Miss Randolph, ma'am, there's no durn way I'ma be able to do that high-kick number in these britches."

"Jen!!! I need you!" I'm so glad she's here to help me get through these dress rehearsals. Though she buys most of her duds at Barneys, she's actually pretty nimble with a needle and thread. Wearing a big smile, she trots over with her little Nantucket basket that does double duty as her sewing kit. She has been smiling ever since I dropped her off at Willie T.'s yesterday afternoon when she flew in from L.A. I haven't asked for any of the details, but her smile says it all.

"Miss Randolph, can I talk to you for a minute?" Qiana crosses the stage to where I'm standing. She is decked out in a navy blue suit, a necktie and an ash-blond wig that's a cross between Principal Hardy's carefully crafted hairdo and a late '60s Glen Campbell.

"Sure, Qiana, what's up?"

"Miss Randolph, I wanted to give this to you." Qiana hands me a small gift bag with a sketch of a large blue baby rattle on one side. Qiana grins at me, and Kiley leaves Pearce to sidle up alongside her friend and watch me open my present. I pull out a soft piece of cloth. I unfold the cloth to find that it is an Angela Davis t-shirt like the one I used to have and that I've seen Qiana wear throughout the summer. Something falls with a thud on the floor, and I bend down to pick up a book that dropped out when I unfolded the shirt. It's a dog-eared copy of Angela Davis's *Women, Race and Class.*

"That shirt's clean," Qiana says. "My mama got it from the church when she was laid off. I see your mother bringin' stuff to the church all the time when I'm over there with Marcellus, so I figured it might be the one you used to have. And even if it's not, I thought you might like to have one again."

I feel the tears coming, and I can't contain them.

"And I bought that book at the library. They sell old books for like a nickel. Both me and Kiley read it already, and we thought you might like it."

I wrap my arms around Qiana and Kiley in a clumsy group hug and give each of them a kiss on the cheek.

"I don't know what to say. Thank you, guys. I can't tell you how much this means to me." I wipe my eyes with Angela Davis. "Now go finish getting ready before I start blubbering again and have to shut down this rehearsal before it even starts."

They both give me another hug and then head back to their marks on the other side of the stage so we can start the big opening number.

"Hey, Jo!" Davis yells from the band pit. "You think we can start this thing before sun-up?"

"*Places, everybody!*" I call out in my biggest stage voice. I peek out from behind the curtain and give Davis a thumbs up.

A few days later, the auditorium begins to fill up with all sorts of folks, young and old and in-between. Droves of people pile into the auditorium to watch this weird little production of ours. There was such a large demand for tickets that we had to add two additional shows.

My whole family is here, even Uncle Buddy and Aunt Lula, though I'm sure she won't hear a thing. Uncle Buddy is seated at the end of the row they have taken up, his walker beside him in the aisle. He is swigging from a flask that he not-so discreetly tucked into the front pocket of his plaid cotton shirt. I wave at my family as I cross the stage carrying a clipboard with my pre-curtain to-do list. I see that Uncle Harvey is wearing his "W" cap today, so Daddy is sitting as far away from him as possible. Mommy is smiling and nodding at all the townsfolk she knows, while Memphis is passing lemon drops down the aisle as bribes to Ann Marie's boys.

I head back behind stage and almost trip over some thick speaker wires. "Nelson!" I yell for my fifteen year old stage manager. "Can you tape these down, please?"

"Looks like it's gonna be a full house," Davis drawls behind me. I feel his torso against my back, and his breath blows the stray hairs at the top of my head.

"I hope we pull off this thing you've gotten us into, Farenthold."

"As I recall, Randolph, this thing is all your doing. You came up with the idea, remember?"

"I was attempting to be sarcastic when I said we should do this,

Davis." I finally turn around to look up at Davis' grinning face. "You were the one that blabbed it to Hardy before I could get a word in edgewise. If it's a flop, it'll be all your fault. But everyone will blame me, of course."

"Sometimes there's a method to my madness. By the way, Jo, I want to introduce you to someone." Davis waves over a petite, very tan woman with a long, black ponytail. My eyes narrow to better focus on who she is. I hear a small squeal and finally broaden my focus and realize that she's holding the hand of Davis's mop-haired little boy. She releases Cody's hand, and he runs toward Davis and body slams himself against Davis's legs. He wraps his little arms around Davis' kneecaps.

Davis kneels down to Cody's eye level. He grasps my hand but continues to look at the little boy. "Cody. Hey, man, I want you to meet somebody." Davis finally looks up at me. "This is Daddy's friend, Jo."

I kneel down and smile at Cody. "Hi, handsome," I say and raise my palm as if about to take a pledge. Cody giggles and gives me a high five.

Davis rises, lifting Cody up in his arms as he stands. He gives him a kiss on the cheek. "Daddy has to work now, so you're gonna go with Mai. Be a good boy, OK?"

Davis shakes his head as he waves goodbye to Cody. "There's no way he's gonna make it through this thing. That poor woman is gonna be outside chasing him around the hallway all evening. But who knows? Maybe I'll get lucky."

I brush my bare knees below the edge of my skirt. "Not a chance, man. I have three nephews, and I've never seen them sit still for more than five minutes except when they're asleep."

"Jo! Jo! We made it, Jo!!!" Rudy's arms are outstretched in my direction as he rushes toward me. "This is my friend, Jones. Jones, this is Jo. Isn't this just fabulous!" Rudy gushes. A nice-looking, nicely tanned man with close-cropped, silver-streaked hair and sleek, black-rimmed glasses extends his hand as Rudy wraps his arms around me, practically knocking me down on my backside.

"Hello, Jones, I'm Jo. And this is Davis, who co-wrote this thing with me. We appreciate you coming all the way down here to check us out."

Jones nods appreciatively in Davis's direction as Rudy tackles Davis in one of his clinch holds.

"Girl, look at you. A dress, heels." Rudy whistles appreciatively as I spin around for his benefit. "Come on, Jones, let's let these two work their magic. We better find some seats before it gets too crowded out there."

"I guess I should get going myself." Davis gives me a kiss on the cheek and starts to move in the direction of some gesturing jocks. "I better get these boys situated so I can check on the musicians. I'll be down in the pit if you need me."

As I peek out again at the audience, I notice that the house is now packed, not only with spectators, but also reporters and Midland's very own version of paparazzi. The next thing I know, Principal Hardy is standing next to me perusing the crowd as well.

"This is just fine, Jo. It's mighty fine. You know, this is not just entertainment. This is a wonderful way to get all the parents and the whole community involved in what we're doing here at this school. Maybe it'll help 'em care about us a little more than they usually do." His smile is wide and true.

"I certainly hope so, Principal Hardy. I guess I better get going. It's almost time to start up."

"Oh, run along, then. Don't let me keep you." He pats me on the back and continues to watch the crowd.

I round up my first group of performers, and make sure that they're all on their marks and ready to start on cue once the music starts and the curtains part. When I'm finally ready to let go, I step off the stage and give Principal Hardy a nod. He strides out before the tall, closed curtains and begins to introduce our production. His face is flush with enthusiasm, and he grins from ear-to-ear in the flickering glow of the shutterbugs' flashes.

And then they're off. I'm overwhelmed as I watch all my kids fall in line and perform their parts like pros. Though we intended to mock Midland when we created them, our song and dance numbers are quite the hit with the crowd. I listen to the dialogue I penned and the lyrics

Davis pounded out on the piano as if hearing them for the first time. They're far more fun than ironic, the jokes joyful and far less mean than what was going through our heads when Davis and I made them up. The kids are full of life and bring down the house with their performances, especially Clance's over-the-top Coach, Qiana's bellicose head of the booster club, and the high-kicking halfbacks that cause people to clutch their sides and hoot with laughter.

The whole crazy thing is a big crazy hit. When the curtain closes for the last time, the crowd jumps to their feet and hollers and claps for the kids to come out again and again to take a bow. Though these may all be friends and family, this feels like a lot more than polite support. The kids wave me out onto the stage. I walk out to join them, and Tomás and Tyrone surprise me with two large bouquets of long-stemmed roses. I step to the edge of the stage and reach my hand down toward Davis, who takes it and climbs onto the stage to join me. We take two more bows with the kids, never letting go of each other's hands. I can't help but smile as I scan the cheering crowd. Until I catch sight of one face in the back of the room as the curtain closes for the last time.

Ravi.

CHAPTER 28 ♡

Backstage I accept more hugs than I can count from the kids, my family, my friends, other faculty members, complete strangers. I keep smiling and joking with everyone. Maybe if I fake it enough, the joy will fill the pit in my stomach.

I suddenly spot Ravi backstage, staring straight at me. I can't do anything but stare back. I can't believe it has been, what, three months since I saw him last? I can't move or speak. Ravi also doesn't move or speak and continues his stare down.

All of a sudden, Davis appears and places a hand on my shoulder.

"Hey, Jo, we're gonna start heading over to my place. I told the kids—" He abruptly stops speaking and turns his head to see what I'm staring at like a zombie.

"It's him." I say softly.

"I figured as much," Davis responds. "You need me to talk to him?"

"No, Davis. I need to have this conversation. It's long overdue."

"Well, I was gonna see if you could bring a few of the kids over to my place in your car, but I'll ask your family if they can help out. OK?"

"Yeah, OK. You go on ahead. I'll meet you over there."

"You sure?" Davis looks concerned.

I smile at him, a genuine smile this time. "Everything's gonna be OK," I say. "For a change."

Davis walks away and the crowd backstage disperses. I walk toward Ravi. We both hesitate to say or do anything when I reach him. Then Ravi extends his arms in my direction, and I accept and return his hug.

He kisses me on the cheek. "You look gorgeous, darling. Of course."

"I wouldn't say 'of course.' But thank you."

Out of the corner of my eye, I notice Paula, Jen and Rudy heading in my direction. I turn and wave them off. "It's OK. Why don't y'all head over to the party? I'll meet you there."

"But," Paula begins.

"It's OK, Paula," I say. "Really. I need to do this." I turn back to Ravi. "Wanna walk me to my classroom?"

"Sure," he says. He smiles at the mention of "my classroom."

He follows me out to the corridor. "That was fantastic, Jo," he finally says. He scans the flyers and drawings posted on the bulletin boards and dry erase boards lining the hallway. "I never would have imagined, but you seem to be doing really well for yourself here."

He looks down at my face and begins to stutter. "I didn't mean . . . I mean, of course you will do well at whatever you do. I just meant . . ."

"I know what you meant, Ravi." His gaze drops to his feet. "What are you doing here?" I ask with genuine interest, not annoyance, to my surprise.

"I don't know, Jo," he says without looking up. "I just wanted to *seeee* you and talk to you before all this movie business starts up again. No lawyers. Just one-on-one, like real people. When your lawyer said that you were tied up until after this musical, I decided to come down."

"And Danielle didn't mind?" I ask. Ravi looks at me again. He appears surprised at how calm I am. I'm surprised at how calm I am.

"Danielle and me. That situation is still a work in progress. But I think we've finally agreed that even though it's not working out anymore, we don't have to torture each other. And we can keep our personal business and other business separate. I offered to give her half of anything I make on the movie and the series on top of what she's entitled to as the executive producer. She turned it down, but she seemed to appreciate the offer. And for me, I've tried to let go of this really rigid idea I had about how I wanted to do this movie and what I wanted it to be. I even started listening to Regan. She actually has some good ideas! Making this film was such an obsession for me, I turned into the kind of person I never wanted to be. And I hurt a lot of people. So, I'm sorry

Jo. I'm sorry for everything. I guess that's what I really came here to say."

We reach the door of my classroom and I motion for Ravi to come inside. I close the door behind me.

"Have a seat," I say to him. He selects one of the student's desks, and I settle into the desk next to his. "Actually, Ravi, I'm the one that owes *you* an apology."

"Really, Jo, you don't—"

I raise my hand to cut him off. "Yes, I do. I need to say this. I'm responsible for the fire at your house."

He stares at me, but his expression doesn't change. He knew all along. "It wasn't intentional, Ravi, really it wasn't. It was a stupid mistake that got out of control. But it doesn't matter if I meant to do it or not. I let my temper get the best of me and acted really irresponsibly. Not only did I destroy your house, but I could have hurt people as well."

His eyes soften, but he doesn't say anything.

"I finally have to own up to what I've done, Ravi. I have to stop running from it. You can call the police or your insurance company or your lawyer or the media or whatever you want to do. I'm not going to deny it anymore."

The tension I felt on sight of Ravi in the auditorium is gone. The months of agonizing and fear and regret leave my body all at once, and I exhale a large gush of air from my lungs as a reflex.

Ravi clutches my hand. "You don't know how much it means to me to hear you say that, Jo. I don't want to fight with you anymore. I want to move forward. Let's just get this movie done and see where it takes us."

I lean over from my desk/chair and reach out for him. He returns my awkward hug. We embrace each other for what feels like a long time before I finally let go. I stand and say, "We're having a little party for the kids at my co-worker's . . . at my friend's house. You wanna come?"

Ravi stands as well. "No, that's OK, Jo. I'll leave you to your celebration. You can drop me off at my hotel, though, if you don't mind. I came straight from the airport, and I'm not sure how one hires a taxi around here."

As we reach the driveway at the entrance of the Marriott, we exchange another platonic but warm hug. I don't leave the car but wave in his direction until he disappears through the automatic doors. I pull away from the hotel and head to Davis' place.

My family and friends have fully made themselves at home at Davis' house. Jen is cuddled up next to Willie T. on a lounge chair with a plate of salad greens on her lap. I guess she hasn't figured out that it's OK for girls to eat ribs and cheeseburgers in front of guys in this part of the world. I notice Daddy chatting and laughing with Davis near the punch bowl. Memphis is holding two fingers above his head like horns and is chasing my nephews and Cody around the yard like a rabid bull. I fill a Styrofoam cup with alcohol-free, high-fructose-corn-syrup-enhanced fruit drink and head out to the backyard.

"Miss Randolph?" Qiana sidles up to me clutching a matching Styrofoam cup of sugar water

"Hi, Qiana. I know I said it already, but you did an *amazing* job. And I had the nerve to ask you whether you were really interested in acting! Remember that? I, of all people, should know that some of the most outstanding actors are quiet, shy types. Like DeNiro and Greta Garbo. They're not hyperactive, extroverted Carol Channing types like myself."

Qiana stares at me with a slightly confused expression.

"What's up?" I ask.

"Um, I was just wonderin' if you decided whether you're goin' back to California or if you're gonna stay here and teach us this year?"

Qiana looks anxious. I feel that nasty lump growing in the back of my throat again.

"To be honest, Qiana, I'm not sure what my future holds." I take another sip of my fake fruit punch. "I've got a contractual commitment to finish a film back in L.A. that'll probably run over into the beginning of the school year. So I don't think I'll be teaching English or drama this fall semester."

Qiana drops her eyes into her cup. "Me and Kiley figured that a big movie star like you wouldn't hang around here."

I reach out and touch her shoulder. "Hey, Qiana, you've got my phone number and my email address. And you've gotta know that I loved teaching you this summer. Being here this summer reminded me what drew me to acting in the first place. It's what made me stop feeling like I was always out of place when I was growing up here in Midland. I'd almost forgotten why I became an artist, what it even means to be a real artist. For a long time, acting has just been my job, not really a passion."

"I wish I could have a job like that," Qiana says in a small voice. "I'd rather do what you do than break my back for nothin' like my mama does."

I know she's right. I know how fortunate I am. And to think of how close I came to throwing it all away. "You're right, of course. Petting a puppy in a dog food ad is a much easier way to pay your rent than working in a petroleum plant. But I'm one of the lucky ones. Most actors are waiting tables and typing documents from midnight to 6:00 A.M. to make ends meet. Like I told you, it's a tough business. But if you work really hard and try not to be discouraged, I know you'll end up in a good place. It may not be where you thought you'd end up, but you'll probably end up where you ought to be."

"So are you gonna end up back in California or here in Midland?" My foray into touchy-feeliness hasn't distracted Qiana in the least. I smile at her stubbornness.

"I can't commit to teaching English full-time in August. But if I can work it out, I'm gonna try to work with the drama program part-time or maybe on a project-by-project basis while I finish what I have to finish in L.A. Long term, who knows? I've got a lot of reasons to spend more time in Midland these days, so you'll see a lot of me, even if you don't see me every day." I glance at Davis who's now walking in our direction. "I don't plan on abandoning you, Qiana."

She smiles into her cup, and I wrap my arms around her shoulders. Davis nears us but doesn't disturb our bear hug. We rock back and forth for a while before we finally release each other. "You can't get rid of me that easy. I am a *huge* pain in the ass."

Qiana walks away to catch up with Kiley. Davis strolls over to join me in her place. We're immediately accosted by what feels like the entirety of Midland's population, all congratulating us and wishing us well on the success of our play. After shaking about a thousand hands, Davis and I finally help ourselves to ribs and coleslaw and try to find a place to sit. The back patio and pool area are swarming with folks, so we head inside to the kitchen. We stand in the corner near the wine rack to have a little space to ourselves as we stuff our faces and lick sauce off our fingers. In all the excitement of the day, I haven't eaten a thing, and I'm starving.

Memphis passes through with a rib in one hand and a beer in the other. "Davis, this is a nice place you got here." Memphis winks at me and then drains the remains of his beer. He sets the empty bottle in a recycling bin beside the counter. "I better get back outside. I told the kids we could play dodge ball. But I don't know if we got room to play with all these people up in here."

"You can take them out front," Davis offers. "Though that might not be such a great idea. The little ones might run out into the street."

"Don't you worry none, Davis. I'll keep an eye on 'em. Jo Ella'll tell you. I can corral those little critters as good as any kindygarden teacher. And I'll bring your babysitter out there to help me. She kinda cute. Where she from? Mexico?"

"Vietnam."

"Cool." Memphis strolls out of the kitchen. He holds the patio door open to allow Uncle Buddy to come in before he heads outside.

"It's too many folks out there for Buddy," he says on sight of us.

"Sir, have a seat here in the den. *Hey guys, outside!*" Davis yells across the kitchen counter at the teenagers lounging in the den and playing Madden Football on his Xbox. They rise obediently and shut off the set before leaving the den for the backyard. Davis unlocks a high cabinet above my head and removes a liter of Jack Daniel's. He pours a generous amount into an etched lowball glass and carries it over to Uncle Buddy.

"Hee hee, thank you, son," Uncle Buddy grins as he accepts the glass with both hands.

"What else you got locked up in there?" I ask as Davis returns the bottle to the shelf. He grins and reaches over my head again. I link my thumbs through his belt loops and hold onto his waist as he retrieves a tall bottle of something clear and slightly gold-tinted before securing the lock on the cabinet.

"Tequila. Premium stuff. I bought it in Guadalajara a couple summers ago. I can't believe I still have it."

"Looks like the party's in here," Rudy taunts as he enters the kitchen with Jones in tow.

"How about a toast?" Davis raises the bottle in their direction.

"Don Julio?" Jones raises his eyebrows and smiles. "Absolutely."

I release Davis and fill my hands with glasses while Davis fetches limes and a tin of course sea salt.

Davis raises his glass with one hand and circles my waist with the other. "*Salud!*"

We all kick back our tequila shots and grimace as we grab our lime slices and then lick a line of salt from the backs of our hands.

"Whew!" Jones releases a whoosh of air from his lips and then snaps his fingers and shakes his hips in time to an old Con Funk Shun song piping through the speakers in the walls.

"Yeaah!" Rudy starts to dance as well. "We came in to talk business with you two. But if the drinks and the music keep up like this, that won't happen. By the way, Davis, this is a gorgeous house." Rudy winks at me and spins in time to the music.

"Business?" Davis refills everyone's glasses.

"Oh, wow. I haven't heard that song in *ages!*" Jones throws back another shot. "Before I get too drunk, I have to tell you that I *loved* your musical. *Loved* it! Would you be interested in trying to do it off-Broadway? We'll have to clear the rights and pay off the original owners of the book and movie, but I think it would still do well. The script . . . I couldn't stop laughing. The music was *so* funny and amazing. And, Jo, if you can pull those kinds of performances from a bunch of high school kids out in the middle of nowhere, I can't even imagine what you could do with a professional cast."

"Probably not as much," I jest as I take another shot of tequila.

"Look, I know you guys have to finish up with this summer school thing. But maybe when classes end, you could come to New York, and we could sit down and talk about it more seriously. That'll give me time to talk to some potential funders and figure out what it might take to get the rights to do it. I would love for you to direct it, Jo, and for you to direct the music, Davis. It will take us a while to raise the cash and put the team together and start work shopping it. Maybe you both can move camp to New York for a bit."

"Wow!" I try to say more, but 'wow' is all that comes out.

Davis tightens his grip on my waist. "Thank you, Jones. I think we're just a little stunned. This thing started as a little joke between the two of us and now . . . Let us talk this through a bit and then come back to you."

"Do you think you might at least come up to New York in August to kick some ideas around? No strings? My company will put you up, of course."

Davis looks down at me and shrugs a 'why not?' "Sure," he says.

"Great!"

Davis gives Rudy and Jones a refill, and they start a funky conga line out of the kitchen to a Foxy jam. As they soul step out the door, Mommy scoots past them into the house with a wailing Cody Farenthold in her arms. His head is on her shoulder, and his little hands clutch her blouse as he howls, huge tears streaming down his face. In an instant Davis releases me and his tequila glass and moves toward Mommy with his arms outstretched. Mommy shoos him away.

"Oh, Davis, we just have a little scratch here." Mommy's voice is soft and syrupy. "All we need is a nice Band-Aid to make it all better."

"There's a first-aid kit in the cupboard. Mrs. Randolph, are you sure I can't . . ."

"Now, Davis," Mommy talks slowly as if Davis is the three year old, not Cody. "I'm a grandmother. And I raised that one over there, so I think I can handle a little drama." She kisses Cody on the top of his fluffy head and pats his hair. "When all the hoo-hah calms down, we find out that everything's not so bad. Isn't that right, Cody?"

Mommy strides past us to the pantry and pulls out a white metal box. "I'll take this outside. We'll probably need it again before the night's out. I love Trey dearly, but my grandson seems to invite accidents." In an instant, Mommy is gone.

Davis leans against the counter and doesn't say anything for a long time.

"I'm sorry, Davis. My mother has a habit of taking over."

"It's OK," he smiles. "It's nice, actually. Hey, get your glass and those limes over there." Davis grabs the tequila bottle and my hand and guides me up the stairs. He leads me through the master bedroom to a narrow balcony overlooking the backyard. It's not wide enough for chairs, so Davis sits right down on the wooden slats and pulls me down between his outstretched legs, my back against his torso. He pours us both another glass of tequila, and I cradle my drink as I lean my head against Davis's chest and look down on the dwindling crowd.

"So, what do you think?" he finally asks.

"About what?"

"About the play, about New York, about your movie. About everything, I guess."

"I think directing a play in New York would be amazing! I go back all the time, but I haven't actually lived in New York since my twenties. I loved doing theater, but I could never make a decent enough living there, which is why I moved to L.A. And now my biggest opportunity might be back in New York. How wild is that?"

"Pretty wild," he says flatly.

"Davis, what's wrong?"

"I don't know." Davis pours himself another drink. I stop his hand before he can raise the glass to his lips.

"Davis, don't you think it would be exciting if we got the chance to produce this in New York? I mean, if my TV series becomes a go, it will make the logistics a bit weird for a while. But if this happens, maybe I could make New York my home base again when I'm not shooting in L.A. And you and Cody could come too. New York is such a cool place for kids. Just think of what you could expose him to."

Davis wraps his arms tightly around my waist and presses his head against my shoulder.

"It's weird, Davis. I've been acting for twenty years, more than that if you count stuff I did in school. And not once did I ever think about writing or directing."

"You're really great at it, you know. You did a great job with this thing." Davis's face is still buried against the base of my neck, and his words are a bit muffled.

"I actually loved it." I set down my glass and swivel in order to see Davis's face. "Davis, what's wrong with you?"

Davis lifts his head. "I don't know, Jo. You're right; this all sounds great. Even though it's premature to start planning like this New York thing will actually happen. I'm actually just trying to get my arms around getting Cody settled here and figuring out what we're doing and where you're going once summer school ends."

"I was avoiding thinking about that," I respond. "I have to go back and finish this stupid pilot. But then I'm done for a while and can come back here while I wait to hear what happens with the series."

"But what if it gets picked up? And, by the way, how was it, seeing your ex?"

"Good, actually." Davis's expression sags. "No, Davis, it was good because we cleared the air. Or at least started the process. So maybe it won't be too awkward or painful seeing him every day again."

Davis grimaces. "So I guess everything is all worked out for you then."

"Not at all," I say. "I'm just starting the process to get my life back on track. And what about you and me? That's a pretty big question mark"

"Exactly," Davis says. "I mean, I know how I feel about you and me. But I don't know what to do about it. If I wasn't in the middle of all this transition, I'd probably follow you back to L.A. and wherever else you end up going. But I need to sit still for a while. I kind of like being here and working with these kids. And Cody has been shuffled around from place to place and person to person so much, I'd like for him to have some stability for a change."

"Who knows?" I say with a shrug. "Hardy has already said that he'd love for me to stay on. If the TV series doesn't work out, then maybe I'll come back for good and start teaching. And Paula has turned out to be a great lawyer. She might be able to argue my way out of the contract."

"Well, on one level I'd be happy about that because I don't want you to go. Especially not now, when we're just starting to . . . whatever it is we're starting to do. But I also don't want you to pass up any great opportunities either, particularly if this New York thing turns into something. You could show people that you're not only a talented actress, but that you can also write and direct and produce the whole thing."

"It could be good for you too, you know."

"Yeah, but I'm doing pretty well for myself. I've been branching out and doing things off stage for a while. Now that I'm writing again, I can get steady work writing and producing songs right here in my house. And I can still perform and tour and travel if I feel like it. But I'm finally at a point where I can pick and choose my projects—praise, Jesus, to quote Principal Hardy. You've got some rebuilding to do, Jo. And if you pass up chances to do that, you'll end up regretting it and resenting me."

I've been avoiding thinking about the end of summer, but it's now staring me in the face. "What are we gonna do?" I cry as I clutch Davis's arms around my waist in a tight grip. "Are you sure you can't you come with me to L.A.?"

"If I thought I could do it without reverting back to the person I used to be and the life I used to live, then I would wrap Cody up and follow you to Timbuktu, if that's where you wanted to go. But I'm just being honest with you and myself. Uprooting our lives right now might not have a great result. I'll just cross my fingers that maybe you'll come back to us."

"And what if there's not a place for me here when I get back?"

"This is your home, Jo. There's always a place for you here."

"I don't mean here in Midland, Davis."

Davis doesn't speak for a few moments. "Like I said, there's always a place for you here."

I can't quite pinpoint how I feel. My emotions are a cocktail of sadness and excitement and a small amount of hope, with a splash of uncertainty thrown in just to give it a kick.

"What if some more wanton, Babylonian women wander through Midland while I'm away?" I find myself smiling though my heart is split in two.

"One wanton Babylonian woman in my life is about all I can handle," Davis drawls. "I think you can trust me."

"Famous last words," I say as I raise my glass to toast. "To happy endings, then?"

"To us," he says as he clinks his glass against mine.

I settle myself against Davis's chest. At least for now, all is right with the world. We sit until the party moves on without us, until dusk turns to darkness, and there's only the two of us under the wide, West Texas sky with a bottle of tequila we can no longer see.

ACKNOWLEDGMENTS ♡

I have to thank my husband, Kevin, who has tolerated and supported me and my antics ever since he fished my keys out of a dirty, frozen puddle in Harvard Square in the '80s. And my daughter, Cameron Quinn, the thespian and the Rory to my Lorelei, who has inspired me and made me laugh throughout my long and winding journey with this novel. They don't understand what the heck I'm doing half the time, but I appreciate their blind faith and love more than they realize.

Thanks to the best parents in the world, Elza McKnight, Jr. and Dr. Mamie L. McKnight, who gave me wings, dreams, experiences, a sense of humor and infinite love. And my incredible grandparents, Mamie and James Abernathy, who made the sweetest lemonade out of life's lemons. And my never-forgotten cousin/little brother, Gary Quinn Abernathy, my sparkling Aunt Virginia Douglas, my brilliant Uncles James, Robert, Sonny, Gary and Arthur Abernathy, and Arthur McKnight, their spouses, my cousins and our ancestors that toiled the red East Texas clay and the slings of arrows of Jim Crow and segregation without ever lowering their standards or convictions. Thanks to my Virginian-Philadelphian Chavers and Burton in-laws for their support. And to my awesome extended family—the McKnights, the Abernathys, the Richardsons, the Tysons, the Douglases, the Rambos, the Mitchells, the Broomfields and all my other relatives. We're a crazy-in-love bunch of Texans and Californians—never change!

To my cheerleader, Mona Rae Washington, my guide, Carla Pinza, and my longtime friend, Kim Fusch, who suffered through an early draft and gave me invaluable feedback—thanks for believing in me and motivating me to continue.

To my gurus, Pat Dunn and Jimin Han of Sarah Lawrence College's Writing Institute, Mary LaChapele of Sarah Lawrence's Graduate Writing Program, and the incomparable Heidi Durrow, Barbara Gordon, and Hope Edelman: I couldn't have completed this novel or pursued this path as a writer without your amazing insight, guidance, wisdom and instruction.

To the beautiful Kathy Gurfein, whose generous spirit and support I will always appreciate.

To the great team at She Writes Press and Book Sparks—Brooke Warner, Kamy Wicoff, Cait Levin, Crystal Patriarche, and Robert Soares—without you I'm nothing!

And to my partners in crime: I'm thankful for the years with my Sarah Lawrence writing group (Diane and Barbara, I miss you guys!). And to my fellow Nun Boxers from Djerassi Resident Artists Program—Robin Farmer, Elena Acevedo Dalcourt, Heidi Durrow, Jenn Stroud Rossman, Jessica Sick Haas, Michele Beller, and Romalyn Tilghman—one week with these amazing writers/crazy women (in the best possible sense), and I've never been the same.

ABOUT THE AUTHOR

A native of Dallas, Texas, Ginger McKnight-Chavers is a graduate of Georgetown's School of Foreign Service and Harvard Law School. She was a Kathryn Gurfein Writing Fellow at Sarah Lawrence College, and she currently blogs for the Huffington Post Blue Nation Review and The TexPatch. She lives in Westchester County, New York, with her husband, daughter, and an overweight West Highland White Terrier.

Author photo by Lyan Bernales

SELECTED TITLES FROM SHE WRITES PRESS

She Writes Press is an independent publishing company founded to serve women writers everywhere. Visit us at www.shewritespress.com.

A Tight Grip: A Novel about Golf, Love Affairs, and Women of a Certain Age by Kay Rae Chomic. $16.95, 978-1-938314-76-6. As forty-six-year-old golfer Jane "Par" Parker prepares for her next tournament, she experiences a chain of events that force her to reevaluate her life.

Center Ring by Nicole Waggoner. $17.95, 978-1-63152-034-1. When a startling confession rattles a group of tightly knit women to its core, the friends are left analyzing their own roads not taken and the vastly different choices they've made in life and love.

Play for Me by Céline Keating. $16.95, 978-1-63152-972-6. Middle-aged Lily impulsively joins a touring folk-rock band, leaving her job and marriage behind in an attempt to find a second chance at life, passion, and art.

Warming Up by Mary Hutchings Reed. $16.95, 978-1-938314-05-6. Unemployed and depressed former musical actress Cecilia Morrison decides to start therapy, hoping it will get her out of her slump—but ultimately it's a teen who cons her out of sixty bucks, not her analyst, who changes her life.

Royal Entertainment by Marni Fechter. $16.95, 978-1-938314-52-0. After being fired from her job for blowing the whistle on her boss, social worker Melody Frank has to adapt to her new life as the assistant to an elite New York party planner.

Duck Pond Epiphany by Tracey Barnes Priestley. $16.95, 978-1-938314-24-7. When a mother of four delivers her last child to college, she has to decide what to do next—and her life takes a surprising turn.